FOUr SISTErS

EuroComics.us

Editor Dean Mullaney • Art Director Lorraine Turner
Translation Edward Gauvin

EuroComics is an imprint of IDW Publishing
a Division of Idea and Design Works, LLC
2765 Truxtun Road • San Diego, CA 92106
www.idwpublishing.com

Distributed to the book trade by Penguin Random House
Distributed to the comic book trade by Diamond Book Distributors

ISBN: 978-1-68405-196-0
First Printing, May 2018

Four Sisters: Enid, Volume 1 (original French title: *Quatre soeurs: Enid, volume 1*)
© 2014 Rue de Sèvres
English translation © 2018 Library of American Comics LLC. All rights reserved.

IDW Publishing
Greg Goldstein, President & Publisher
Robbie Robbins, EVP & Sr. Art Director
Chris Ryall, Chief Creative Officer & Editor-in-Chief
Matthew Ruzicka, CPA, Chief Financial Officer
David Hedgecock, Associate Publisher
Laurie Windrow, Senior Vice President of Sales & Marketing
Lorelei Bunjes, VP of Digital Services
Eric Moss, Sr. Director, Licensing & Business Development

Ted Adams, Founder & CEO of IDW Media Holdings

Special thanks to Justin Eisinger, Alonzo Simon, Rick Parker (for lettering on page 53),
and Marija Gaudry of Rue de Sèvres.

Four Sisters

1. Enid

Written by Malika Ferdjoukh and Cati Baur

Illustrations and colors by Cati Baur

Based on the novel by Malika Ferdjoukh

EURO COMICS
ENGLISH EDITION GRAPHIC NOVELS

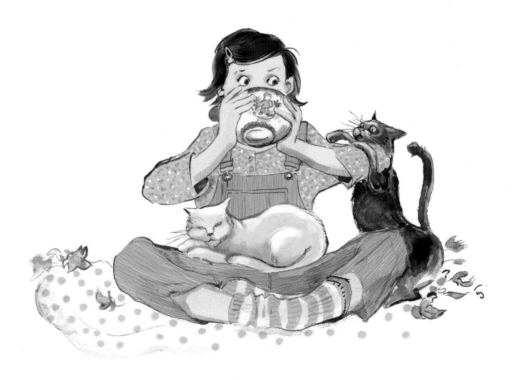

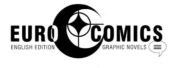

An imprint of IDW PUBLISHING

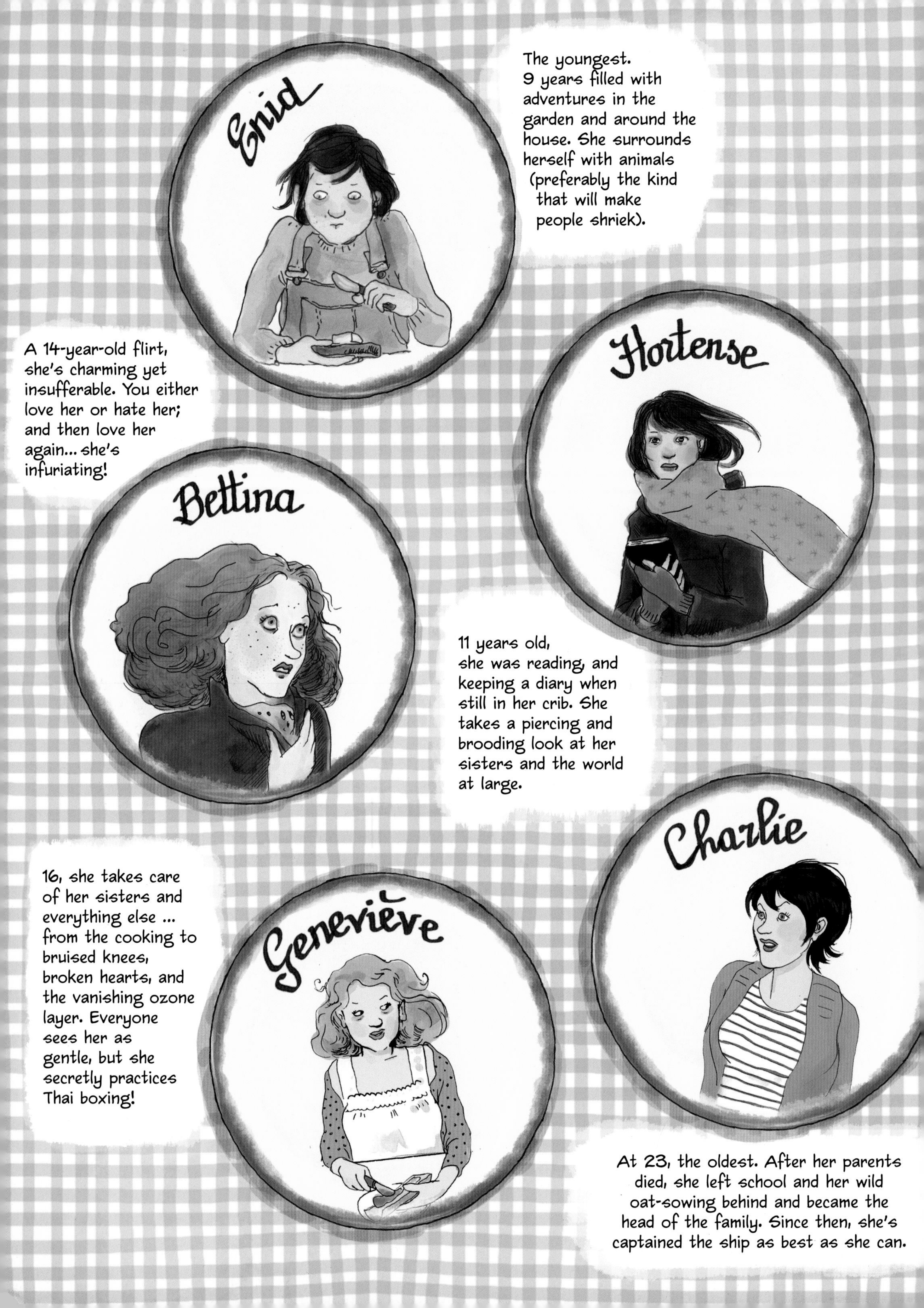
Enid
The youngest. 9 years filled with adventures in the garden and around the house. She surrounds herself with animals (preferably the kind that will make people shriek).
A 14-year-old flirt, she's charming yet insufferable. You either love her or hate her; and then love her again... she's infuriating!
Hortense
Bettina
11 years old, she was reading, and keeping a diary when still in her crib. She takes a piercing and brooding look at her sisters and the world at large.
Charlie
16, she takes care of her sisters and everything else ... from the cooking to bruised knees, broken hearts, and the vanishing ozone layer. Everyone sees her as gentle, but she secretly practices Thai boxing!
Geneviève
At 23, the oldest. After her parents died, she left school and her wild oat-sowing behind and became the head of the family. Since then, she's captained the ship as best as she can.

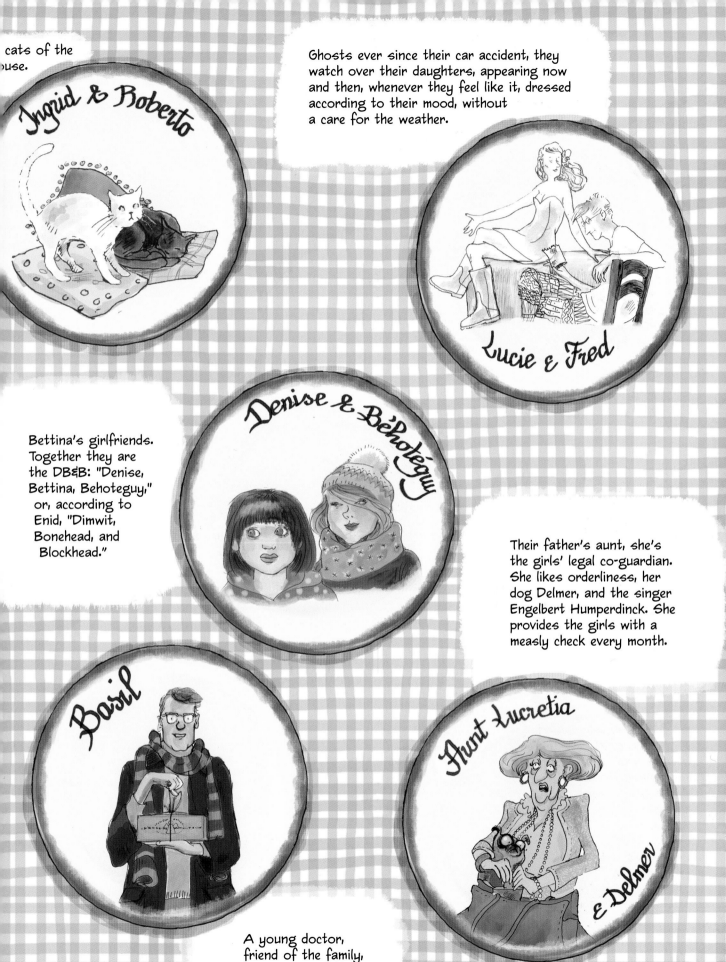

cats of the
ouse.

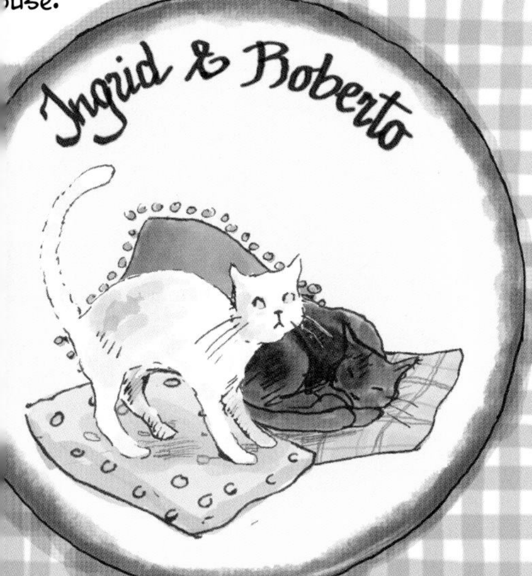
Ingrid & Roberto

Ghosts ever since their car accident, they watch over their daughters, appearing now and then, whenever they feel like it, dressed according to their mood, without a care for the weather.

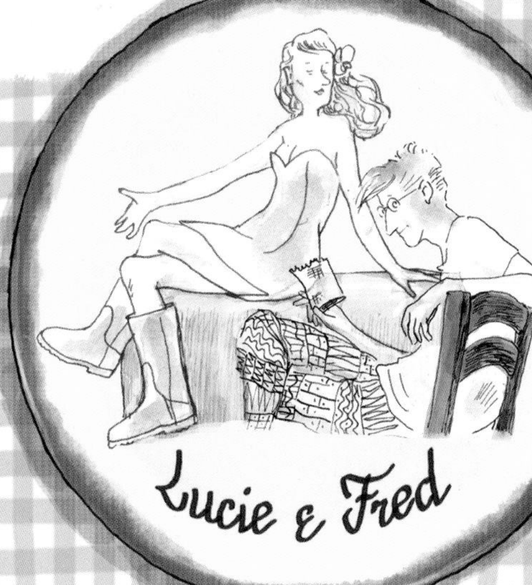
Lucie & Fred

Bettina's girlfriends. Together they are the DB&B: "Denise, Bettina, Behoteguy," or, according to Enid, "Dimwit, Bonehead, and Blockhead."

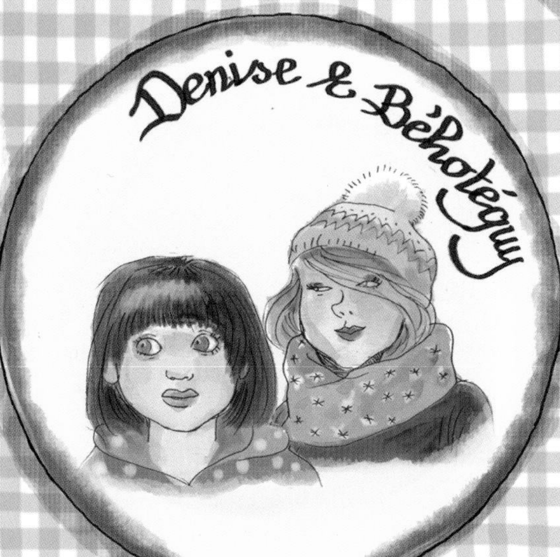
Denise & Béhotéguy

Their father's aunt, she's the girls' legal co-guardian. She likes orderliness, her dog Delmer, and the singer Engelbert Humperdinck. She provides the girls with a measly check every month.

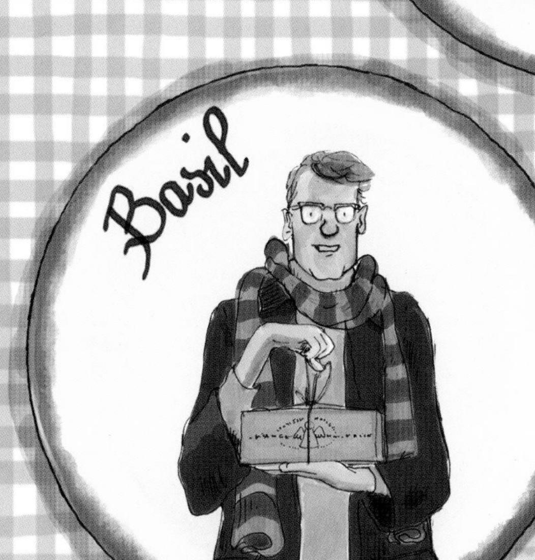
Basil

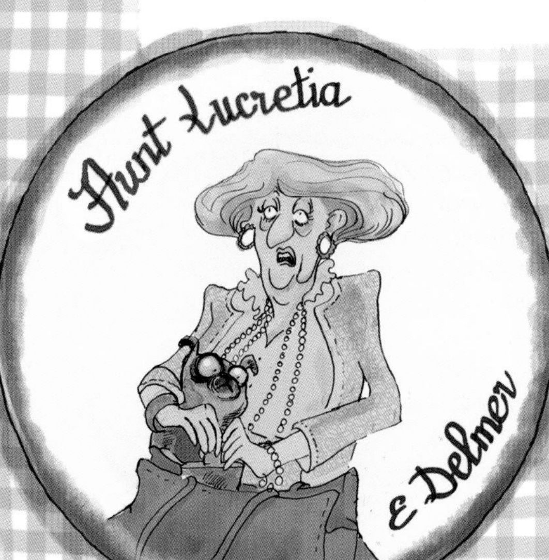
Aunt Lucretia
& Delmer

A young doctor, friend of the family, and Charlie's official boyfriend.

This book is dedicated to my kids: Siméon, Olympe, and Honoré.
And also to the four Cruz sisters, who are dear to me, and especially Mom.
And finally, a big thank you to Nicolas and Malika.
— Cati Baur

Thank you to Louis Delas for this trip back to Vill'Hervé.
— Malika Ferdjoukh

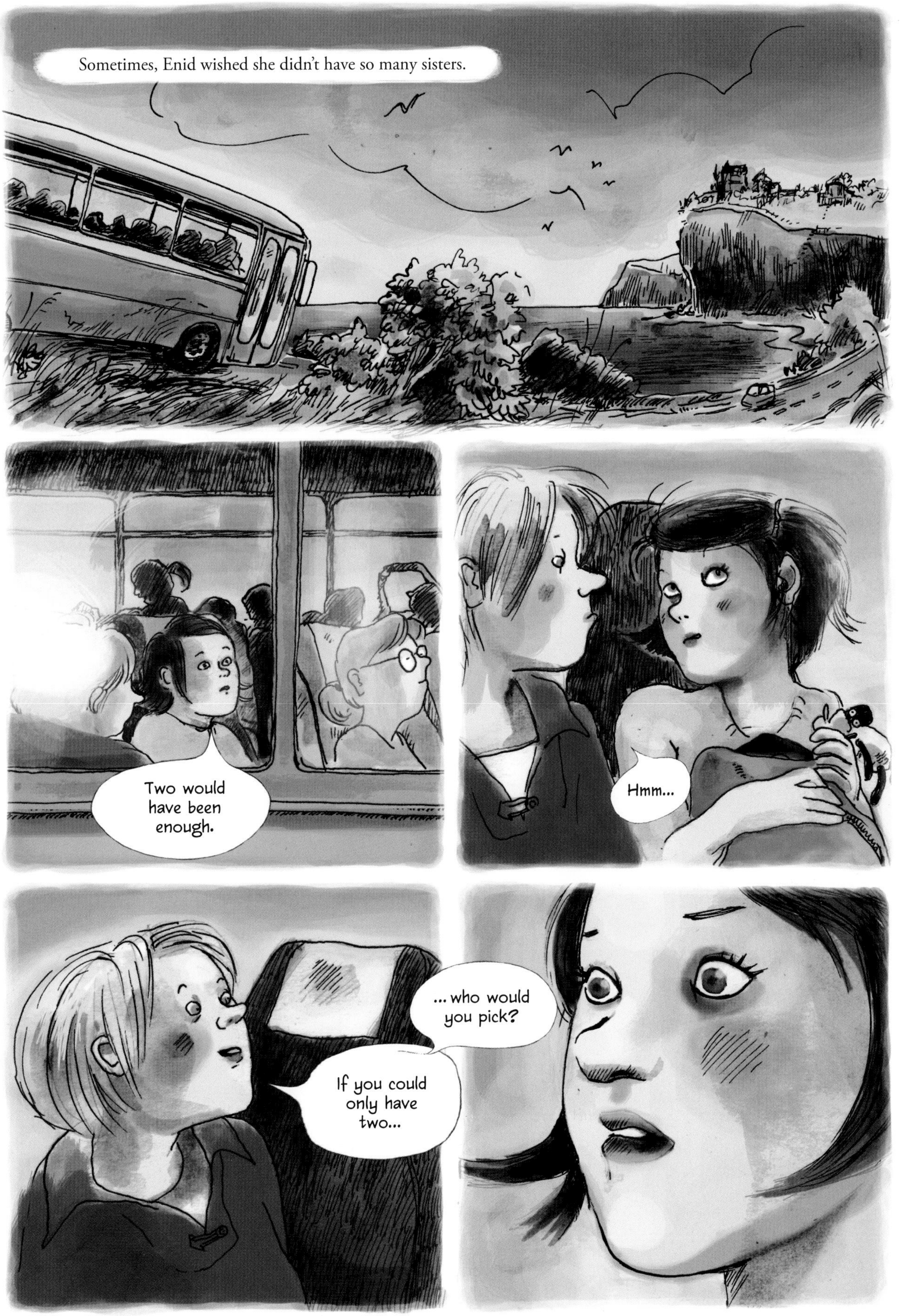
Sometimes, Enid wished she didn't have so many sisters.
Two would have been enough.
Hmm...
If you could only have two...
... who would you pick?

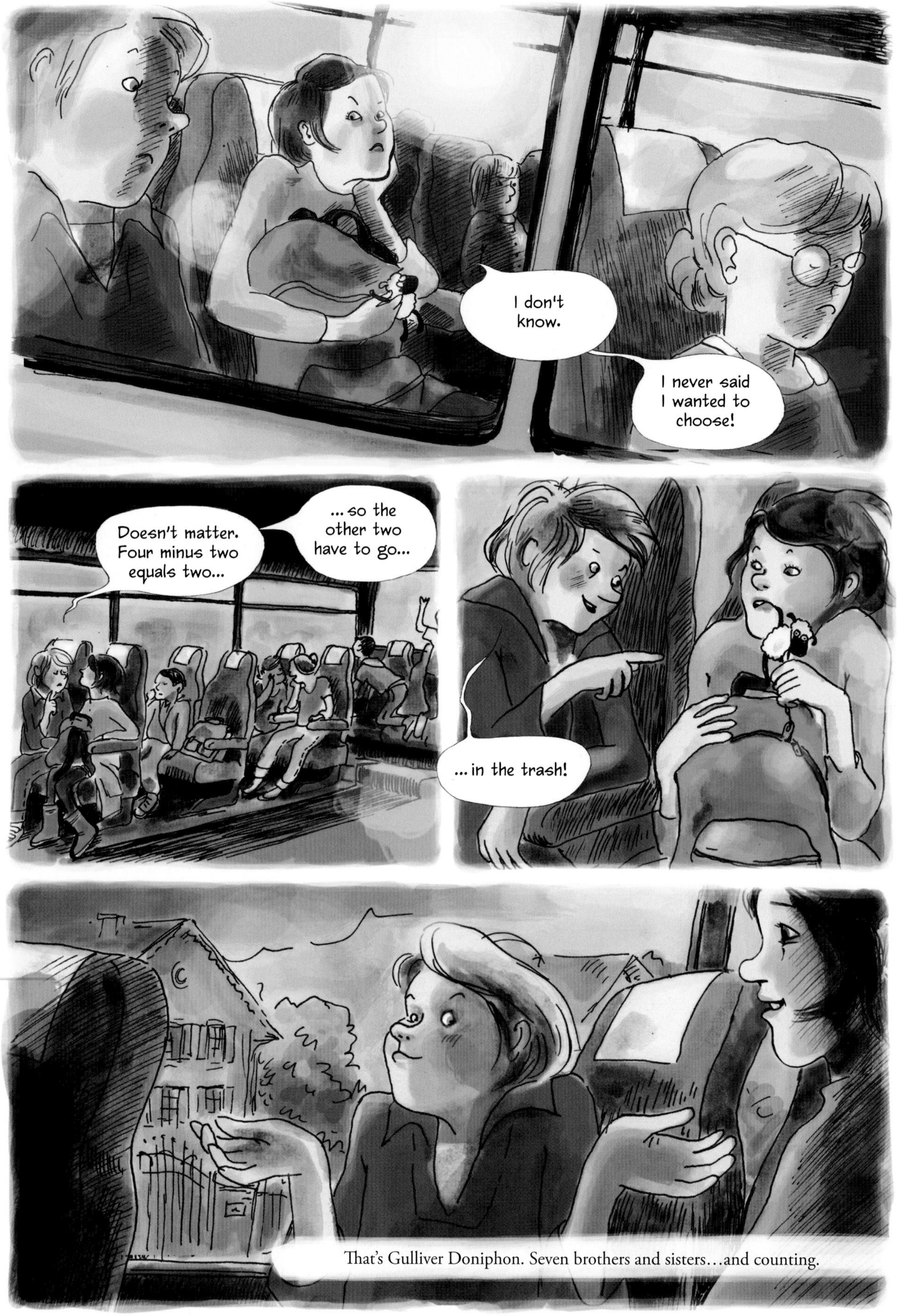
I don't know.
I never said I wanted to choose!
Doesn't matter. Four minus two equals two...
...so the other two have to go...
...in the trash!
That's Gulliver Doniphon. Seven brothers and sisters...and counting.

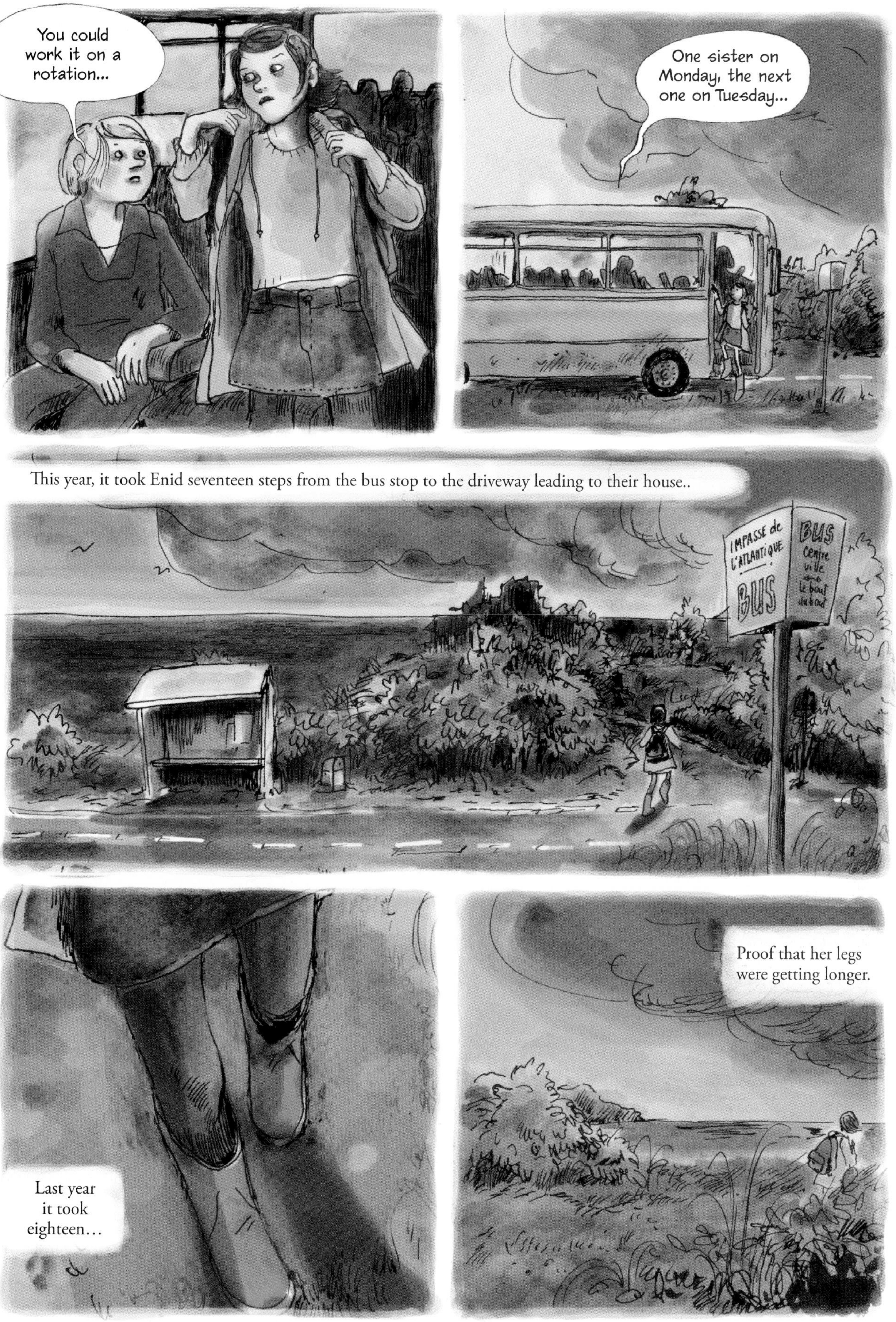
You could work it on a rotation...
One sister on Monday, the next one on Tuesday...
This year, it took Enid seventeen steps from the bus stop to the driveway leading to their house..
IMPASSE de L'ATLANTIQUE
BUS
BUS
centre ville
le bout du bout
Last year it took eighteen…
Proof that her legs were getting longer.

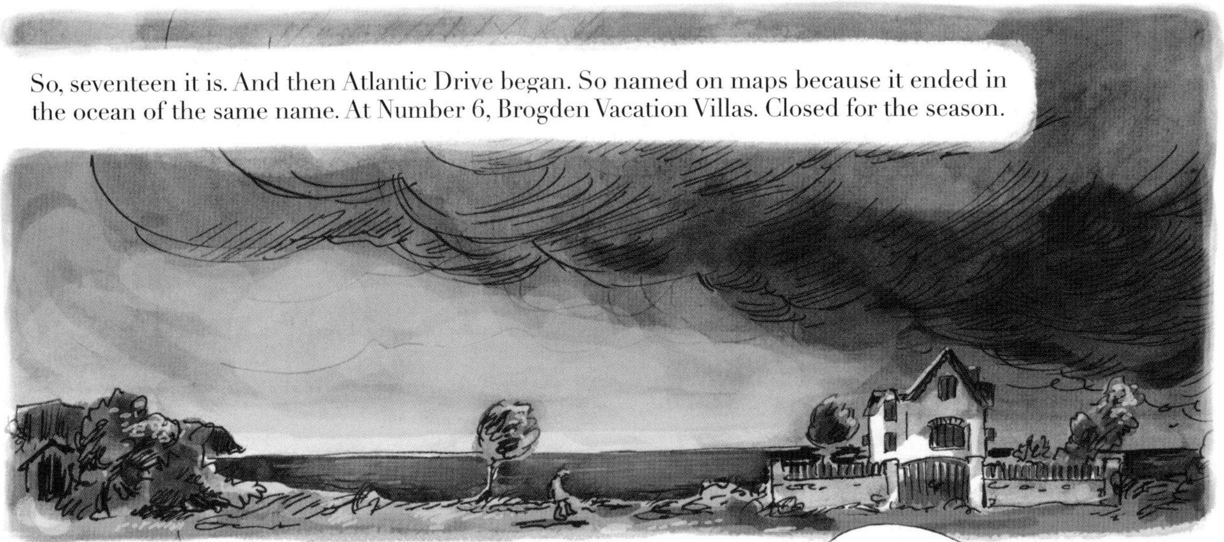
So, seventeen it is. And then Atlantic Drive began. So named on maps because it ended in the ocean of the same name. At Number 6, Brogden Vacation Villas. Closed for the season.

Then, 500 yards of frustrated, misanthropic moorland...

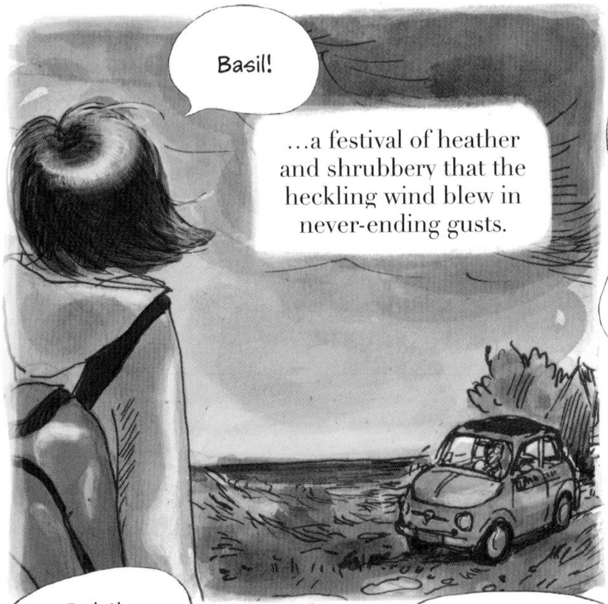
Basil!
...a festival of heather and shrubbery that the heckling wind blew in never-ending gusts.

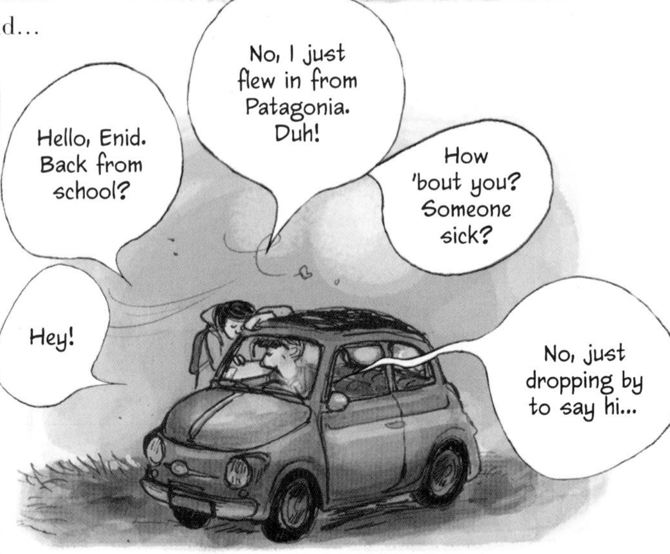
Hey!
Hello, Enid. Back from school?
No, I just flew in from Patagonia. Duh!
How 'bout you? Someone sick?
No, just dropping by to say hi...

Basil was in love with Charlie, the oldest of the Verdelaine sisters. He was a doctor, and also very shy.

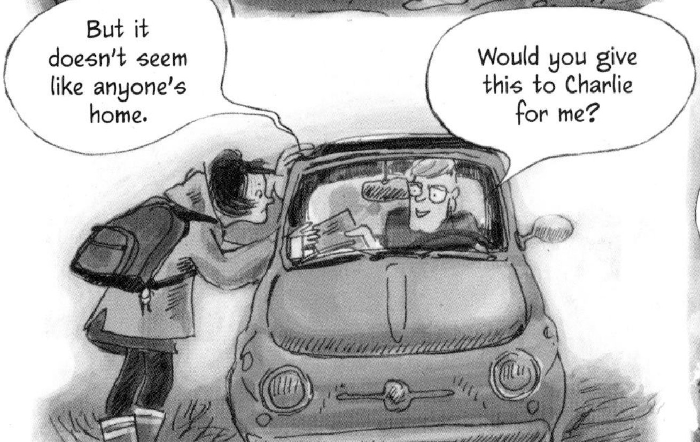
But it doesn't seem like anyone's home.
Would you give this to Charlie for me?

He was an old friend of the family. Actually, you could say he was kind of part of it already, since everyone knew he and Charlie would wind up getting married (even if all that stuff was still very much up in the air)...

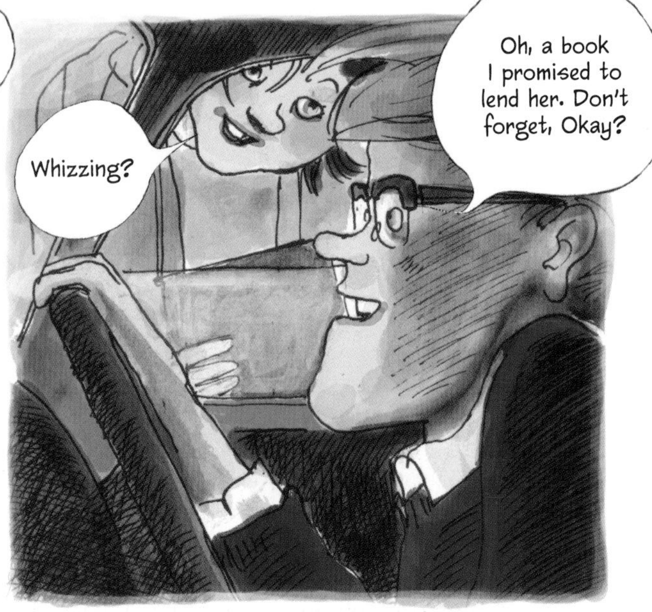
Oh, a book I promised to lend her. Don't forget, Okay?
Whizzing?

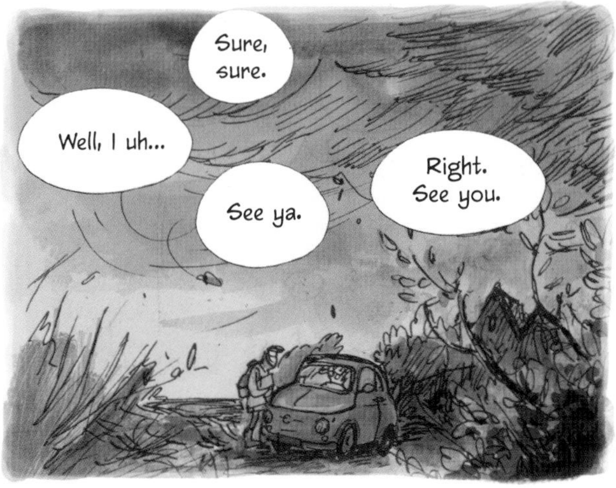
Well, I uh...
Sure, sure.
See ya.
Right. See you.

From deep in the underbrush came much rustling and shuddering, a miniature tumult. Hordes of things hid out there.

Creatures that meant no harm, prying as magpies, airy as sprites, cowardly, mischievous, springy, and quite tiny.

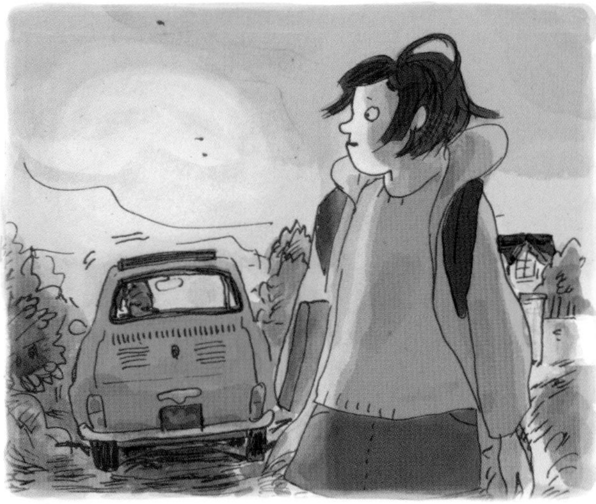

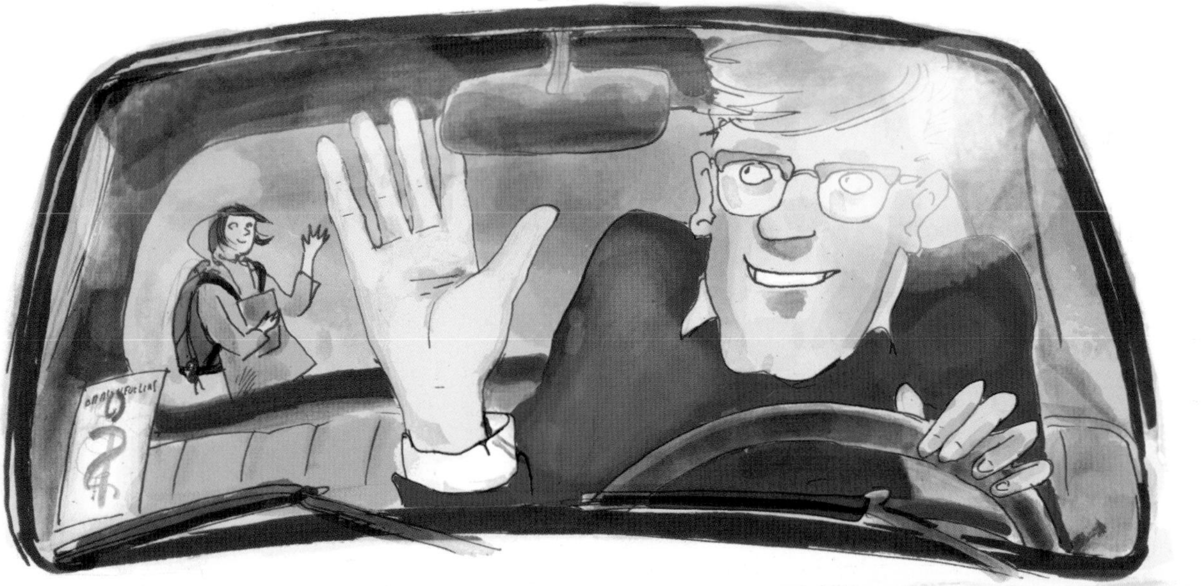

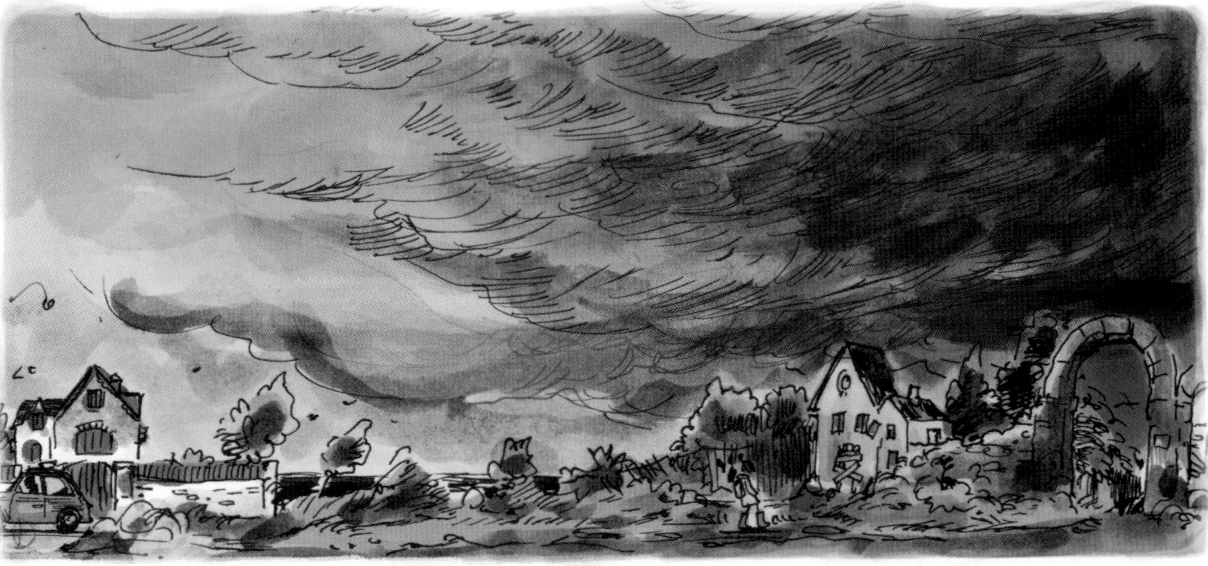

A bit farther off down the road was the caretaker's cottage, empty for years now. And finally...

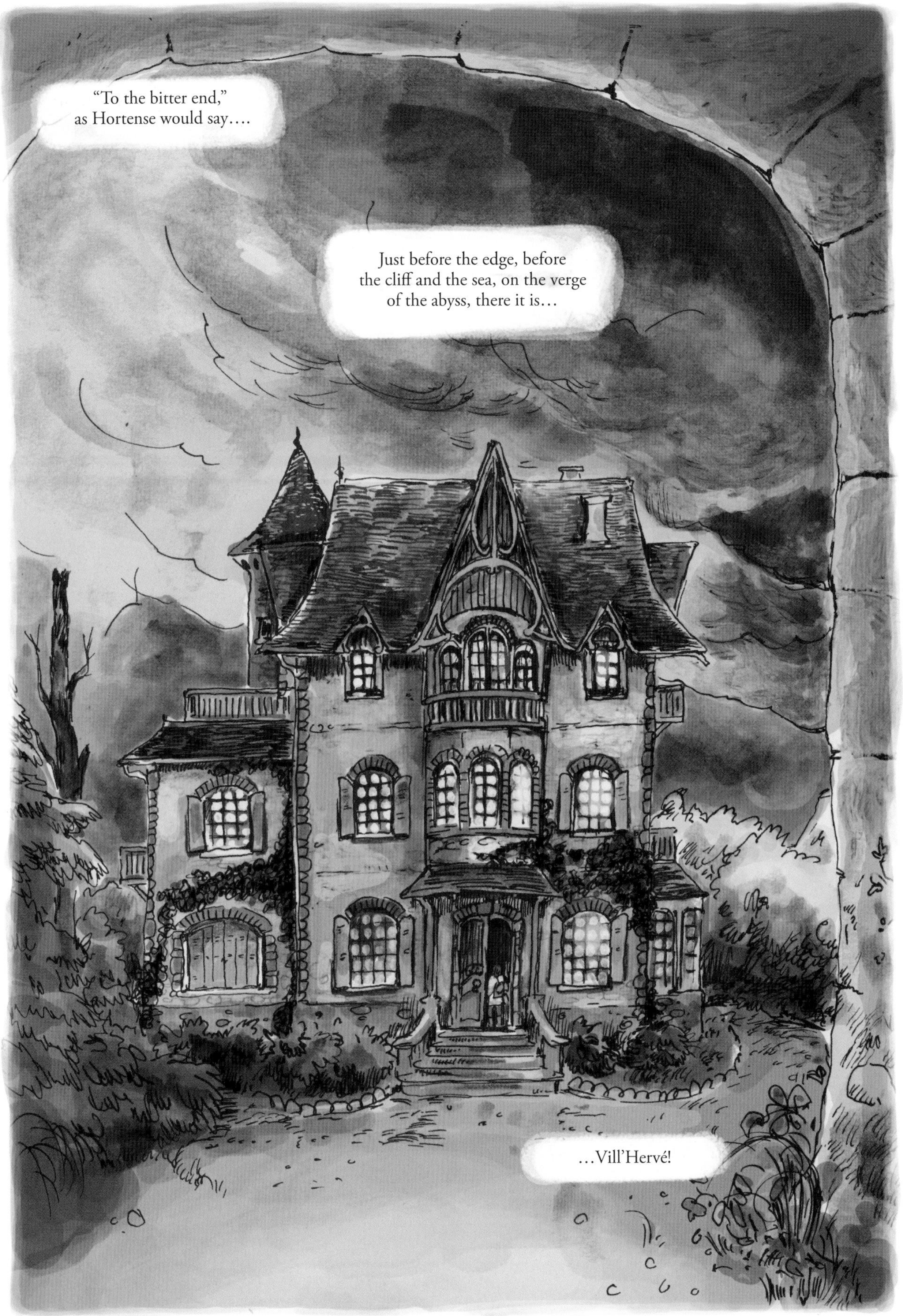
"To the bitter end," as Hortense would say….
Just before the edge, before the cliff and the sea, on the verge of the abyss, there it is…
…Vill'Hervé!

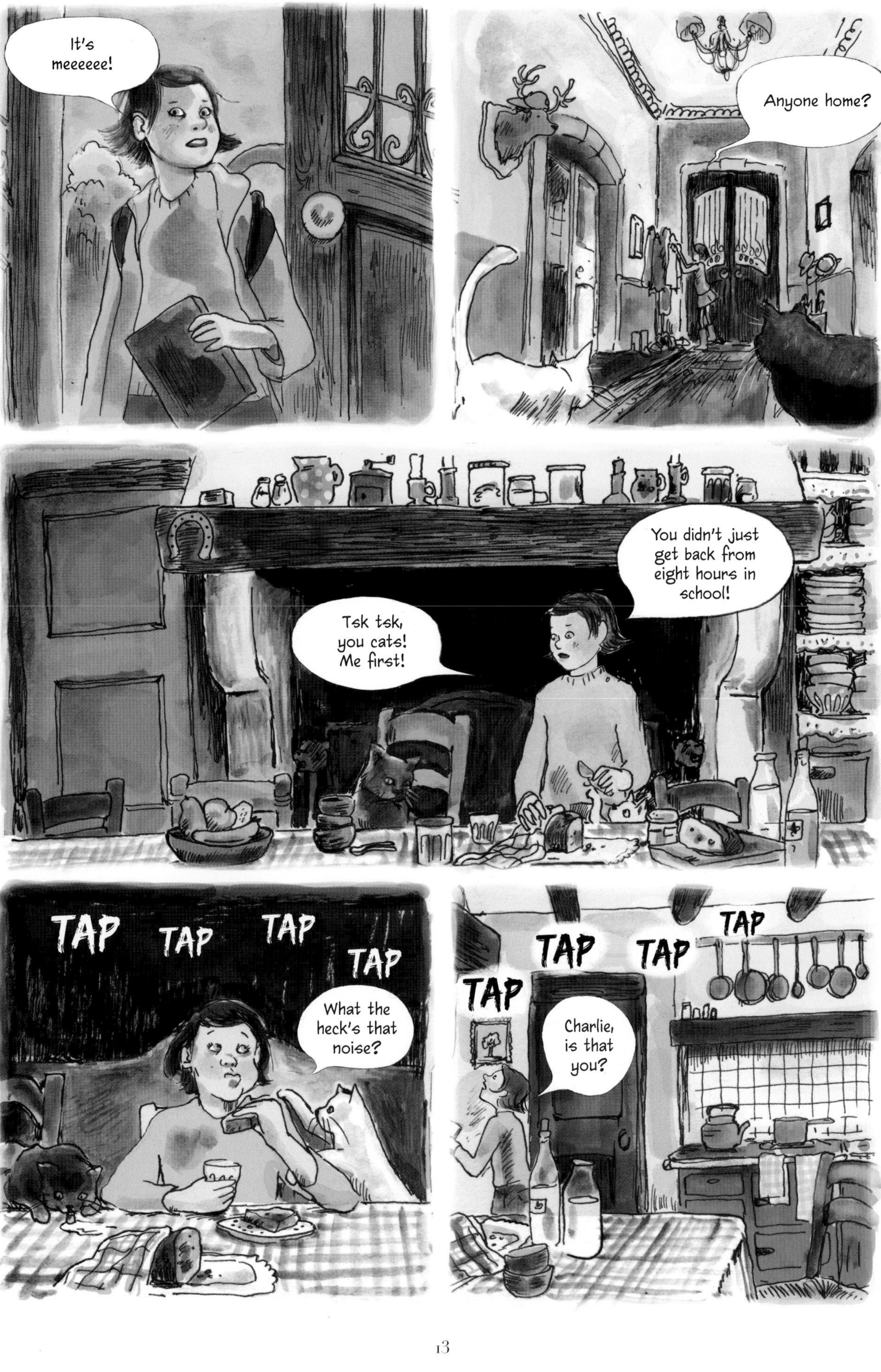
It's meeeeee!
Anyone home?
You didn't just get back from eight hours in school!
Tsk tsk, you cats! Me first!
TAP TAP TAP TAP
What the heck's that noise?
TAP TAP TAP TAP
Charlie, is that you?

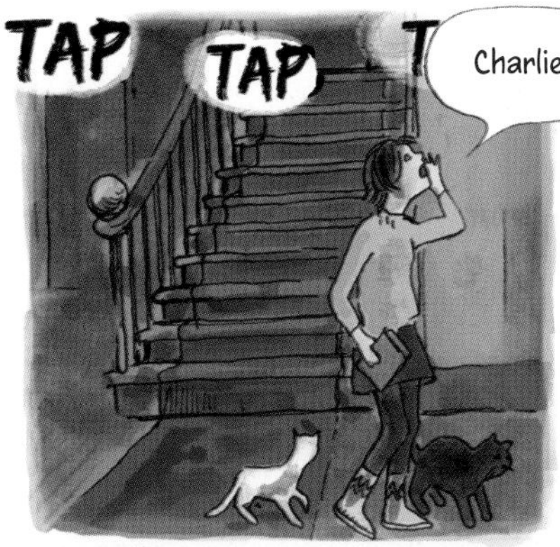
TAP
TAP
TAP
Charlie?

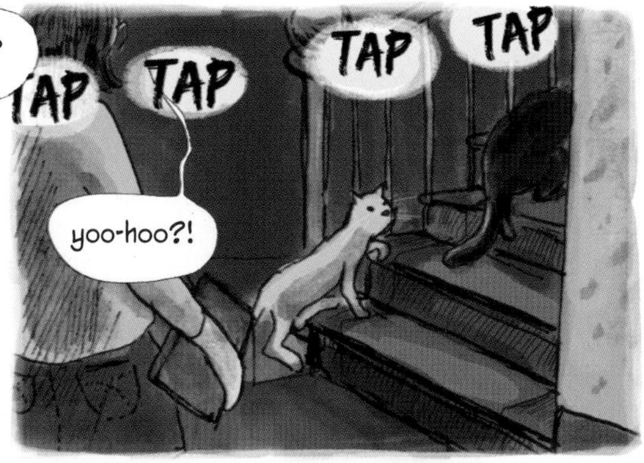
TAP
TAP
yoo-hoo?!
TAP
TAP

That staircase was called the Macaroni. Probably because it was all curvy and kind of smushy, too. It was the main staircase, and led to all four floors of Vill'Hervé.

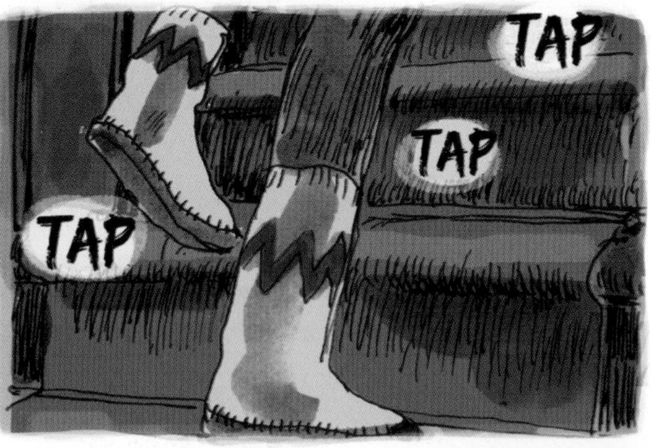
TAP
TAP
TAP

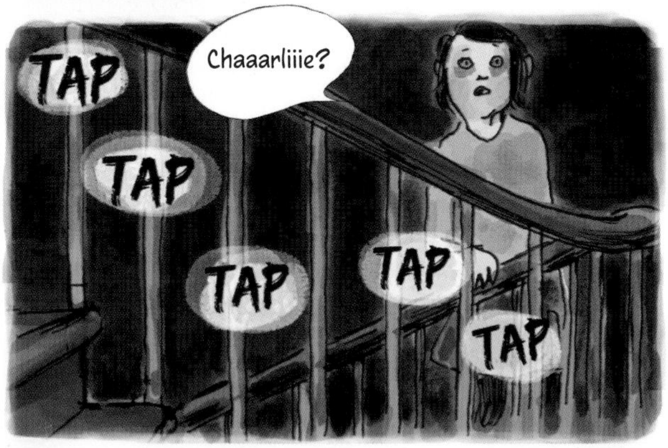
TAP
Chaaarliiie?
TAP
TAP
TAP
TAP

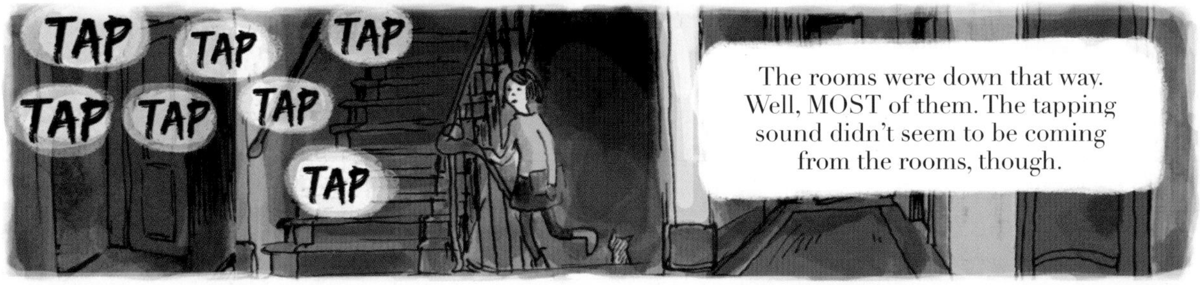
TAP
TAP
TAP
TAP
TAP
TAP
TAP
The rooms were down that way. Well, MOST of them. The tapping sound didn't seem to be coming from the rooms, though.

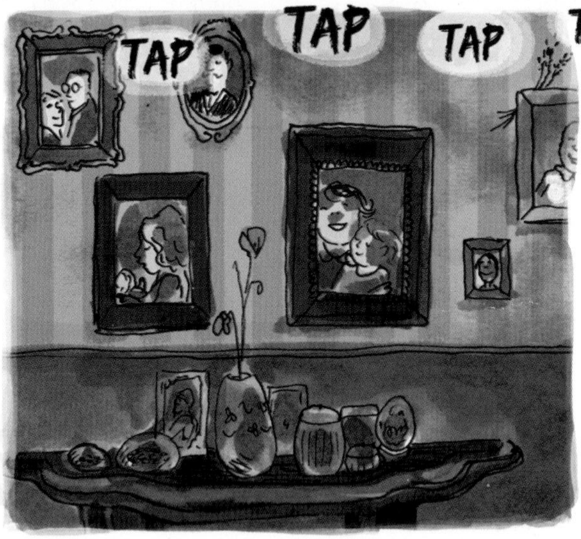
TAP
TAP
TAP
TAP

Now left, after the big red wardrobe. The path was so familiar. Familiar…and yet so terrifying! The double doors, a parlor, and then… THE door. To her parents' room.

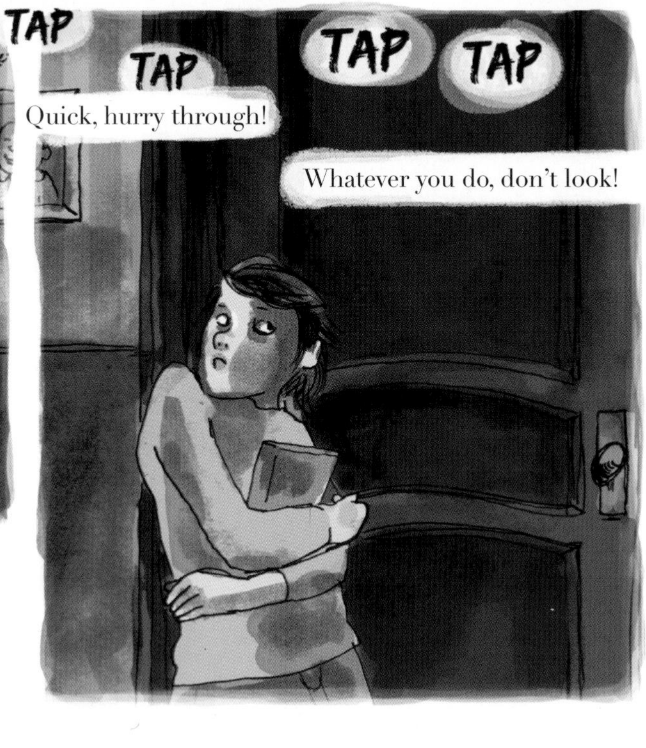
TAP
TAP
TAP
Quick, hurry through!
Whatever you do, don't look!

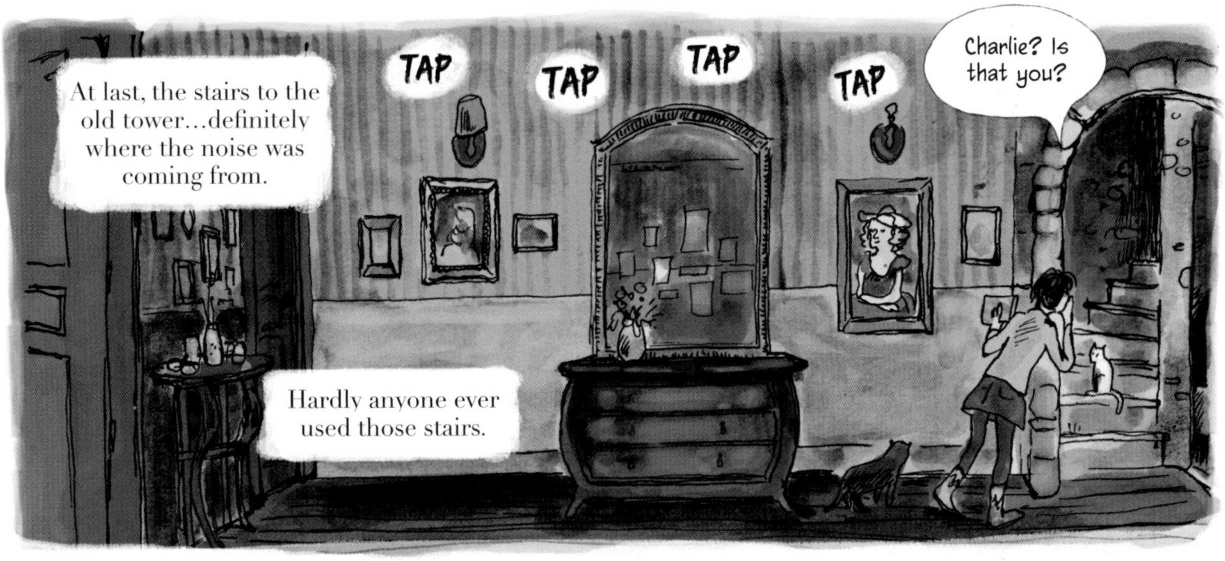
At last, the stairs to the old tower…definitely where the noise was coming from.
TAP
TAP
TAP
TAP
Charlie? Is that you?
Hardly anyone ever used those stairs.

They wound up into the tower, with their steep steps of slippery, perilous stone.
They were pretty, but drafty as could be, and all things considered, kind of gloomy.

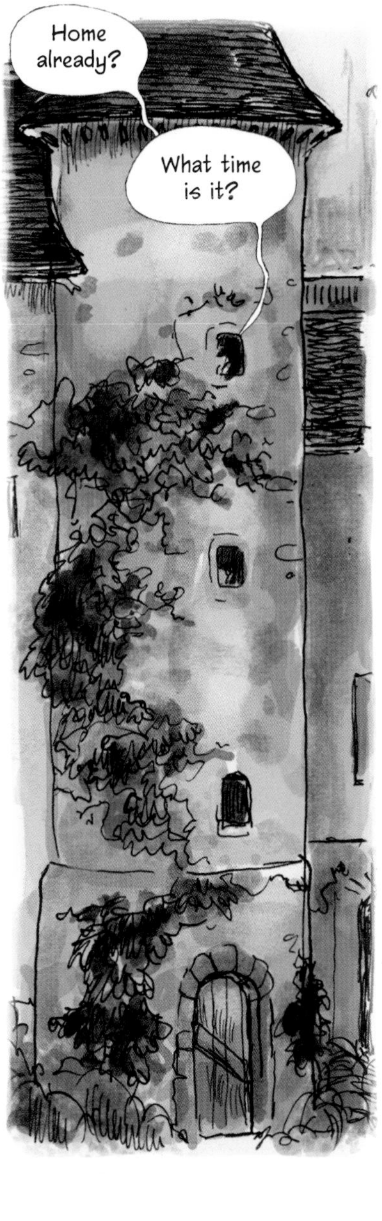
Home already?
What time is it?

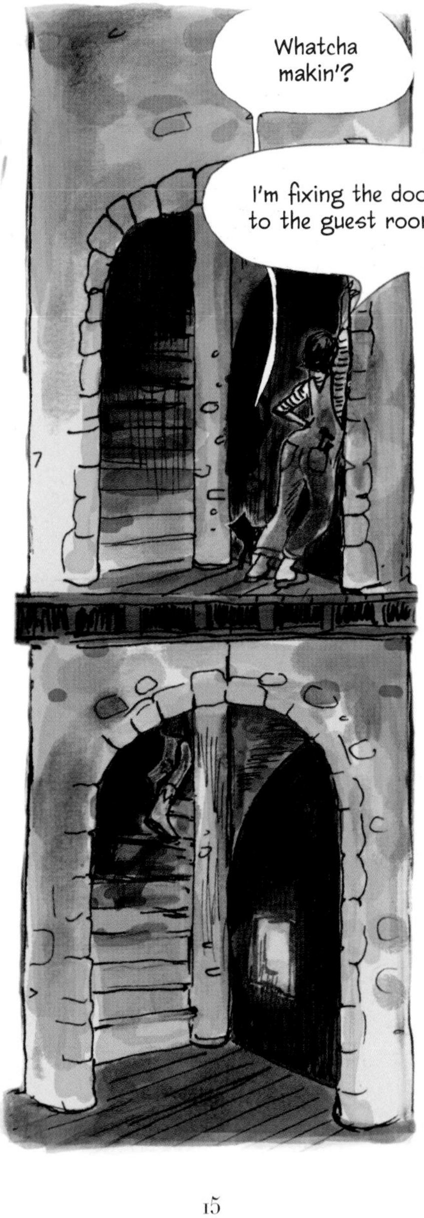
Whatcha makin'?
I'm fixing the door to the guest room.

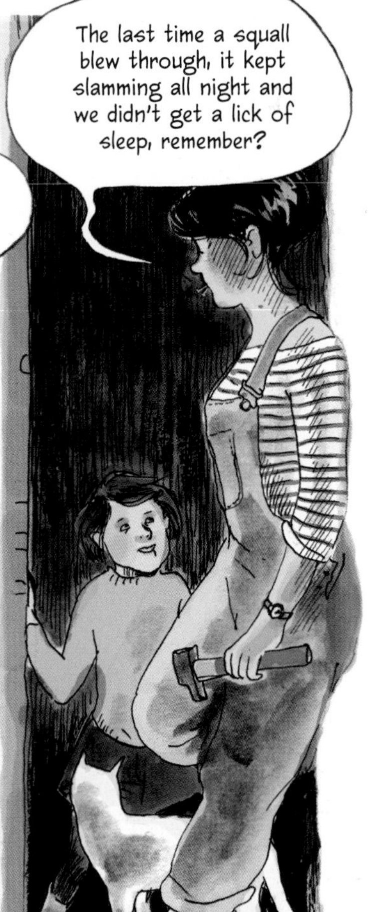
The last time a squall blew through, it kept slamming all night and we didn't get a lick of sleep, remember?

Charlie Verdelaine was 23 years old. She fixed things, cooked, worked in a lab, loved Basil, and looked after everyone else.

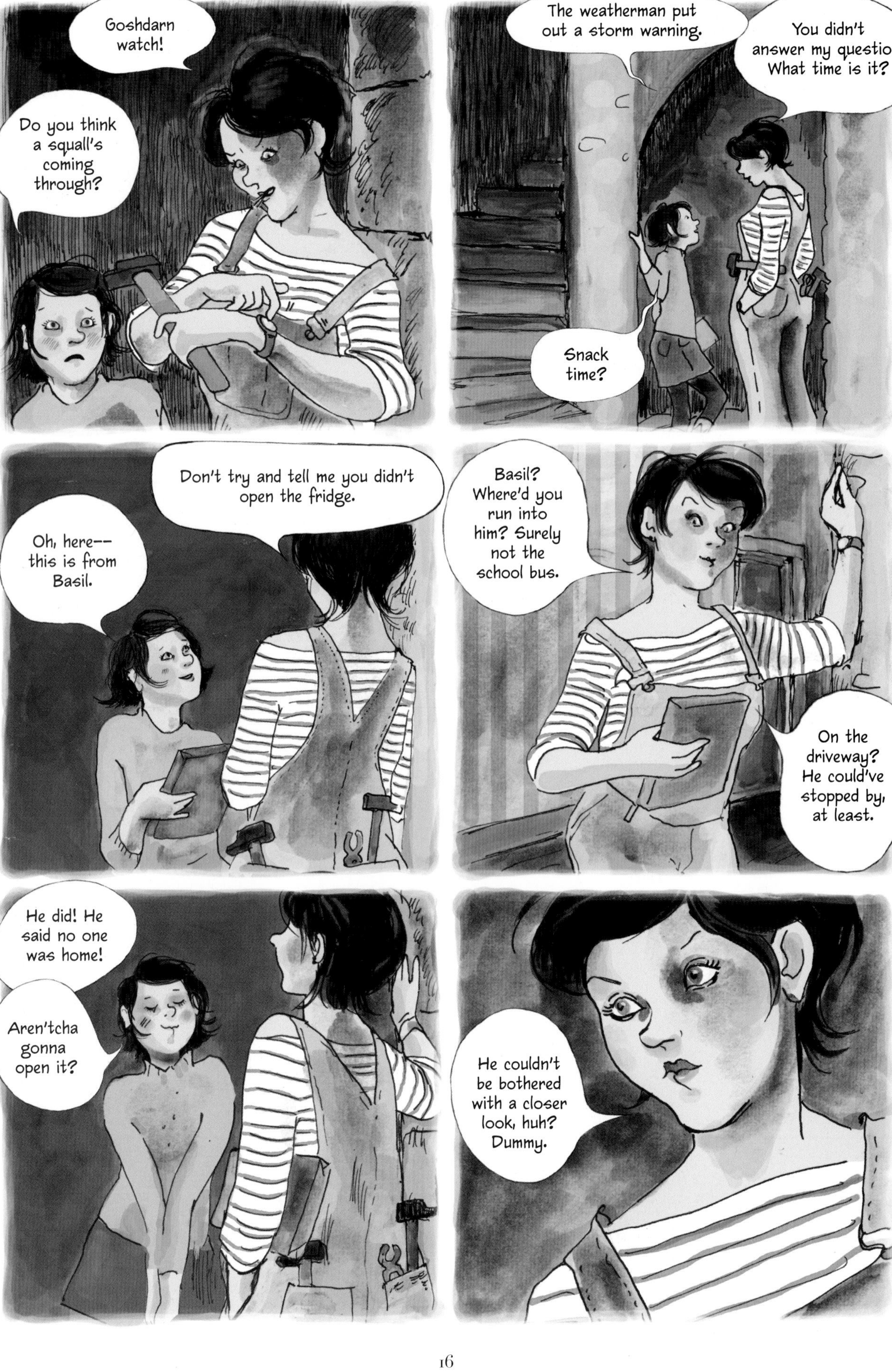
Goshdarn watch!
Do you think a squall's coming through?
The weatherman put out a storm warning.
You didn't answer my question. What time is it?
Snack time?
Don't try and tell me you didn't open the fridge.
Oh, here-- this is from Basil.
Basil? Where'd you run into him? Surely not the school bus.
On the driveway? He could've stopped by, at least.
He did! He said no one was home!
Aren'tcha gonna open it?
He couldn't be bothered with a closer look, huh? Dummy.

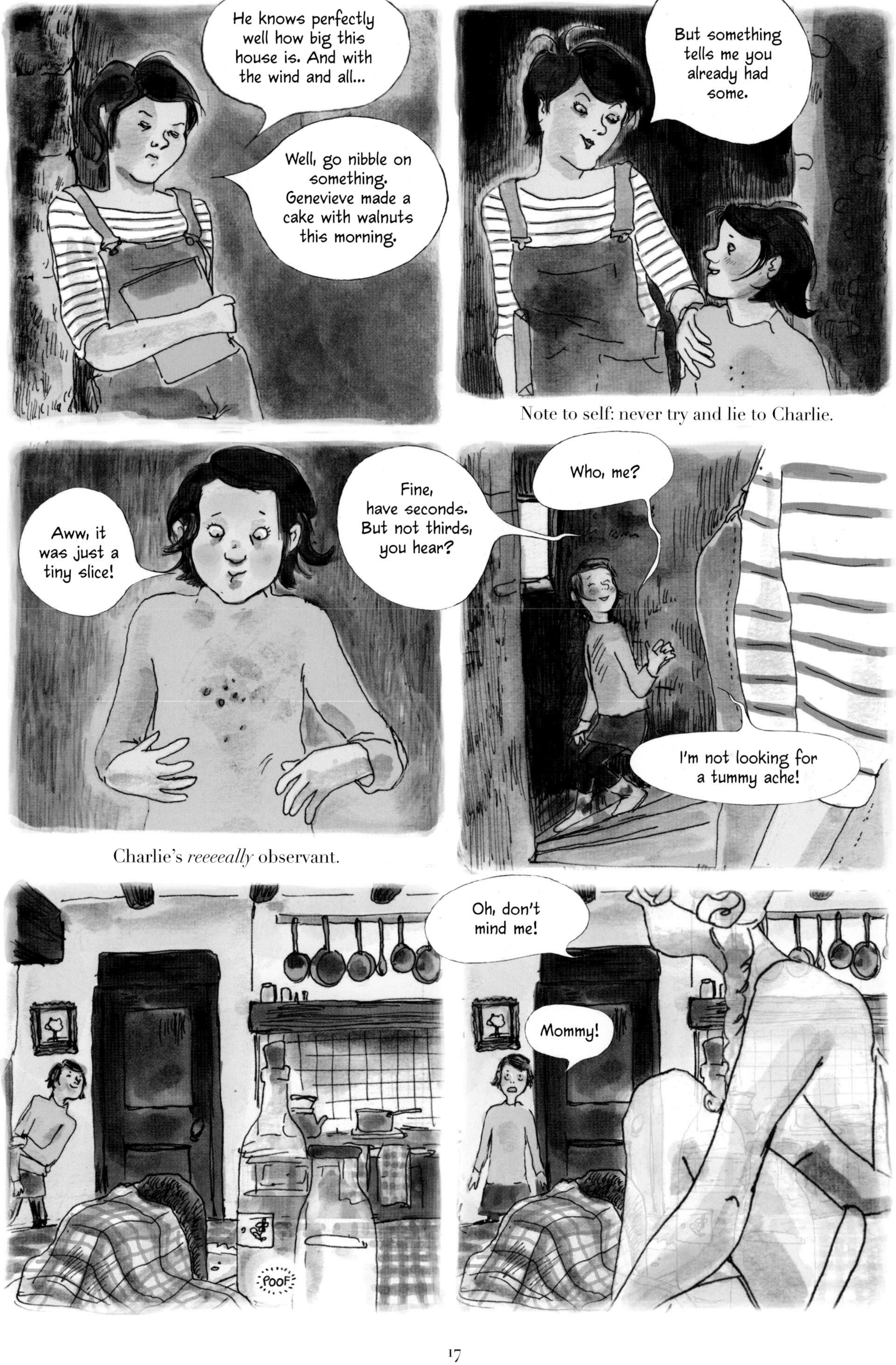
He knows perfectly well how big this house is. And with the wind and all...
Well, go nibble on something. Genevieve made a cake with walnuts this morning.
But something tells me you already had some.
Note to self: never try and lie to Charlie.
Aww, it was just a tiny slice!
Charlie's *reeeeally* observant.
Fine, have seconds. But not thirds, you hear?
Who, me?
I'm not looking for a tummy ache!
POOF
Oh, don't mind me!
Mommy!

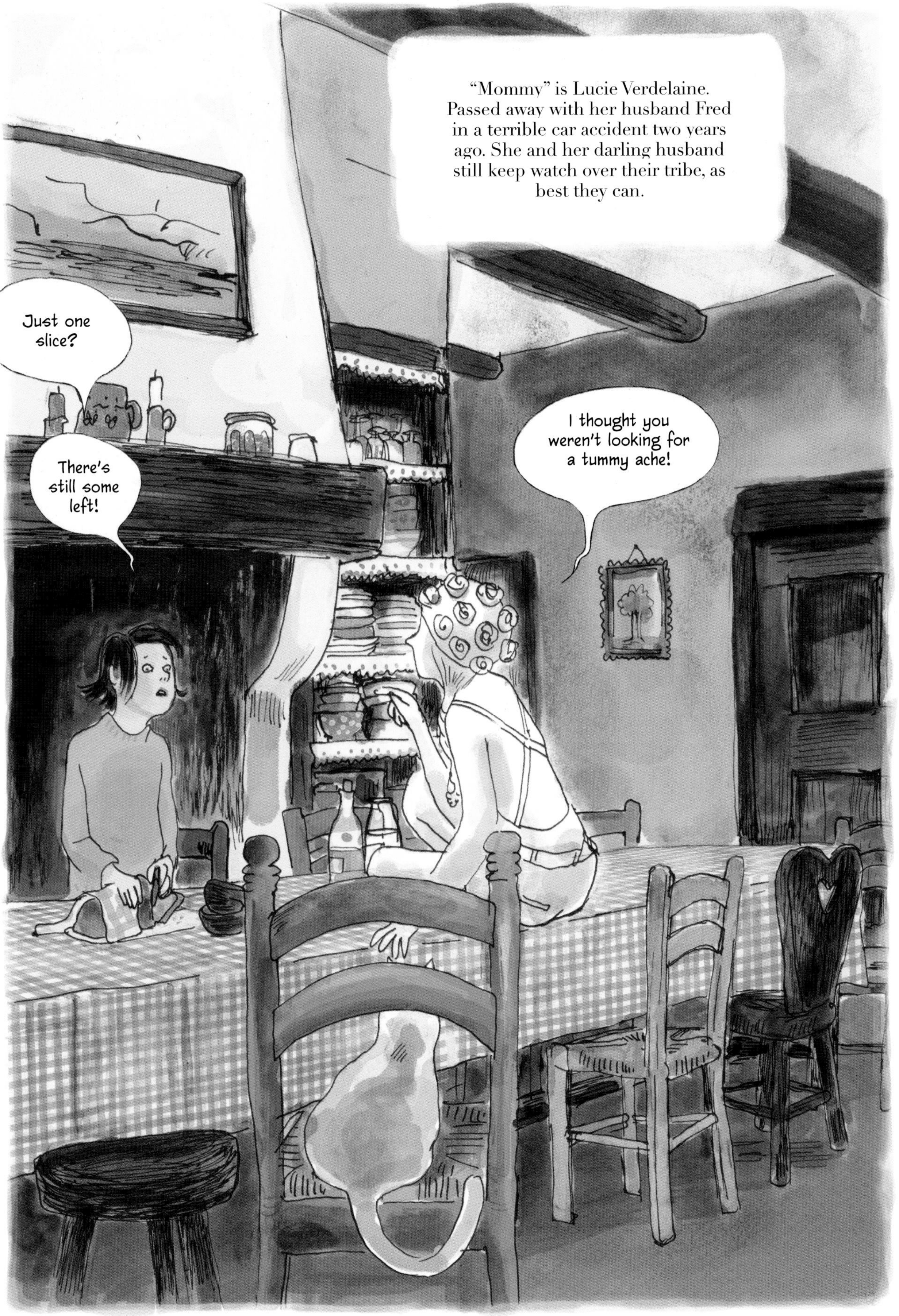
"Mommy" is Lucie Verdelaine. Passed away with her husband Fred in a terrible car accident two years ago. She and her darling husband still keep watch over their tribe, as best they can.
Just one slice?
There's still some left!
I thought you weren't looking for a tummy ache!

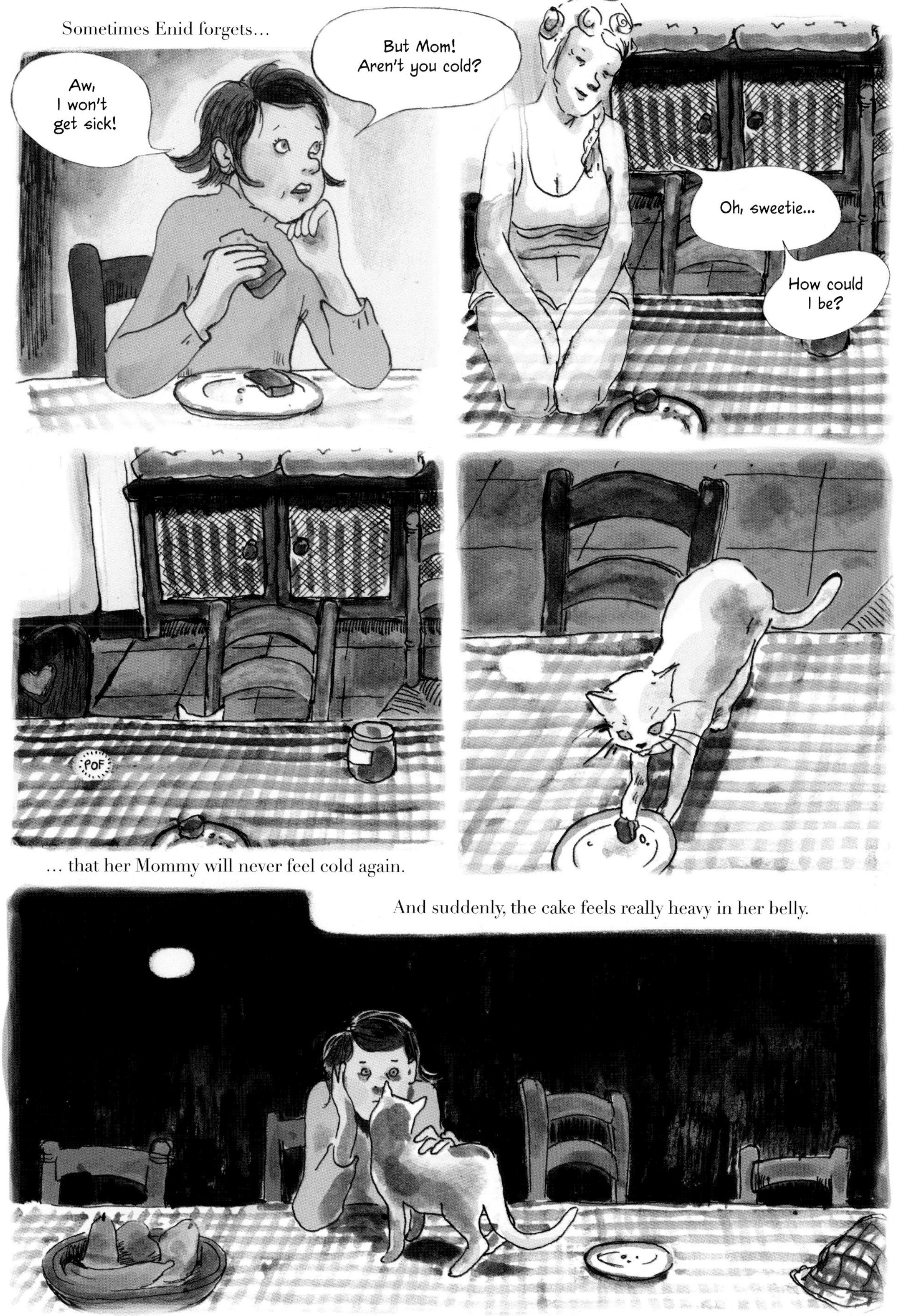
Sometimes Enid forgets...
Aw, I won't get sick!
But Mom! Aren't you cold?
Oh, sweetie...
How could I be?
POF
... that her Mommy will never feel cold again.
And suddenly, the cake feels really heavy in her belly.

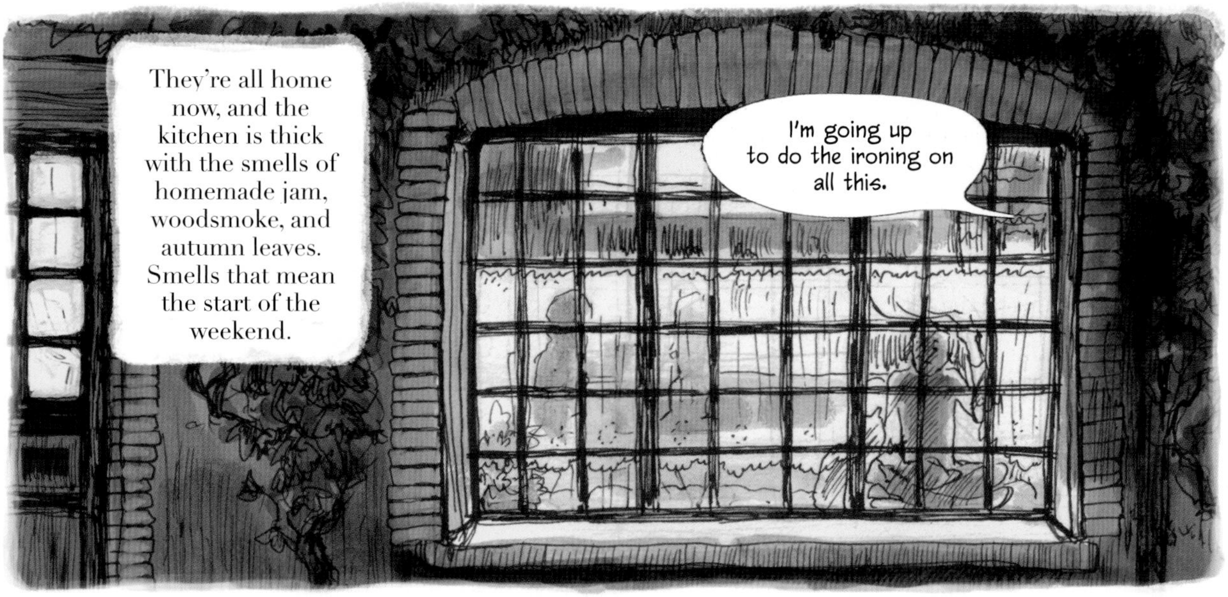
They're all home now, and the kitchen is thick with the smells of homemade jam, woodsmoke, and autumn leaves. Smells that mean the start of the weekend.
I'm going up to do the ironing on all this.

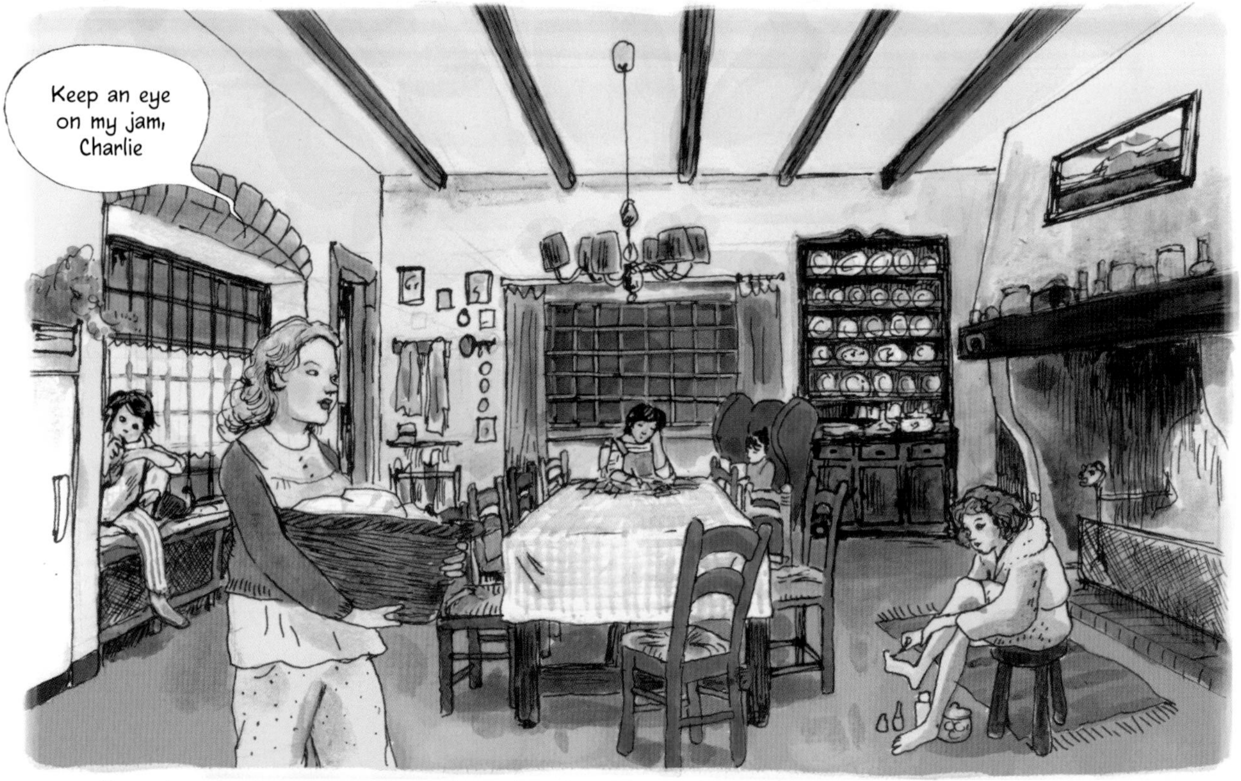
Keep an eye on my jam, Charlie

Genevieve is 16, and her thing is housekeeping. She washes whole bunches of things, irons others, sews buttons back on, and mends socks, roasts, and bakes cakes.

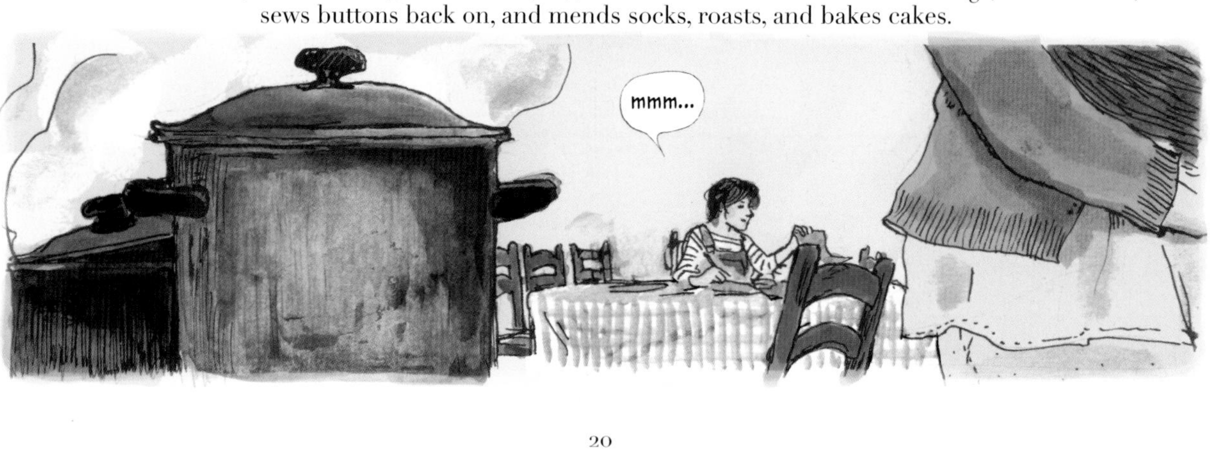
mmm...

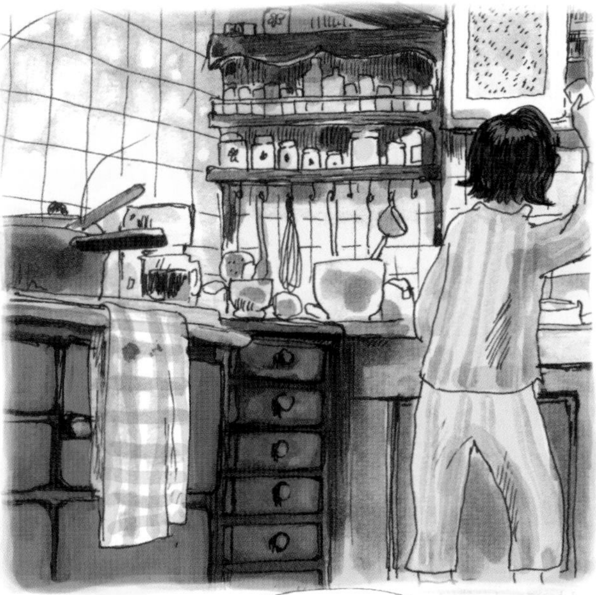

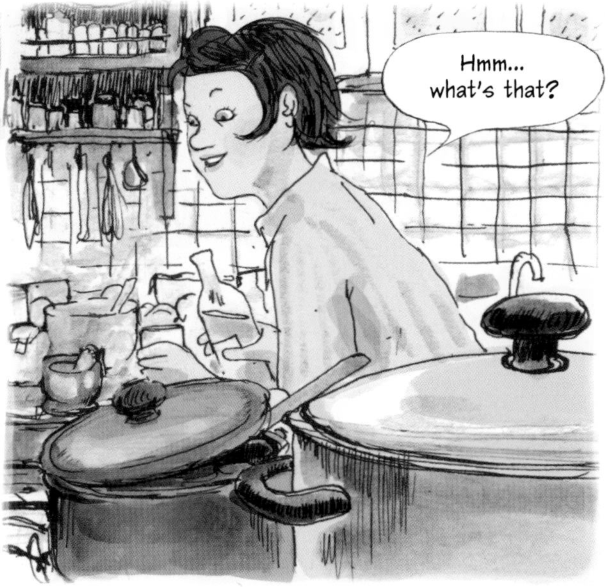
Hmm... what's that?

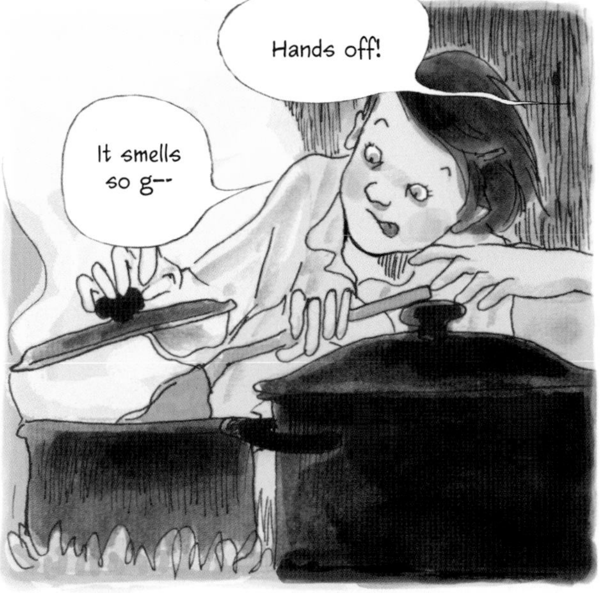
Hands off!
It smells so g--

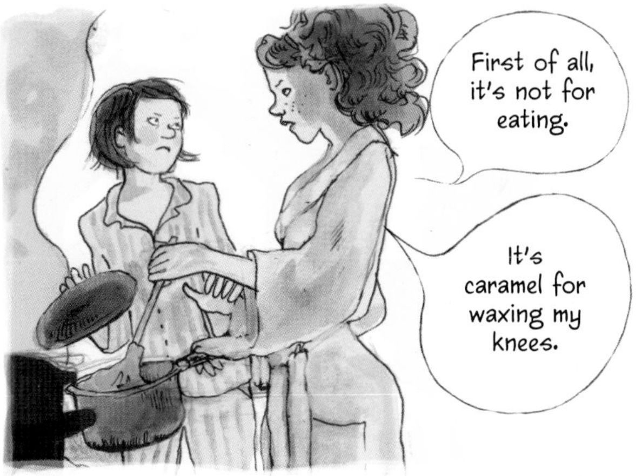
First of all, it's not for eating.
It's caramel for waxing my knees.

Bettina is 14. Her primary activities are: laying siege to the bathroom, watching her never-ending soap opera *Cooper Lane* with her insuff—ahem, inseparable friends, Denise and Behoteguy, and the rest of the time, being a pain to everyone else.

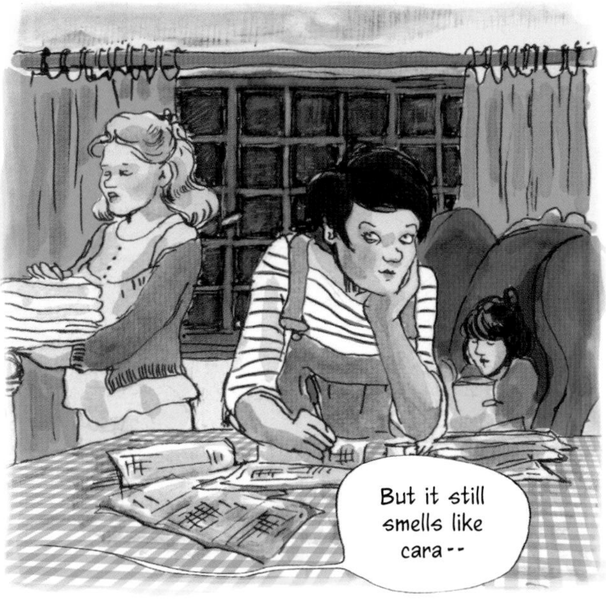
But it still smells like cara--

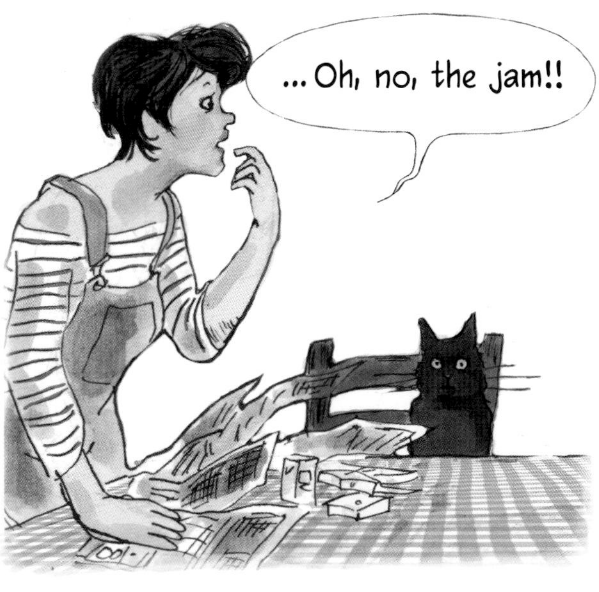
...Oh, no, the jam!!

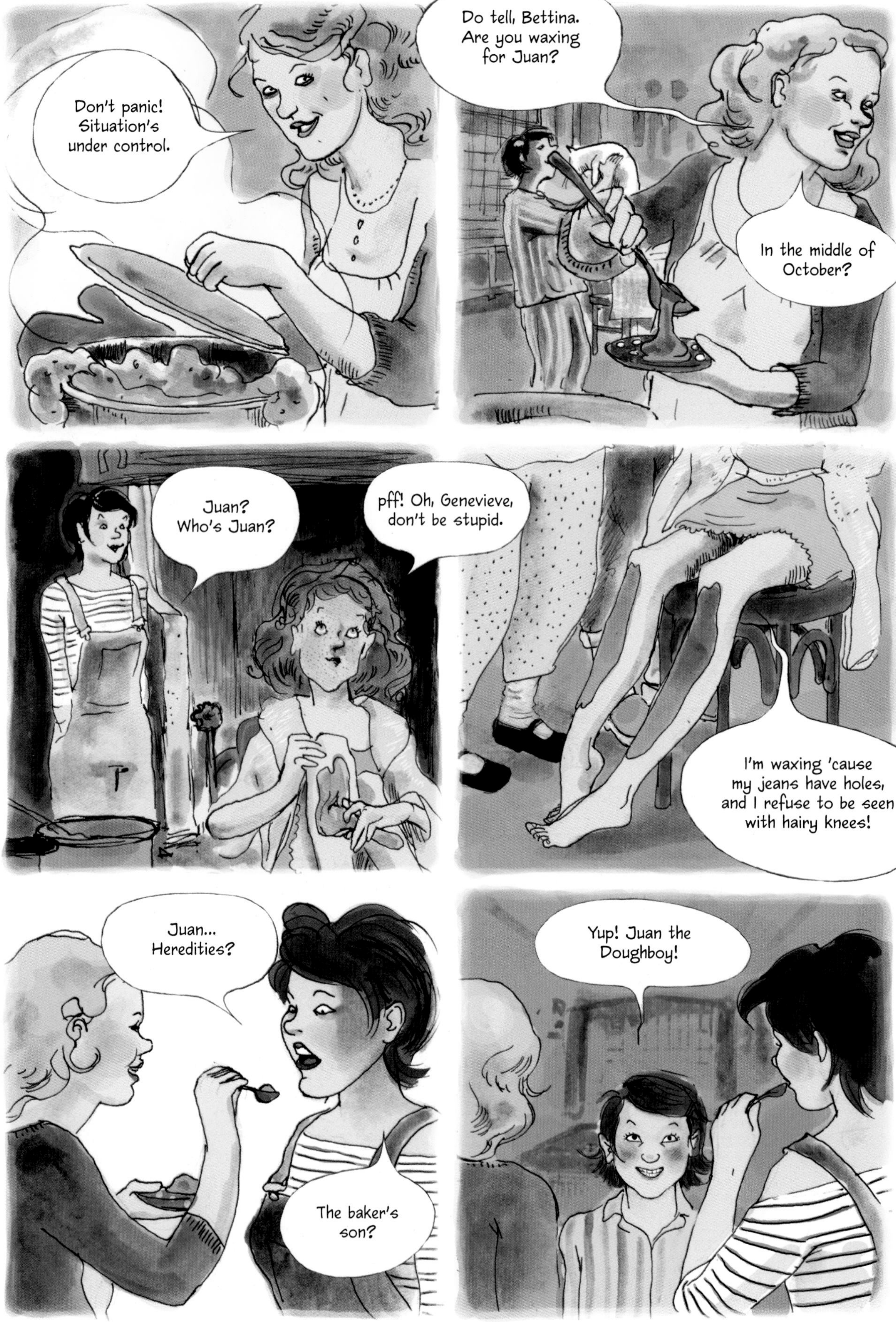
Don't panic! Situation's under control.
Do tell, Bettina. Are you waxing for Juan?
In the middle of October?
Juan? Who's Juan?
pff! Oh, Genevieve, don't be stupid.
I'm waxing 'cause my jeans have holes, and I refuse to be seen with hairy knees!
Juan... Heredities?
The baker's son?
Yup! Juan the Doughboy!

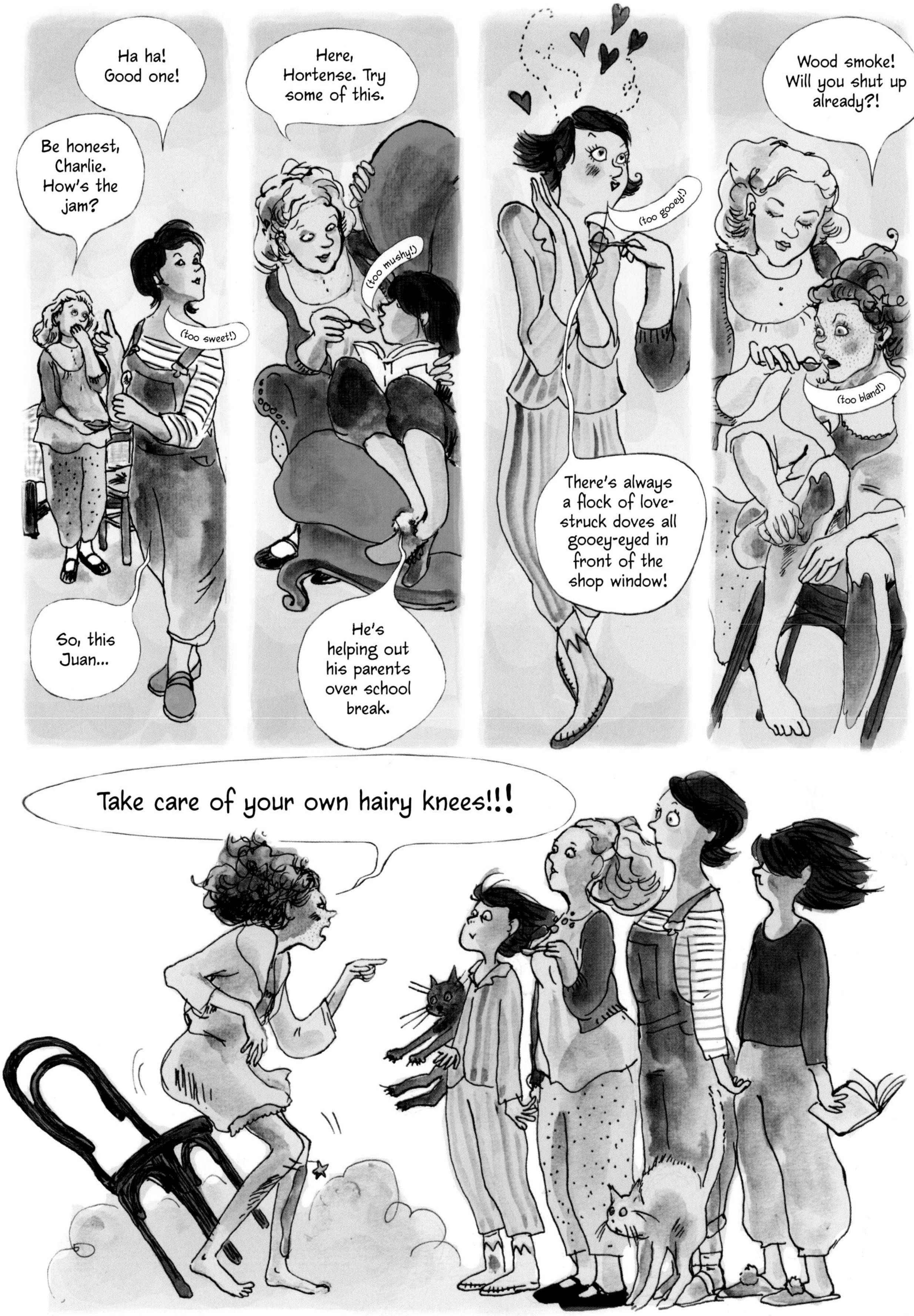
Ha ha! Good one!
Be honest, Charlie. How's the jam?
(too sweet!)
So, this Juan...
Here, Hortense. Try some of this.
(too mushy!)
He's helping out his parents over school break.
(too gooey!)
There's always a flock of love-struck doves all gooey-eyed in front of the shop window!
Wood smoke! Will you shut up already?!
(too bland!)
Take care of your own hairy knees!!!

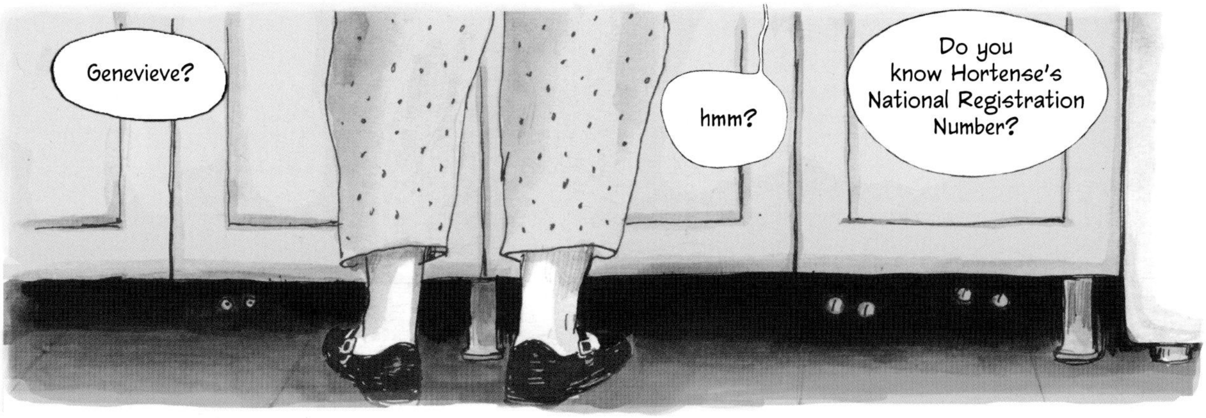
Genevieve?
hmm?
Do you know Hortense's National Registration Number?

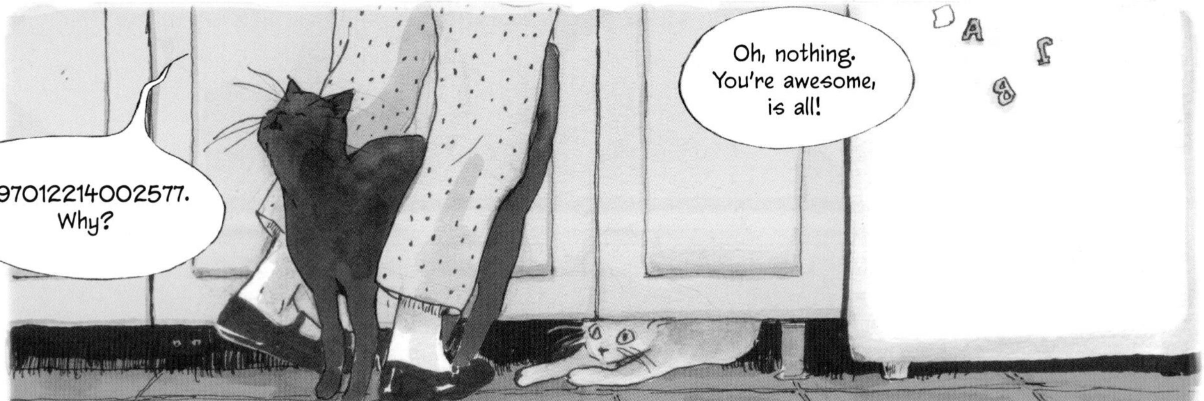
297012214002577. Why?
Oh, nothing. You're awesome, is all!

Charlie always waited till she had a whole stack of government forms before sending them back so she could get reimbursed for some massive amount (which never happened, of course).

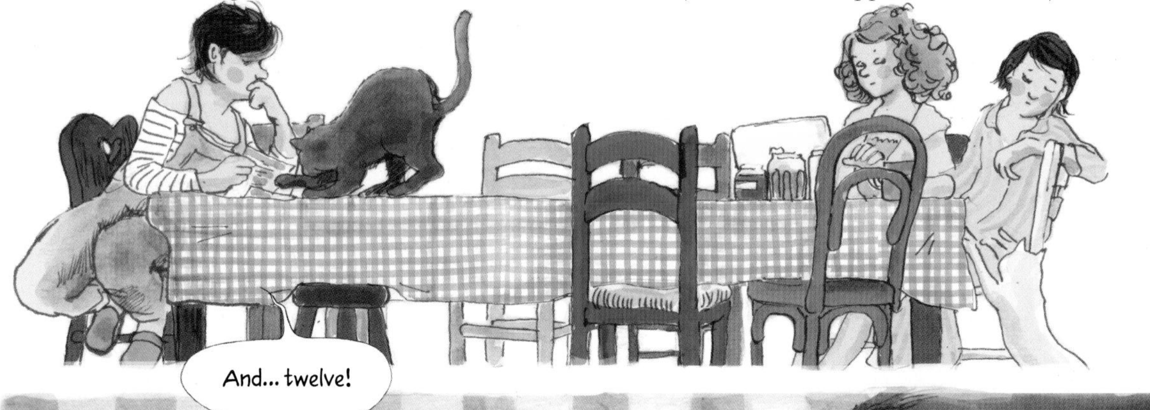
And... twelve!

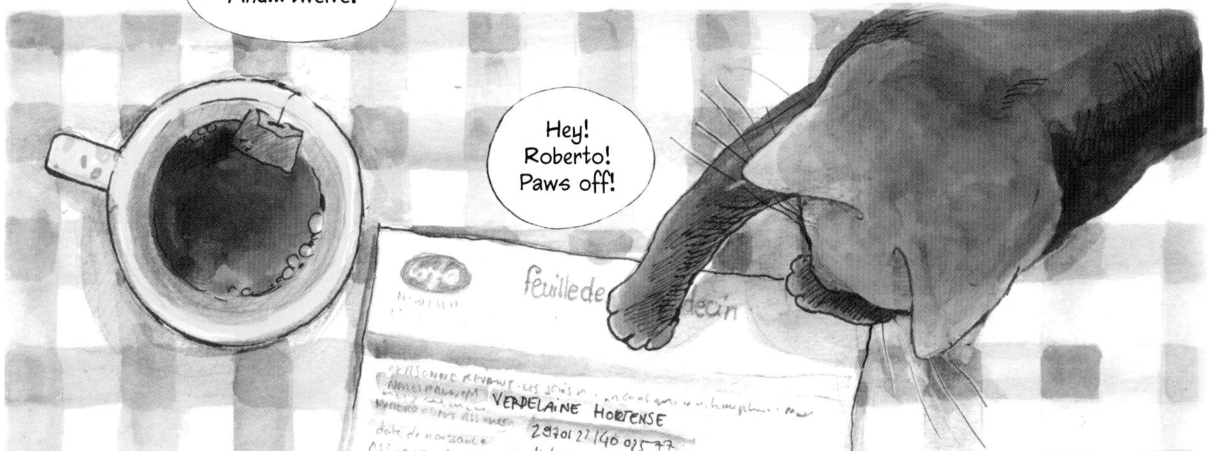
Hey! Roberto! Paws off!
VERDELAINE HORTENSE

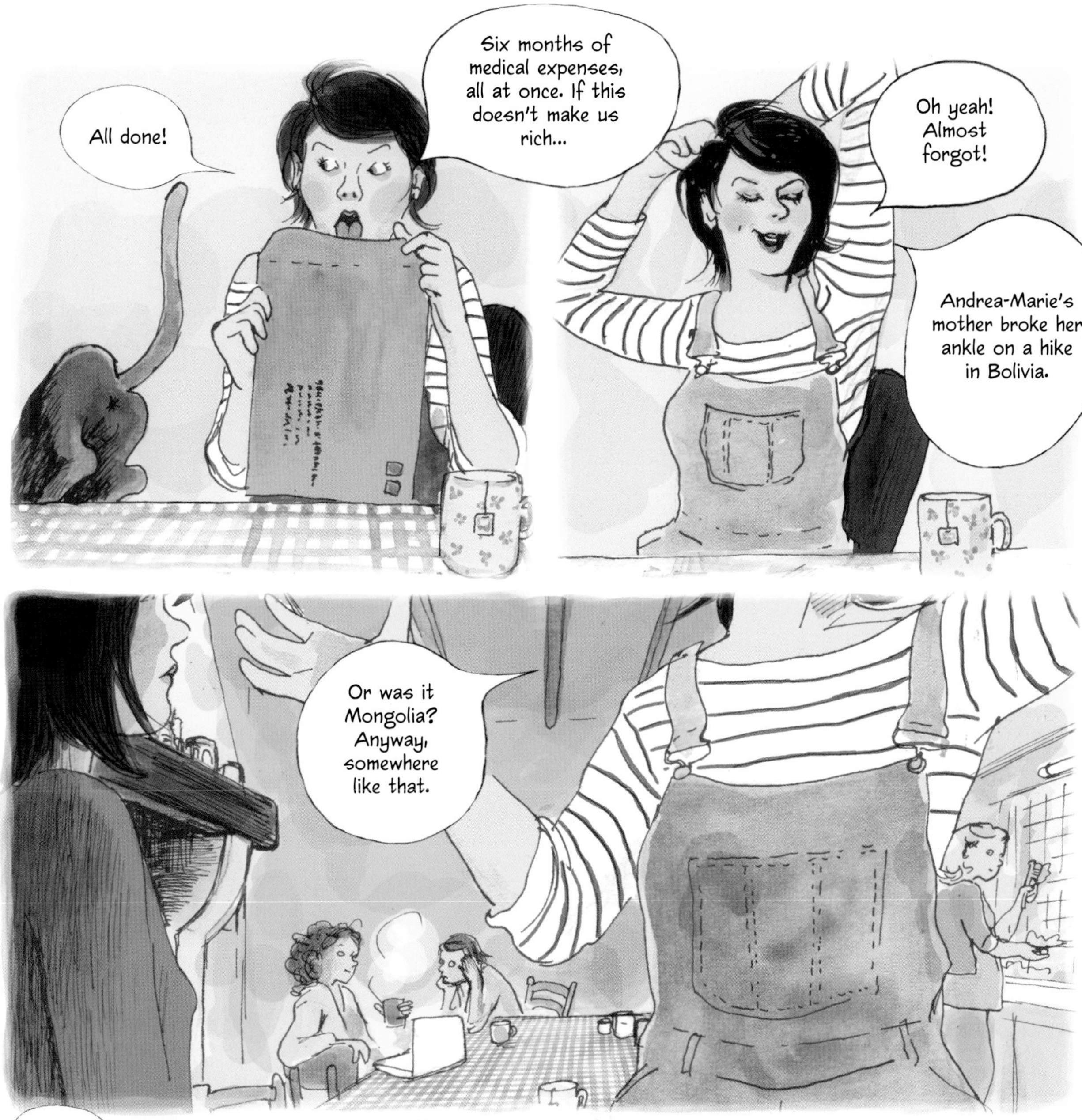
All done!
Six months of medical expenses, all at once. If this doesn't make us rich...
Oh yeah! Almost forgot!
Andrea-Marie's mother broke her ankle on a hike in Bolivia.
Or was it Mongolia? Anyway, somewhere like that.

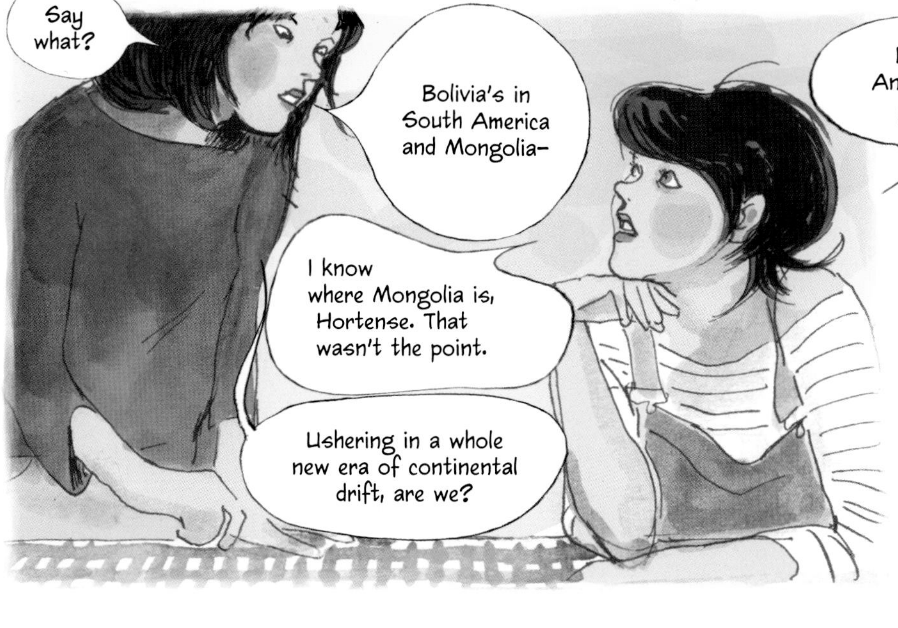
Say what?
Bolivia's in South America and Mongolia–
Back to the point, Andrea-Marie's mother got flown home...
I know where Mongolia is, Hortense. That wasn't the point.
Ushering in a whole new era of continental drift, are we?

Not much has been said yet about Hortense, age 11. She knows lots of things. Who wouldn't, when you've always got your nose buried in a book? In the rare moments when she doesn't, she's busy writing in her diary.

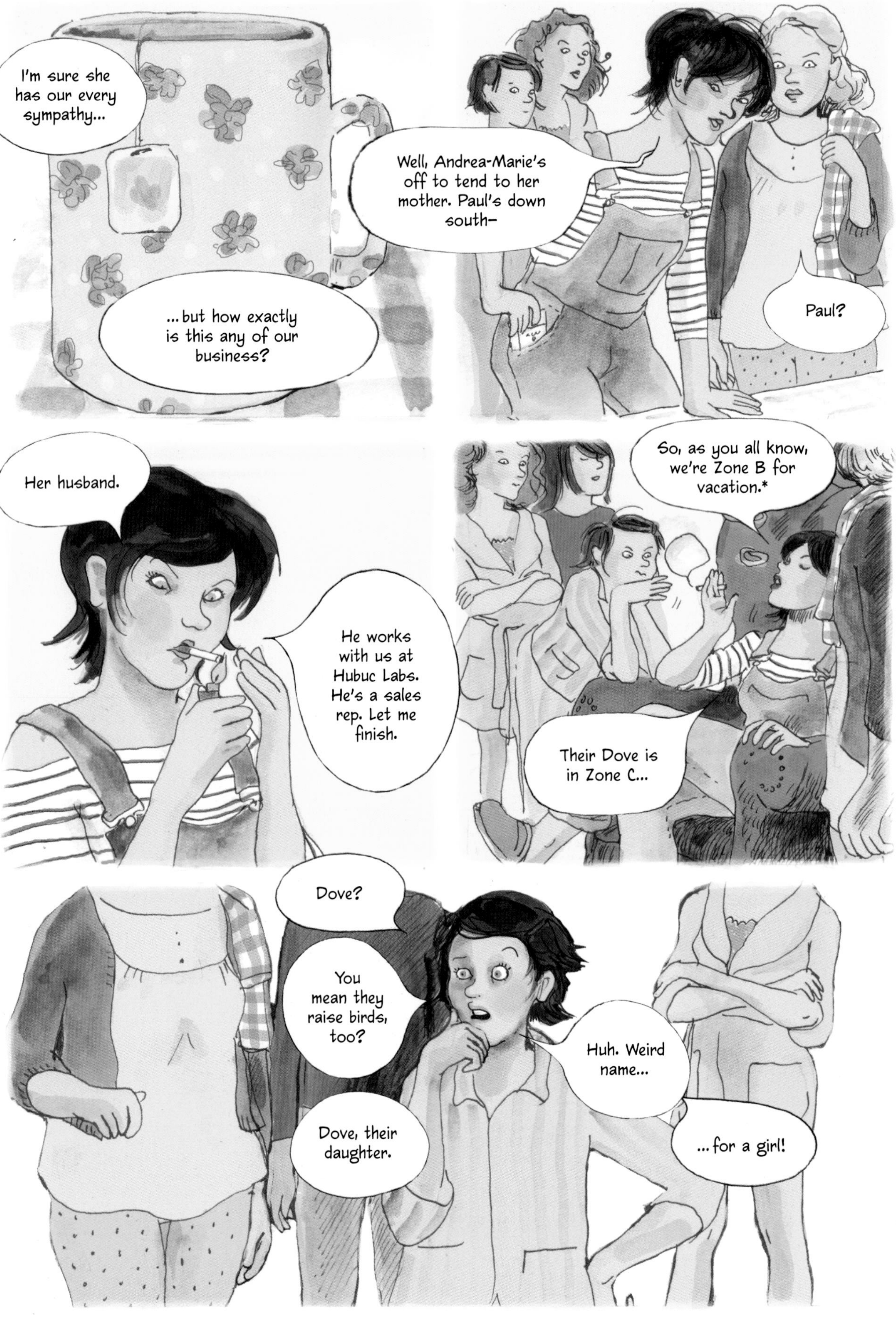
I'm sure she has our every sympathy...
...but how exactly is this any of our business?
Well, Andrea-Marie's off to tend to her mother. Paul's down south–
Paul?
Her husband.
He works with us at Hubuc Labs. He's a sales rep. Let me finish.
So, as you all know, we're Zone B for vacation.*
Their Dove is in Zone C...
Dove?
You mean they raise birds, too?
Dove, their daughter.
Huh. Weird name...
...for a girl!

* To alleviate congestion at popular vacation spots, some school holidays in France are staggered by dividing the country into three zones.

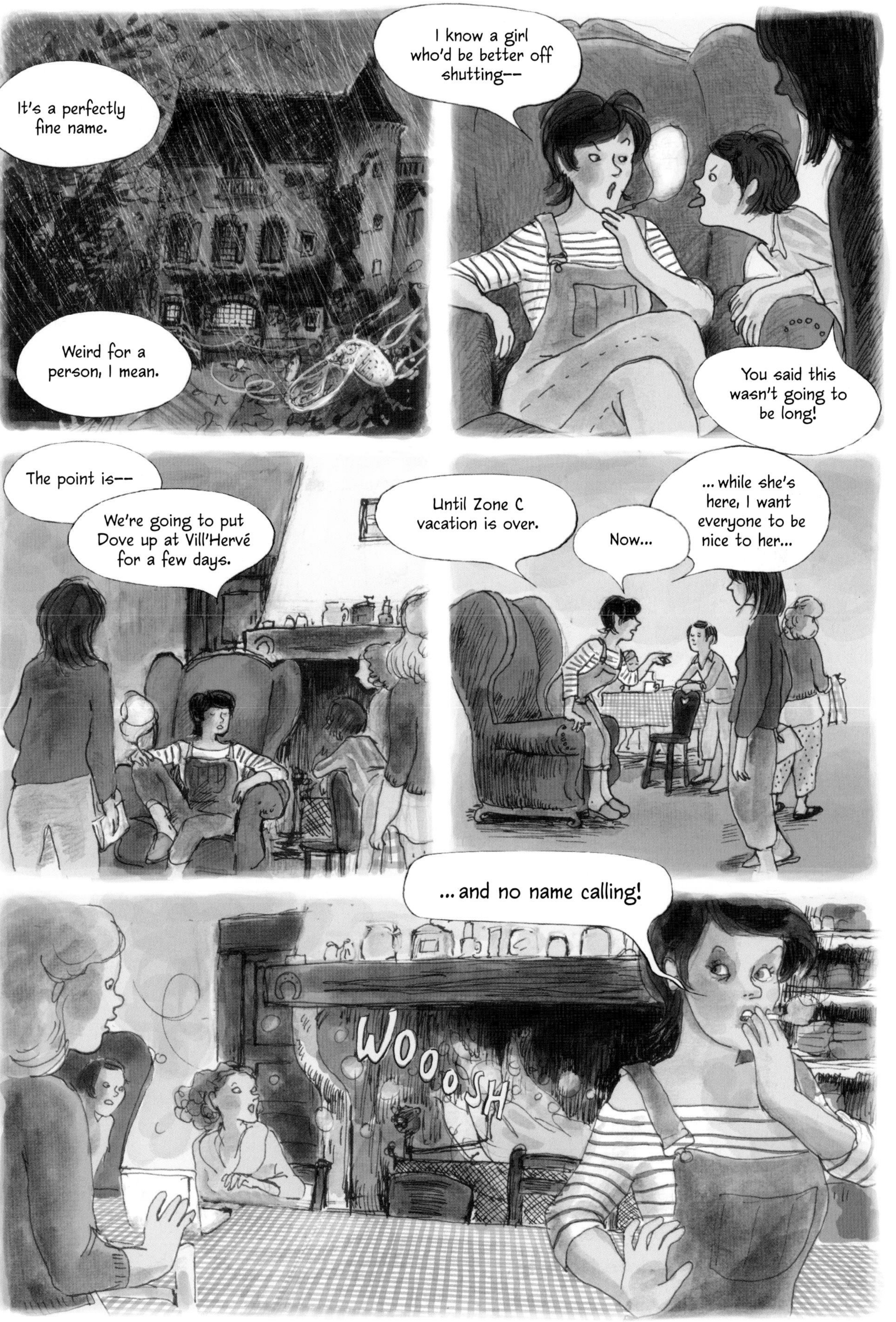
It's a perfectly fine name.
Weird for a person, I mean.
I know a girl who'd be better off shutting--
You said this wasn't going to be long!
The point is--
We're going to put Dove up at Vill'Hervé for a few days.
Until Zone C vacation is over.
Now...
...while she's here, I want everyone to be nice to her...
...and no name calling!
WOOOOSH

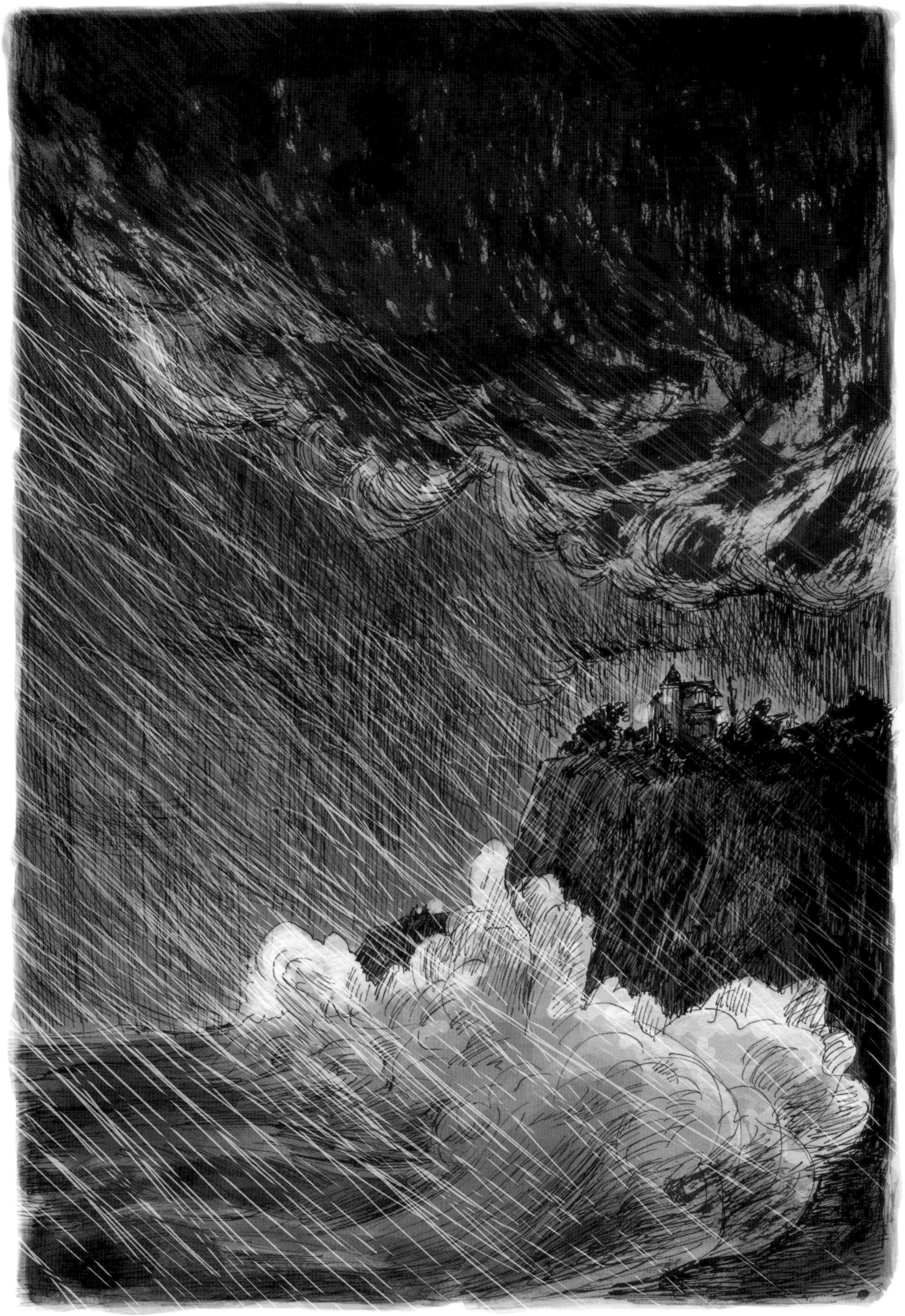

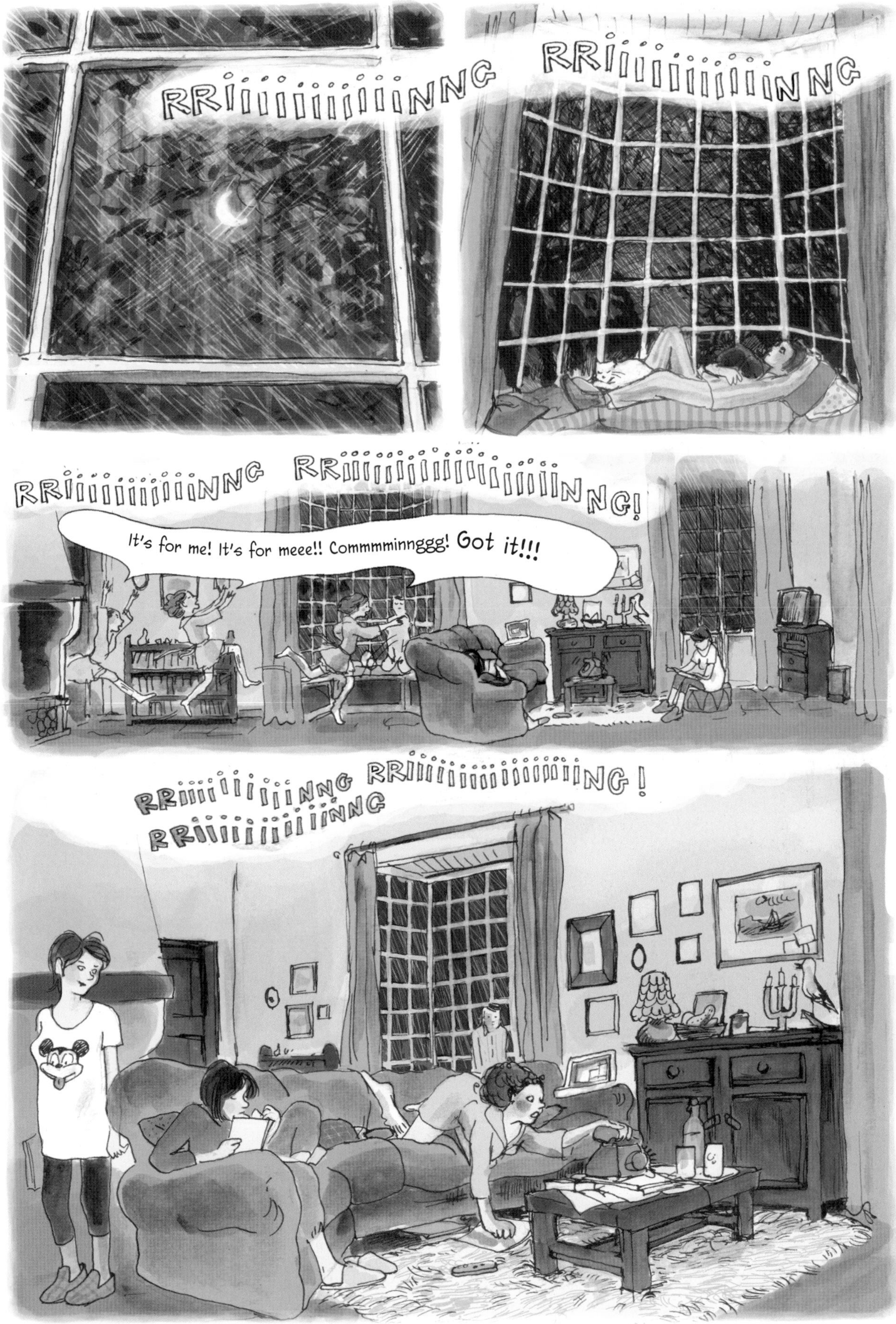
RRIiiiiiiiiiiiNNG
RRIiiiiiiiiiiiiiiNNG
RRIiiiiiiiiiiiiNNG
RRiiiiiiiiiiiiiiiiiiiiiiiiiiNNG!
It's for me! It's for meee!! Commmminnggg! Got it!!!
RRiiiiiiiiiiiiNNG RRIiiiiiiiiiiiiiiiiiiiNG!
RRiiiiiiiiiiiiNNG

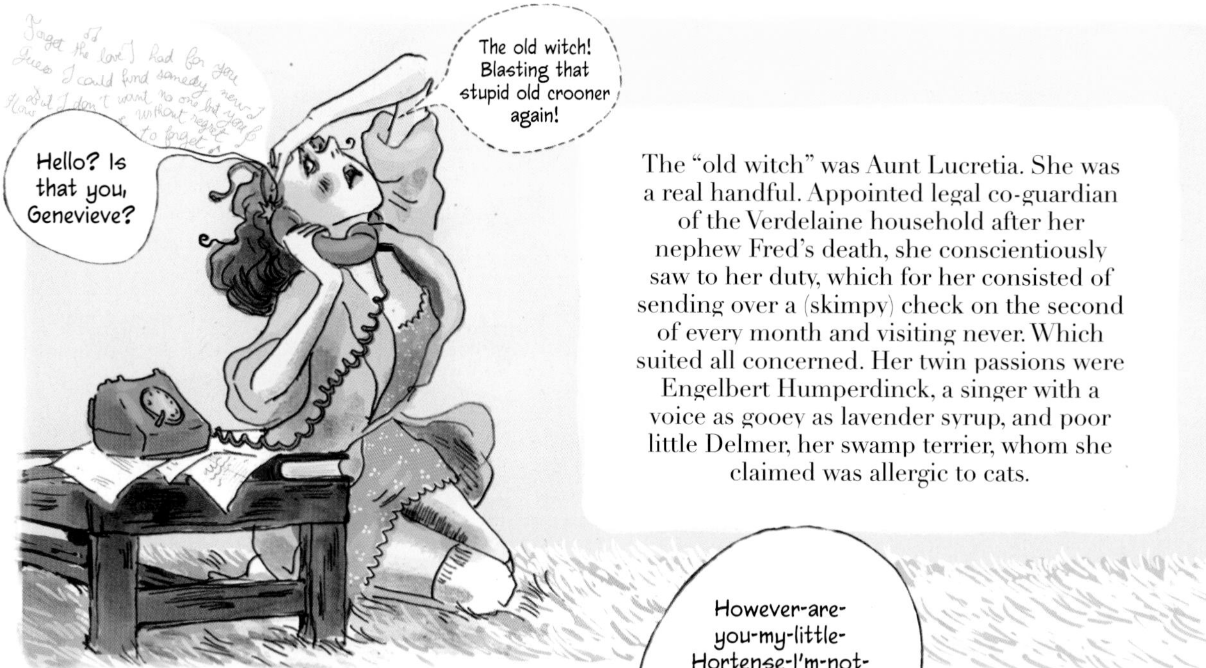
Hello? Is that you, Genevieve?
The old witch! Blasting that stupid old crooner again!
The "old witch" was Aunt Lucretia. She was a real handful. Appointed legal co-guardian of the Verdelaine household after her nephew Fred's death, she conscientiously saw to her duty, which for her consisted of sending over a (skimpy) check on the second of every month and visiting never. Which suited all concerned. Her twin passions were Engelbert Humperdinck, a singer with a voice as gooey as lavender syrup, and poor little Delmer, her swamp terrier, whom she claimed was allergic to cats.

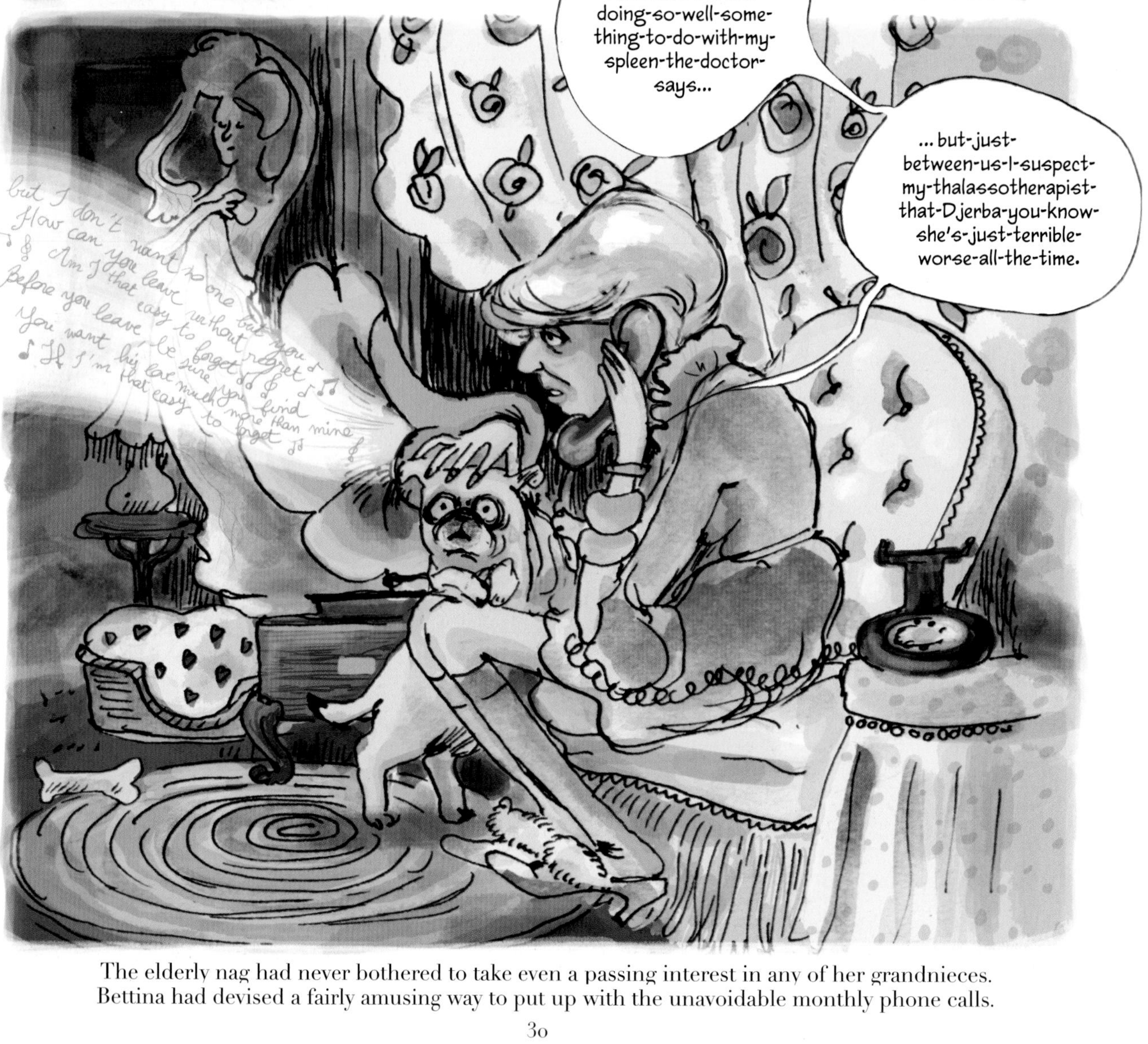
However-are-you-my-little-Hortense-I'm-not-doing-so-well-something-to-do-with-my-spleen-the-doctor-says...
... but-just-between-us-I-suspect-my-thalassotherapist-that-Djerba-you-know-she's-just-terrible-worse-all-the-time.

The elderly nag had never bothered to take even a passing interest in any of her grandnieces. Bettina had devised a fairly amusing way to put up with the unavoidable monthly phone calls.

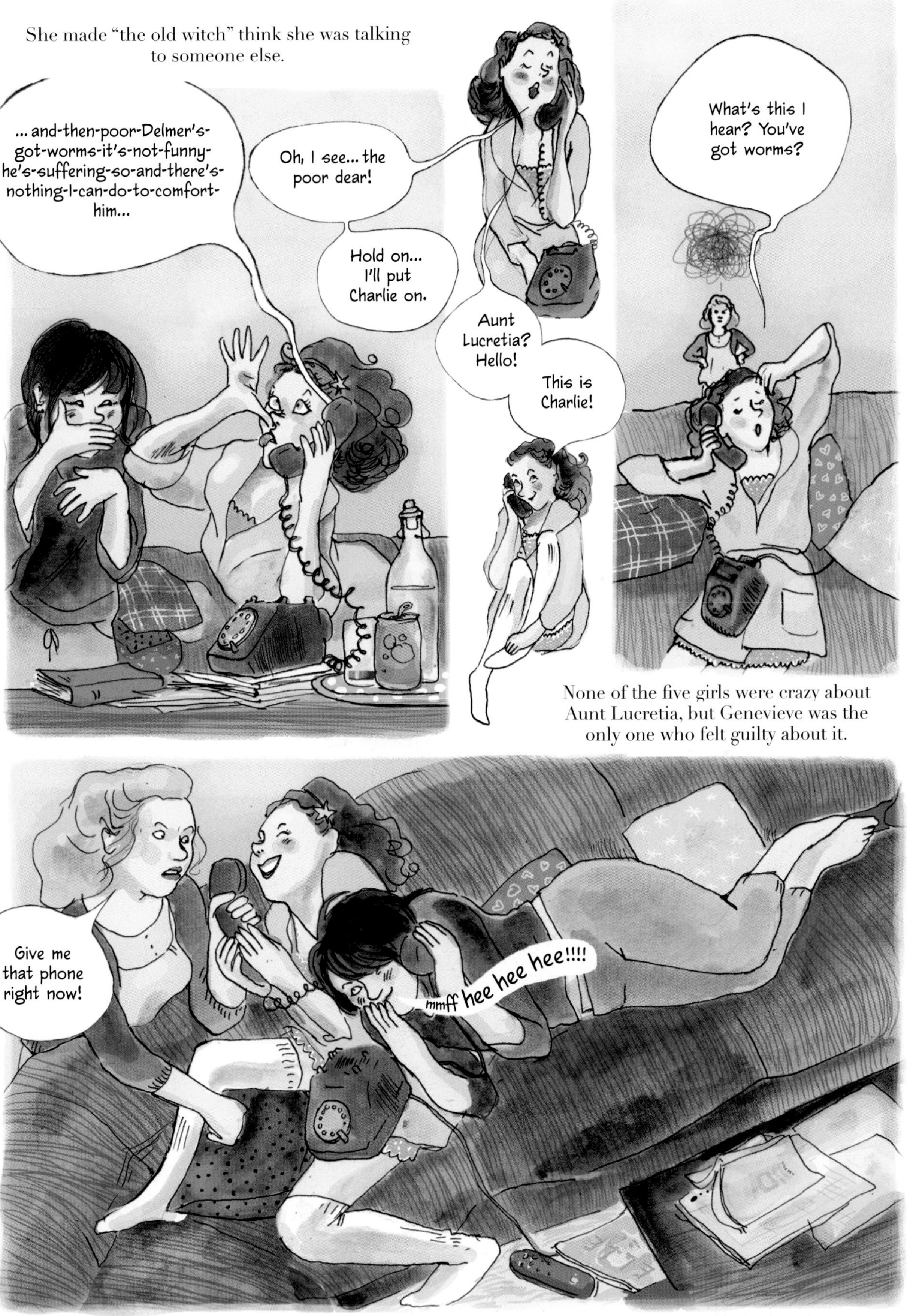
She made "the old witch" think she was talking to someone else.
... and-then-poor-Delmer's-got-worms-it's-not-funny-he's-suffering-so-and-there's-nothing-I-can-do-to-comfort-him...
Oh, I see... the poor dear!
Hold on... I'll put Charlie on.
Aunt Lucretia? Hello!
This is Charlie!
What's this I hear? You've got worms?
None of the five girls were crazy about Aunt Lucretia, but Genevieve was the only one who felt guilty about it.
Give me that phone right now!
mmff hee hee hee!!!!

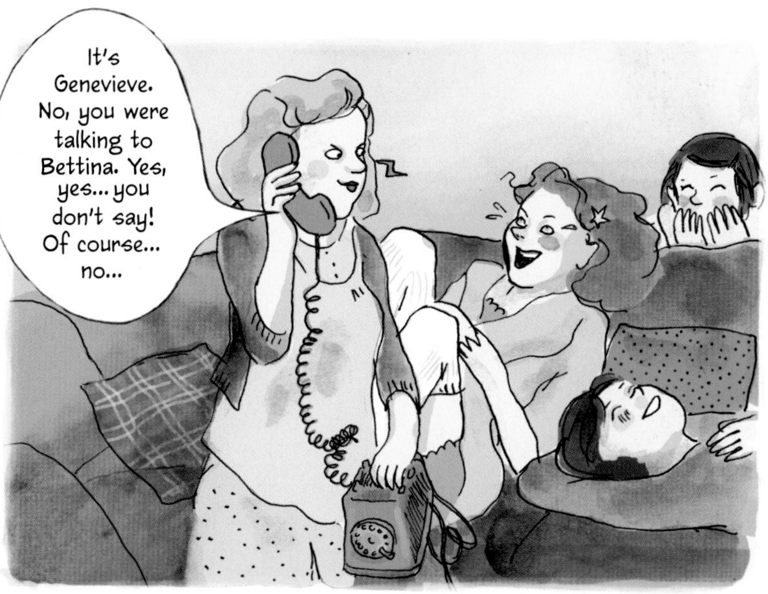
It's Genevieve. No, you were talking to Bettina. Yes, yes... you don't say! Of course... no...

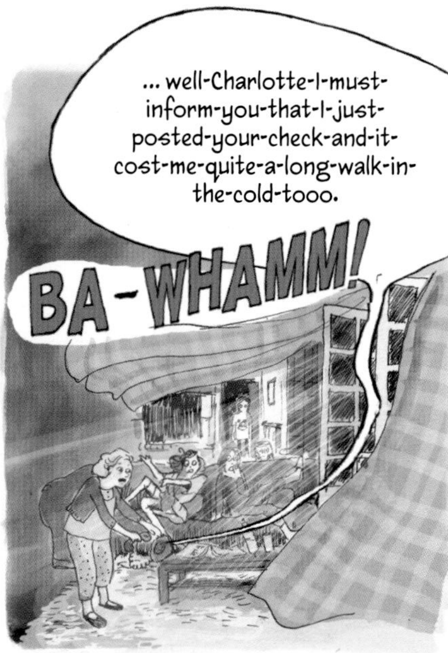
... well-Charlotte-I-must-inform-you-that-I-just-posted-your-check-and-it-cost-me-quite-a-long-walk-in-the-cold-tooo.
BA-WHAMM!

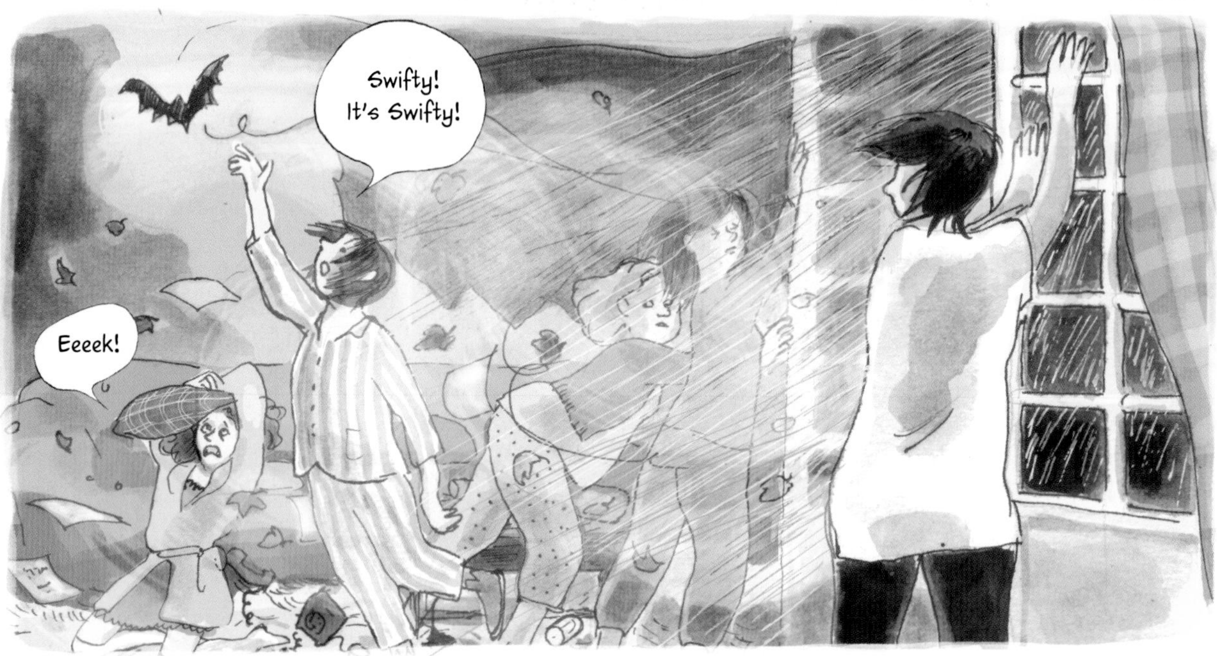
Swifty! It's Swifty!
Eeeek!

Three quick circles and Swifty was off. Swifty was a bat Enid had tamed. Apparently she lived in the dead sycamore, along with Blitz, the squirrel.

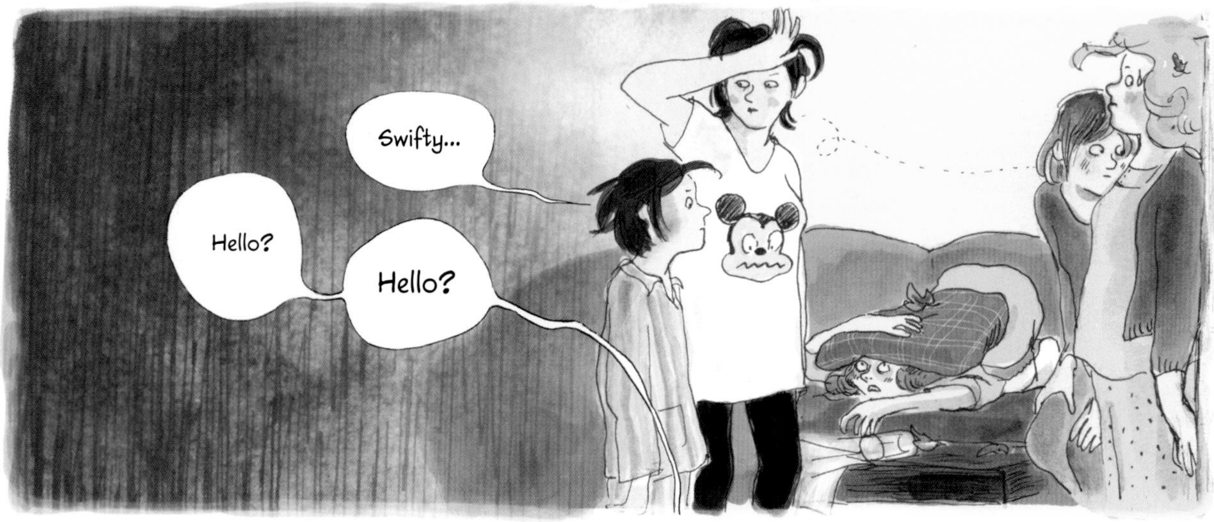
Swifty...
Hello?
Hello?

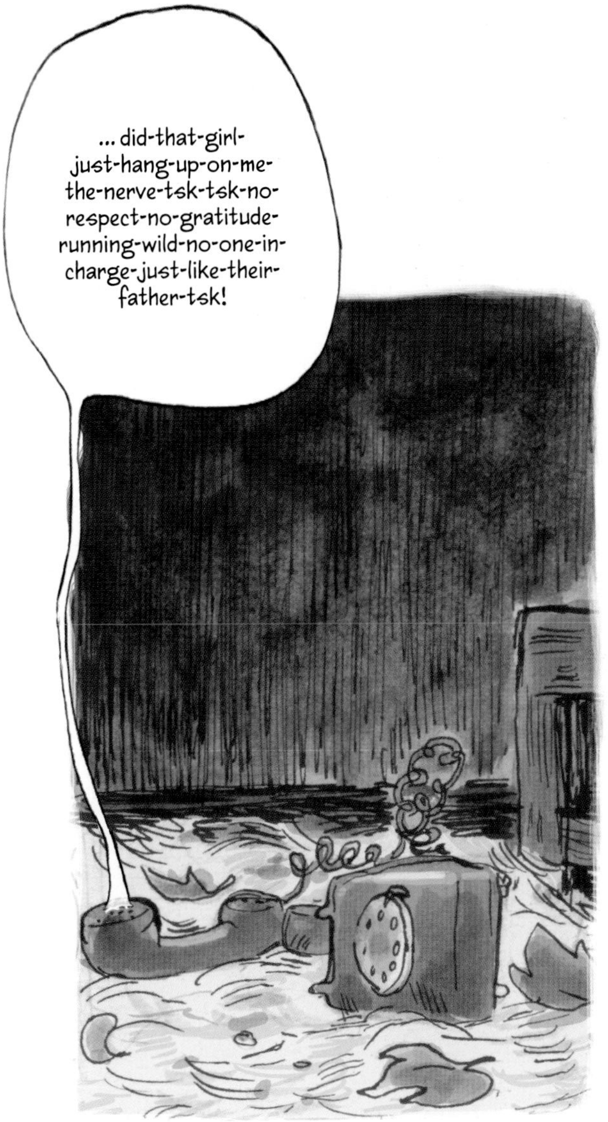
...did-that-girl-just-hang-up-on-me-the-nerve-tsk-tsk-no-respect-no-gratitude-running-wild-no-one-in-charge-just-like-their-father-tsk!

For Charlie, Enid, Genevieve, Bettina, and Hortense Verdelaine, each call from their Aunt Lucretia was like a knife plunged into the still-aching wound of their parents' death.

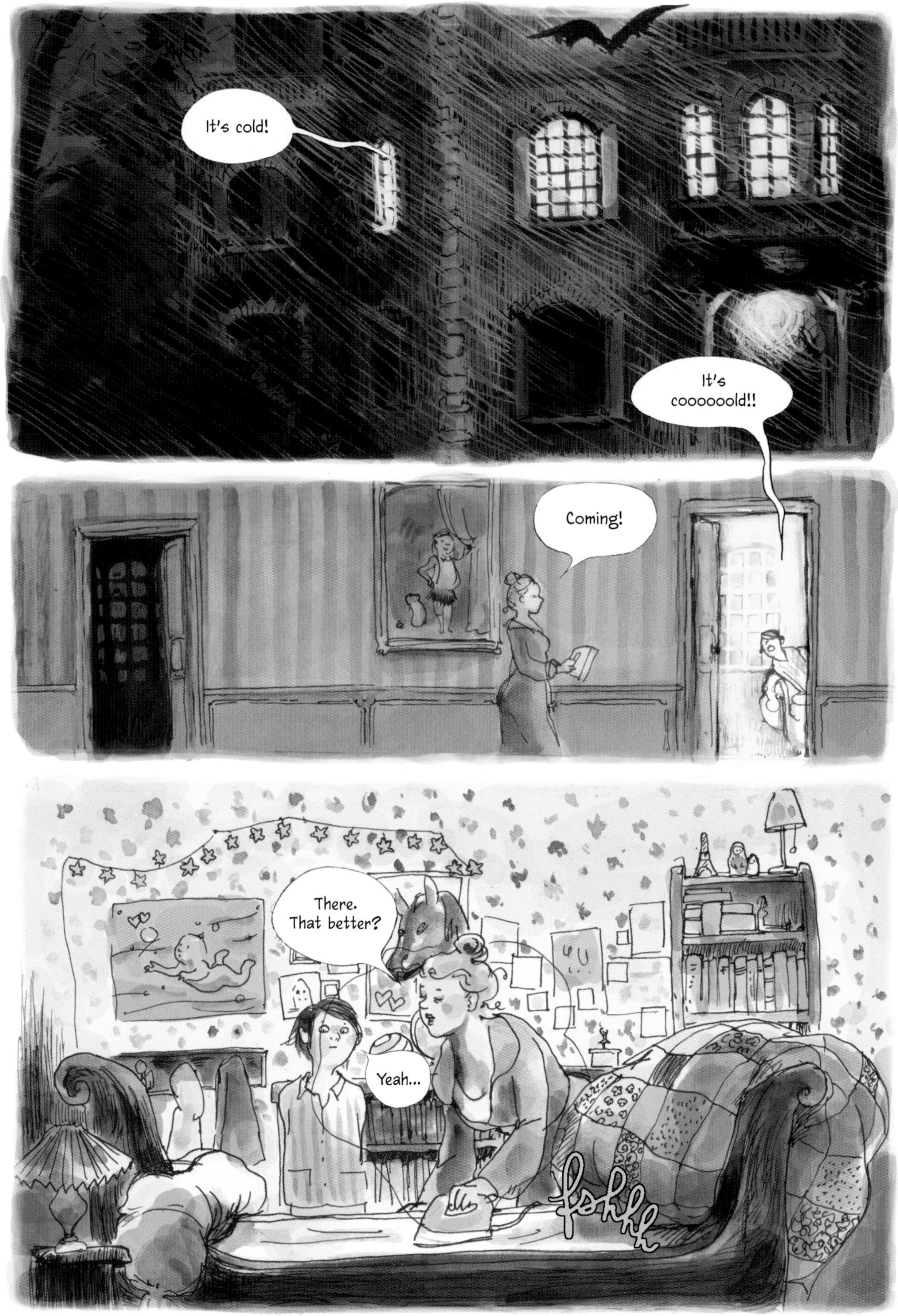
It's cold!
It's coooooold!!
Coming!
There. That better?
Yeah...
fshhh

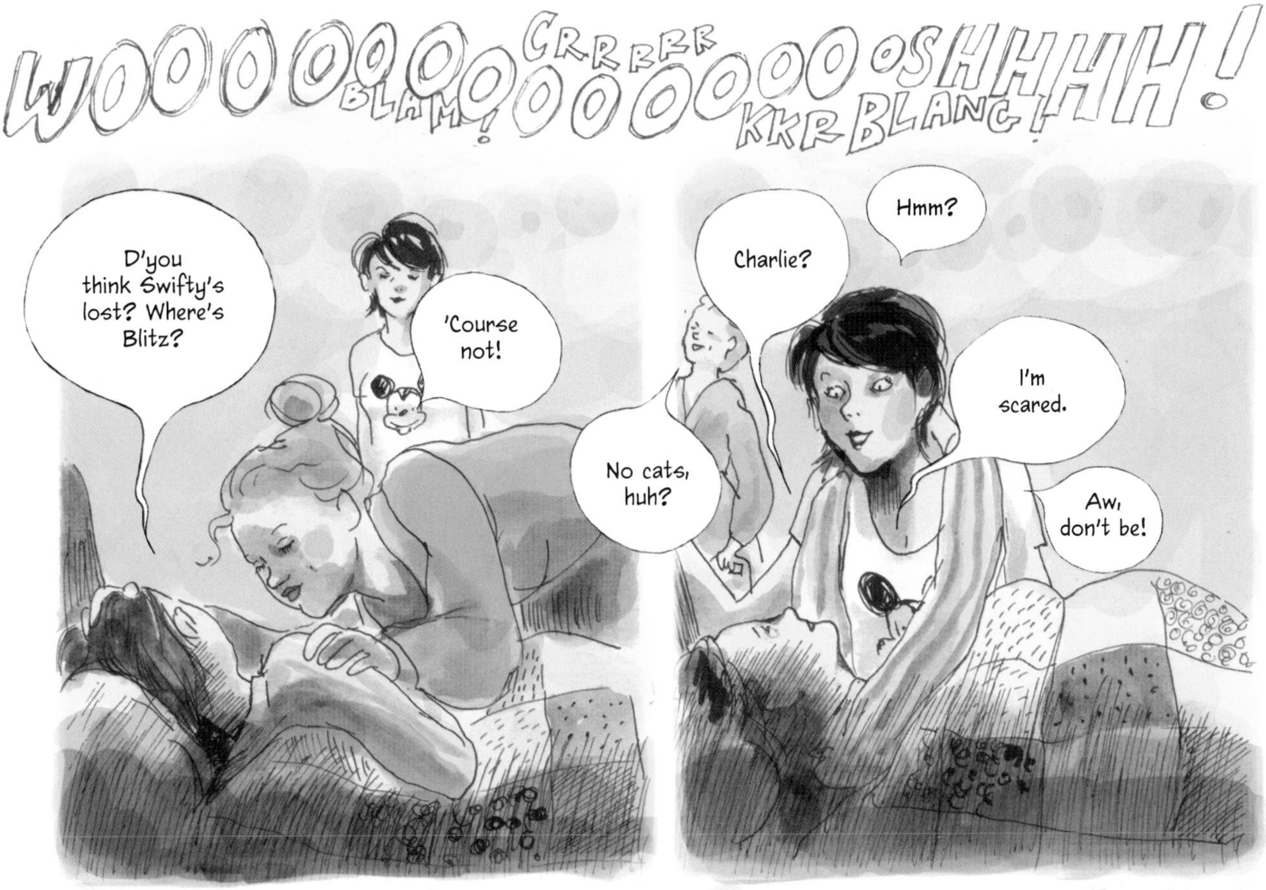
WOOOOOOOOOOOOOOSHHHHH!
CRRRRR
BLAM!
KKR BLANG!
D'you think Swifty's lost? Where's Blitz?
'Course not!
No cats, huh?
Charlie?
Hmm?
I'm scared.
Aw, don't be!

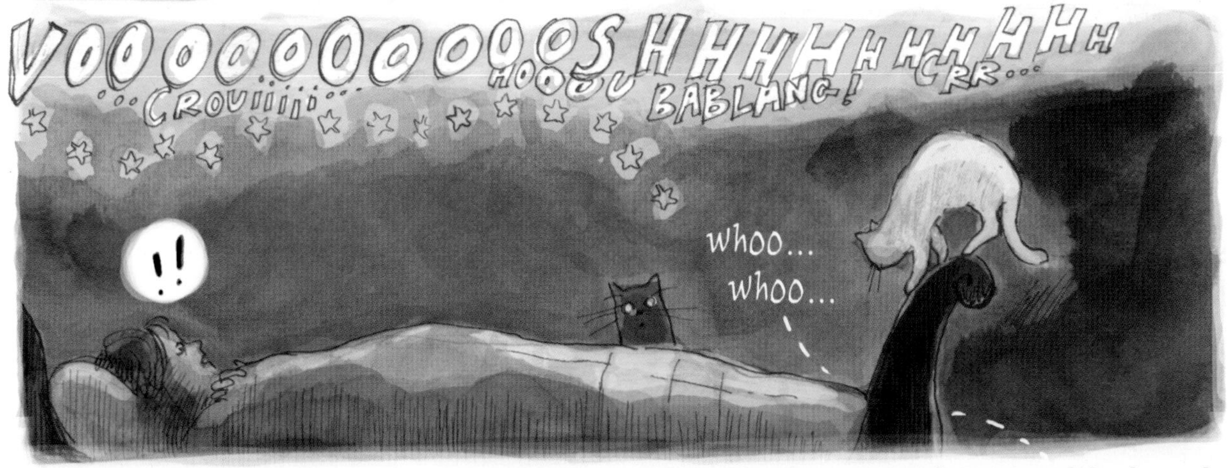
VOOOOOOOOOOOOSHHHHHHHHHH
CROUIIIIII
HOOOOU
BABLANG!
CRR...
!!
whoo...
whoo...

The storm was howling, slamming, creaking, whipping, and shaking, but there was another, more subdued sound…

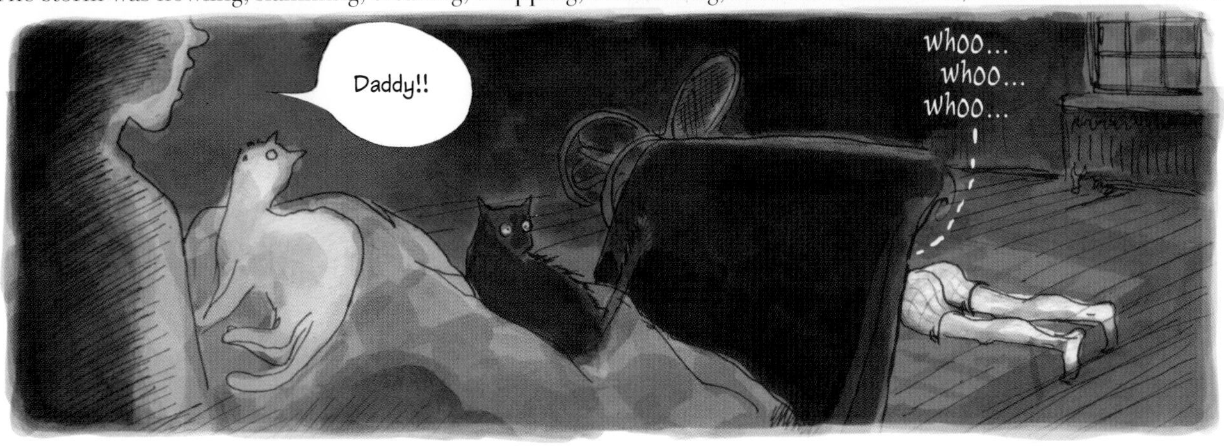
Daddy!!
whoo...
whoo...
whoo...

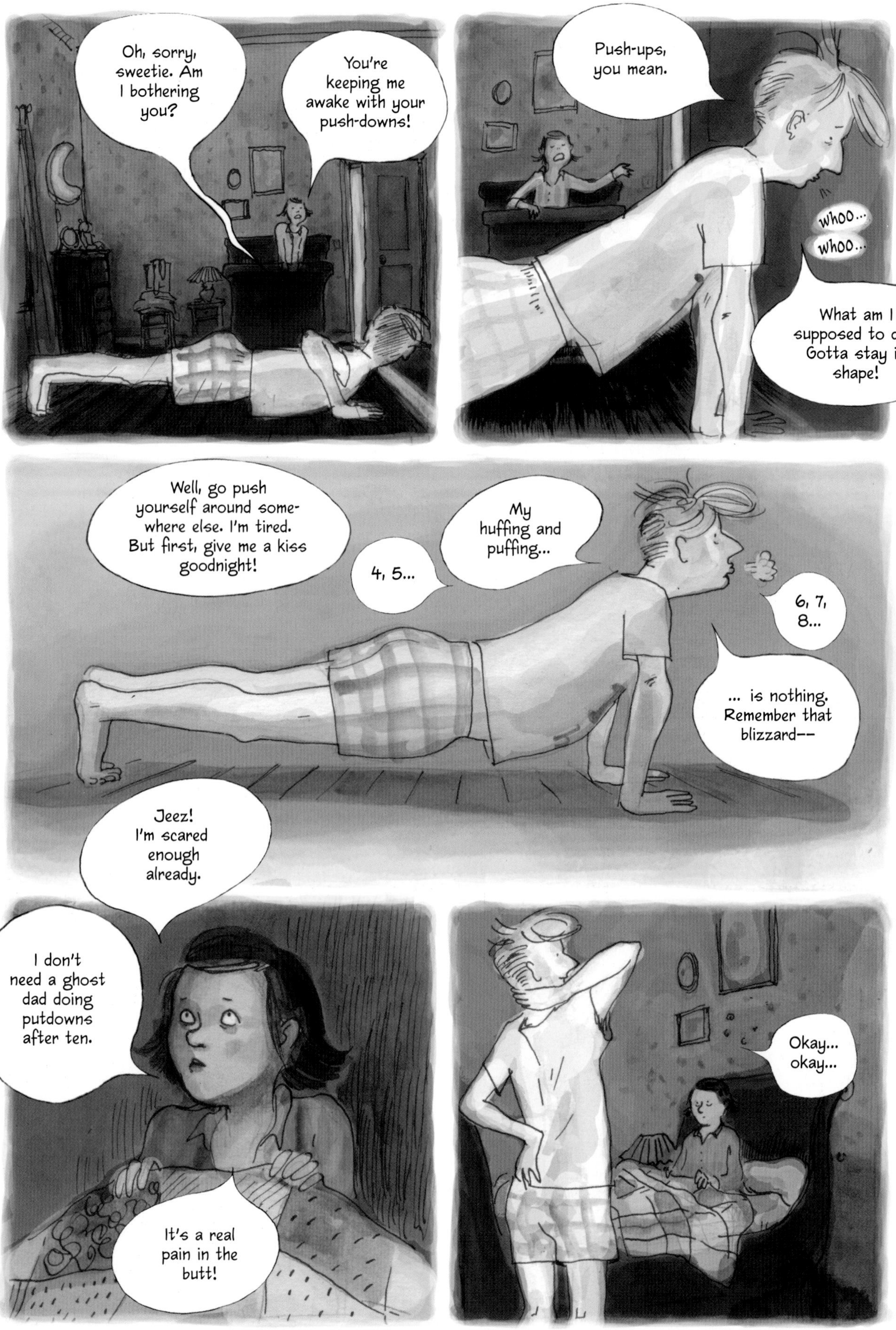
Oh, sorry, sweetie. Am I bothering you?
You're keeping me awake with your push-downs!
Push-ups, you mean.
whoo...
whoo...
What am I supposed to do? Gotta stay in shape!
Well, go push yourself around somewhere else. I'm tired. But first, give me a kiss goodnight!
4, 5...
My huffing and puffing...
6, 7, 8...
... is nothing. Remember that blizzard--
Jeez! I'm scared enough already.
I don't need a ghost dad doing putdowns after ten.
It's a real pain in the butt!
Okay... okay...

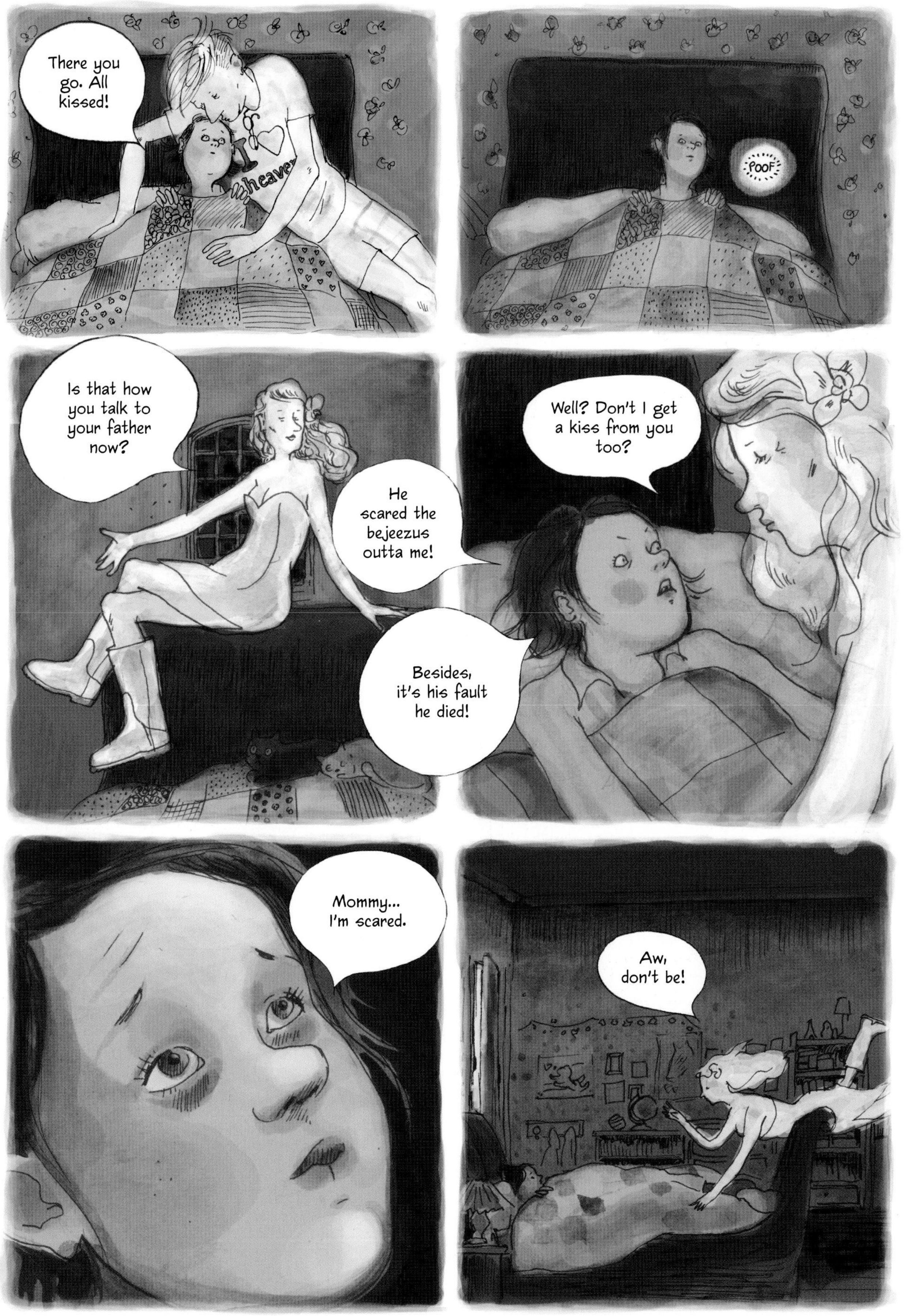
There you go. All kissed!
I ♡ heaven
POOF
Is that how you talk to your father now?
He scared the bejeezus outta me!
Besides, it's his fault he died!
Well? Don't I get a kiss from you too?
Mommy... I'm scared.
Aw, don't be!

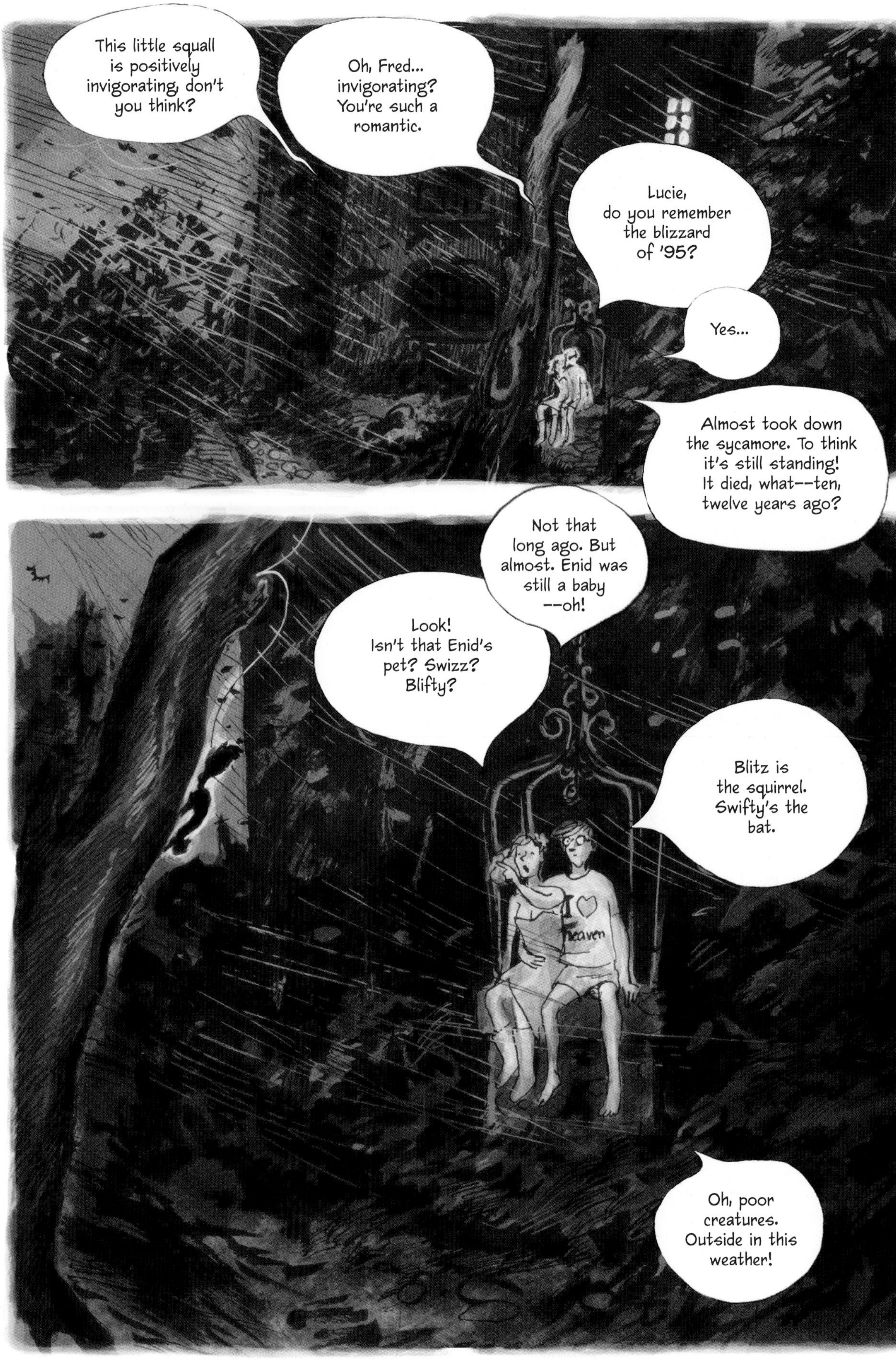
This little squall is positively invigorating, don't you think?
Oh, Fred... invigorating? You're such a romantic.
Lucie, do you remember the blizzard of '95?
Yes...
Almost took down the sycamore. To think it's still standing! It died, what--ten, twelve years ago?
Not that long ago. But almost. Enid was still a baby --oh!
Look! Isn't that Enid's pet? Swizz? Blifty?
Blitz is the squirrel. Swifty's the bat.
Oh, poor creatures. Outside in this weather!

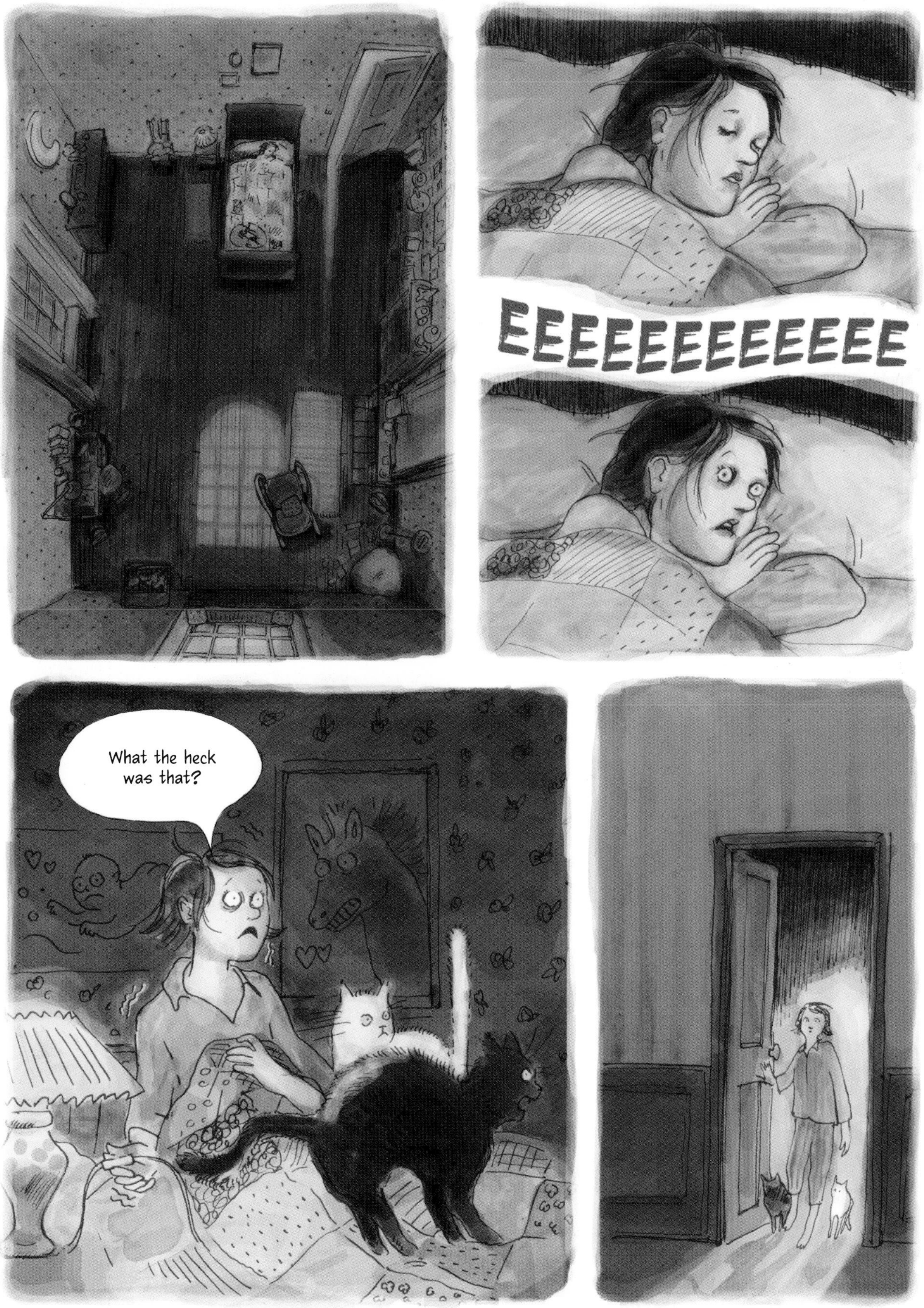
EEEEEEEEEEEEE
What the heck was that?

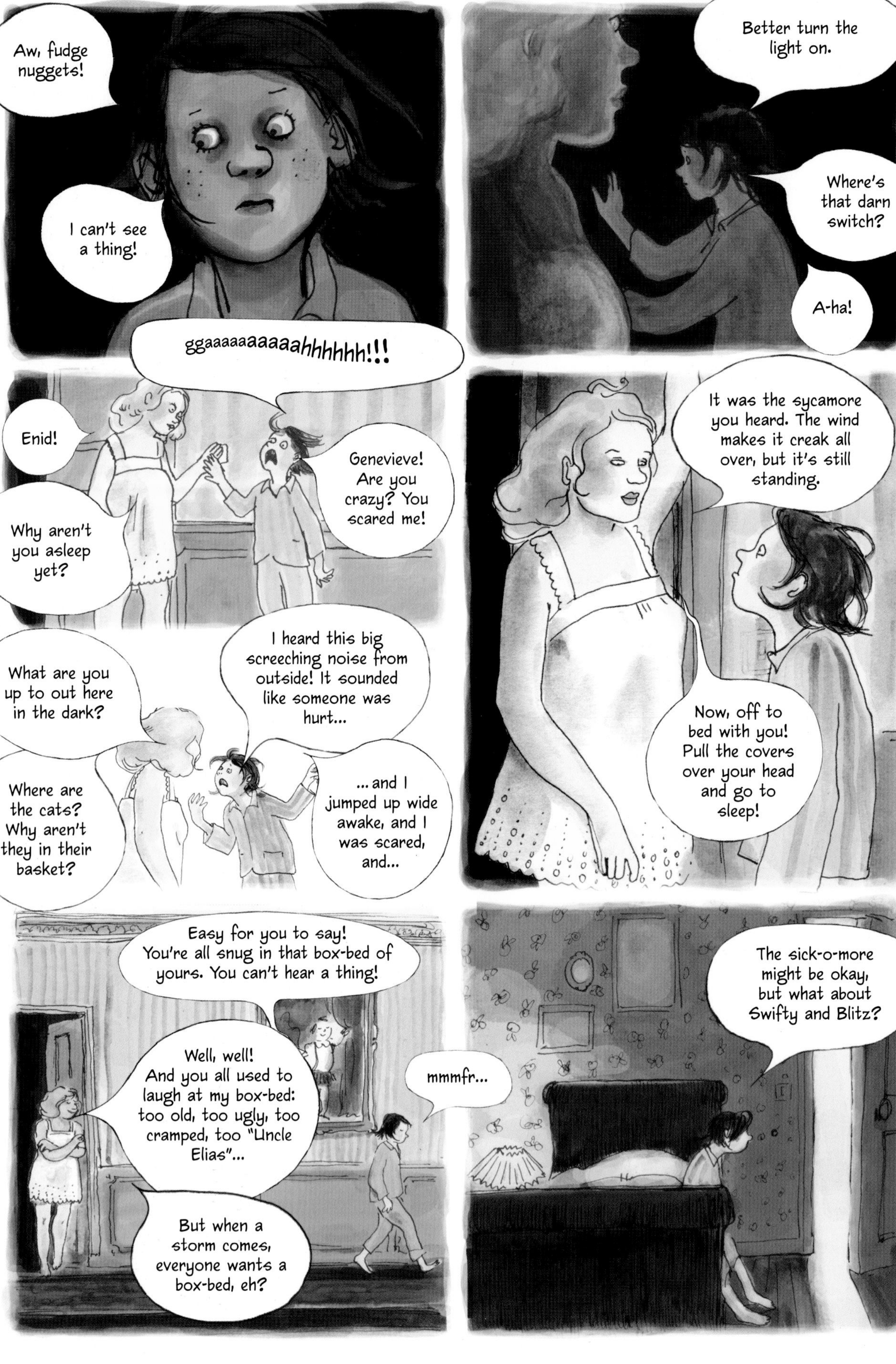

Aw, fudge nuggets!
I can't see a thing!
Better turn the light on.
Where's that darn switch?
A-ha!
ggaaaaaaaaaaahhhhhh!!!
Enid!
Genevieve! Are you crazy? You scared me!
Why aren't you asleep yet?
What are you up to out here in the dark?
I heard this big screeching noise from outside! It sounded like someone was hurt...
Where are the cats? Why aren't they in their basket?
...and I jumped up wide awake, and I was scared, and...
It was the sycamore you heard. The wind makes it creak all over, but it's still standing.
Now, off to bed with you! Pull the covers over your head and go to sleep!
Easy for you to say! You're all snug in that box-bed of yours. You can't hear a thing!
Well, well! And you all used to laugh at my box-bed: too old, too ugly, too cramped, too "Uncle Elias"...
But when a storm comes, everyone wants a box-bed, eh?
mmmfr...
The sick-o-more might be okay, but what about Swifty and Blitz?

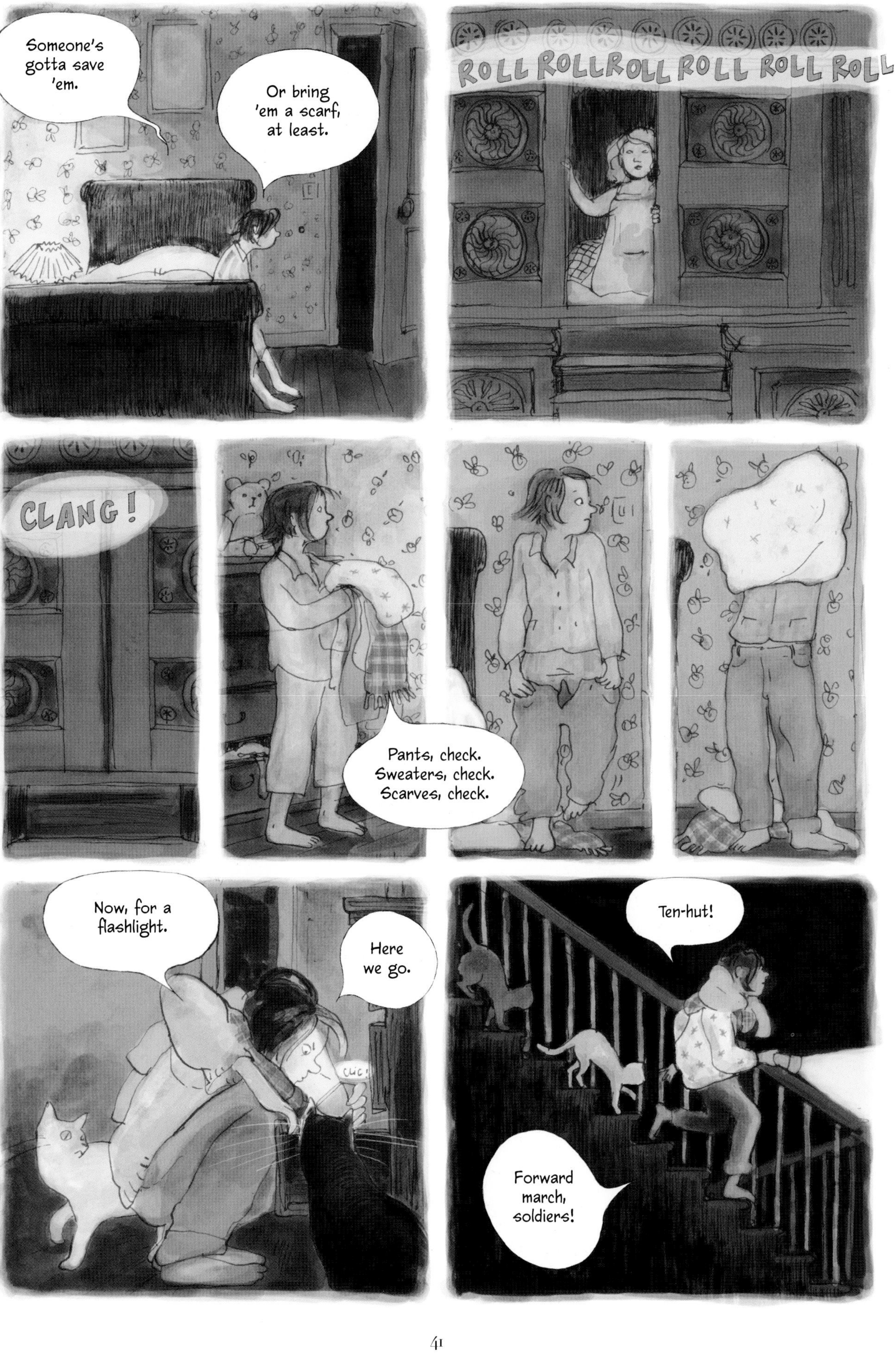
Someone's gotta save 'em.
Or bring 'em a scarf, at least.
ROLL ROLL ROLL ROLL ROLL ROLL
CLANG!
Pants, check. Sweaters, check. Scarves, check.
Now, for a flashlight.
Here we go.
Ten-hut!
Forward march, soldiers!

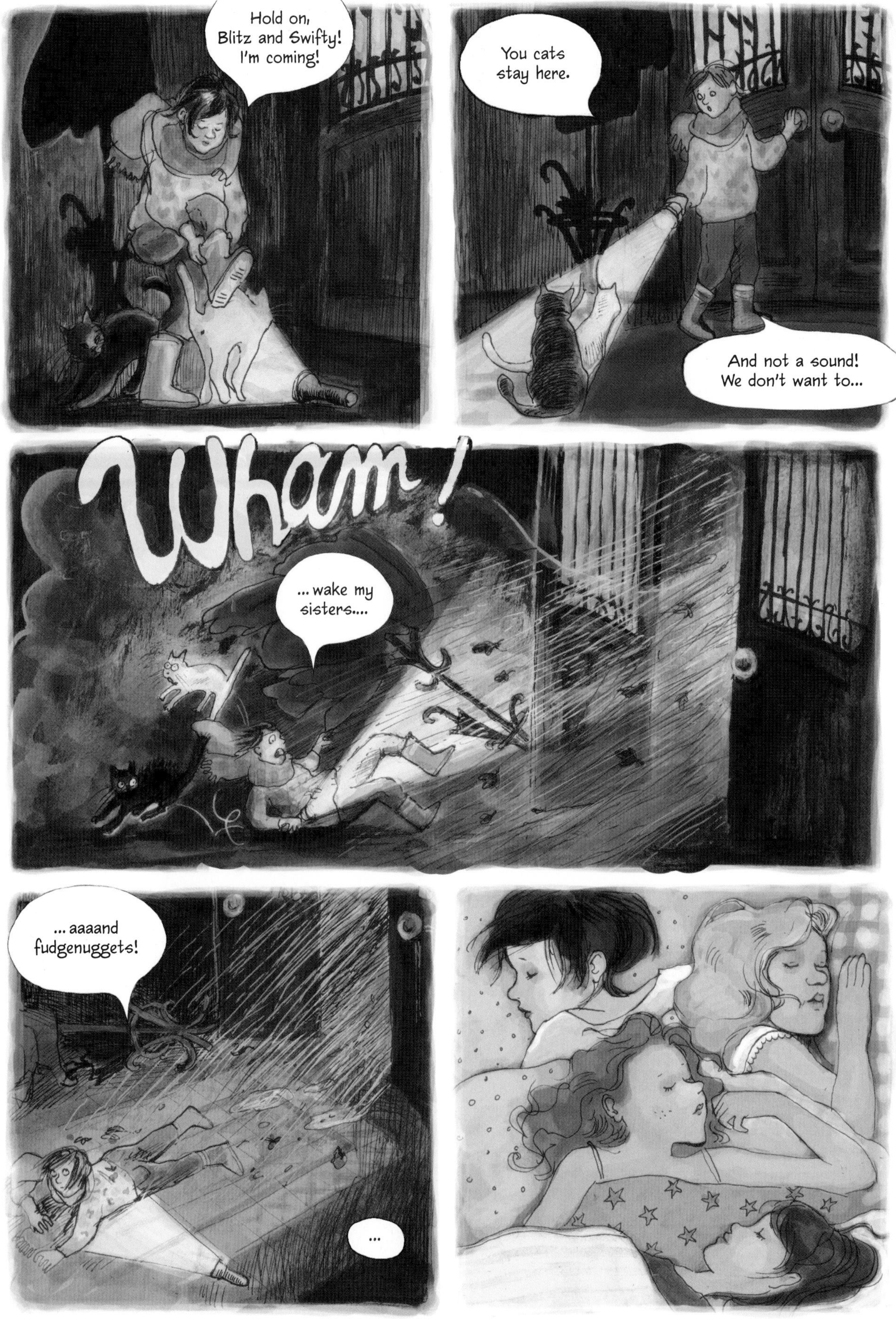
Hold on, Blitz and Swifty! I'm coming!
You cats stay here.
And not a sound! We don't want to...
Wham!
... wake my sisters....
... aaaand fudgenuggets!
...

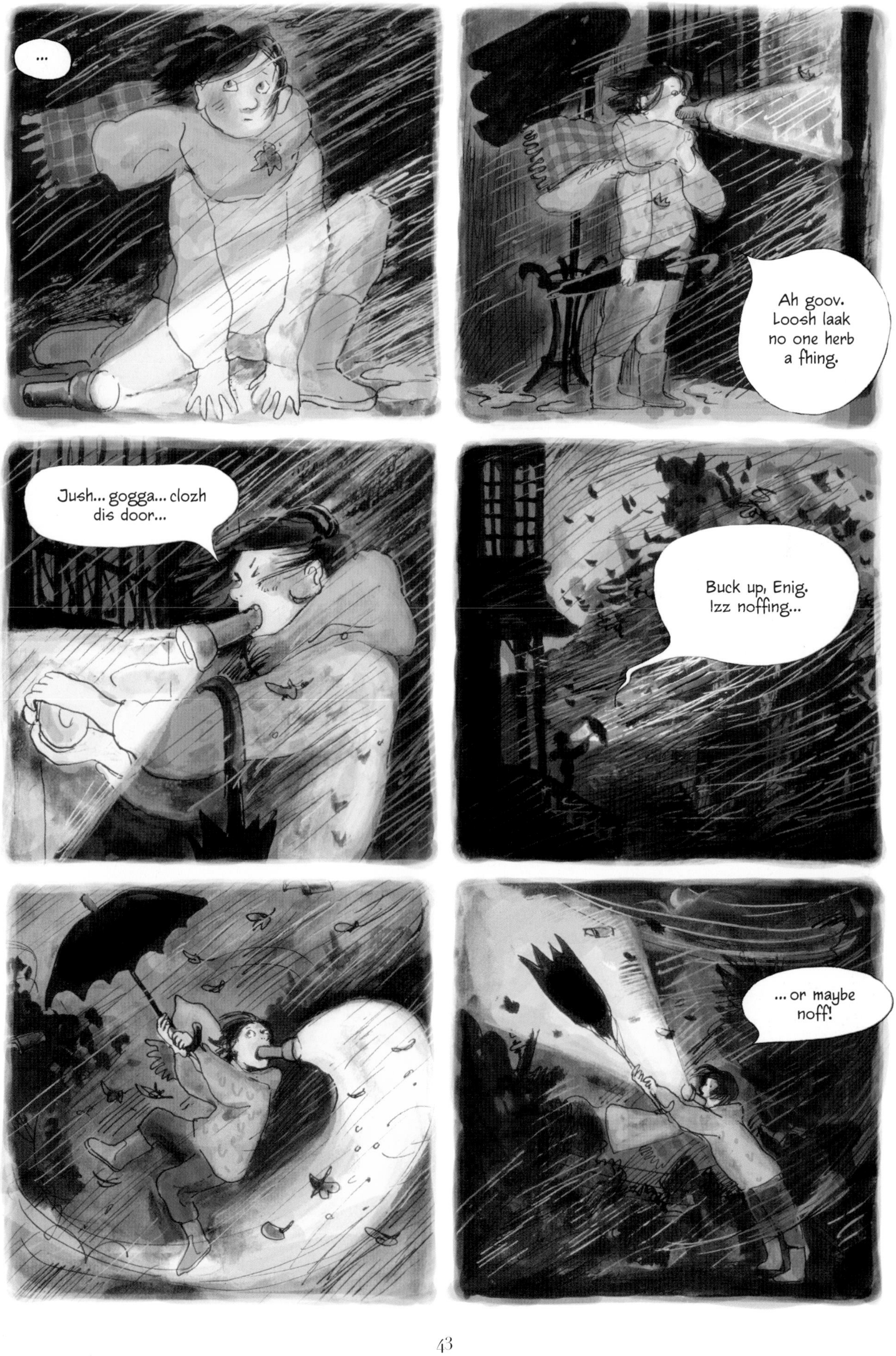
...
Ah goov. Loosh laak no one herb a fhing.
Jush... gogga... clozh dis door...
Buck up, Enig. Izz noffing...
...or maybe noff!

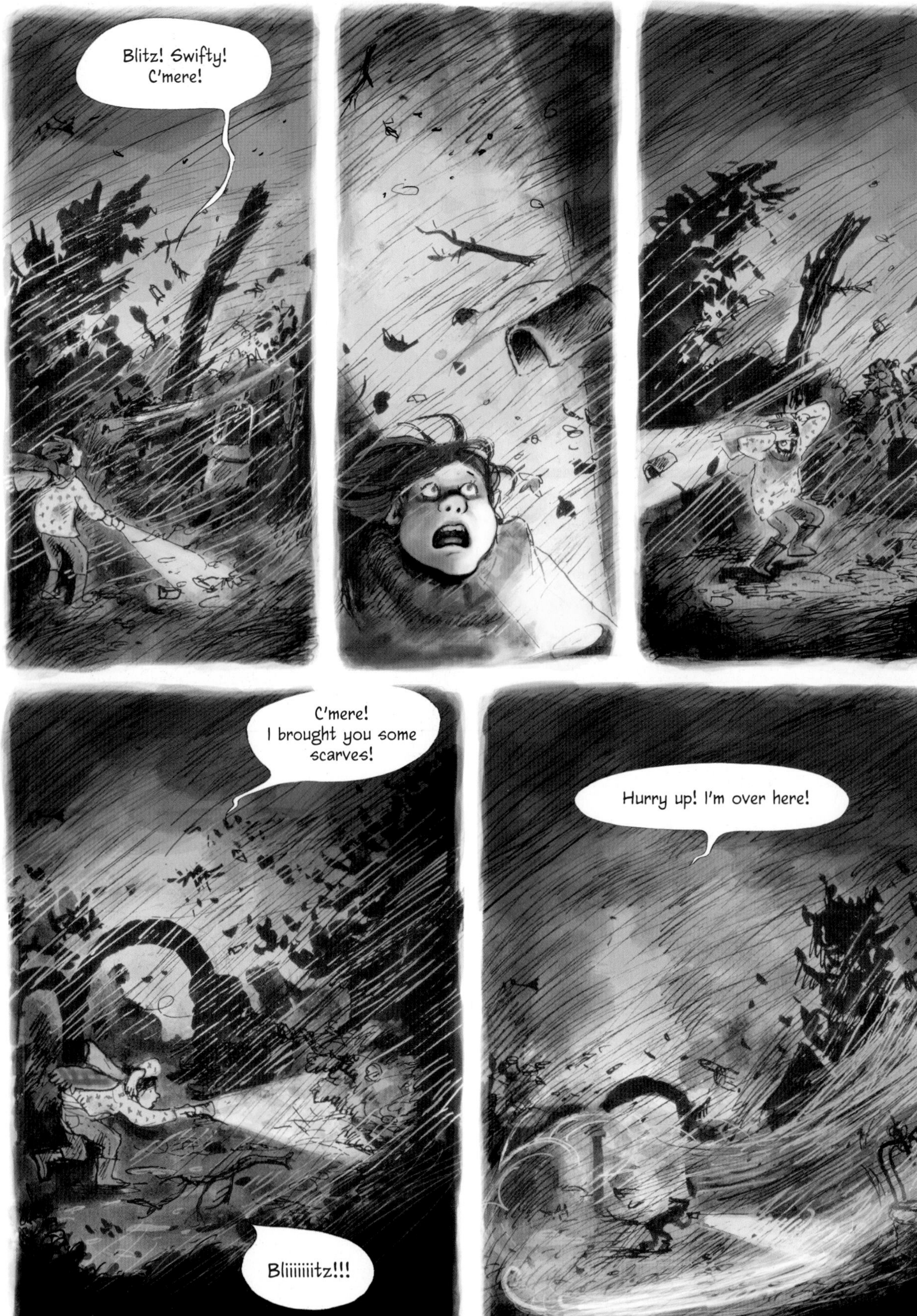
Blitz! Swifty! C'mere!
C'mere! I brought you some scarves!
Bliiiiiitz!!!
Hurry up! I'm over here!

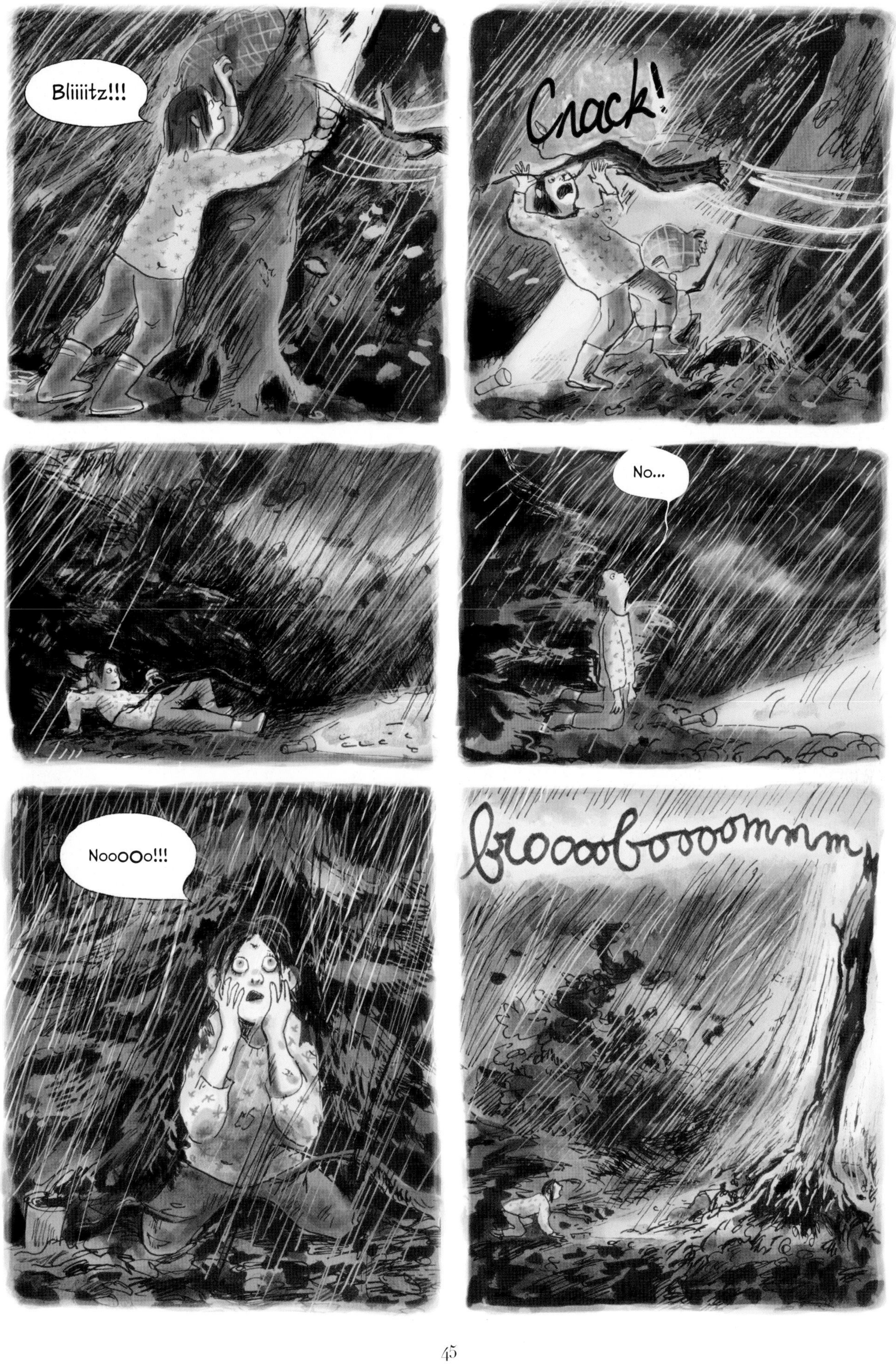
Bliiiitz!!!
Crack!
No...
NooOOo!!!
brooobooommm

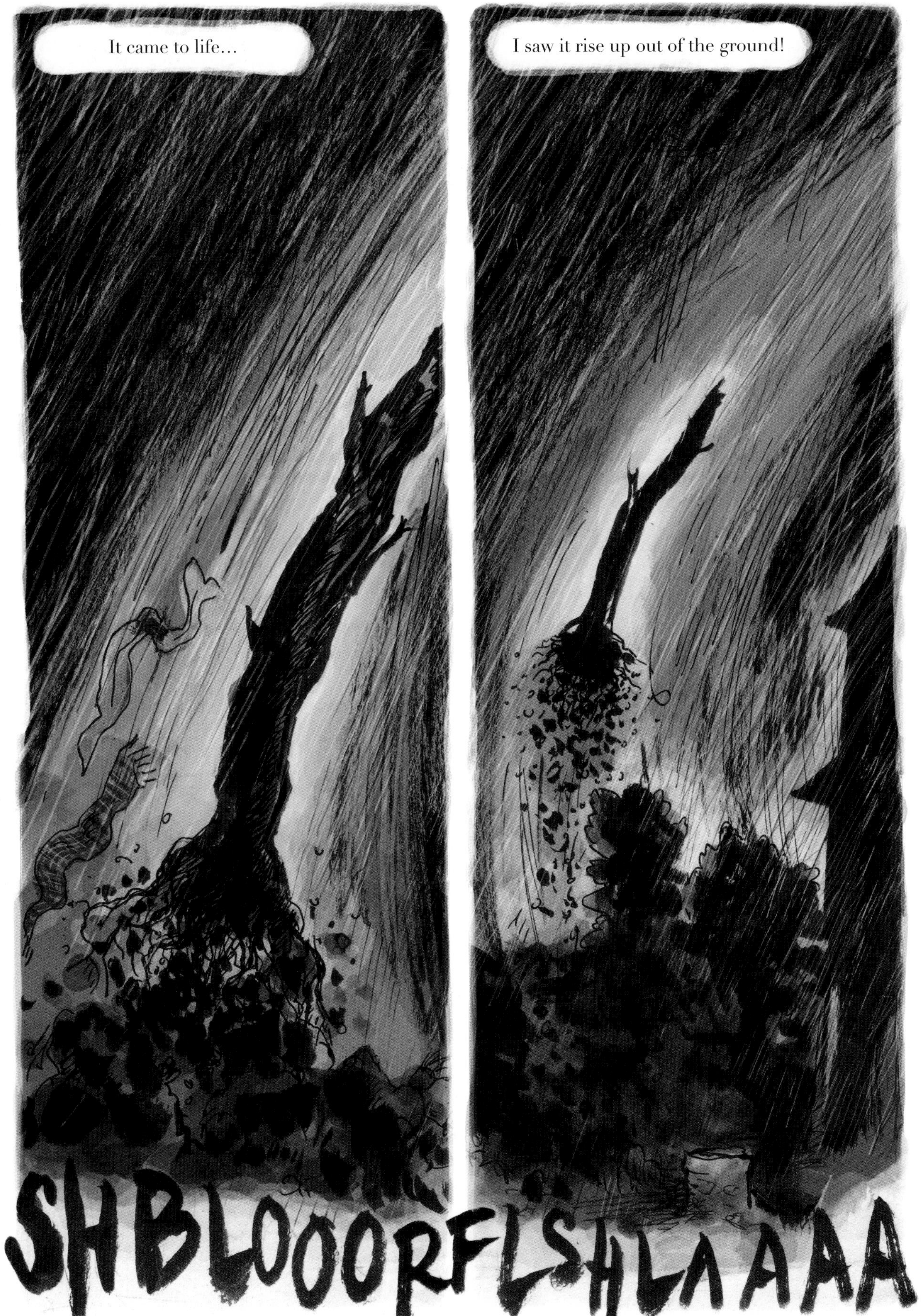
It came to life...
I saw it rise up out of the ground!
SHBLOOORFLSHLAAAA

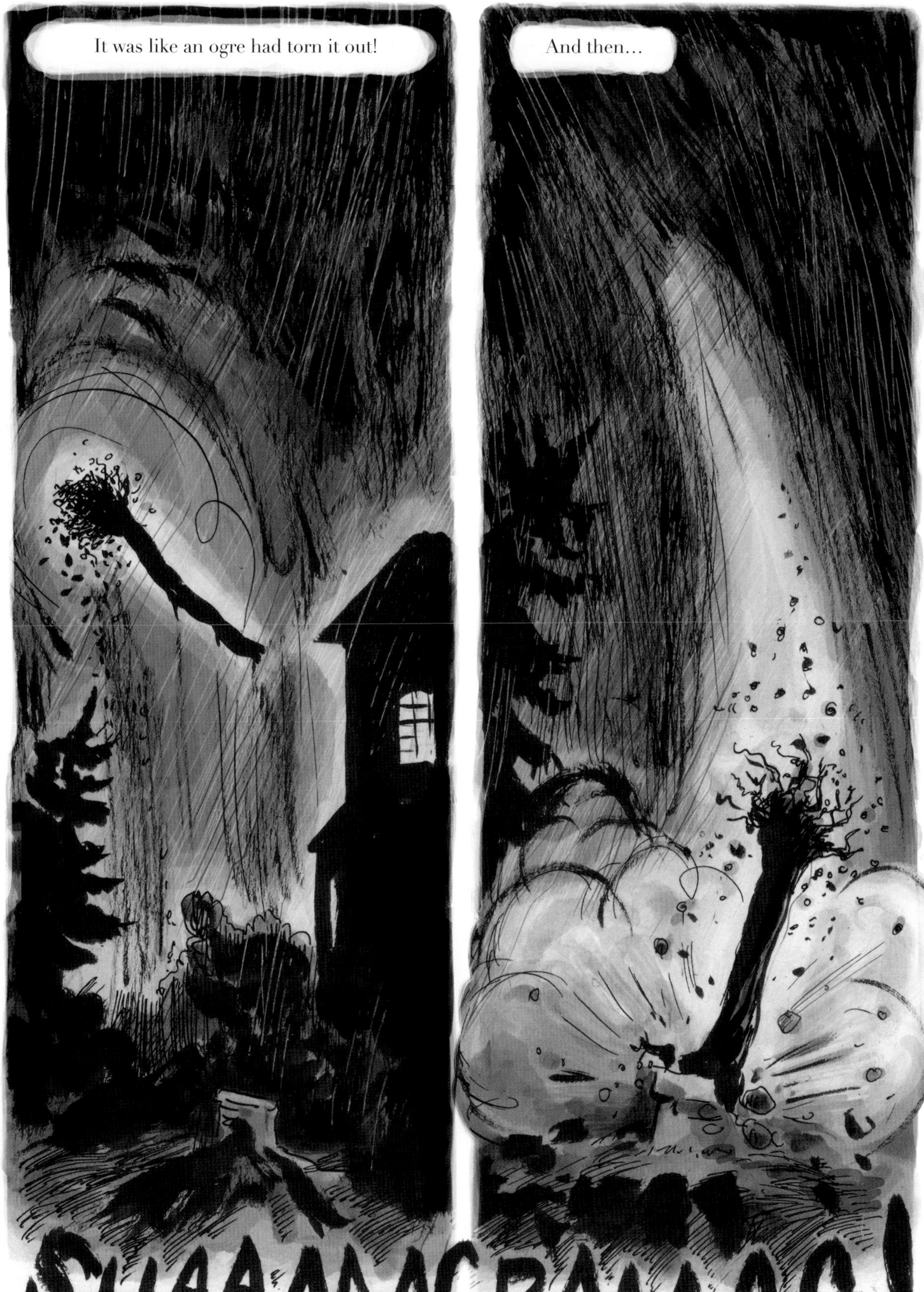
It was like an ogre had torn it out!
And then…
SHAAAAACRAAAAC!

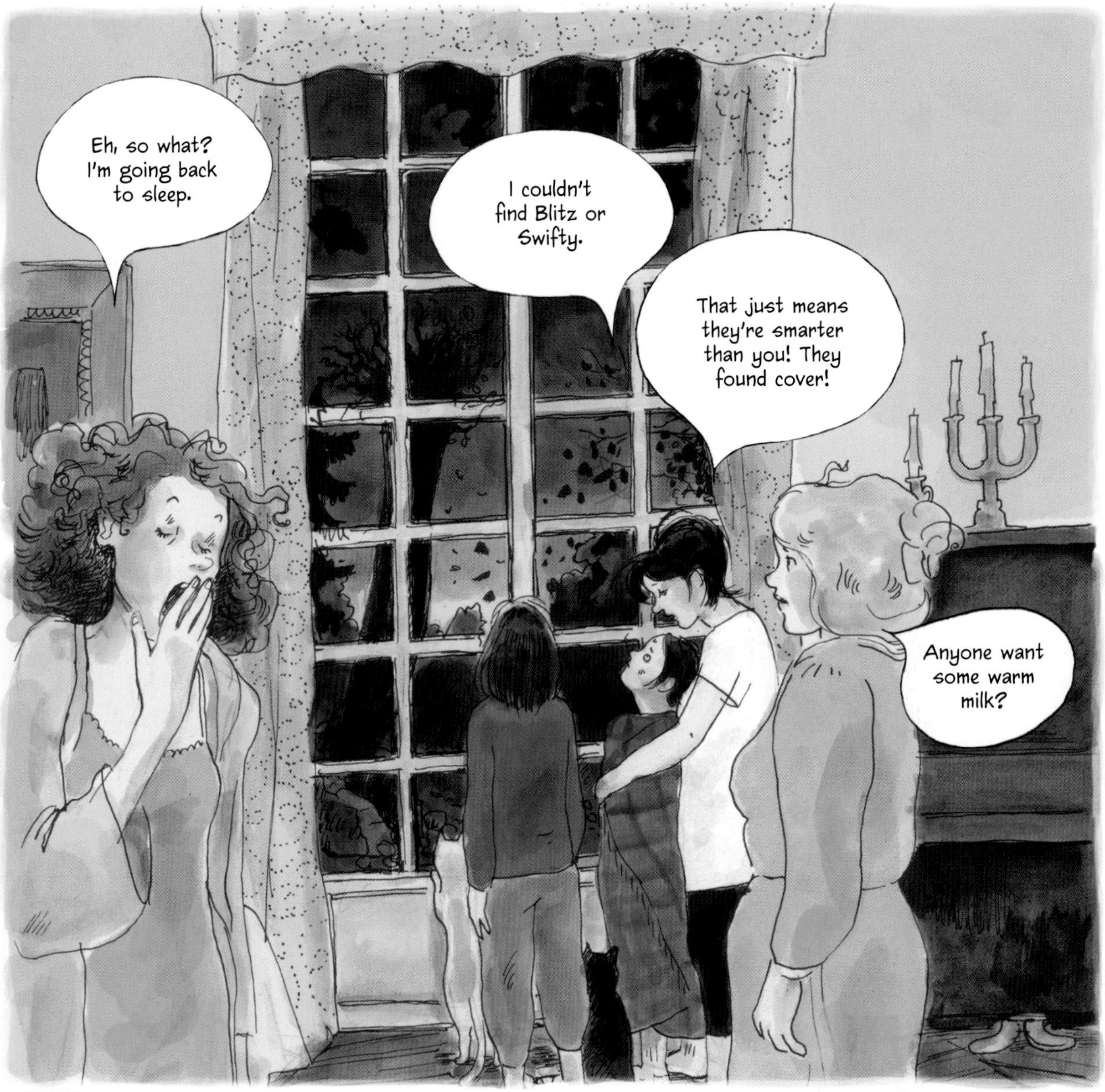
Eh, so what? I'm going back to sleep.
I couldn't find Blitz or Swifty.
That just means they're smarter than you! They found cover!
Anyone want some warm milk?

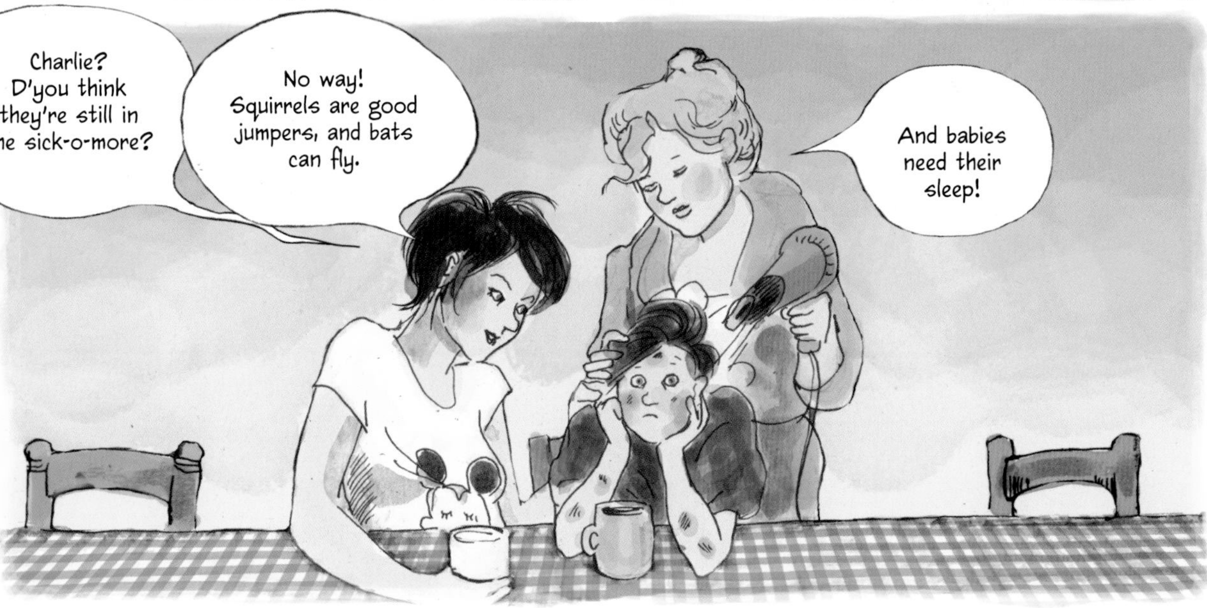
Charlie? D'you think they're still in the sick-o-more?
No way! Squirrels are good jumpers, and bats can fly.
And babies need their sleep!

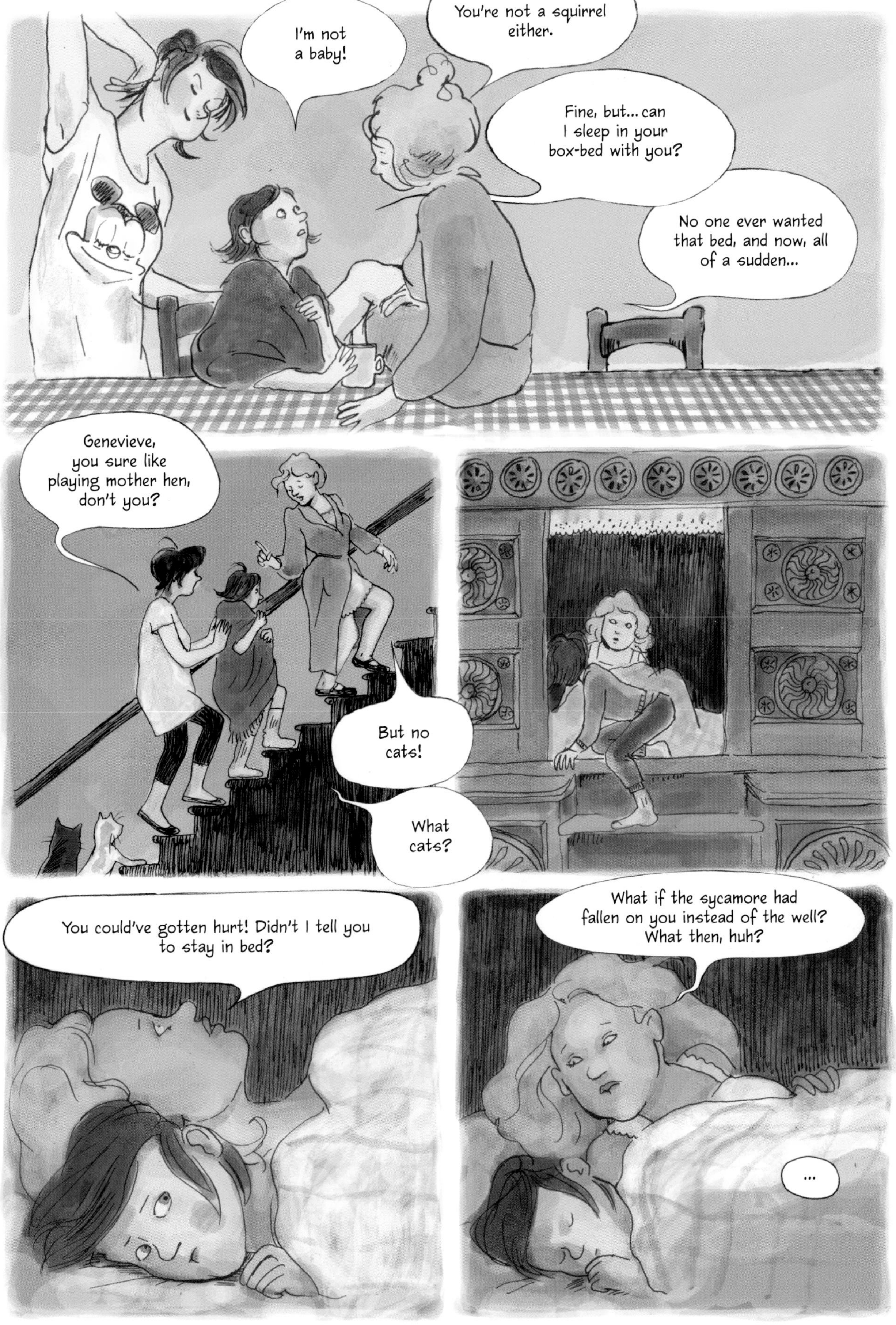
I'm not a baby!
You're not a squirrel either.
Fine, but... can I sleep in your box-bed with you?
No one ever wanted that bed, and now, all of a sudden...
Genevieve, you sure like playing mother hen, don't you?
But no cats!
What cats?
You could've gotten hurt! Didn't I tell you to stay in bed?
What if the sycamore had fallen on you instead of the well? What then, huh?
...

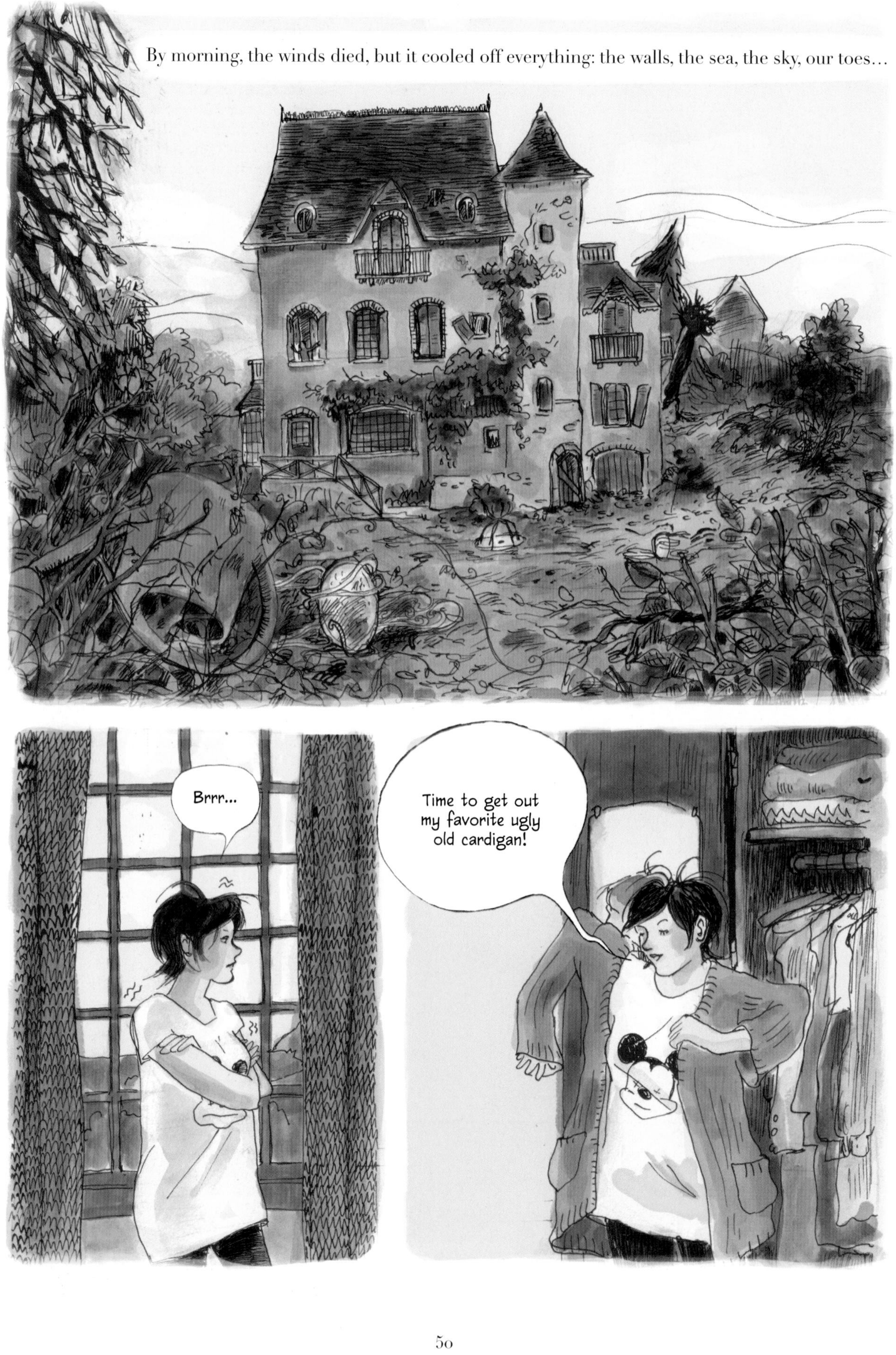
By morning, the winds died, but it cooled off everything: the walls, the sea, the sky, our toes…
Brrr…
Time to get out my favorite ugly old cardigan!

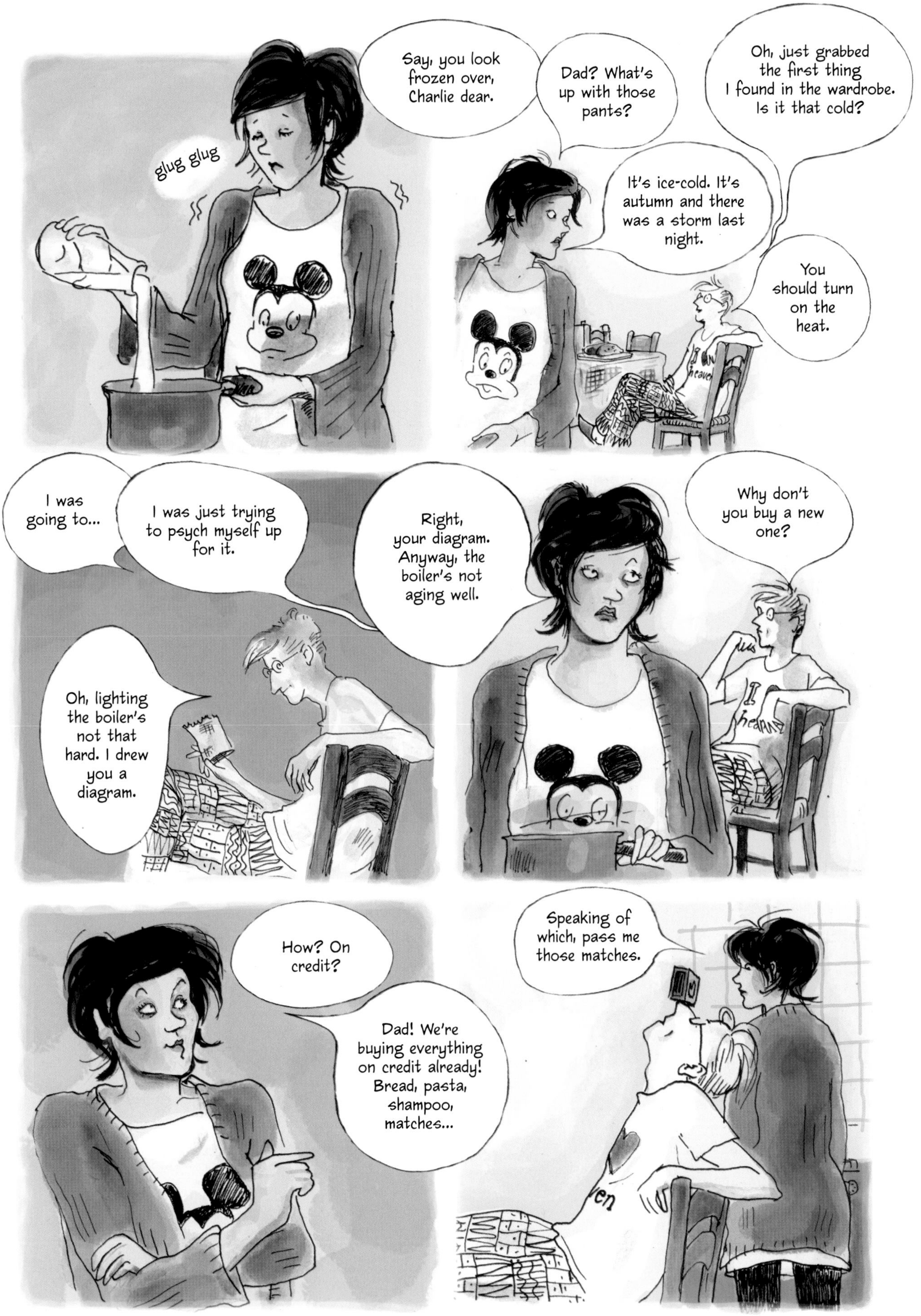
glug glug
Say, you look frozen over, Charlie dear.
Dad? What's up with those pants?
Oh, just grabbed the first thing I found in the wardrobe. Is it that cold?
It's ice-cold. It's autumn and there was a storm last night.
You should turn on the heat.
I was going to...
I was just trying to psych myself up for it.
Oh, lighting the boiler's not that hard. I drew you a diagram.
Right, your diagram. Anyway, the boiler's not aging well.
Why don't you buy a new one?
How? On credit?
Dad! We're buying everything on credit already! Bread, pasta, shampoo, matches...
Speaking of which, pass me those matches.

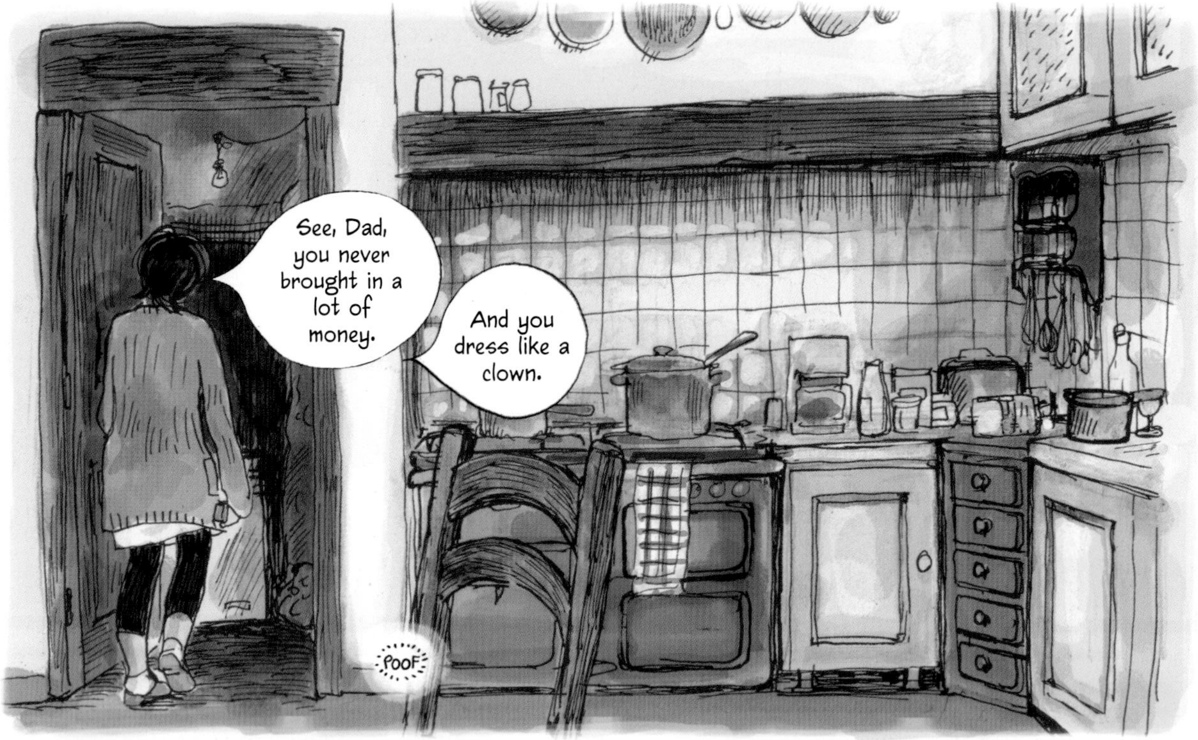
See, Dad, you never brought in a lot of money.
And you dress like a clown.
POOF

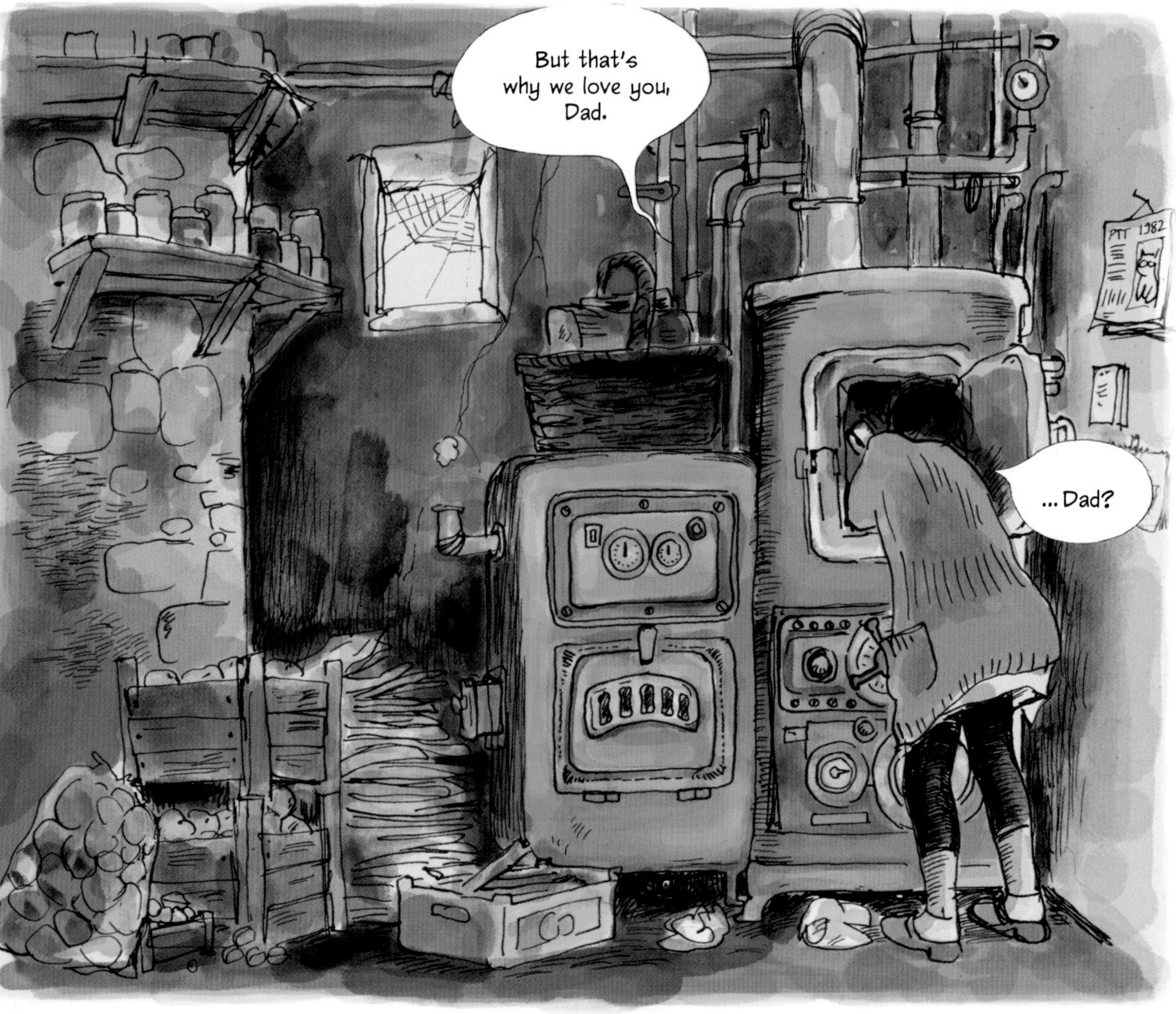
But that's why we love you, Dad.
PTT 1982
...Dad?

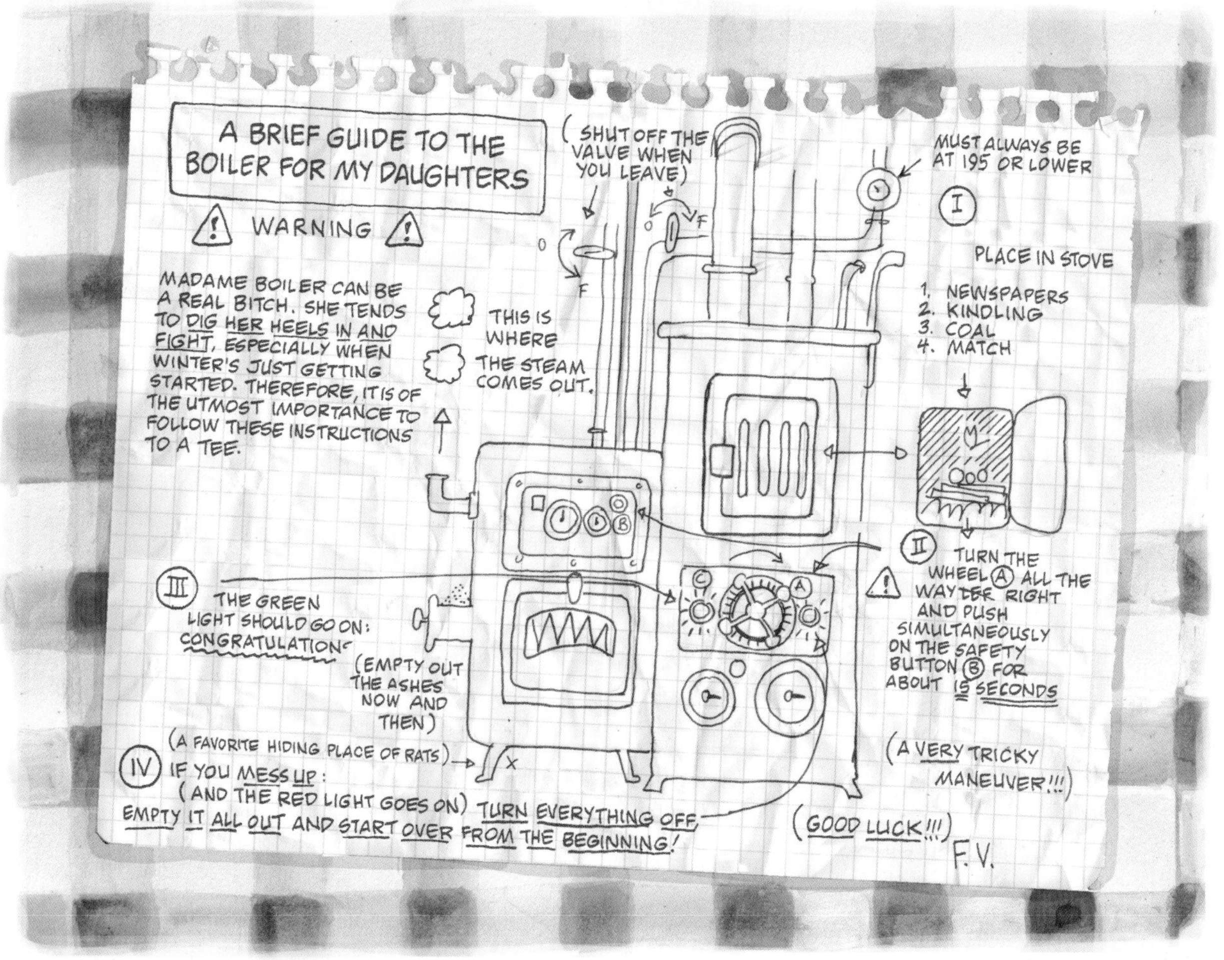
A BRIEF GUIDE TO THE BOILER FOR MY DAUGHTERS
WARNING
MADAME BOILER CAN BE A REAL BITCH. SHE TENDS TO DIG HER HEELS IN AND FIGHT, ESPECIALLY WHEN WINTER'S JUST GETTING STARTED. THEREFORE, IT IS OF THE UTMOST IMPORTANCE TO FOLLOW THESE INSTRUCTIONS TO A TEE.
(SHUT OFF THE VALVE WHEN YOU LEAVE)
THIS IS WHERE THE STEAM COMES OUT.
MUST ALWAYS BE AT 195 OR LOWER
I
PLACE IN STOVE
1. NEWSPAPERS
2. KINDLING
3. COAL
4. MATCH
II
TURN THE WHEEL A ALL THE WAY RIGHT AND PUSH SIMULTANEOUSLY ON THE SAFETY BUTTON B FOR ABOUT 15 SECONDS
(A VERY TRICKY MANEUVER!!!)
III
THE GREEN LIGHT SHOULD GO ON: CONGRATULATIONS
(EMPTY OUT THE ASHES NOW AND THEN)
(A FAVORITE HIDING PLACE OF RATS)
IV
IF YOU MESS UP: (AND THE RED LIGHT GOES ON) TURN EVERYTHING OFF, EMPTY IT ALL OUT AND START OVER FROM THE BEGINNING!
(GOOD LUCK!!!)
F.V.

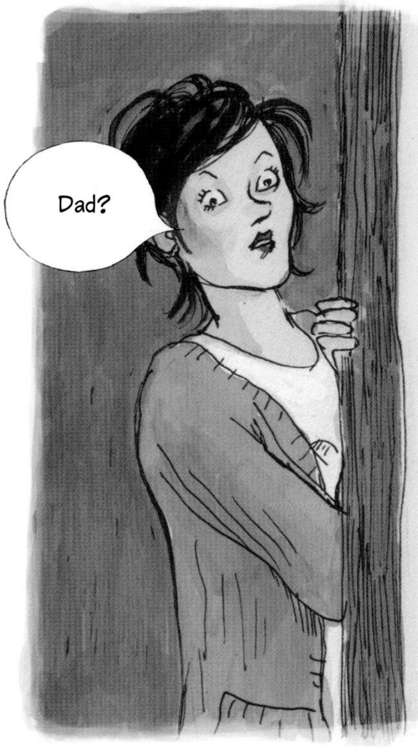
Dad?

If my sisters knew that I, Charlie Verdelaine, 23 years of age and level-headed to a fault, had taken up talking to the ghost of our dear departed father almost two years ago now…

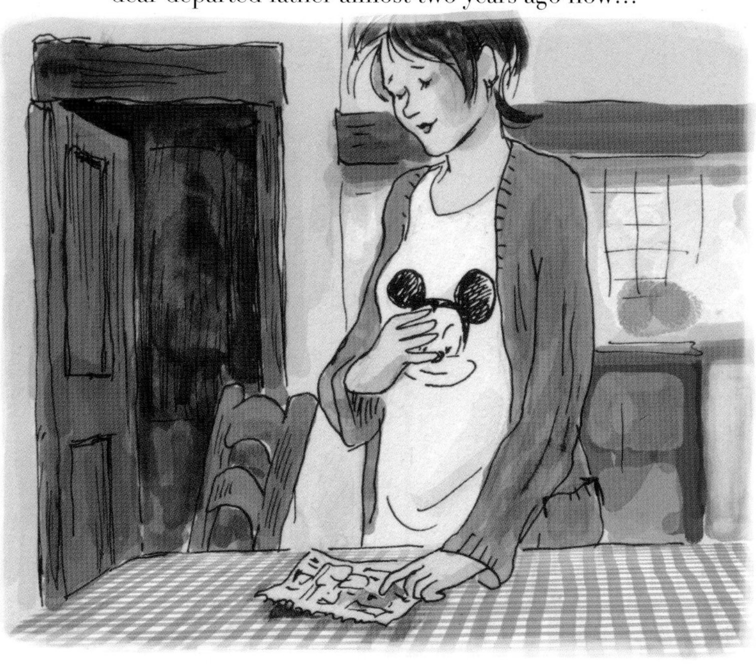

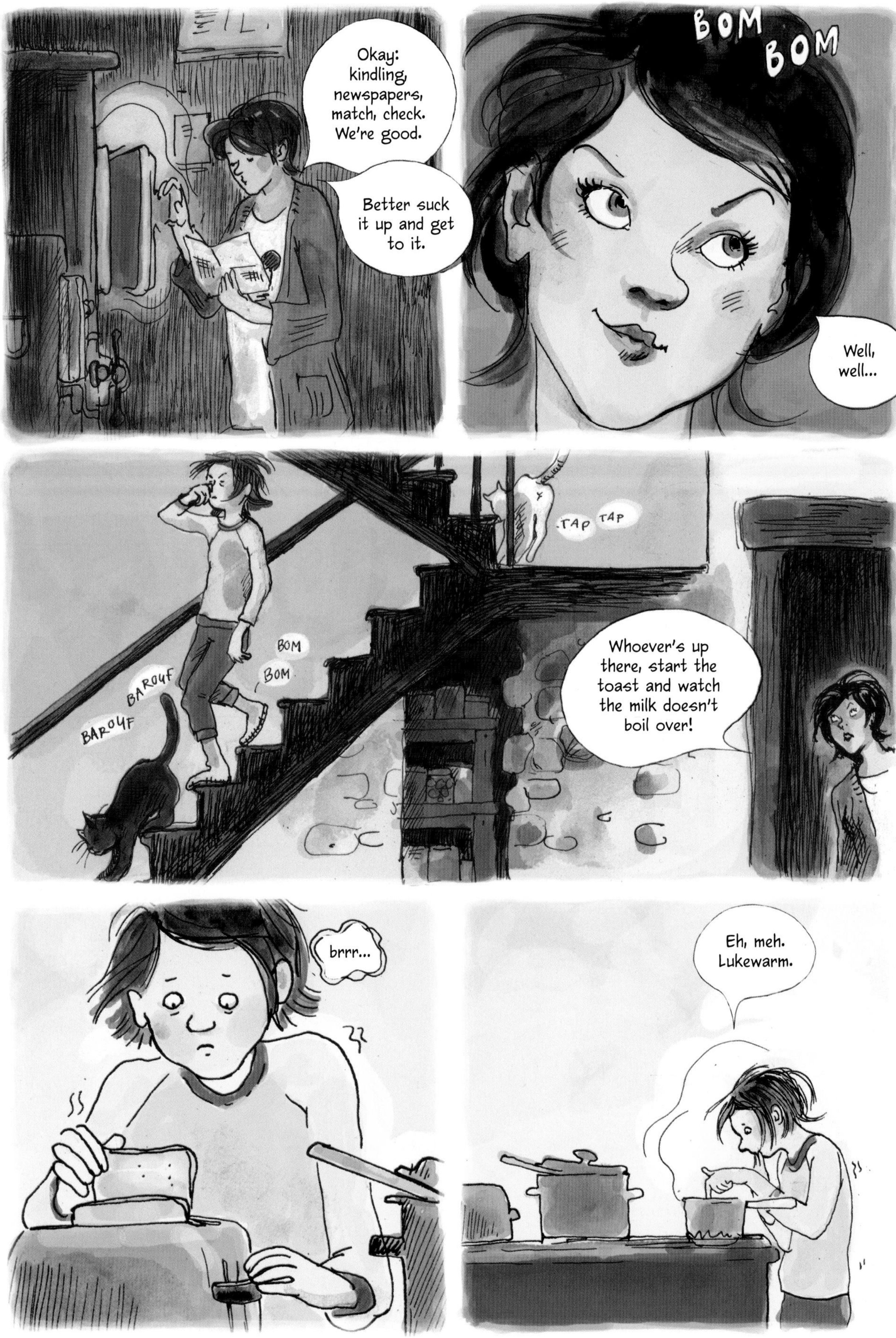
Okay: kindling, newspapers, match, check. We're good.
Better suck it up and get to it.
BOM BOM
Well, well...
TAP TAP
BOM
BOM
BAROUF
BAROUF
Whoever's up there, start the toast and watch the milk doesn't boil over!
brrr...
Eh, meh. Lukewarm.

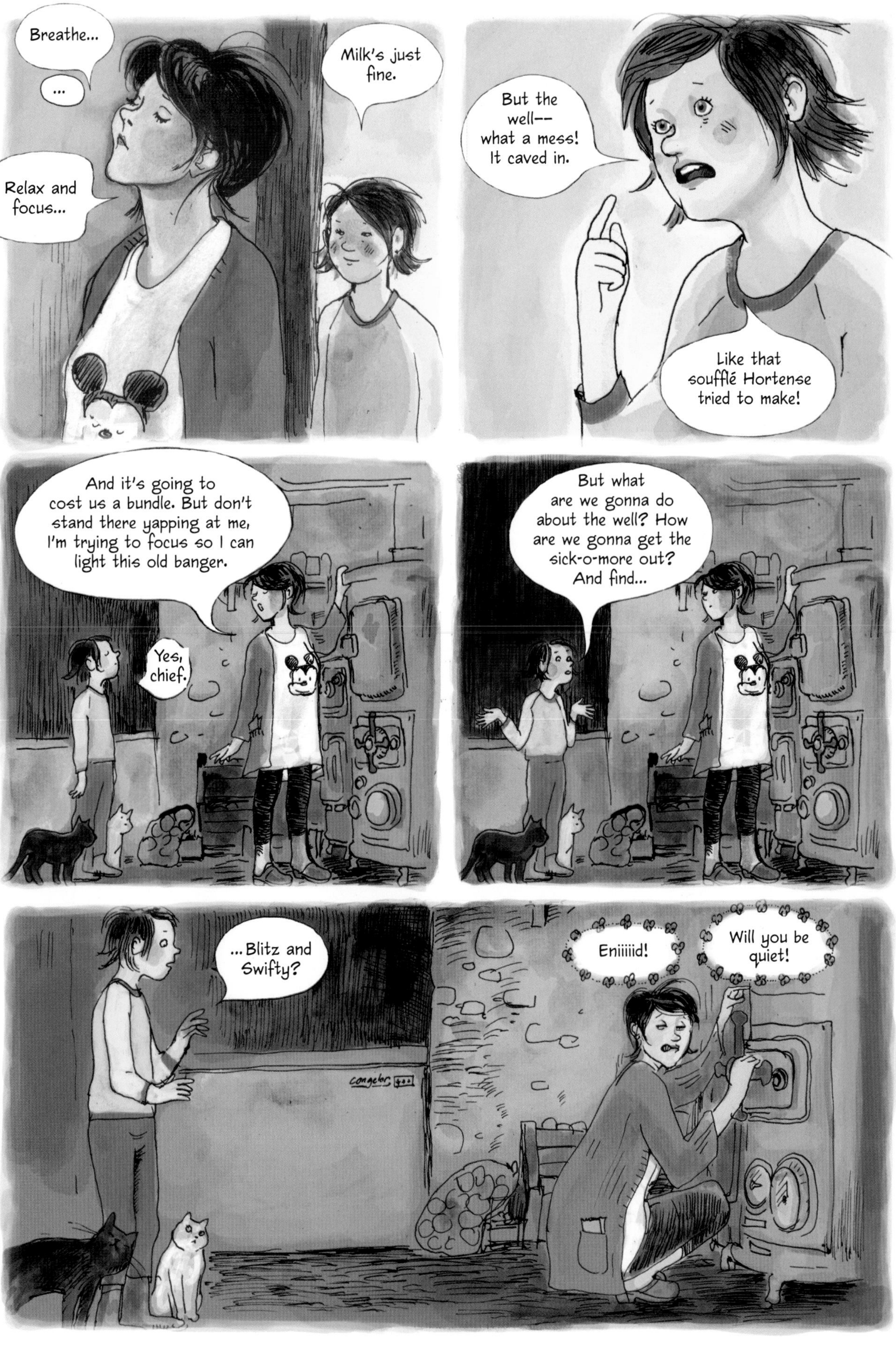
Breathe...
...
Relax and focus...
Milk's just fine.
But the well-- what a mess! It caved in.
Like that soufflé Hortense tried to make!
And it's going to cost us a bundle. But don't stand there yapping at me, I'm trying to focus so I can light this old banger.
Yes, chief.
But what are we gonna do about the well? How are we gonna get the sick-o-more out? And find...
...Blitz and Swifty?
Eniiiiid!
Will you be quiet!

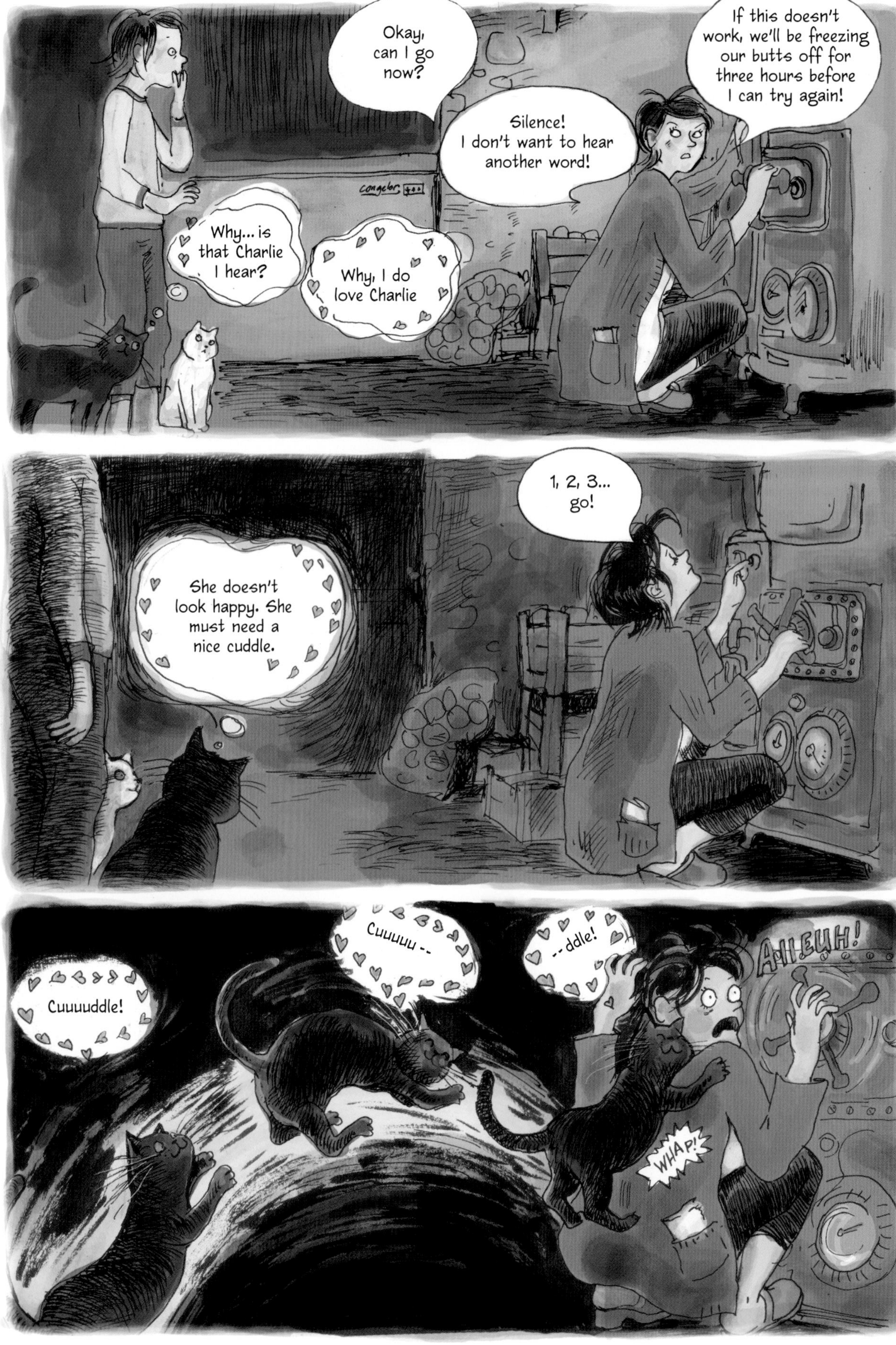

Okay, can I go now?
If this doesn't work, we'll be freezing our butts off for three hours before I can try again!
Silence! I don't want to hear another word!
Why... is that Charlie I hear?
Why, I do love Charlie
1, 2, 3... go!
She doesn't look happy. She must need a nice cuddle.
Cuuuuddle!
Cuuuuu --
-- ddle!
AIIEUH!
WHAP!

fsshhh
Roberto!
Roberto...
vrush vrush vrush
tap tap
DOGGONE
DEGENE
FELINE
EATING
LAMEBRA
YOU MAKE
SACK OF
FURBAG
FLEA
ahem...
ANIMAL
ME SICK!!!
So we just leave the stove on unattended now?

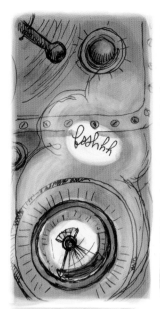

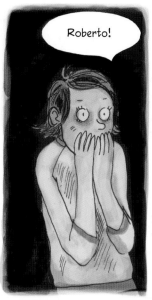

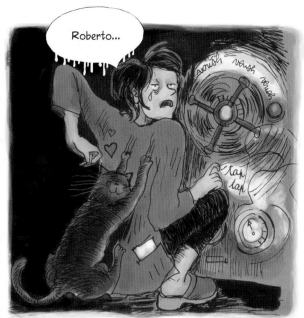

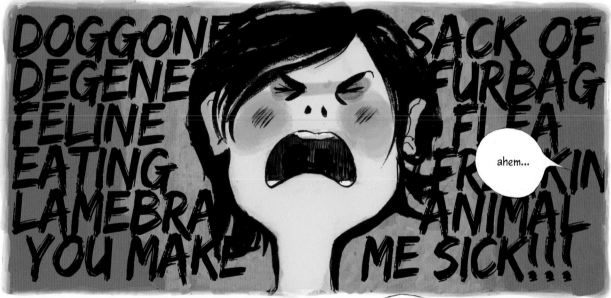

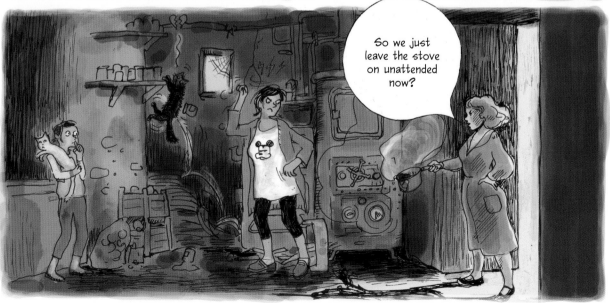

That morning. Mr. Philip Belmondoe (plumbing, painting, landscaping, decorating, masonry, chimneys, tiling: "We get the job done."), lover of strawberry-flavored chewing gum and meteorological metaphors, came by and gave his unimpeachable professional opinion.

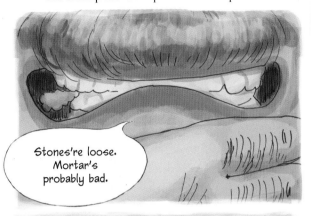

Stones're loose. Mortar's probably bad.

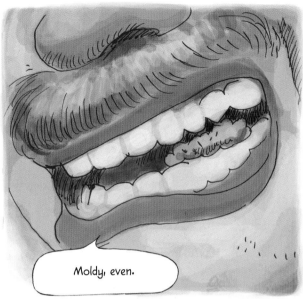

Moldy, even.

All it took was the tree hitting just one...

...and wham!

Snowballed!

Snow-balled?

Poor ol' fella...

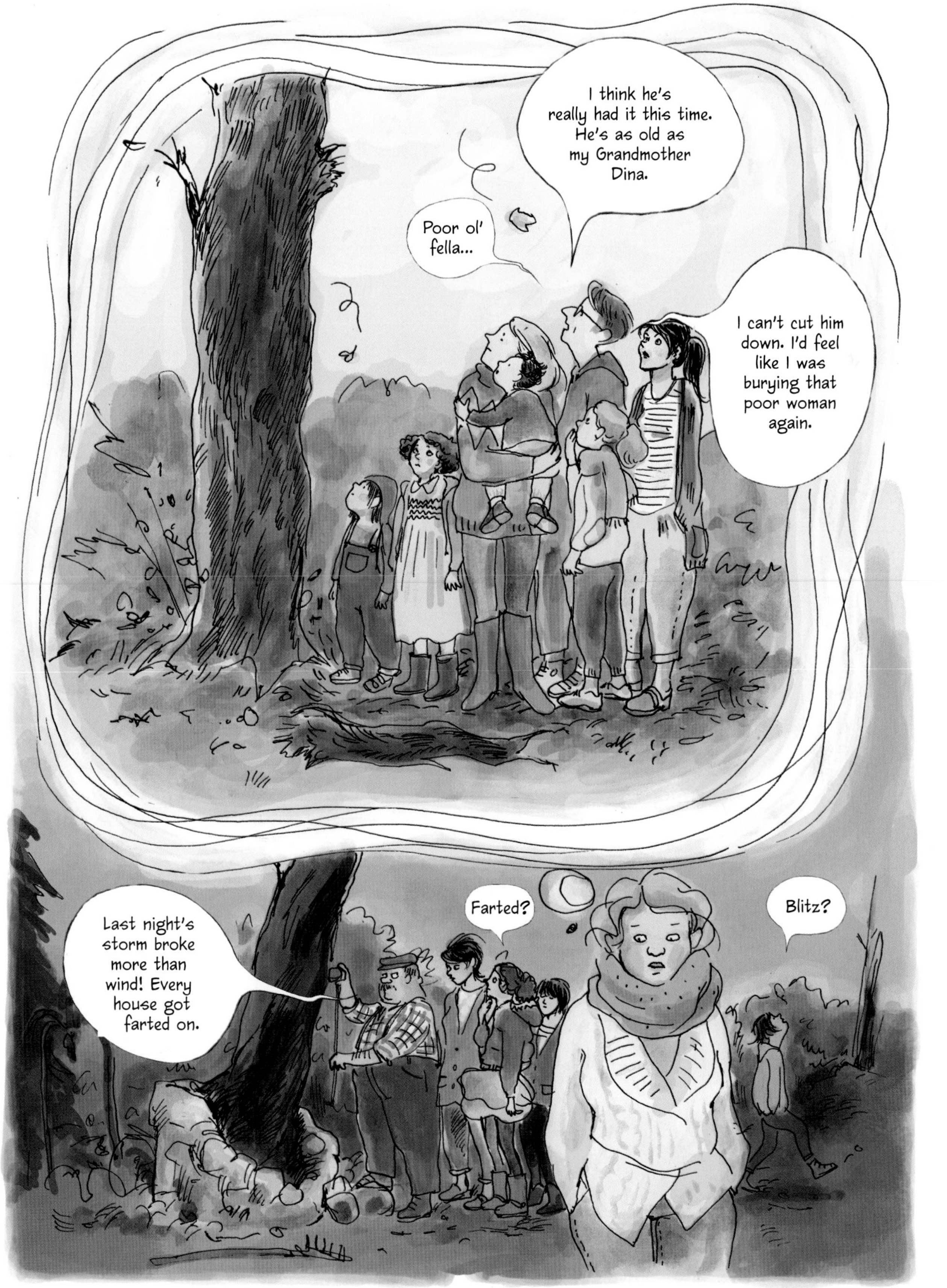
Poor ol' fella...
I think he's really had it this time. He's as old as my Grandmother Dina.
I can't cut him down. I'd feel like I was burying that poor woman again.
Last night's storm broke more than wind! Every house got farted on.
Farted?
Blitz?

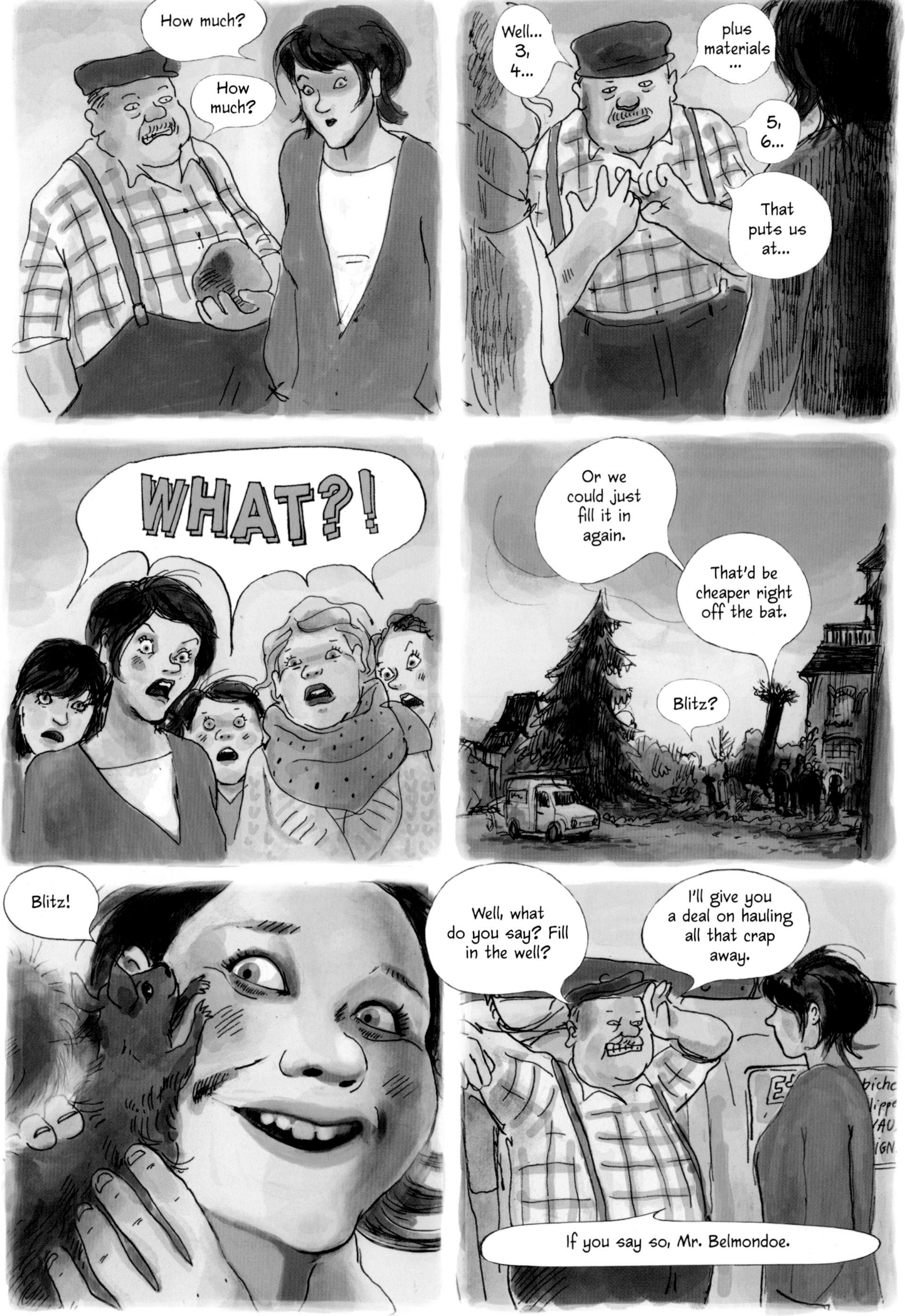
How much?
How much?
Well... 3, 4...
plus materials ...
5, 6...
That puts us at...
WHAT?!
Or we could just fill it in again.
That'd be cheaper right off the bat.
Blitz?
Blitz!
Well, what do you say? Fill in the well?
I'll give you a deal on hauling all that crap away.
If you say so, Mr. Belmondoe.

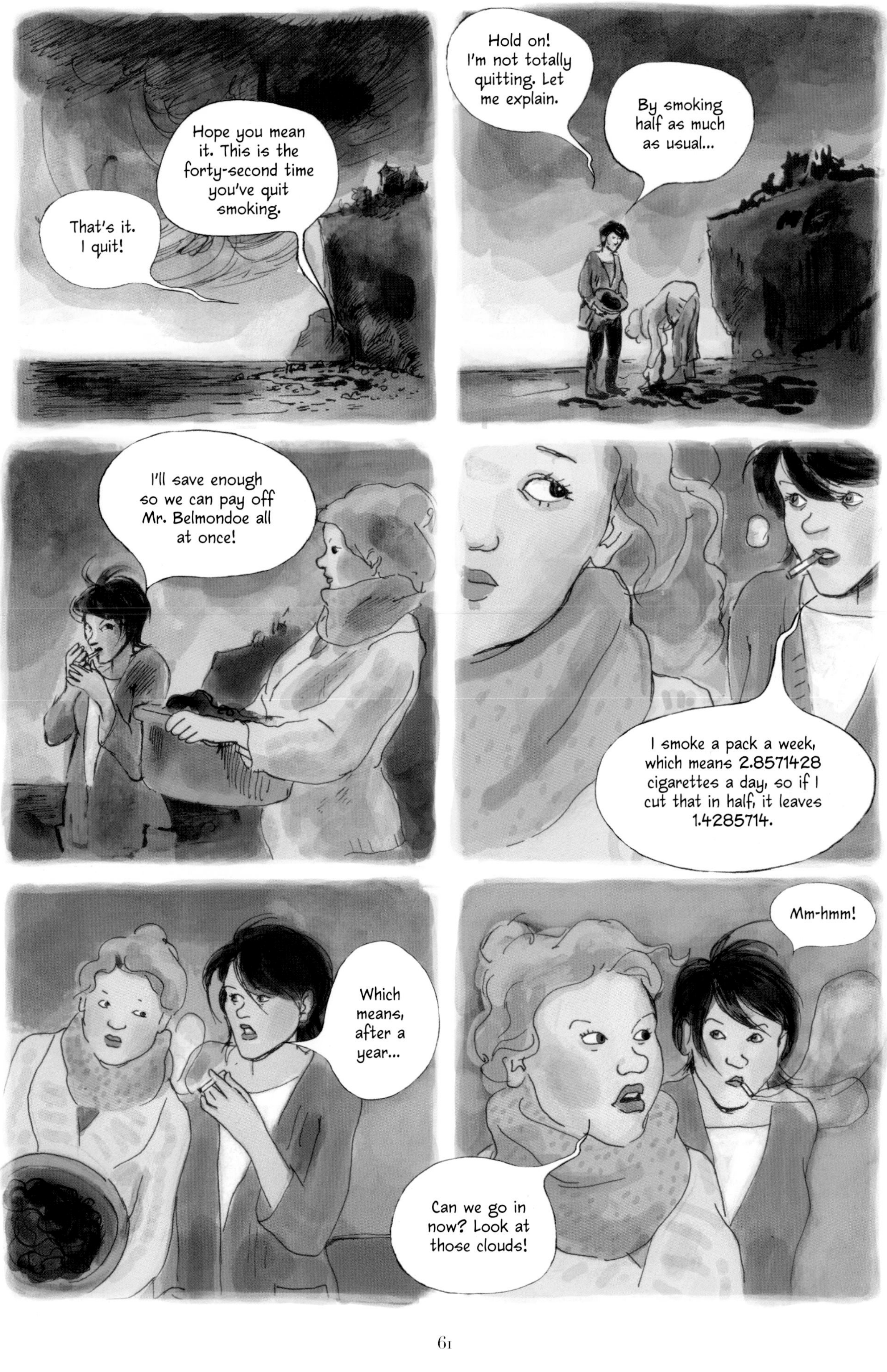
That's it. I quit!
Hope you mean it. This is the forty-second time you've quit smoking.
Hold on! I'm not totally quitting. Let me explain.
By smoking half as much as usual...
I'll save enough so we can pay off Mr. Belmondoe all at once!
I smoke a pack a week, which means 2.8571428 cigarettes a day, so if I cut that in half, it leaves 1.4285714.
Which means, after a year...
Mm-hmm!
Can we go in now? Look at those clouds!

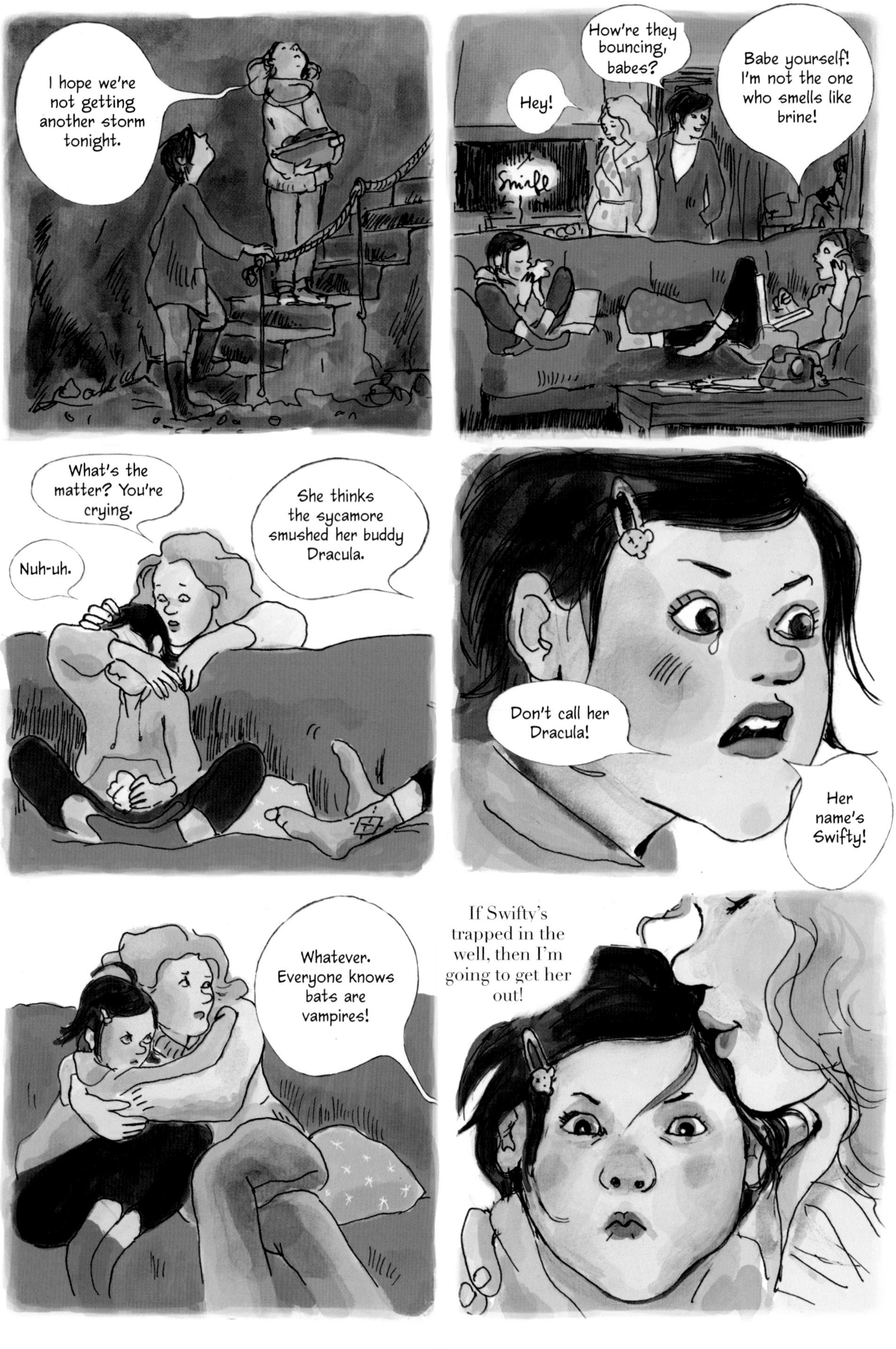
I hope we're not getting another storm tonight.
Hey!
How're they bouncing, babes?
Babe yourself! I'm not the one who smells like brine!
Smirfle
What's the matter? You're crying.
Nuh-uh.
She thinks the sycamore smushed her buddy Dracula.
Don't call her Dracula!
Her name's Swifty!
Whatever. Everyone knows bats are vampires!
If Swifty's trapped in the well, then I'm going to get her out!

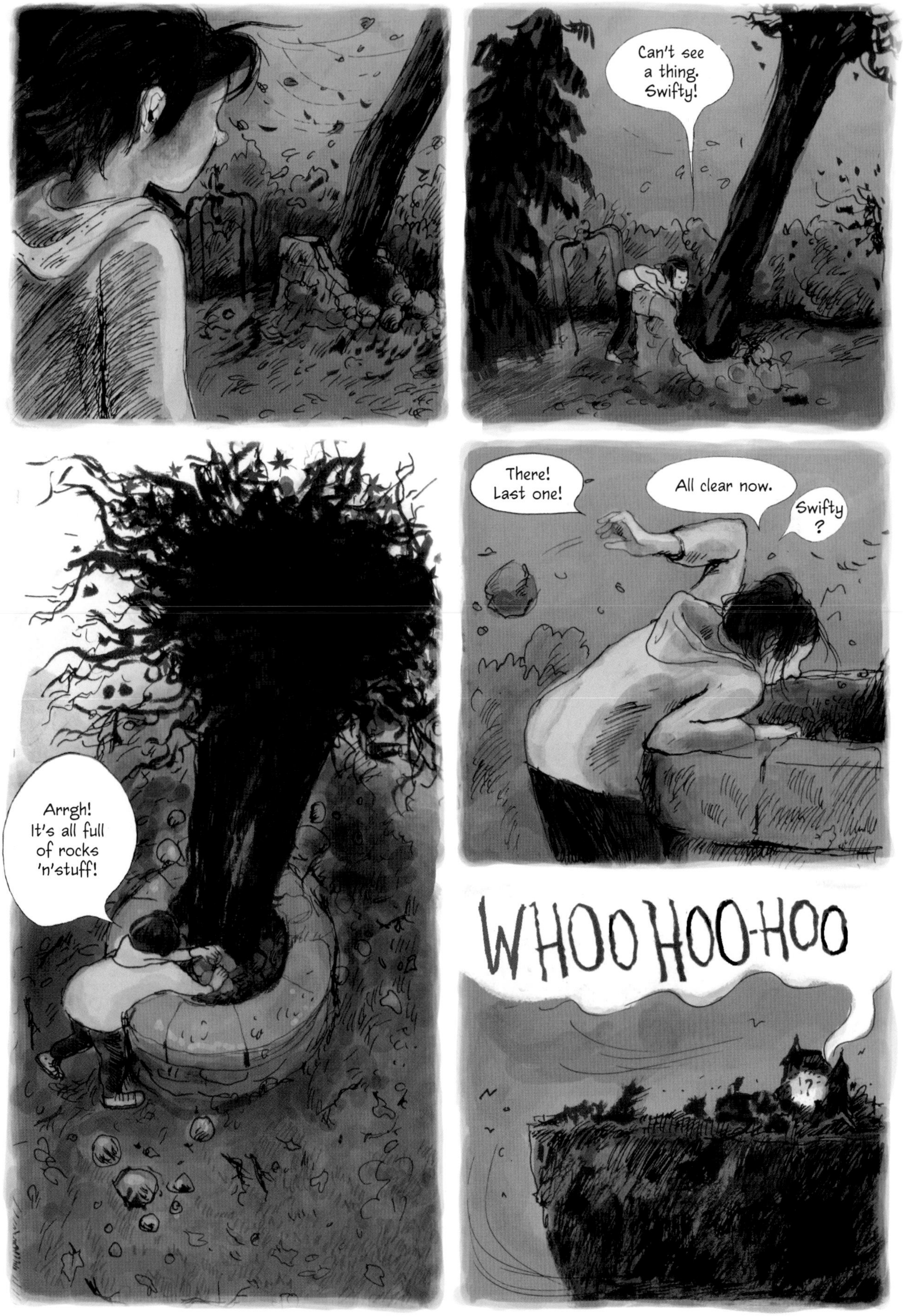
Can't see a thing. Swifty!
Arrgh! It's all full of rocks 'n'stuff!
There! Last one!
All clear now.
Swifty ?
WHOO HOO-HOO

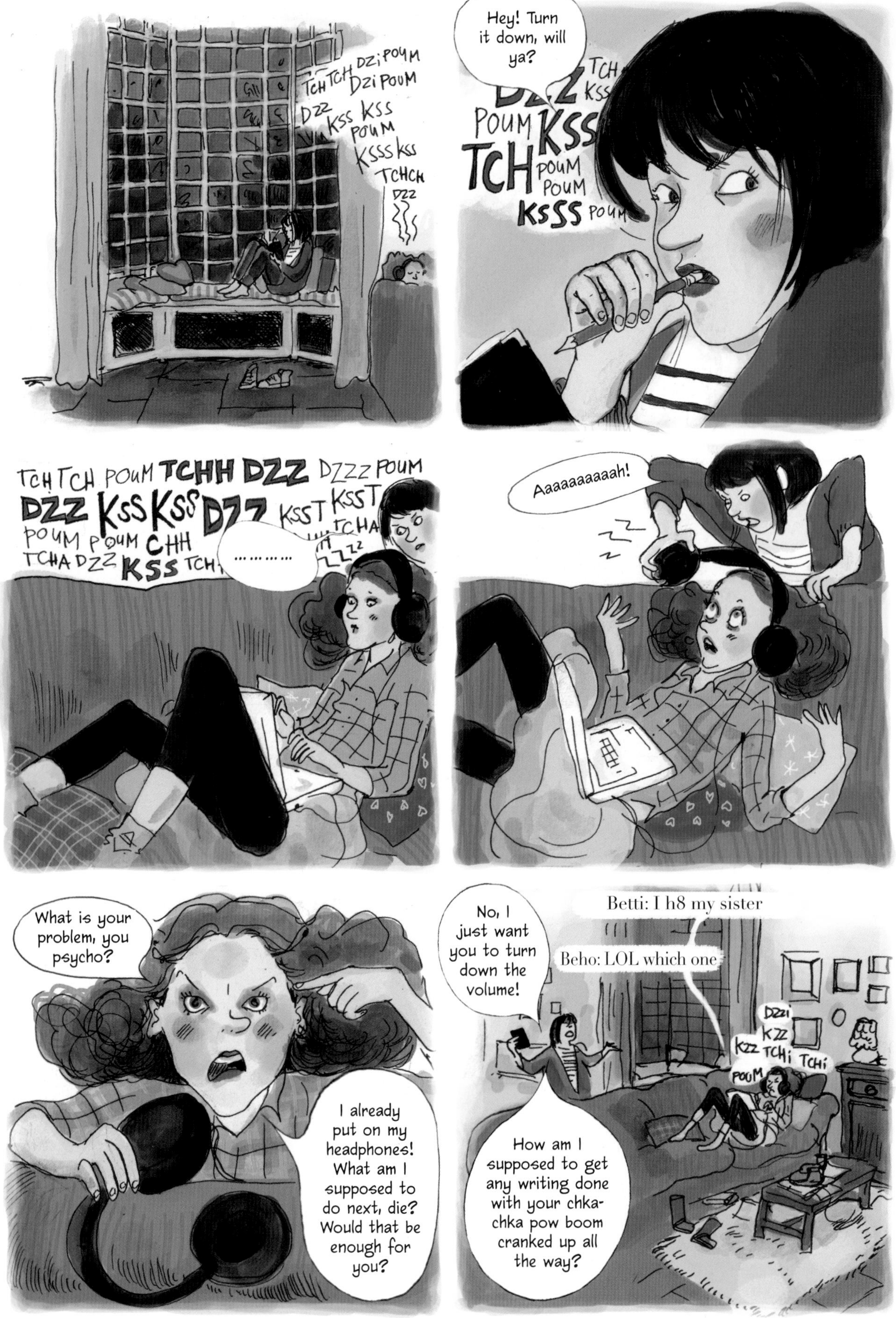

TCH TCH DZi POUM
DZi POUM
DZZ KSS KSS
POUM
KSSS KSS
TCHCH
DZZ
Hey! Turn it down, will ya?
DZZ TCH KSS
POUM KSS
TCH POUM POUM
KSSS POUM
TCH TCH POUM TCHH DZZ DZZZ POUM
DZZ KSS KSS DZZ KSST KSST
POUM POUM CHH TCHA
TCHA DZZ KSS TCH
………
Aaaaaaaaaah!
What is your problem, you psycho?
I already put on my headphones! What am I supposed to do next, die? Would that be enough for you?
No, I just want you to turn down the volume!
Betti: I h8 my sister
Beho: LOL which one
DZZi
KZZ
KZZ TCHi TCHi
POUM
How am I supposed to get any writing done with your chka-chka pow boom cranked up all the way?

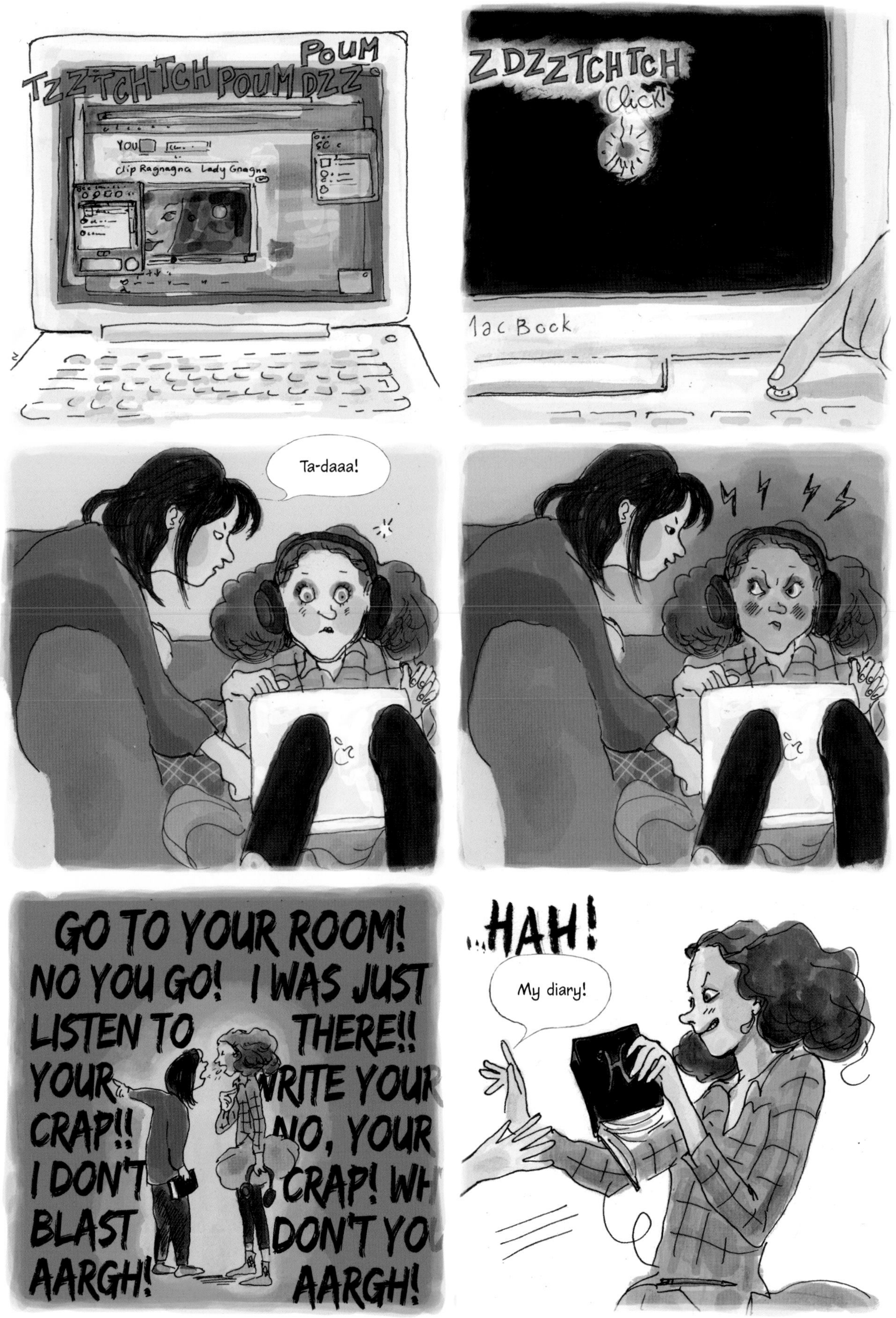
TZZTCHTCH POUM DZZ POUM
YOU
Clip Ragnagna Lady Gnagna
ZDZZZTCHTCH
Click!
Ta-daaa!
GO TO YOUR ROOM!
NO YOU GO! I WAS JUST
LISTEN TO THERE!!
YOUR WRITE YOUR
CRAP!! NO, YOUR
I DON'T CRAP! WH
BLAST DON'T YO
AARGH! AARGH!
...HAH!
My diary!

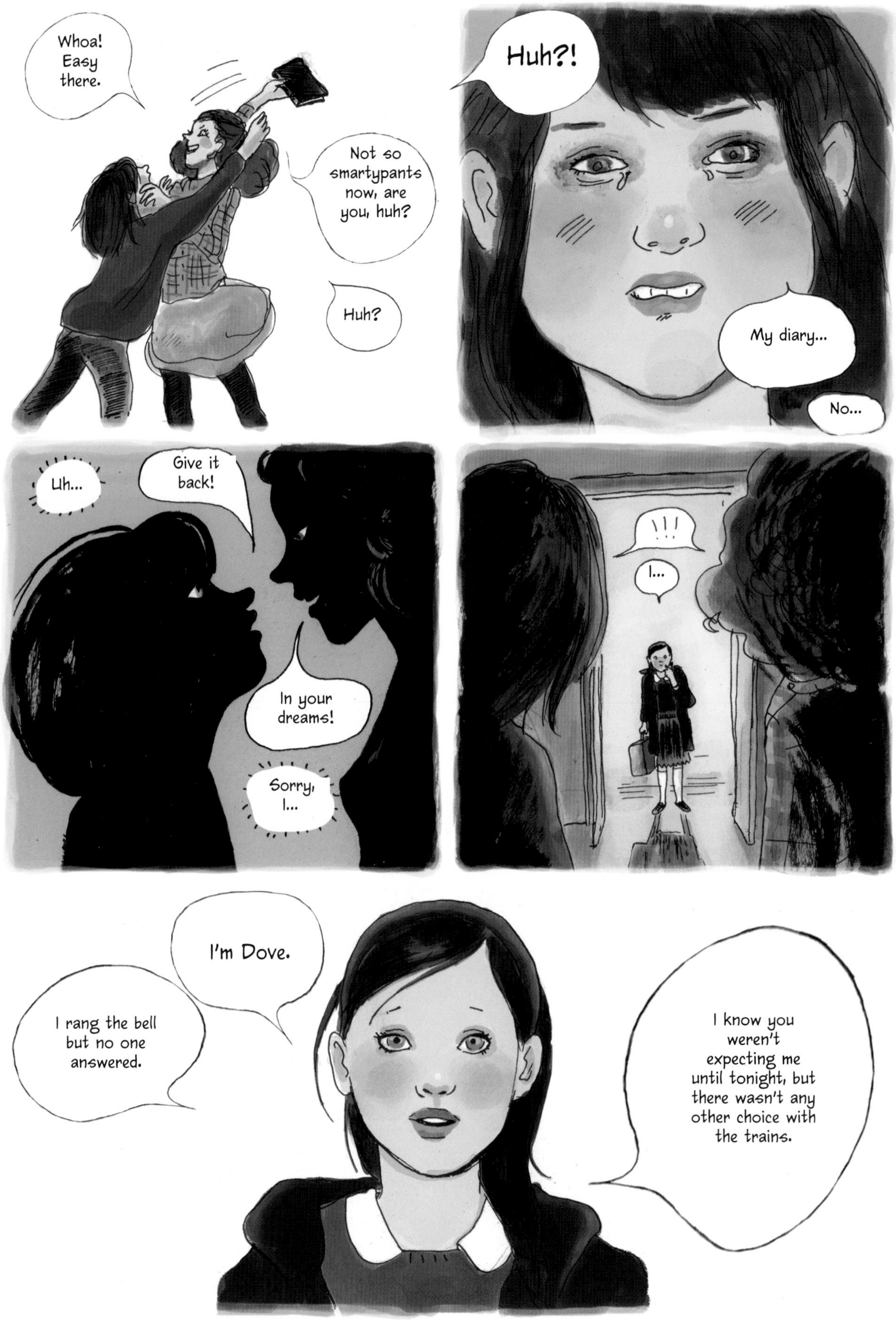

Whoa! Easy there.
Not so smartypants now, are you, huh?
Huh?
Huh?!
My diary...
No...
Uh...
Give it back!
In your dreams!
Sorry, I...
!!!
I...
I'm Dove.
I rang the bell but no one answered.
I know you weren't expecting me until tonight, but there wasn't any other choice with the trains.

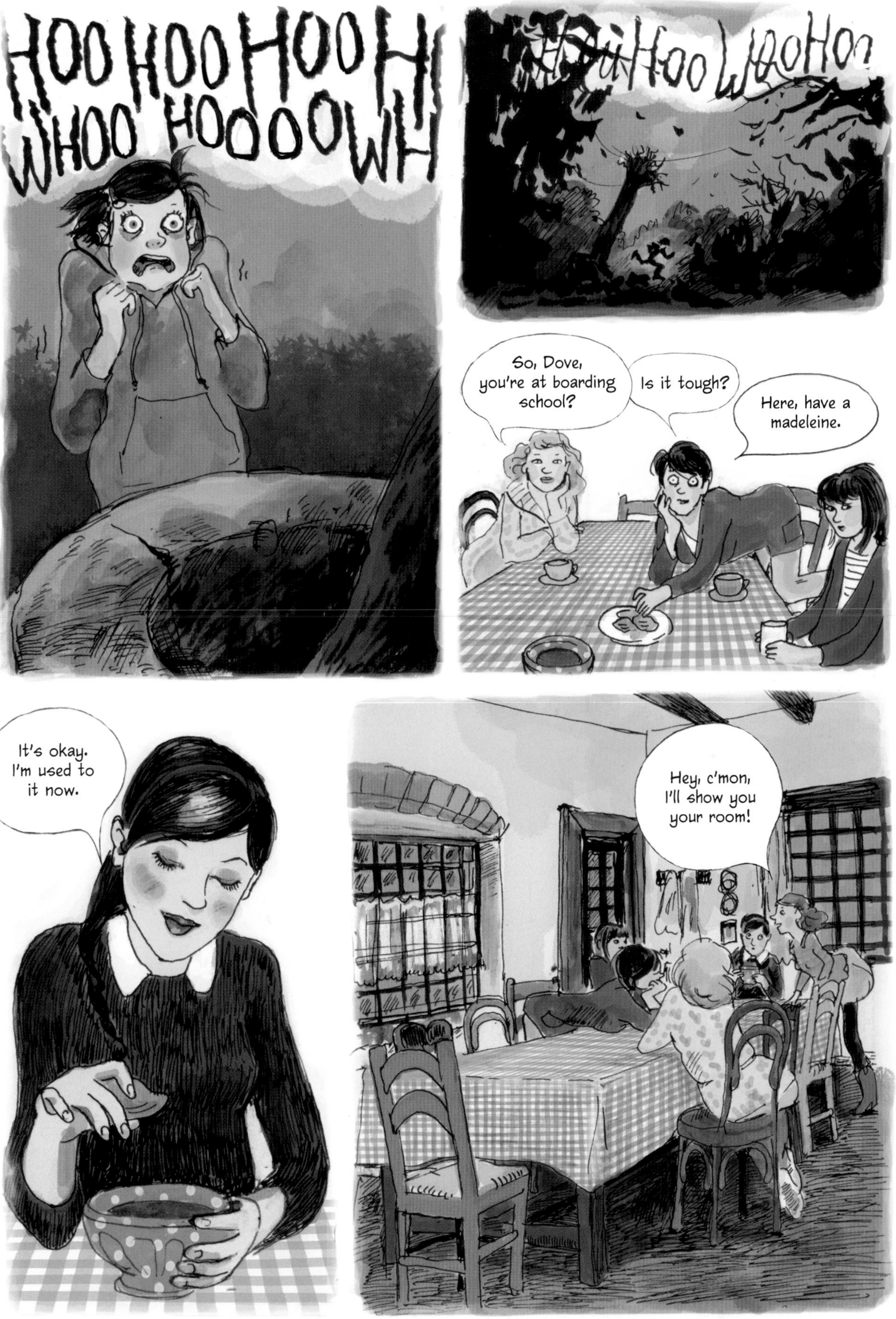
HOO HOO HOO H
WHOO HOOOOOWH
So, Dove, you're at boarding school?
Is it tough?
Here, have a madeleine.
It's okay. I'm used to it now.
Hey, c'mon, I'll show you your room!

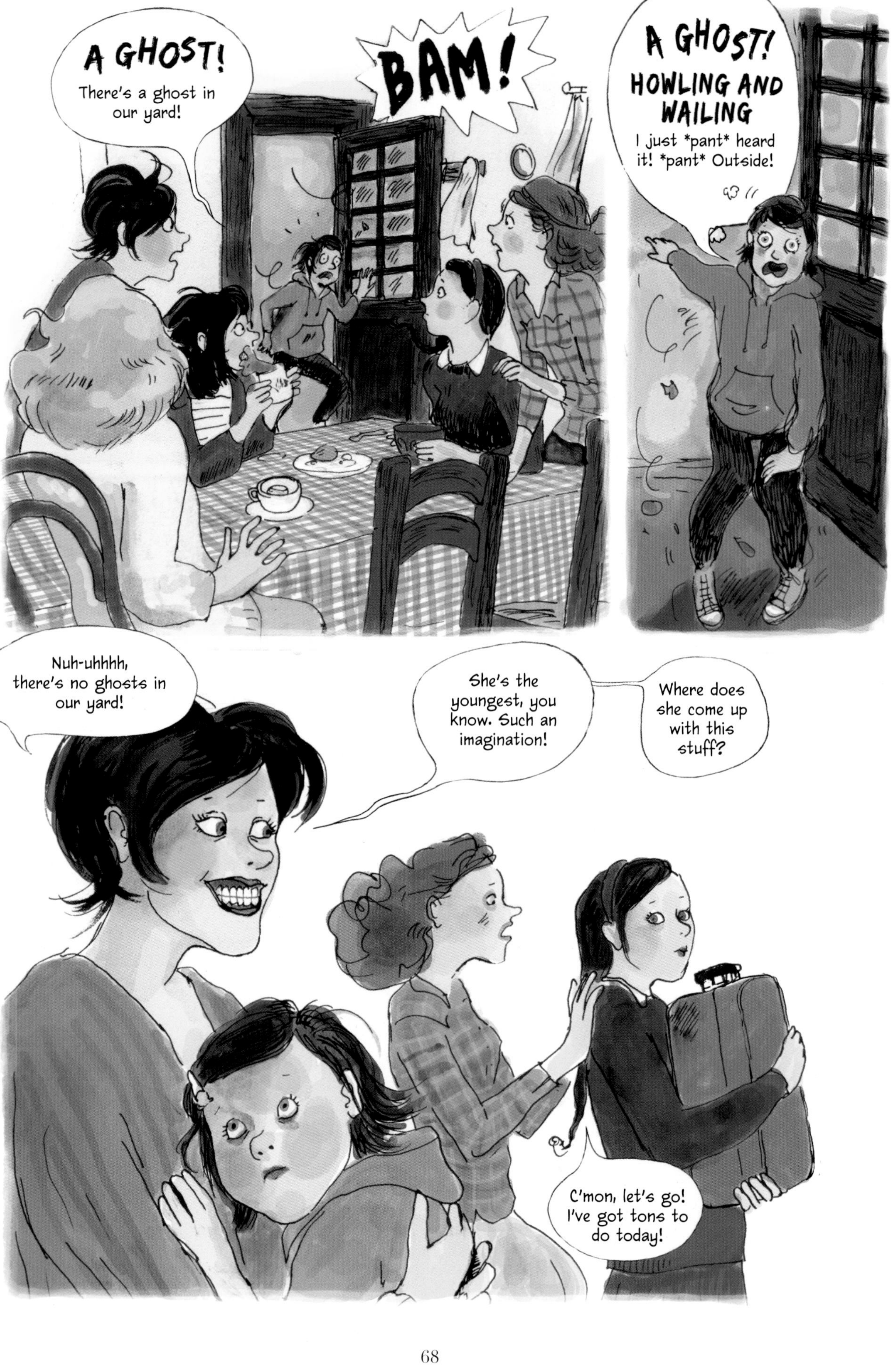
A GHOST!
There's a ghost in our yard!
BAM!
A GHOST!
HOWLING AND WAILING
I just *pant* heard it! *pant* Outside!
Nuh-uhhhh, there's no ghosts in our yard!
She's the youngest, you know. Such an imagination!
Where does she come up with this stuff?
C'mon, let's go! I've got tons to do today!

Of the five sisters, Bettina was the only one with her own bathroom (it was always a real pigsty). The trade-off, by mutual agreement, was that she lived by herself on the third floor, by the tower.

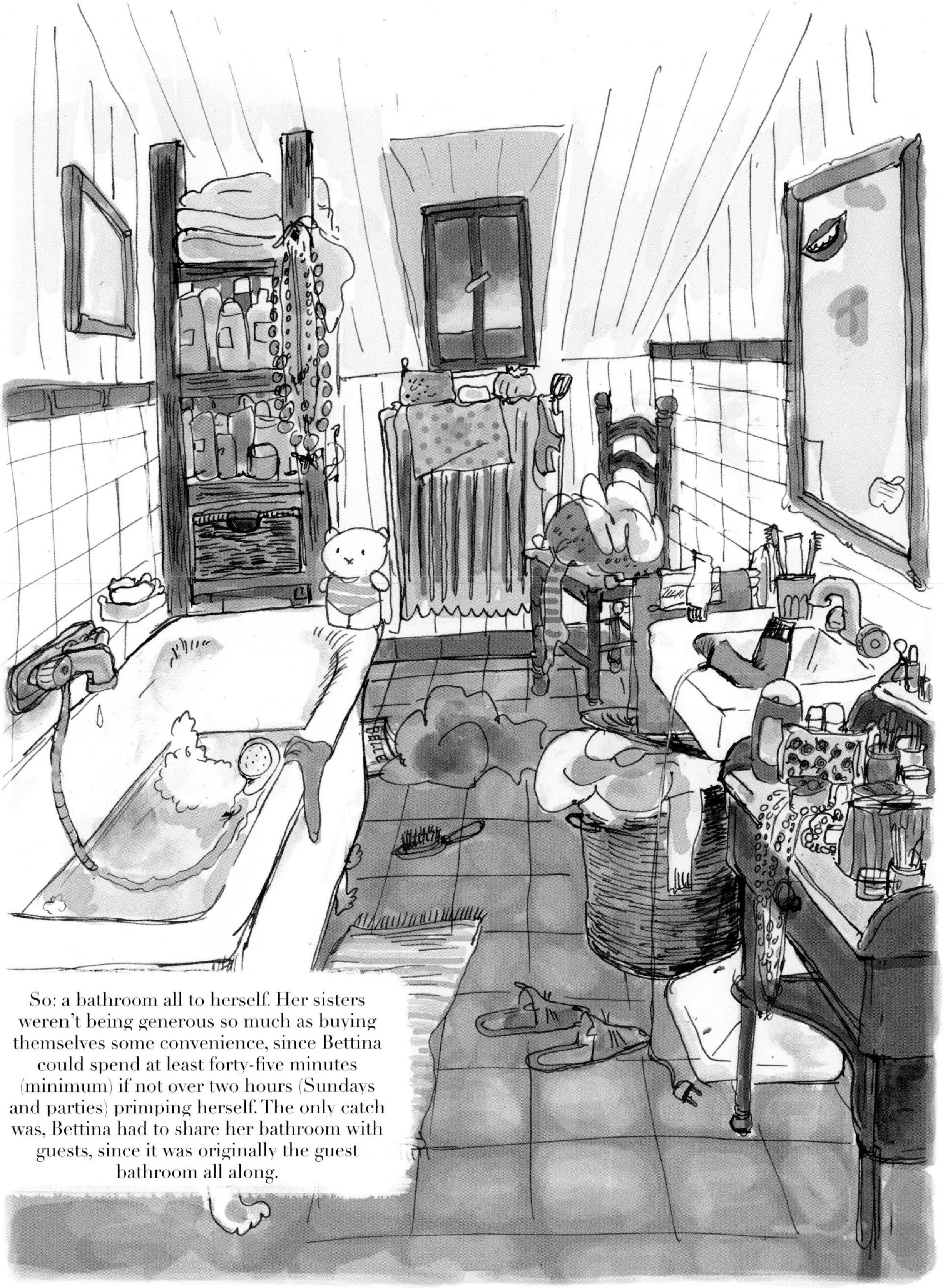
So: a bathroom all to herself. Her sisters weren't being generous so much as buying themselves some convenience, since Bettina could spend at least forty-five minutes (minimum) if not over two hours (Sundays and parties) primping herself. The only catch was, Bettina had to share her bathroom with guests, since it was originally the guest bathroom all along.

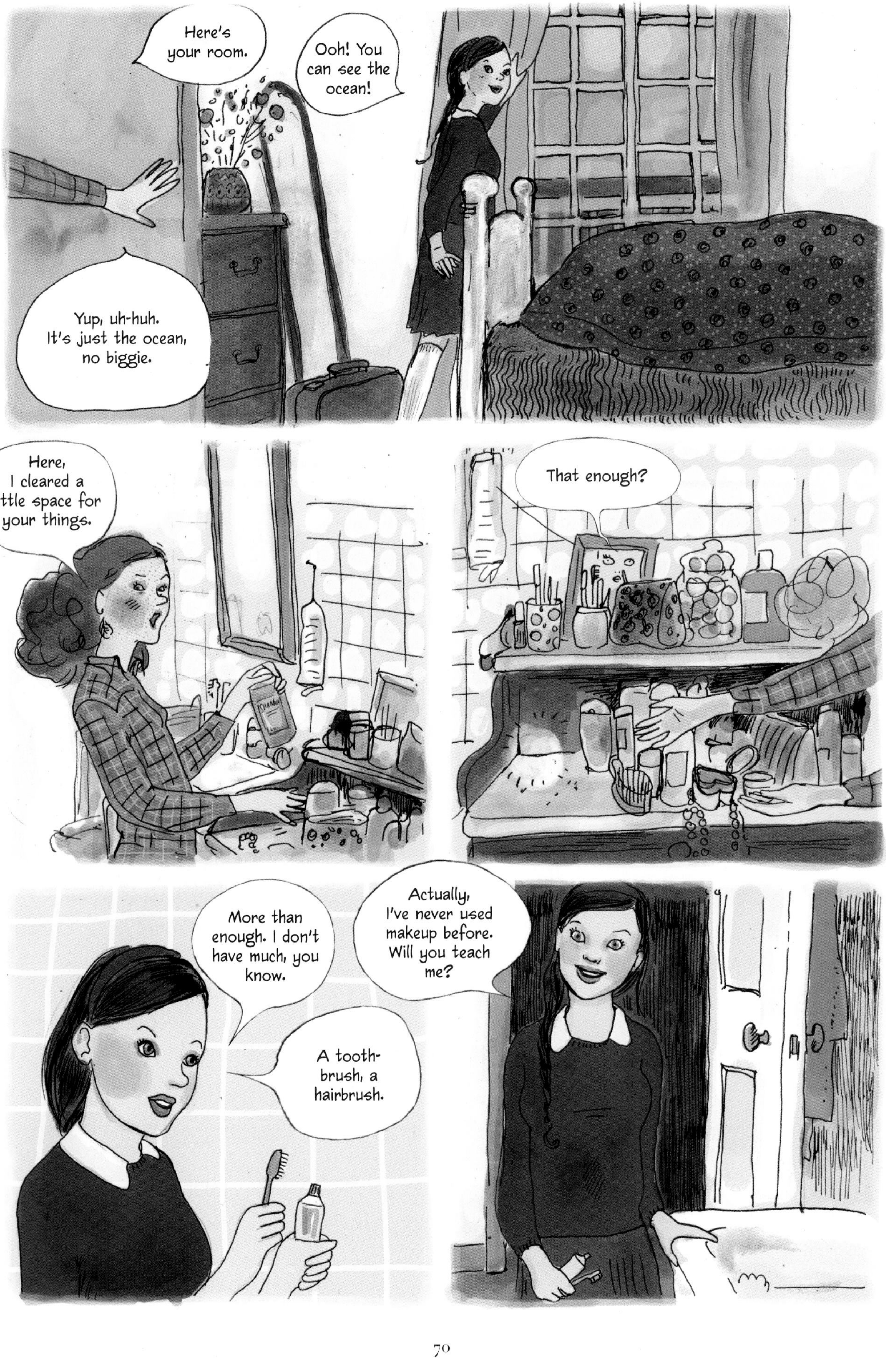
Here's your room.
Ooh! You can see the ocean!
Yup, uh-huh. It's just the ocean, no biggie.
Here, I cleared a little space for your things.
That enough?
More than enough. I don't have much, you know.
A toothbrush, a hairbrush.
Actually, I've never used makeup before. Will you teach me?

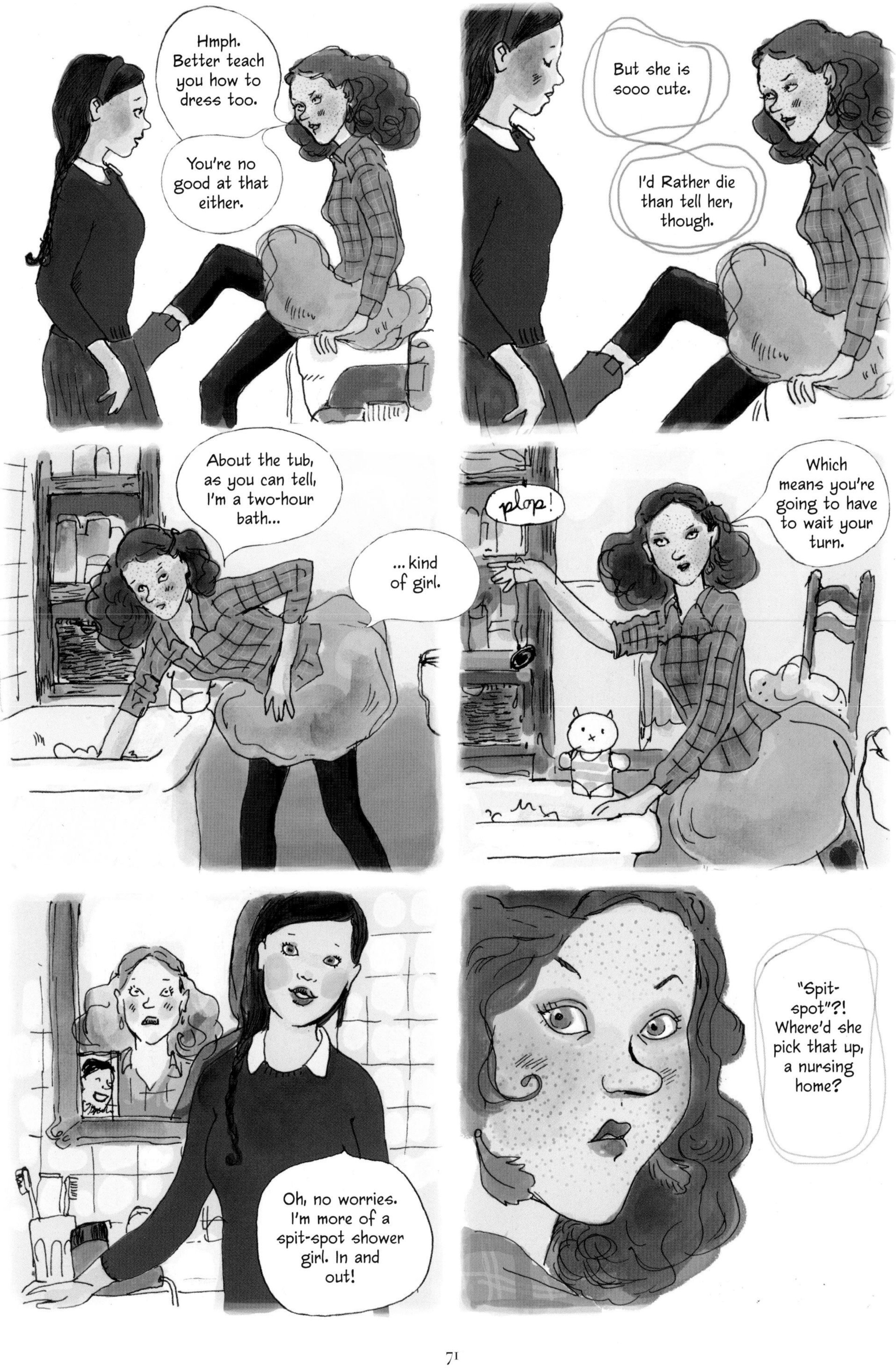

Hmph. Better teach you how to dress too.
You're no good at that either.
But she is sooo cute.
I'd Rather die than tell her, though.
About the tub, as you can tell, I'm a two-hour bath...
...kind of girl.
plop!
Which means you're going to have to wait your turn.
Oh, no worries. I'm more of a spit-spot shower girl. In and out!
"Spit-spot"?! Where'd she pick that up, a nursing home?

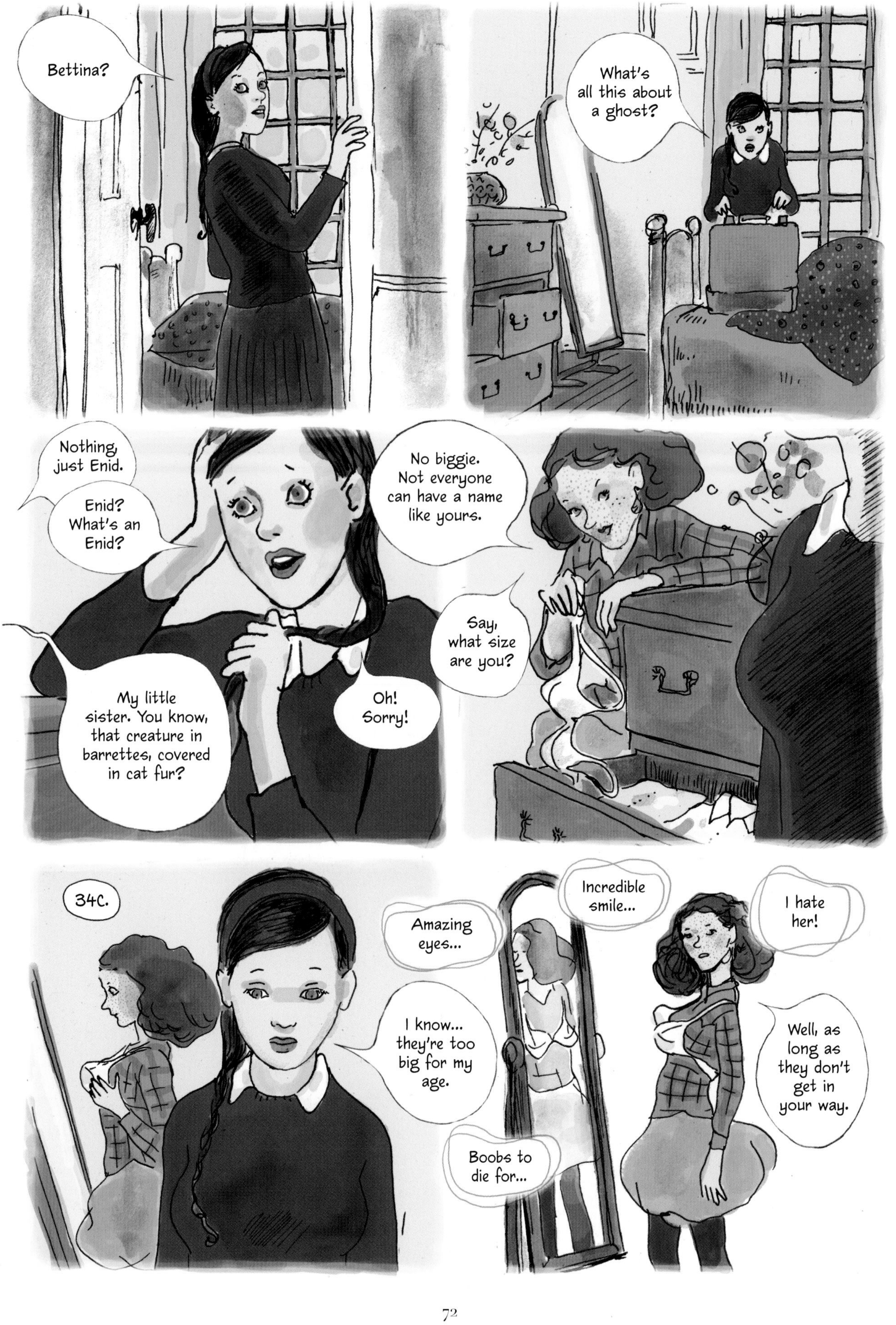
Bettina?
What's all this about a ghost?
Nothing, just Enid.
Enid? What's an Enid?
My little sister. You know, that creature in barrettes, covered in cat fur?
Oh! Sorry!
No biggie. Not everyone can have a name like yours.
Say, what size are you?
34C.
I know... they're too big for my age.
Amazing eyes...
Incredible smile...
Boobs to die for...
I hate her!
Well, as long as they don't get in your way.

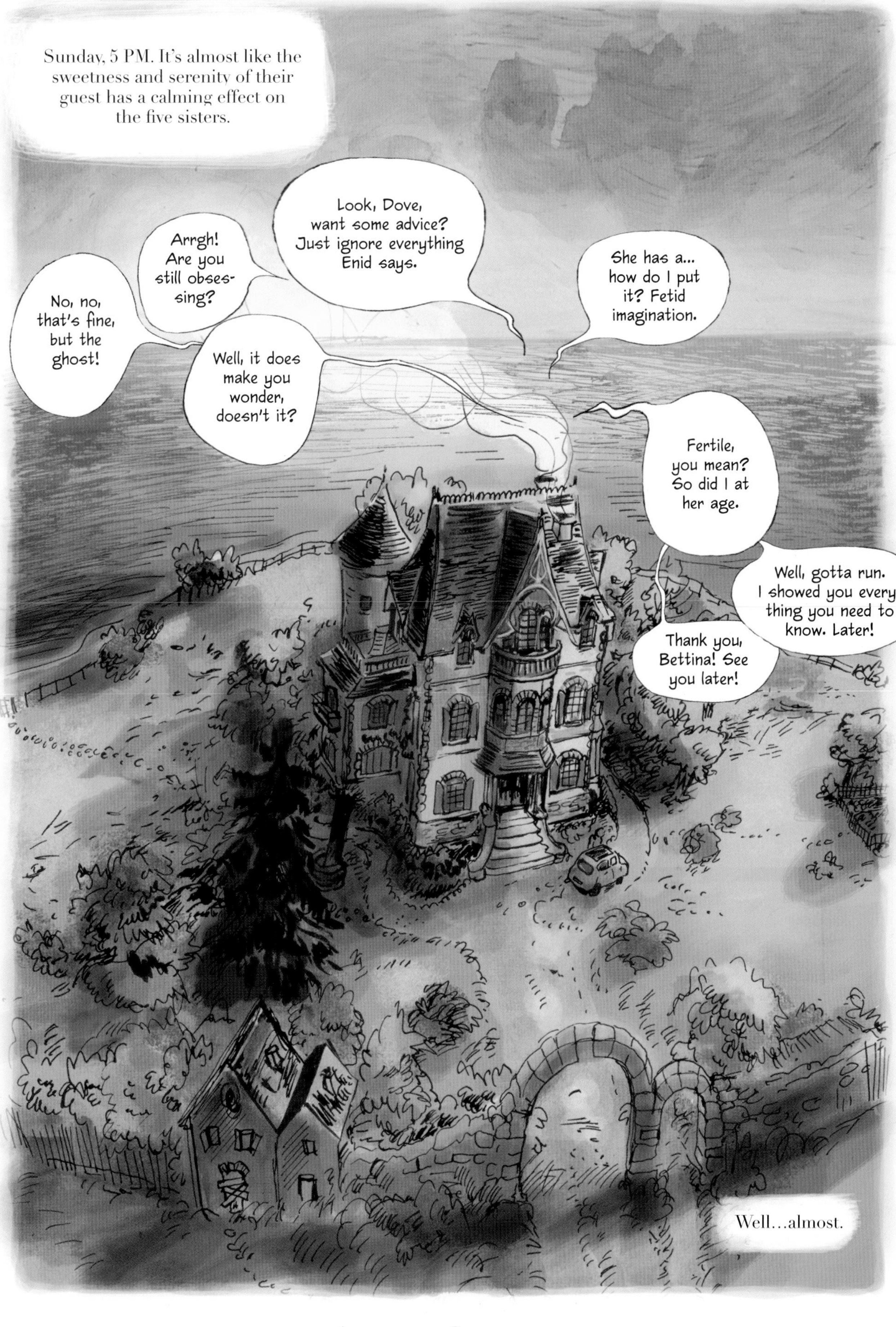
Sunday, 5 PM. It's almost like the sweetness and serenity of their guest has a calming effect on the five sisters.
No, no, that's fine, but the ghost!
Arrgh! Are you still obsessing?
Well, it does make you wonder, doesn't it?
Look, Dove, want some advice? Just ignore everything Enid says.
She has a... how do I put it? Fetid imagination.
Fertile, you mean? So did I at her age.
Well, gotta run. I showed you everything you need to know. Later!
Thank you, Bettina! See you later!
Well...almost.

Dove reminded Charlie of her mom's little red-and-gold girls' novels, in a crate in the attic.

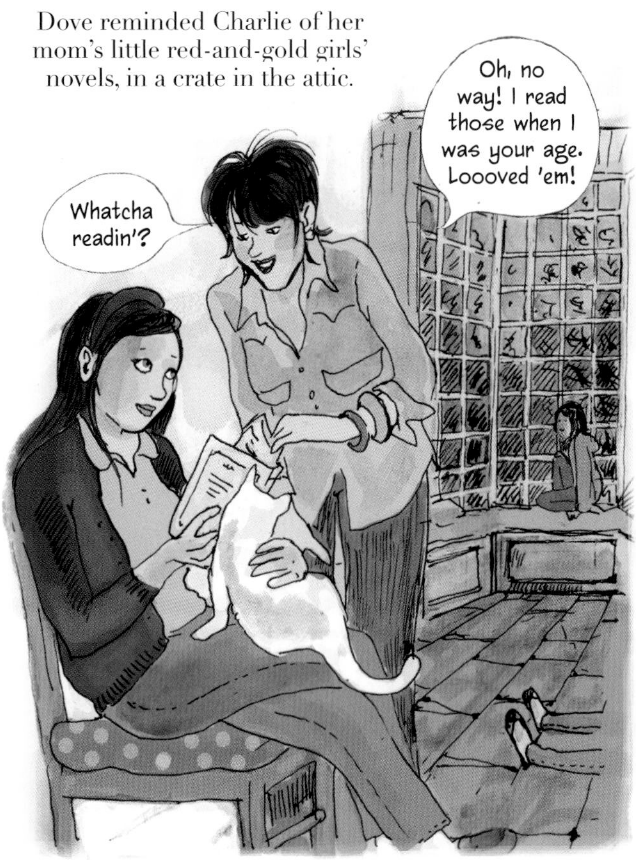
Whatcha readin'?
Oh, no way! I read those when I was your age. Loooved 'em!

She reminded Enid of Aunt Lucretia's knitted tea-cozy.

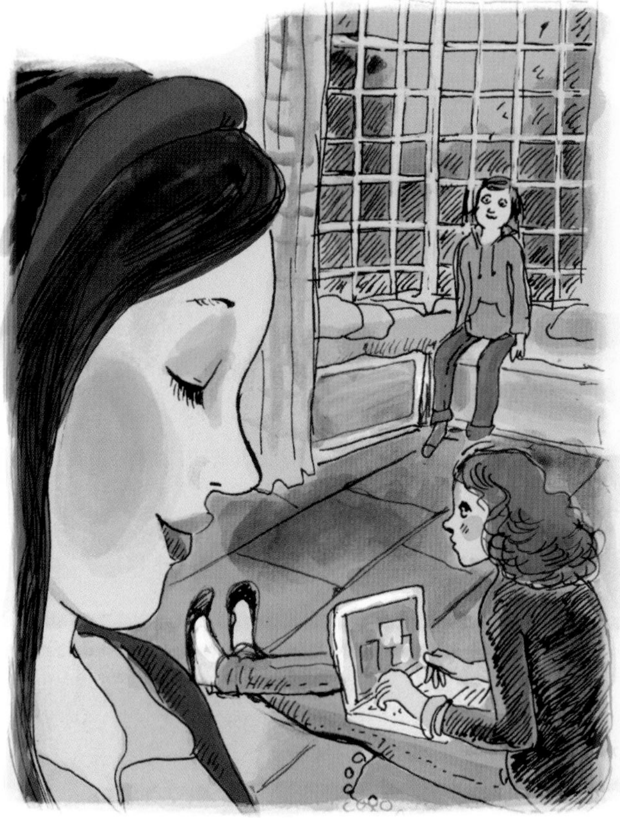

To Bettina, she was something smart and boring, like a game of Trivial Pursuit with no winner.

To Genevieve, she was that lace Peter Pan collar folded neatly away in a wardrobe upstairs.

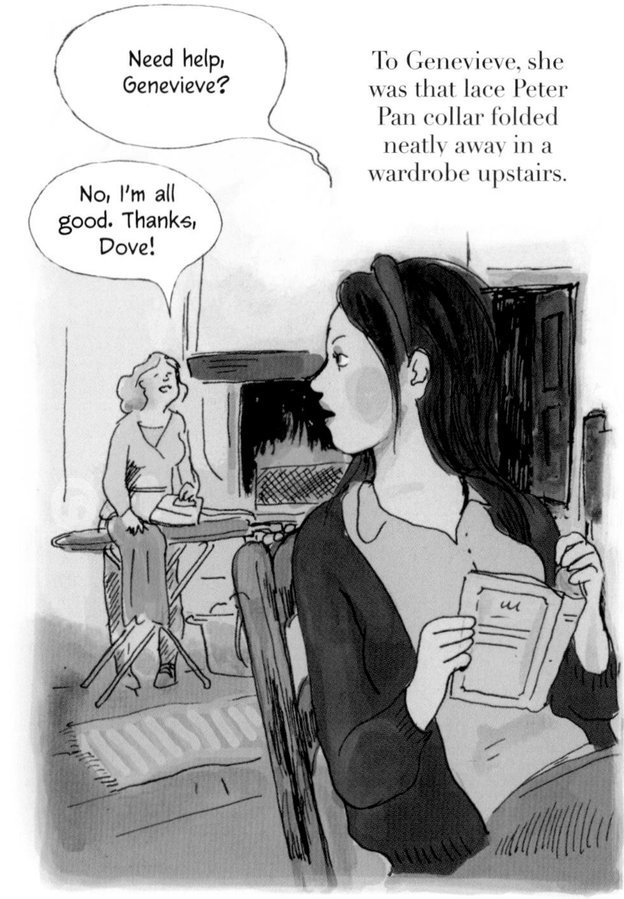
Need help, Genevieve?
No, I'm all good. Thanks, Dove!

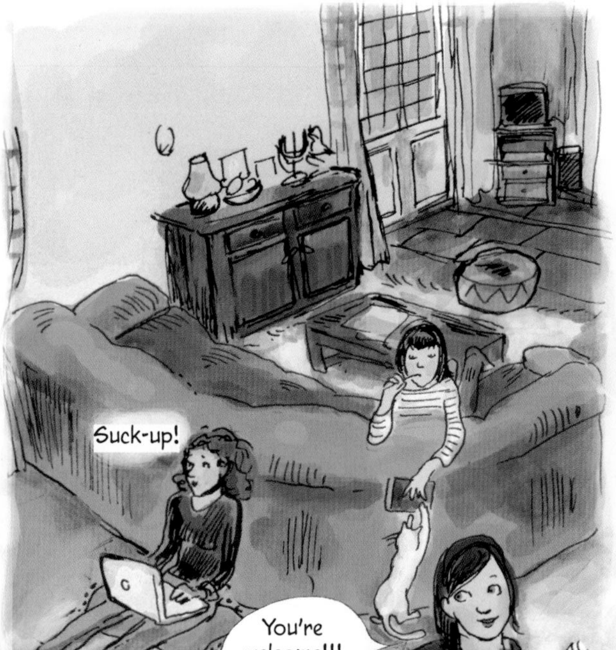
Suck-up!
You're welcome!!!

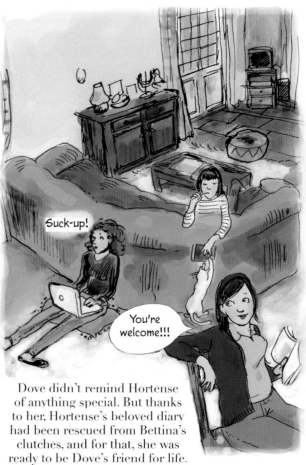

Dove didn't remind Hortense of anything special. But thanks to her, Hortense's beloved diary had been rescued from Bettina's clutches, and for that, she was ready to be Dove's friend for life.

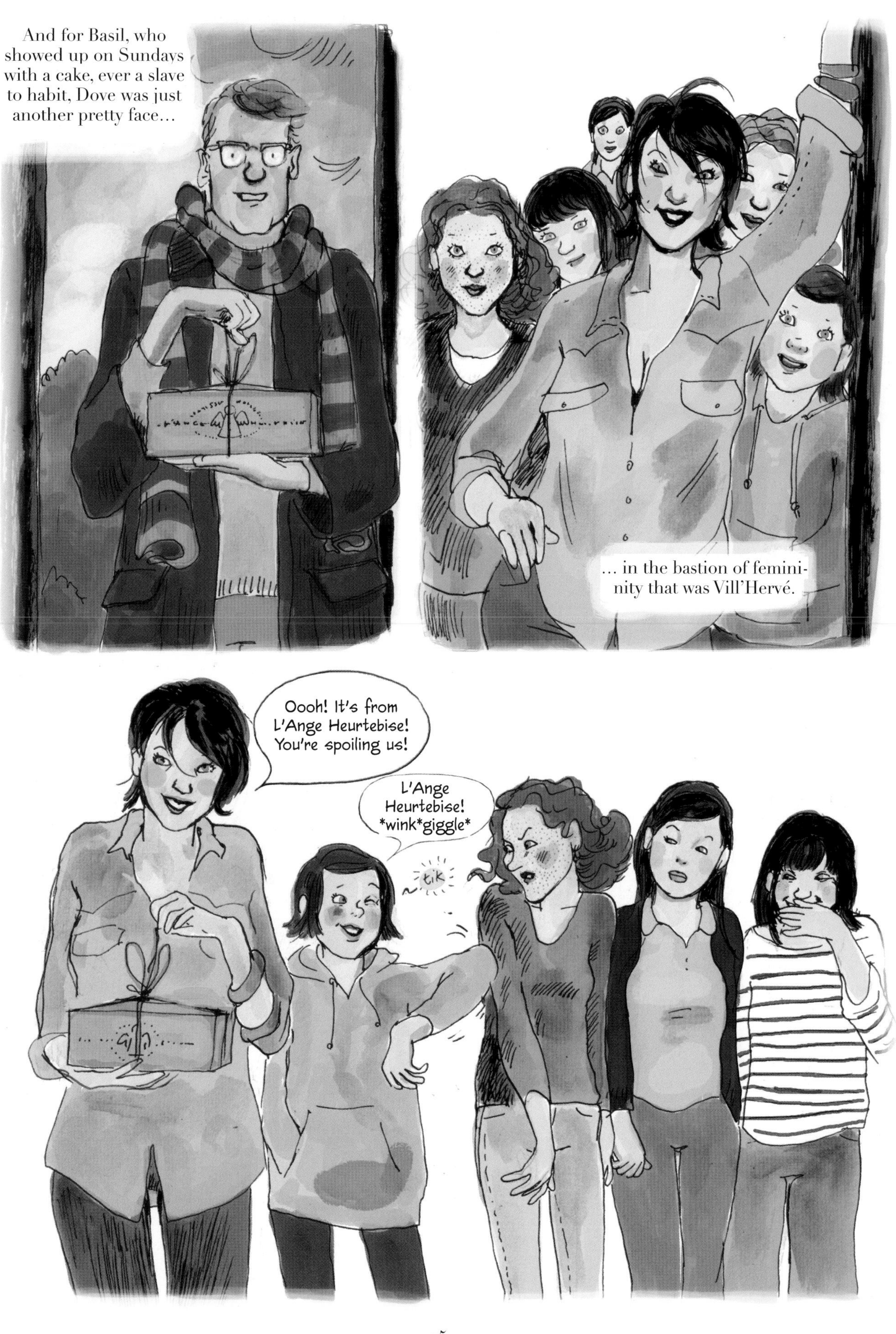
And for Basil, who showed up on Sundays with a cake, ever a slave to habit, Dove was just another pretty face…
… in the bastion of femininity that was Vill'Hervé.
Oooh! It's from L'Ange Heurtebise! You're spoiling us!
L'Ange Heurtebise! *wink*giggle*
tik

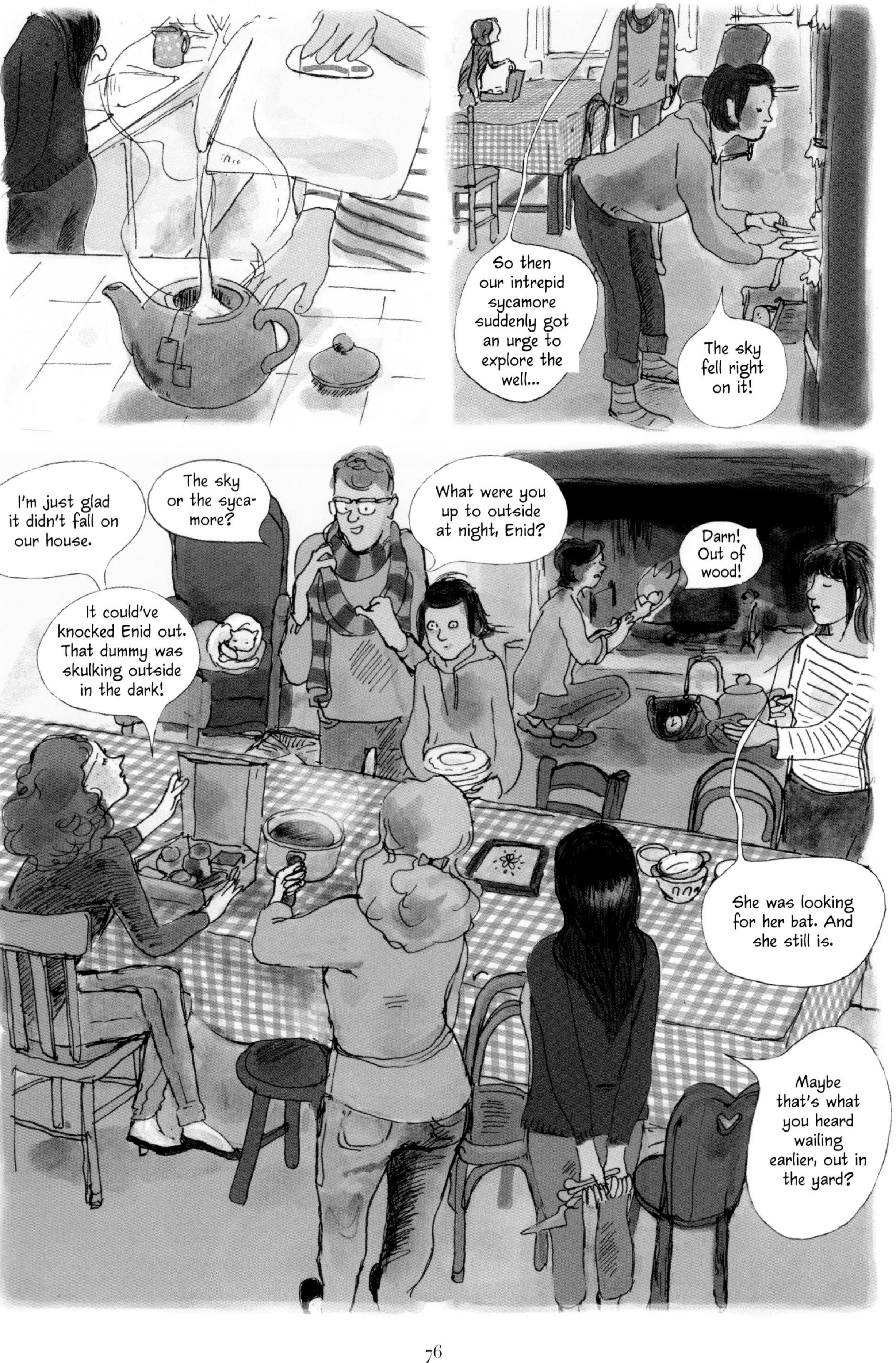
So then our intrepid sycamore suddenly got an urge to explore the well...
The sky fell right on it!
I'm just glad it didn't fall on our house.
The sky or the sycamore?
What were you up to outside at night, Enid?
Darn! Out of wood!
It could've knocked Enid out. That dummy was skulking outside in the dark!
She was looking for her bat. And she still is.
Maybe that's what you heard wailing earlier, out in the yard?

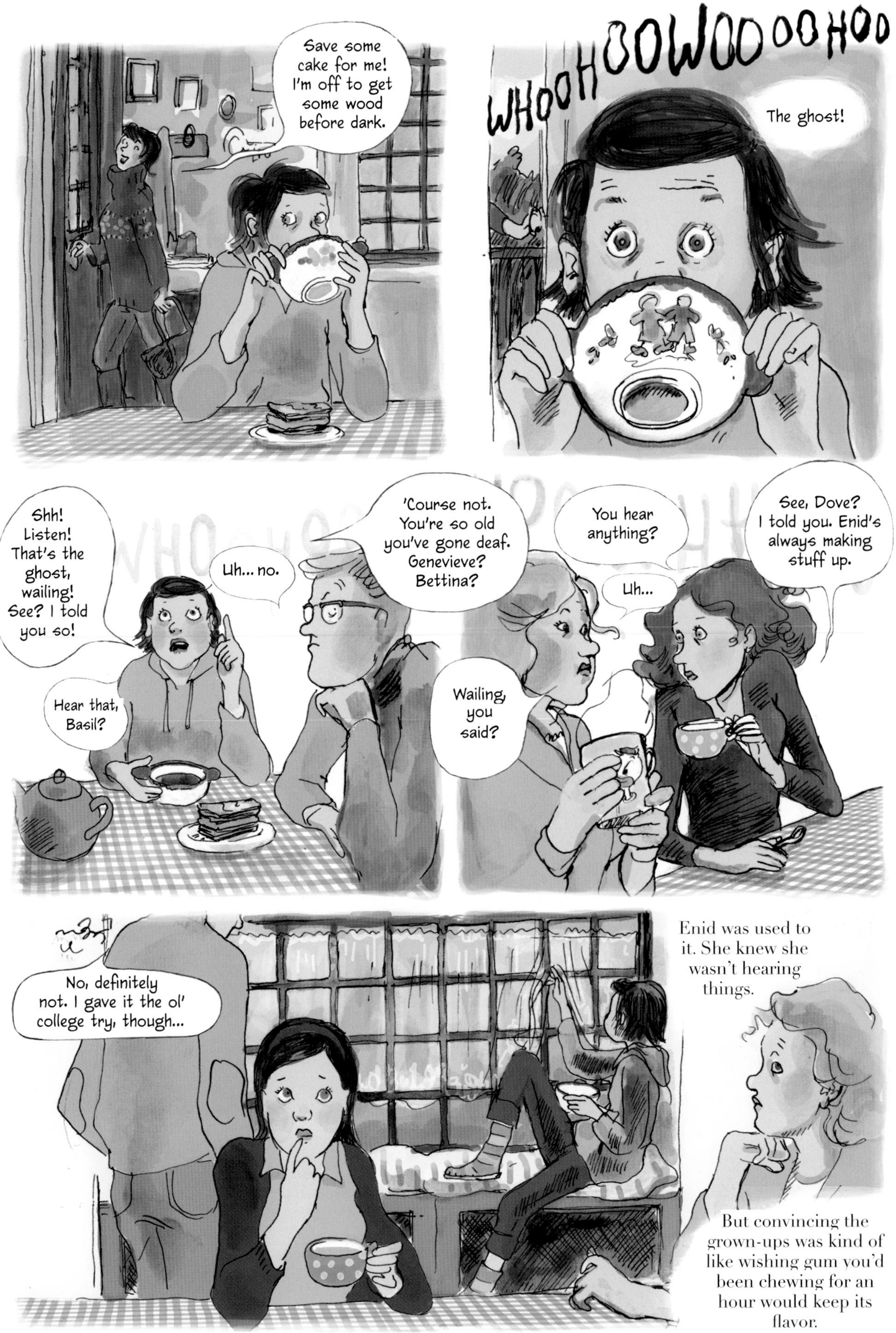
Save some cake for me! I'm off to get some wood before dark.
WHOOHOOWOOOOHOO
The ghost!
Shh! Listen! That's the ghost, wailing! See? I told you so!
Uh... no.
'Course not. You're so old you've gone deaf. Genevieve? Bettina?
Hear that, Basil?
You hear anything?
Uh...
See, Dove? I told you. Enid's always making stuff up.
Wailing, you said?
No, definitely not. I gave it the ol' college try, though...
Enid was used to it. She knew she wasn't hearing things.
But convincing the grown-ups was kind of like wishing gum you'd been chewing for an hour would keep its flavor.

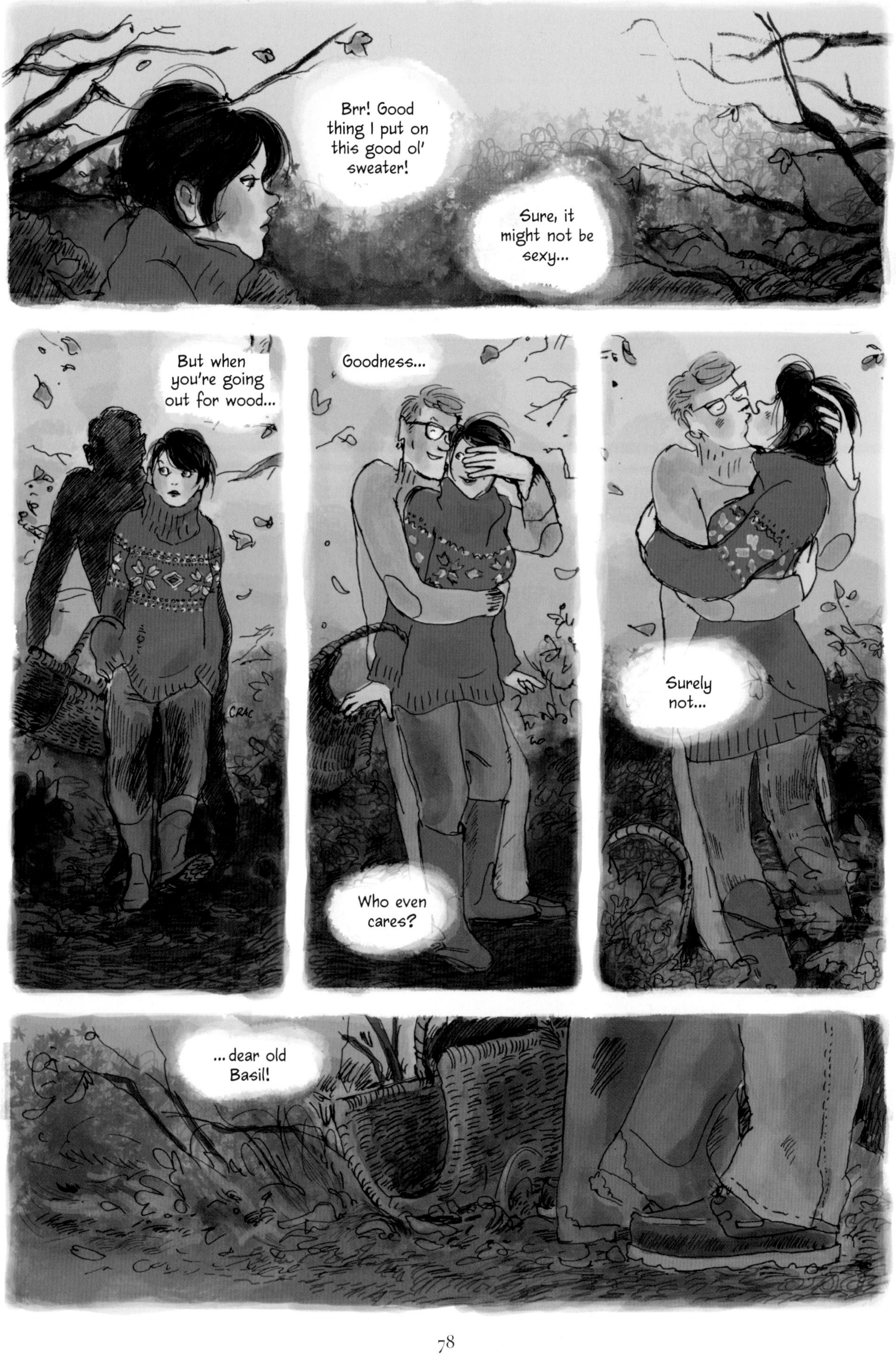

Brr! Good thing I put on this good ol' sweater!
Sure, it might not be sexy...
But when you're going out for wood...
CRAC
Goodness...
Who even cares?
Surely not...
...dear old Basil!

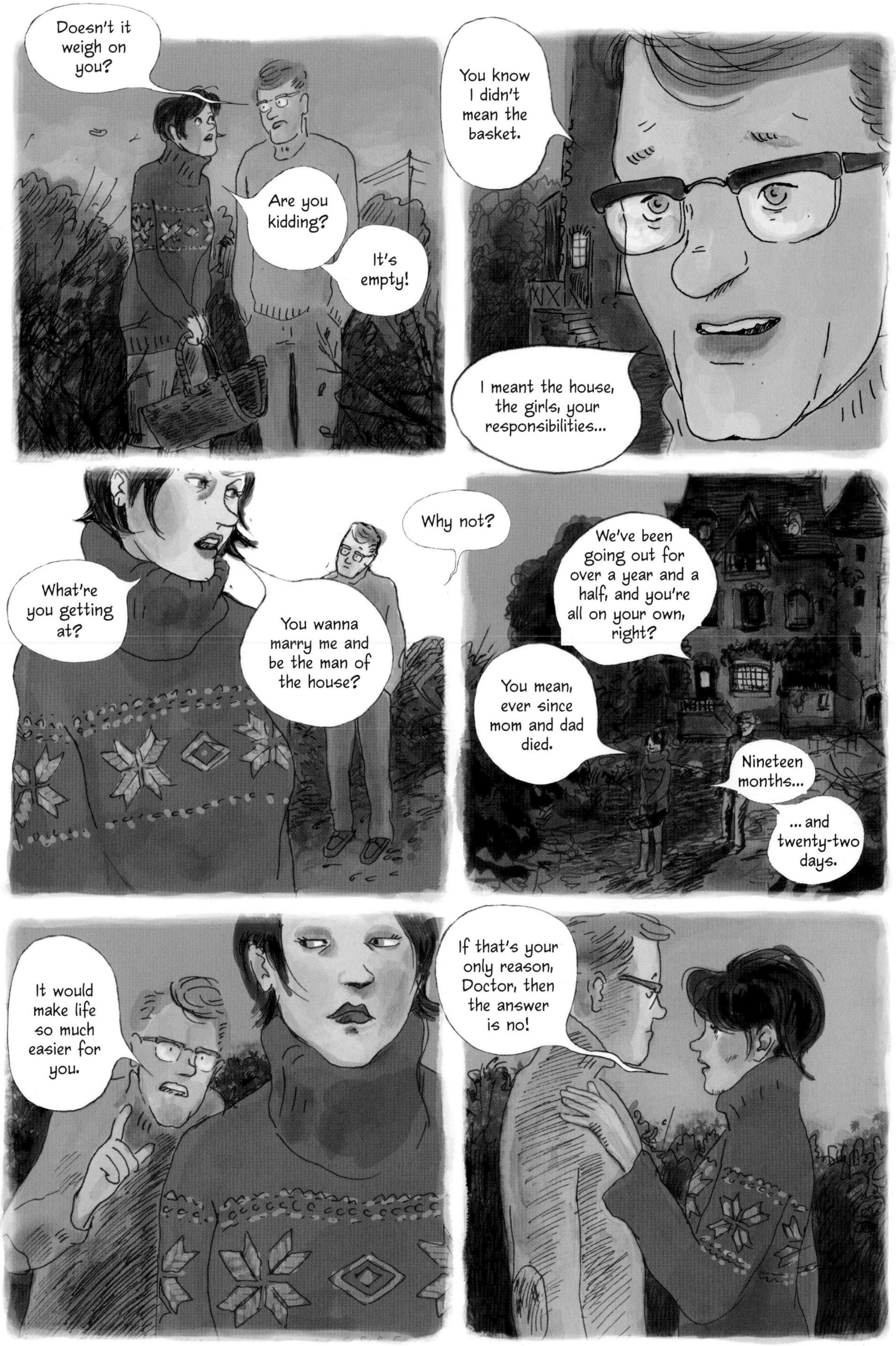
Doesn't it weigh on you?
Are you kidding?
It's empty!
You know I didn't mean the basket.
I meant the house, the girls, your responsibilities...
What're you getting at?
You wanna marry me and be the man of the house?
Why not?
We've been going out for over a year and a half, and you're all on your own, right?
You mean, ever since mom and dad died.
Nineteen months...
... and twenty-two days.
It would make life so much easier for you.
If that's your only reason, Doctor, then the answer is no!

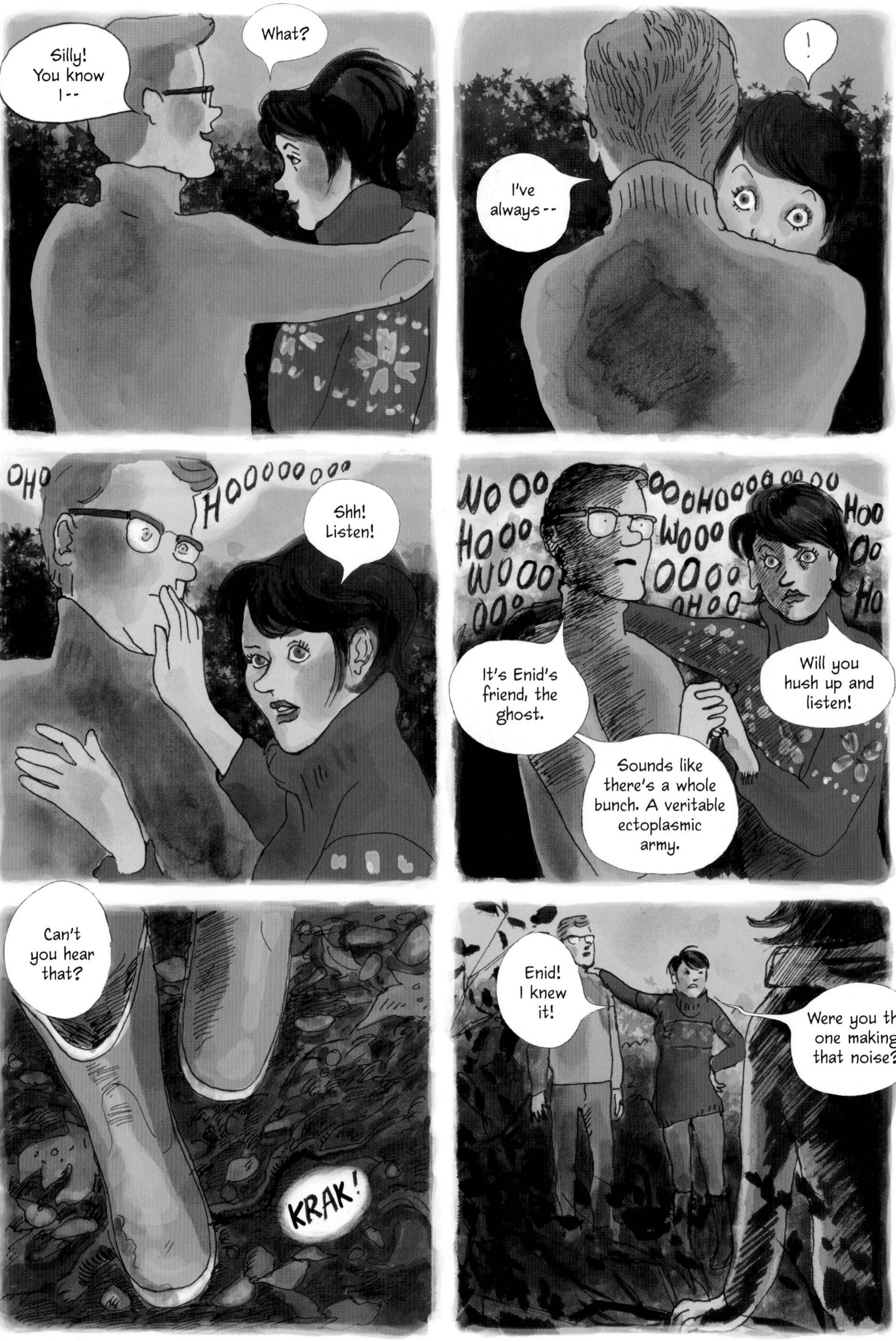
Silly! You know I--
What?
!
I've always--
OHO
HOOOOOOOO
Shh! Listen!
It's Enid's friend, the ghost.
Sounds like there's a whole bunch. A veritable ectoplasmic army.
Will you hush up and listen!
Can't you hear that?
KRAK!
Enid! I knew it!
Were you the one making that noise?

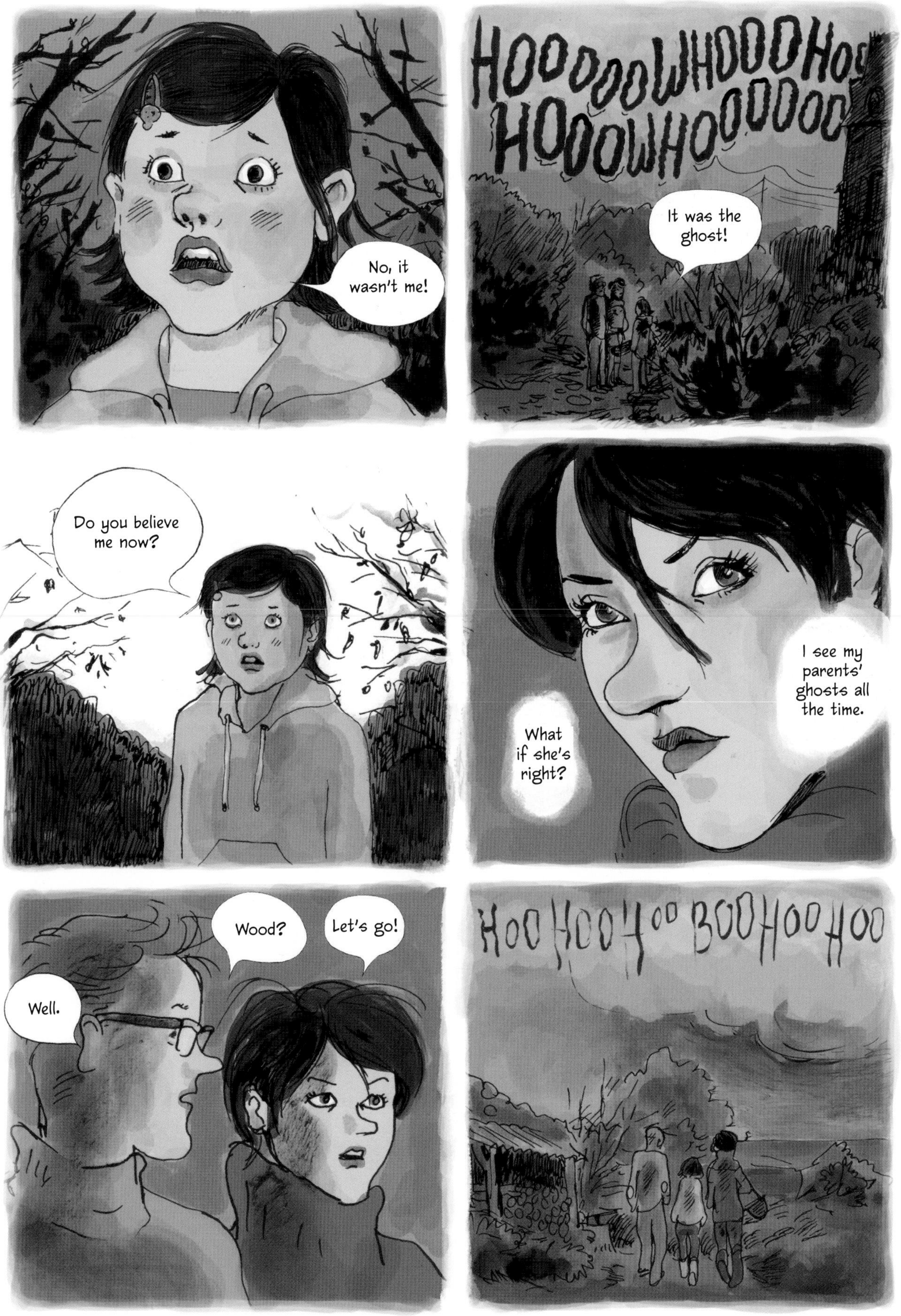
No, it wasn't me!
HOOOOOWHOOOHOO HOOOWHOOOOOO
It was the ghost!
Do you believe me now?
I see my parents' ghosts all the time.
What if she's right?
Well.
Wood?
Let's go!
HOO HOOHOO BOOHOOHOO

Monday, 5 PM. It won't be long before the autumn evening sweeps the leaves from the trees, and students hurry toward the buses that have begun their nightly ballet around the school.

If you ask me, it's got something to do with Swifty and her disappearance.

Swifty's the squirrel?

No, the bat! I've told you a hundred times. Blitz is the squirrel, and he just moved out of the tree. But I haven't seen Swifty since the storm.

Are you sure she's not... your ghost?

Swifty's not dead. She has wings.

When the sycamore fell, she took off. I just know it!

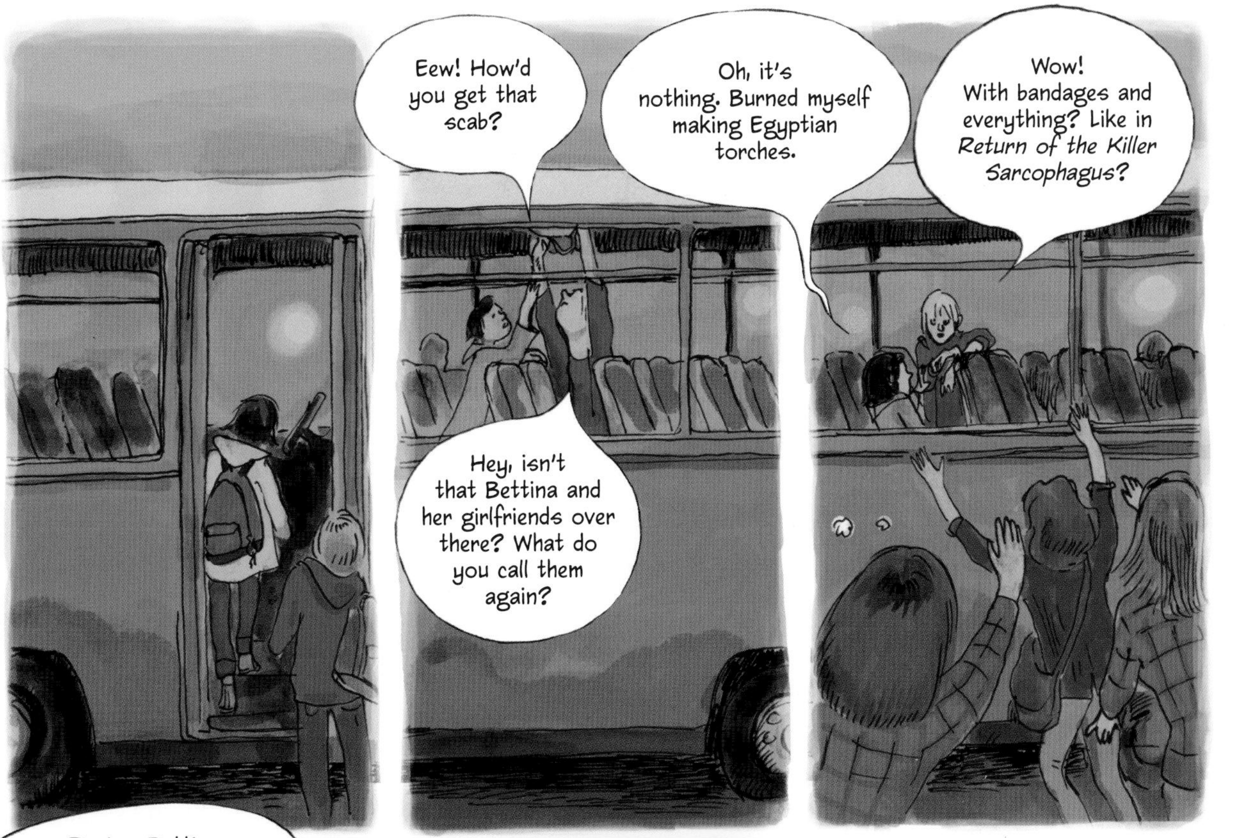
Eew! How'd you get that scab?
Oh, it's nothing. Burned myself making Egyptian torches.
Wow! With bandages and everything? Like in *Return of the Killer Sarcophagus*?
Hey, isn't that Bettina and her girlfriends over there? What do you call them again?

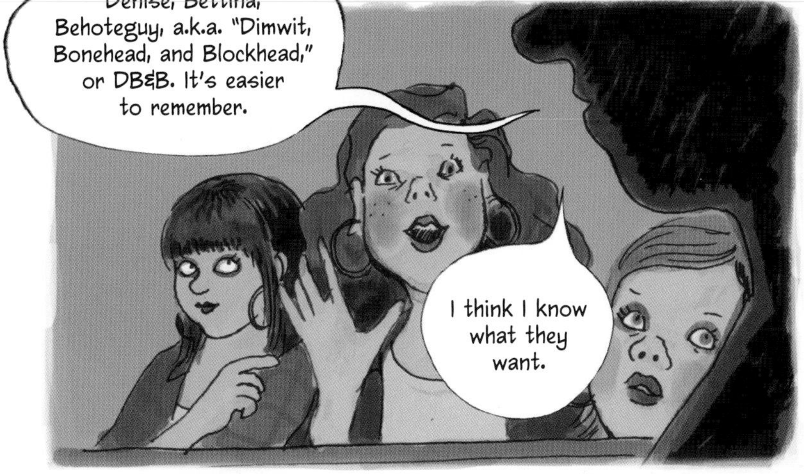
Denise, Bettina, Behoteguy, a.k.a. "Dimwit, Bonehead, and Blockhead," or DB&B. It's easier to remember.
I think I know what they want.

Enid knew perfectly well that DB&B had no desire to be saddled with a kid sister. Charlie was no fool, and forbade Bettina from missing the bus on purpose to hang out in town—but having a kid sister around made it look more on the up-and-up.

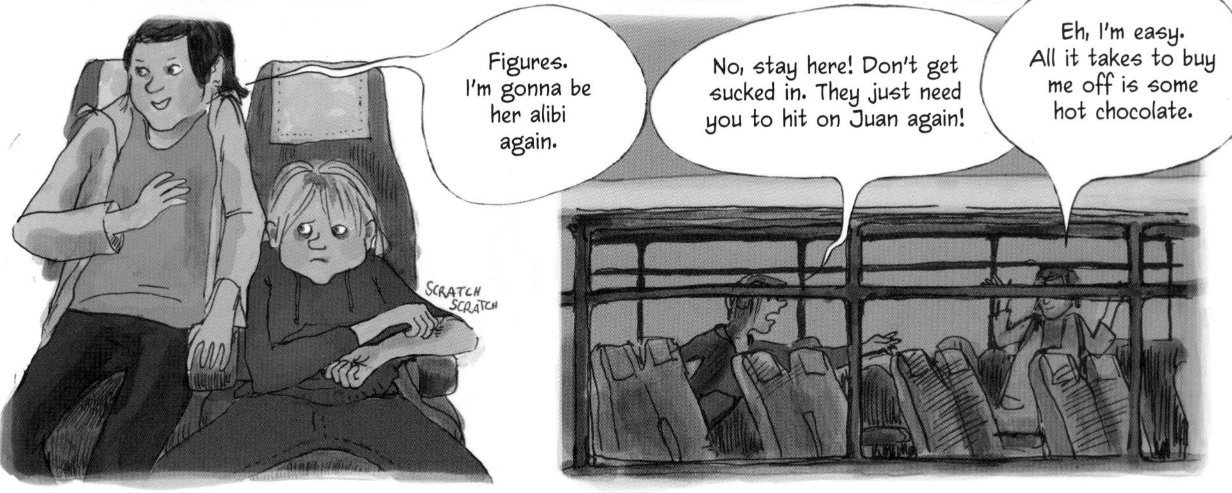
Figures. I'm gonna be her alibi again.
SCRATCH SCRATCH
No, stay here! Don't get sucked in. They just need you to hit on Juan again!
Eh, I'm easy. All it takes to buy me off is some hot chocolate.

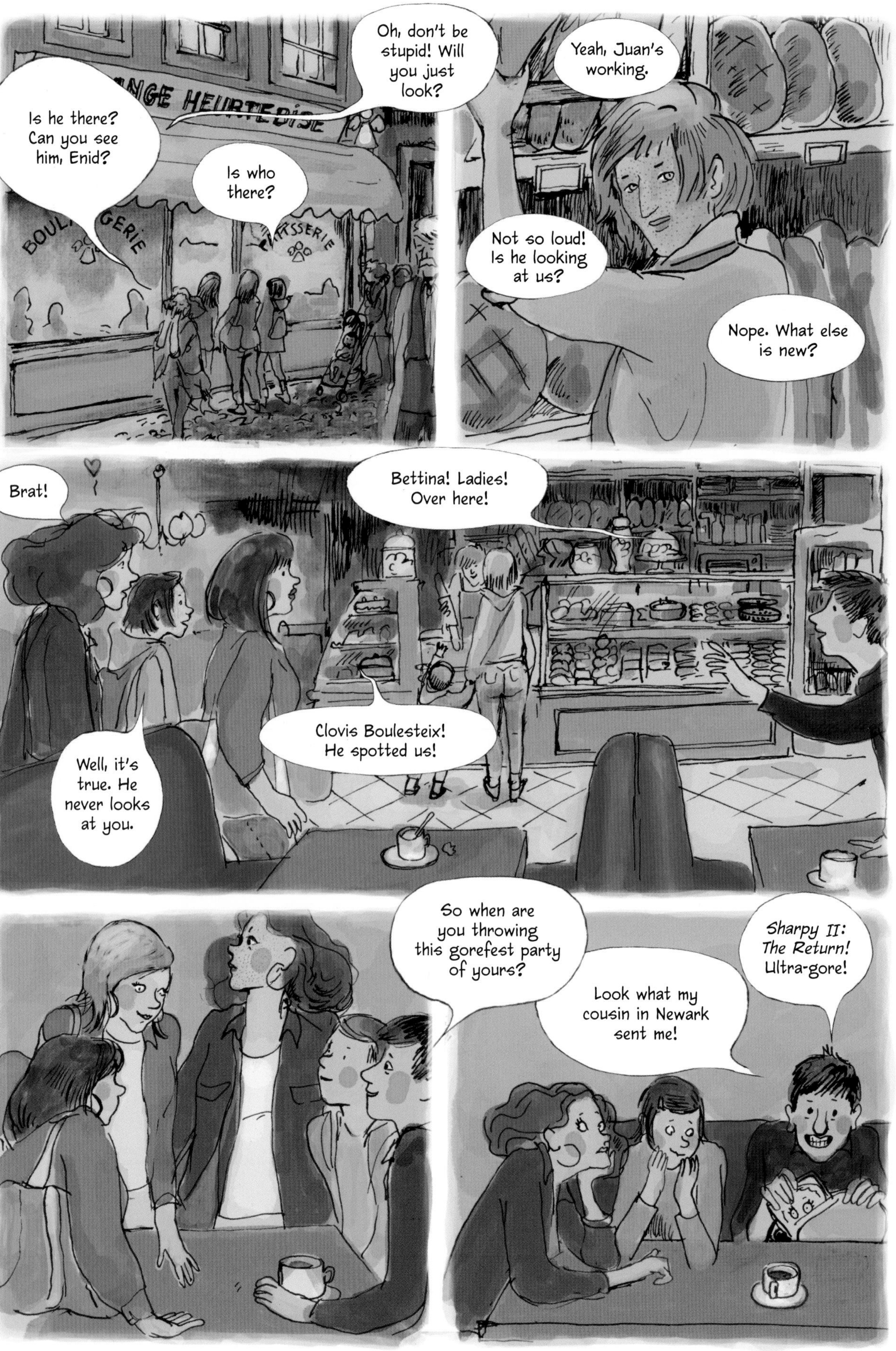
Is he there? Can you see him, Enid?
Is who there?
Oh, don't be stupid! Will you just look?
Yeah, Juan's working.
Not so loud! Is he looking at us?
Nope. What else is new?
Brat!
Well, it's true. He never looks at you.
Clovis Boulesteix! He spotted us!
Bettina! Ladies! Over here!
So when are you throwing this gorefest party of yours?
Look what my cousin in Newark sent me!
Sharpy II: The Return! Ultra-gore!

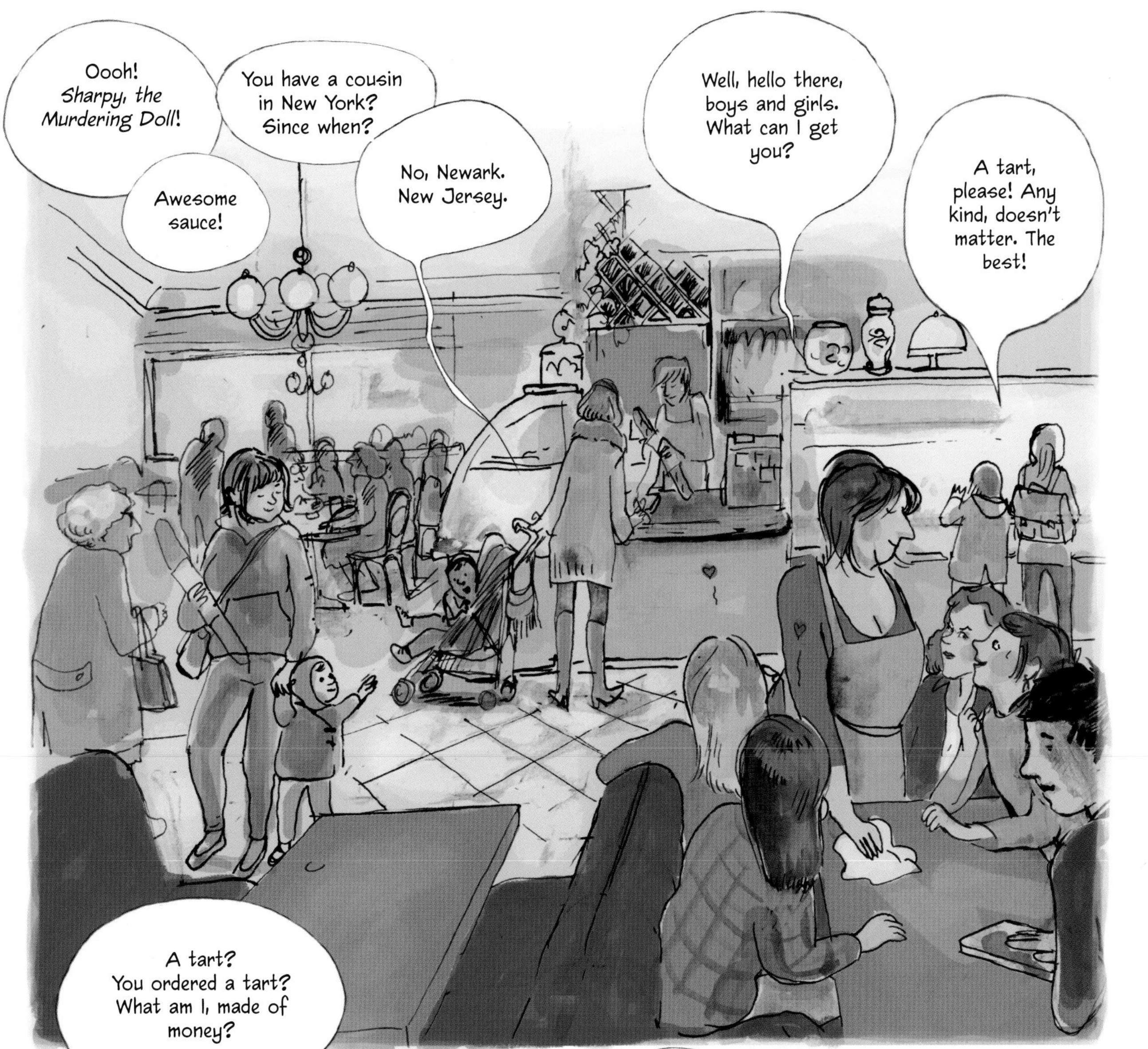
Oooh! Sharpy, the Murdering Doll!
You have a cousin in New York? Since when?
Awesome sauce!
No, Newark. New Jersey.
Well, hello there, boys and girls. What can I get you?
A tart, please! Any kind, doesn't matter. The best!

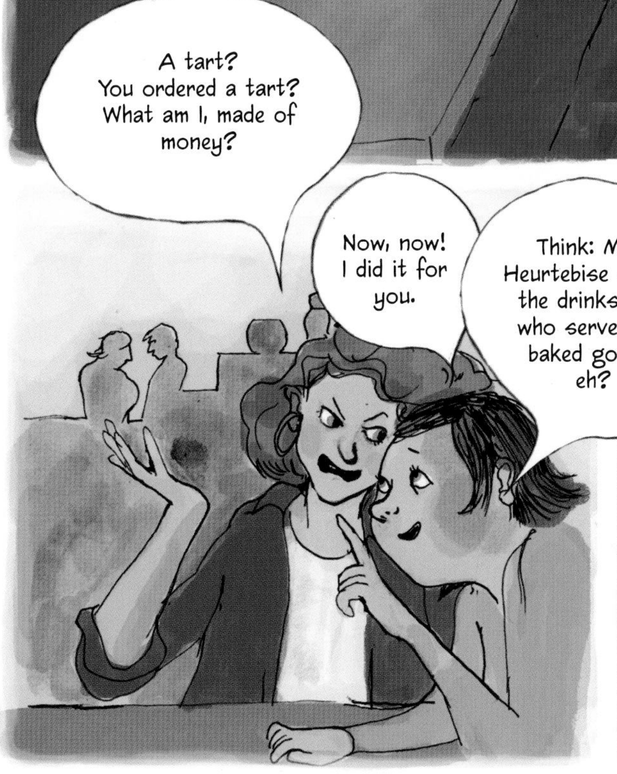
A tart? You ordered a tart? What am I, made of money?
Now, now! I did it for you.
Think: Mrs. Heurtebise serves the drinks. But who serves the baked goods, eh?

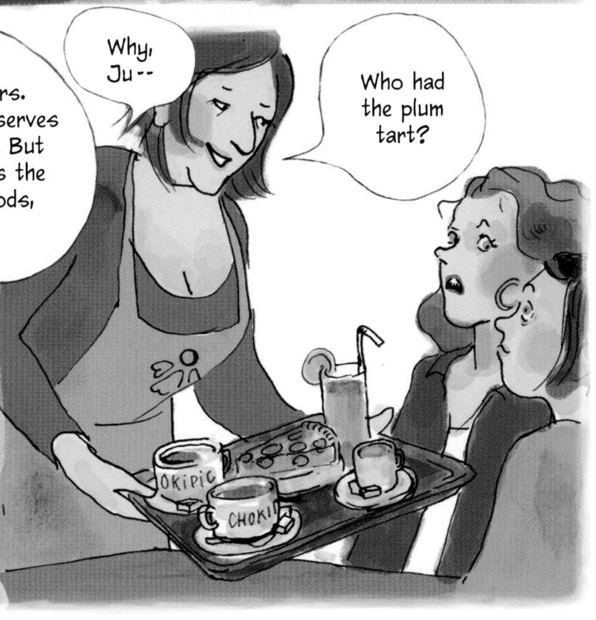
Why, Ju--
Who had the plum tart?
OKIPIC
CHOKI

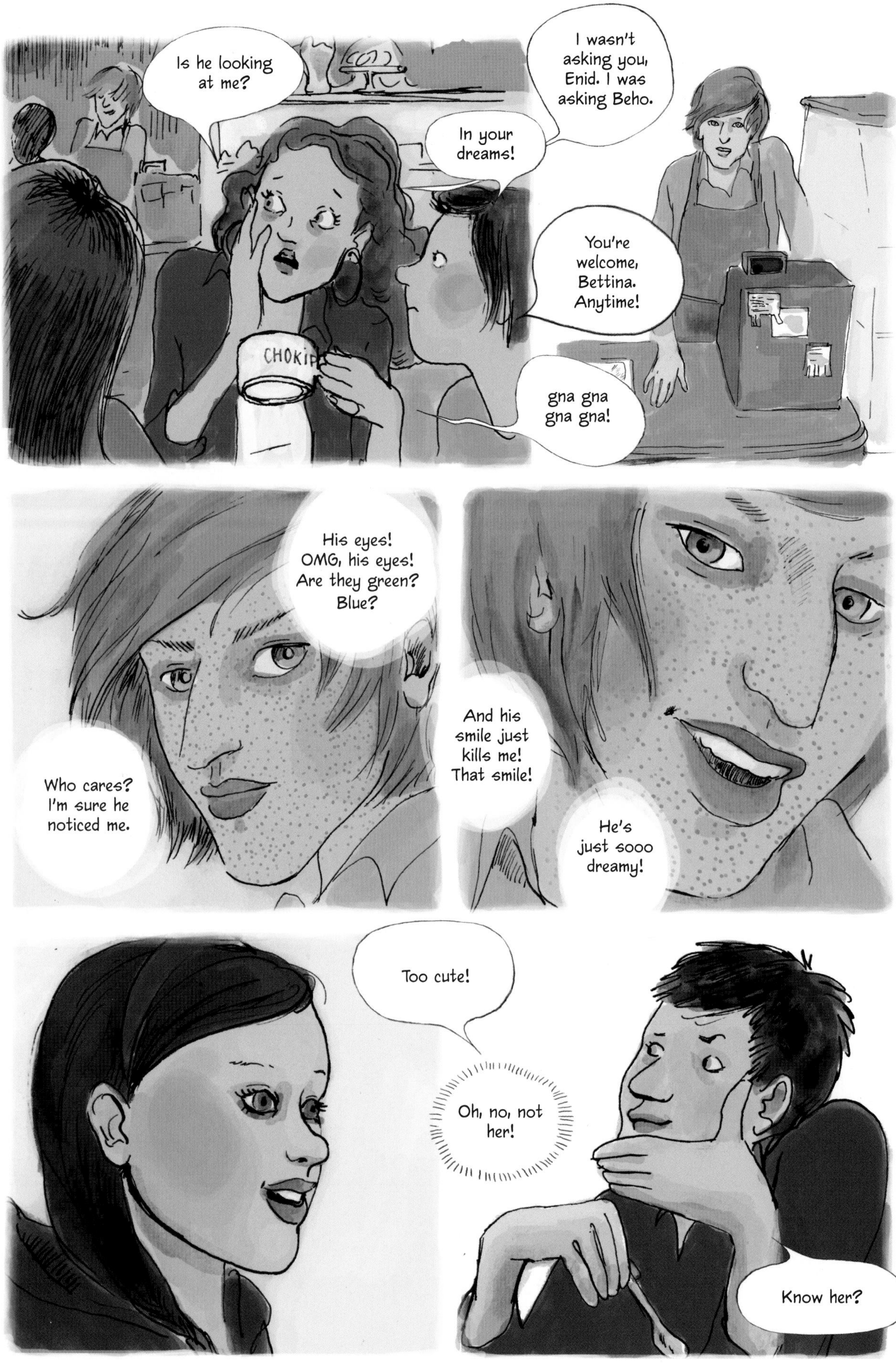
Is he looking at me?
In your dreams!
I wasn't asking you, Enid. I was asking Beho.
You're welcome, Bettina. Anytime!
gna gna gna gna!
CHOKI
His eyes! OMG, his eyes! Are they green? Blue?
Who cares? I'm sure he noticed me.
And his smile just kills me! That smile!
He's just sooo dreamy!
Too cute!
Oh, no, not her!
Know her?

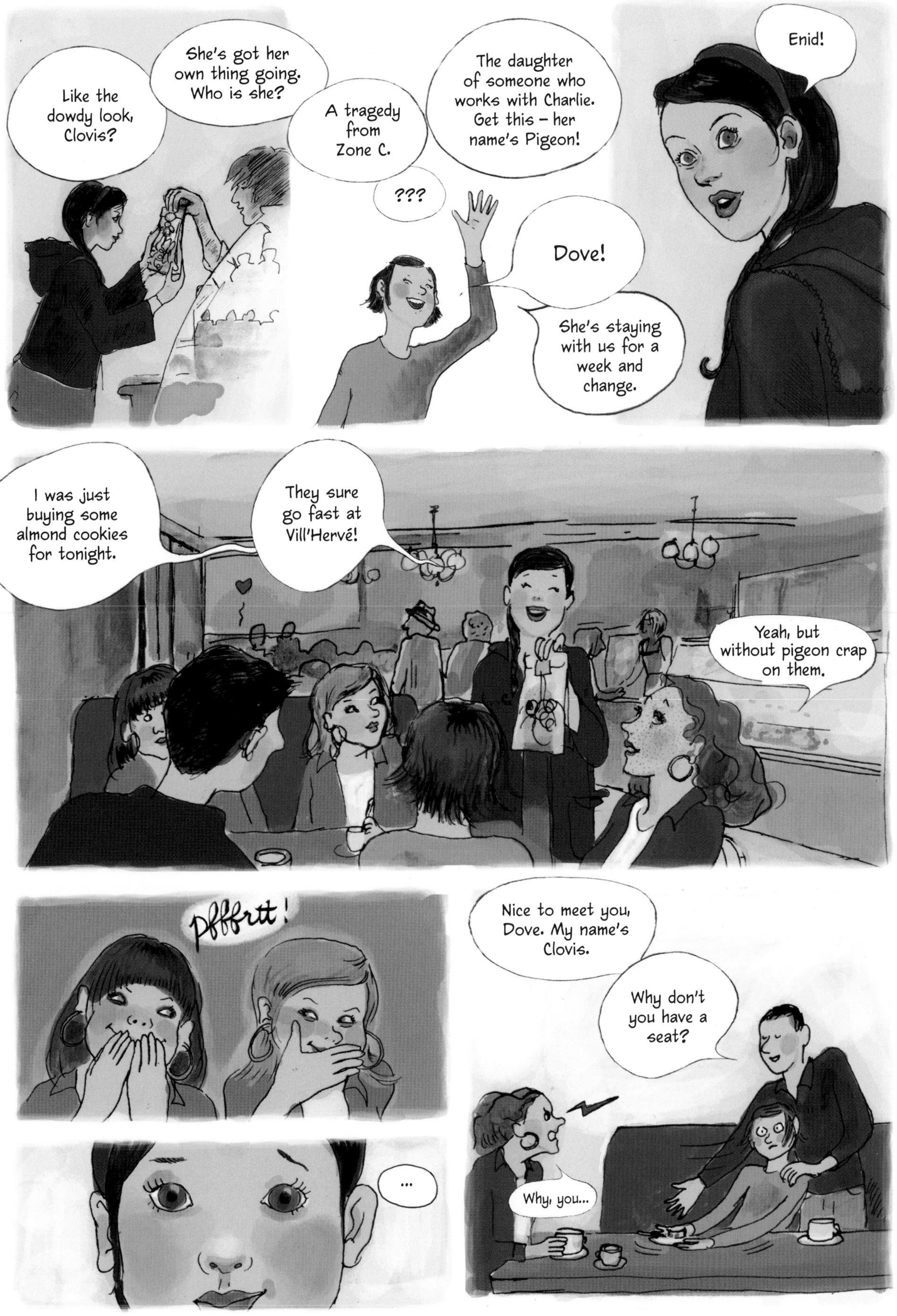

Like the dowdy look, Clovis?
She's got her own thing going. Who is she?
A tragedy from Zone C.
The daughter of someone who works with Charlie. Get this – her name's Pigeon!
???
Dove!
She's staying with us for a week and change.
Enid!
I was just buying some almond cookies for tonight.
They sure go fast at Vill'Hervé!
Yeah, but without pigeon crap on them.
pfffrtt!
...
Nice to meet you, Dove. My name's Clovis.
Why don't you have a seat?
Why, you...

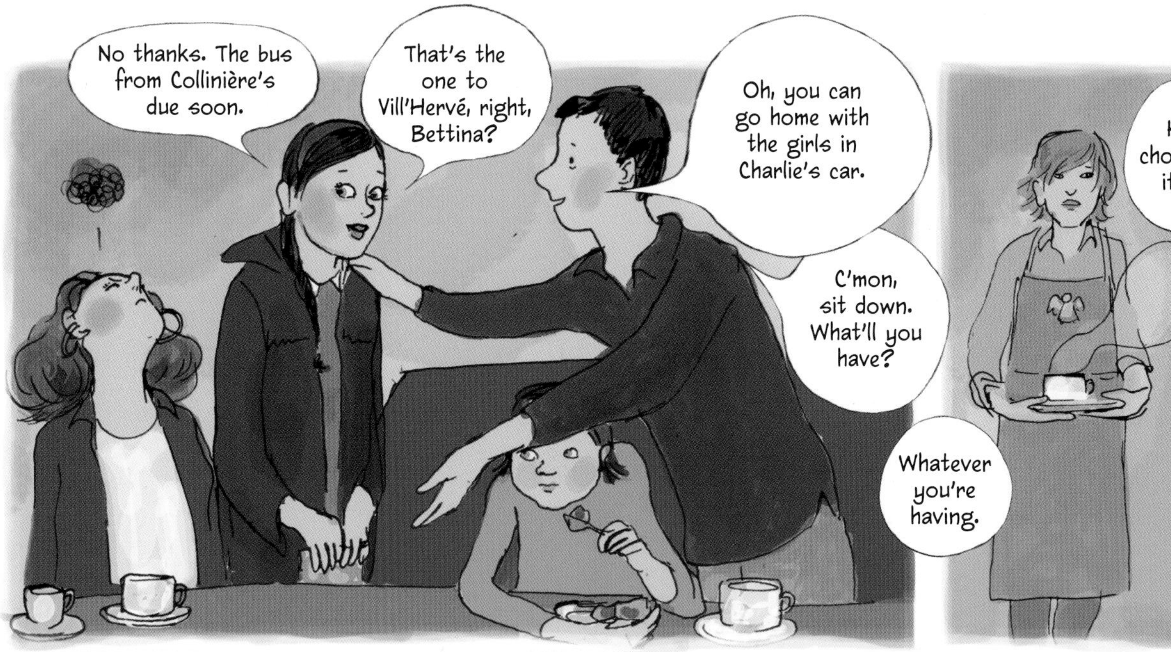
No thanks. The bus from Collinière's due soon.
That's the one to Vill'Hervé, right, Bettina?
Oh, you can go home with the girls in Charlie's car.
C'mon, sit down. What'll you have?
Whatever you're having.
Hot chocolate it is!

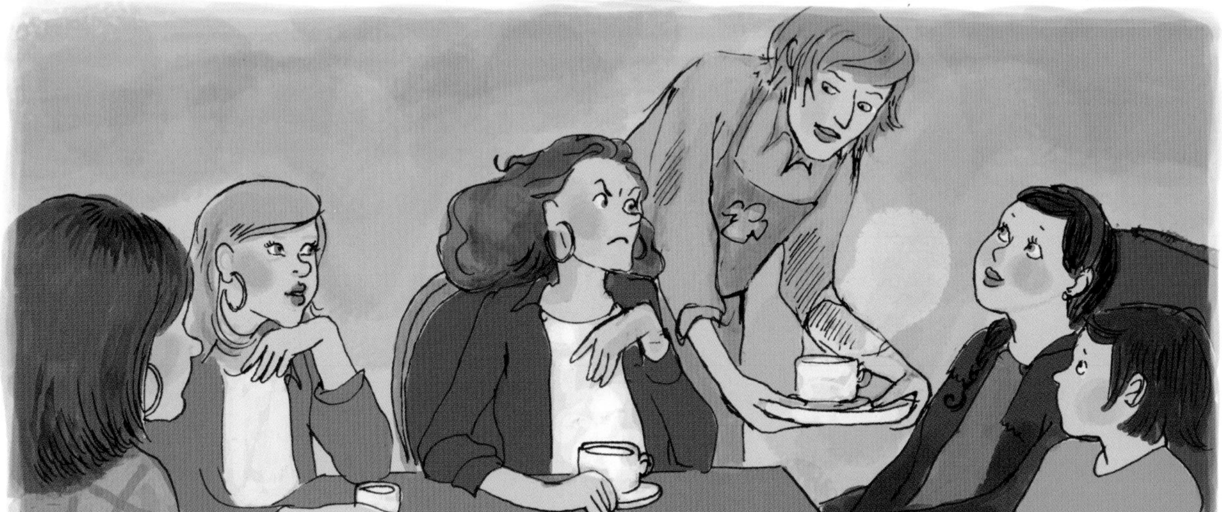

Enid caught the look Juan gave Bettina, but she wondered what it could mean. Bettina, though, was too ruffled to notice anything…

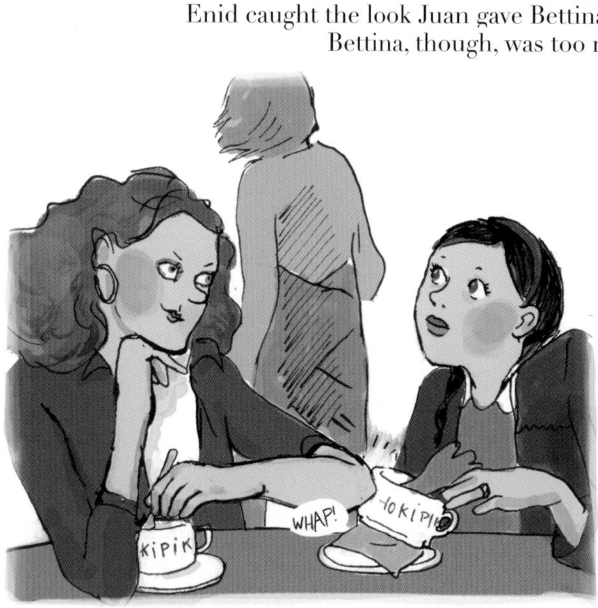
WHAP!
KIPIK

…except for the fact that goody two-shoes Dove definitely needed a little lesson.

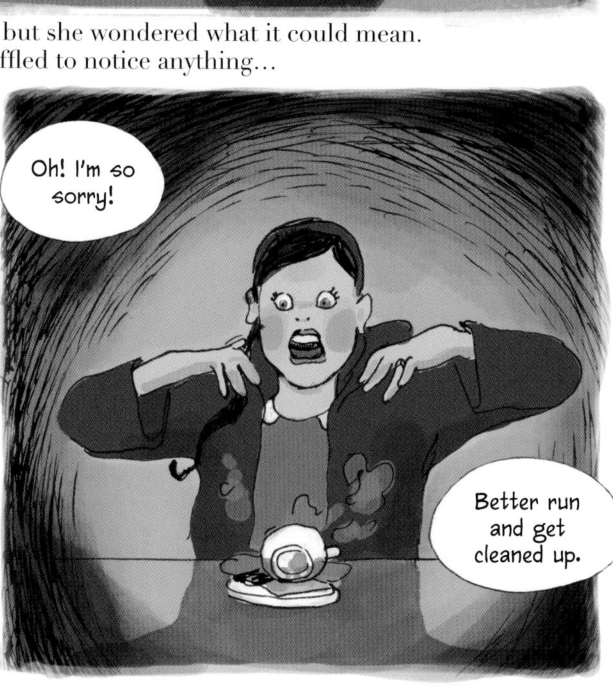
Oh! I'm so sorry!
Better run and get cleaned up.

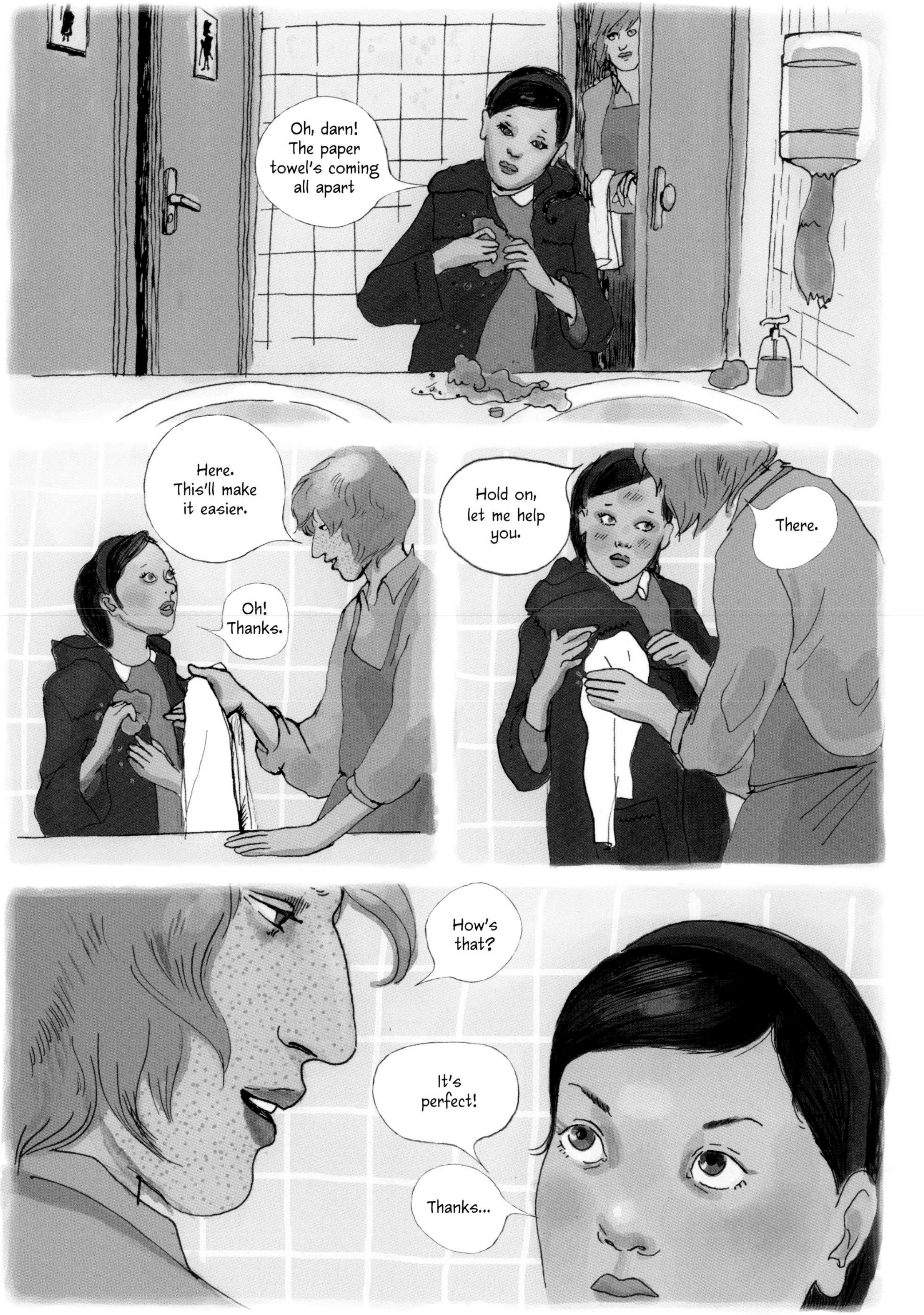
Oh, darn! The paper towel's coming all apart
Here. This'll make it easier.
Oh! Thanks.
Hold on, let me help you.
There.
How's that?
It's perfect!
Thanks...

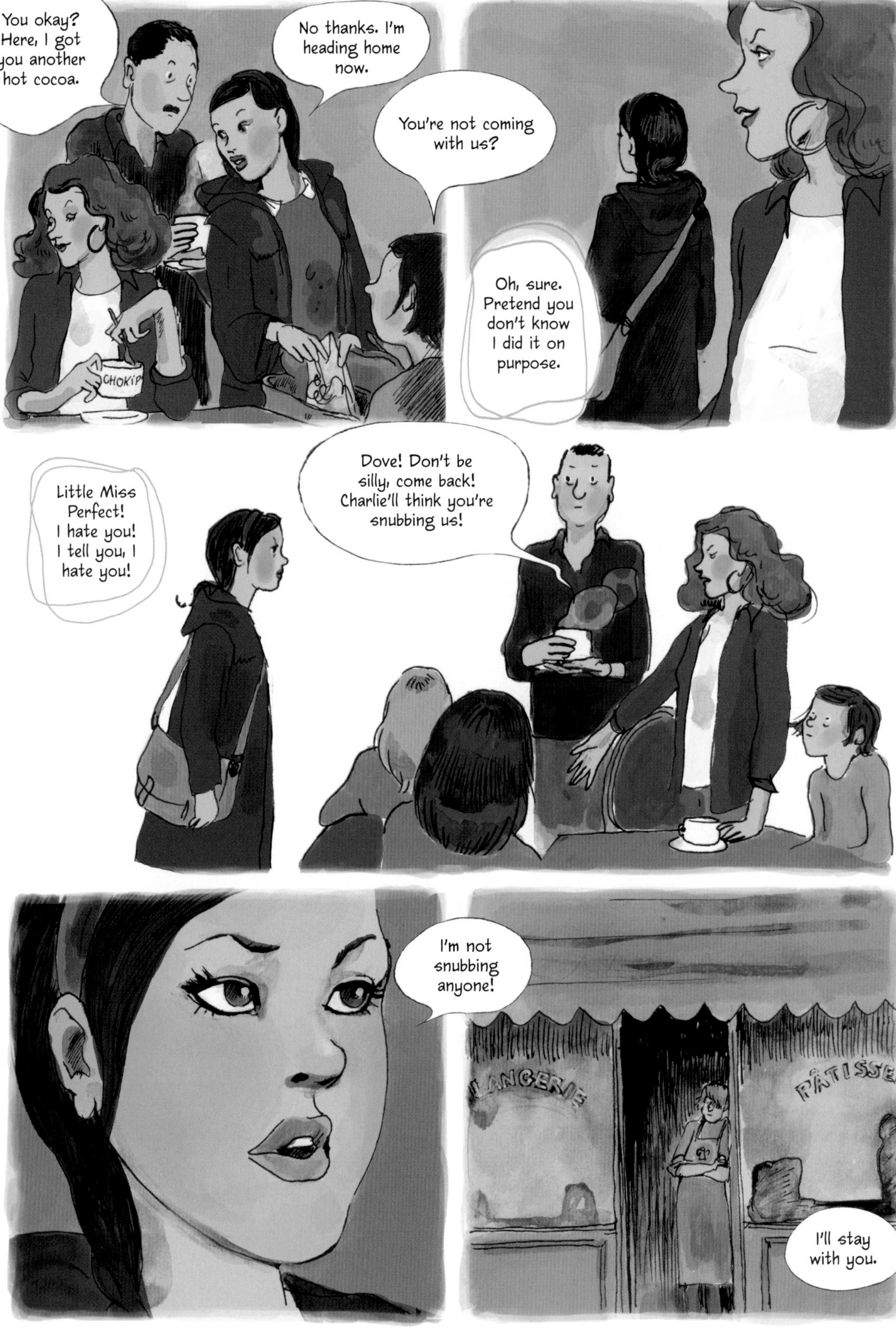
You okay? Here, I got you another hot cocoa.
No thanks. I'm heading home now.
You're not coming with us?
Oh, sure. Pretend you don't know I did it on purpose.
Little Miss Perfect! I hate you! I tell you, I hate you!
Dove! Don't be silly, come back! Charlie'll think you're snubbing us!
I'm not snubbing anyone!
I'll stay with you.

Charlie thought it terrific that Bettina had already taken Dove under her wing.

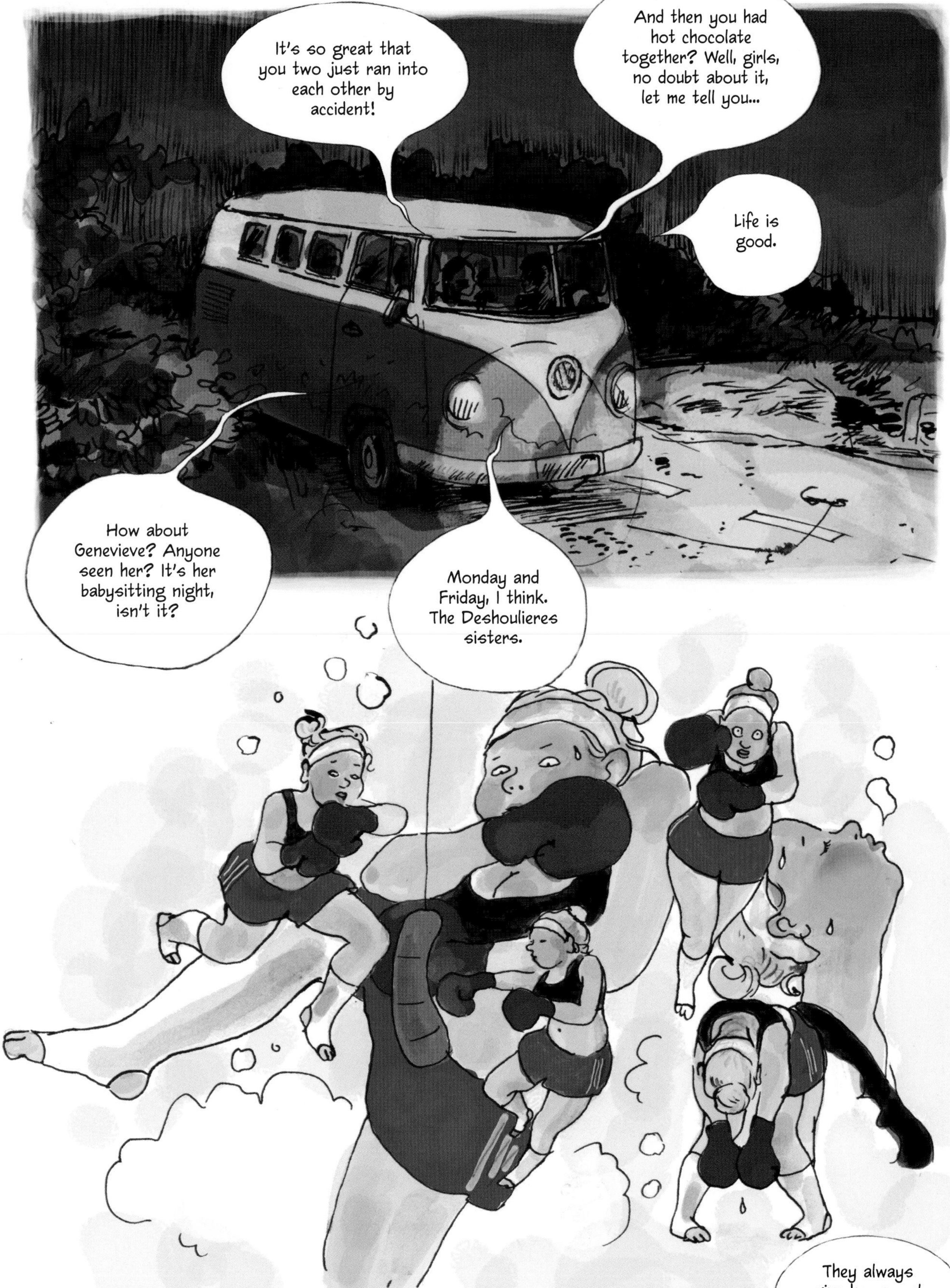

It's so great that you two just ran into each other by accident!
And then you had hot chocolate together? Well, girls, no doubt about it, let me tell you...
Life is good.
How about Genevieve? Anyone seen her? It's her babysitting night, isn't it?
Monday and Friday, I think. The Deshoulieres sisters.
They always give her a real workout.

That night, the ghost seemed particularly active…

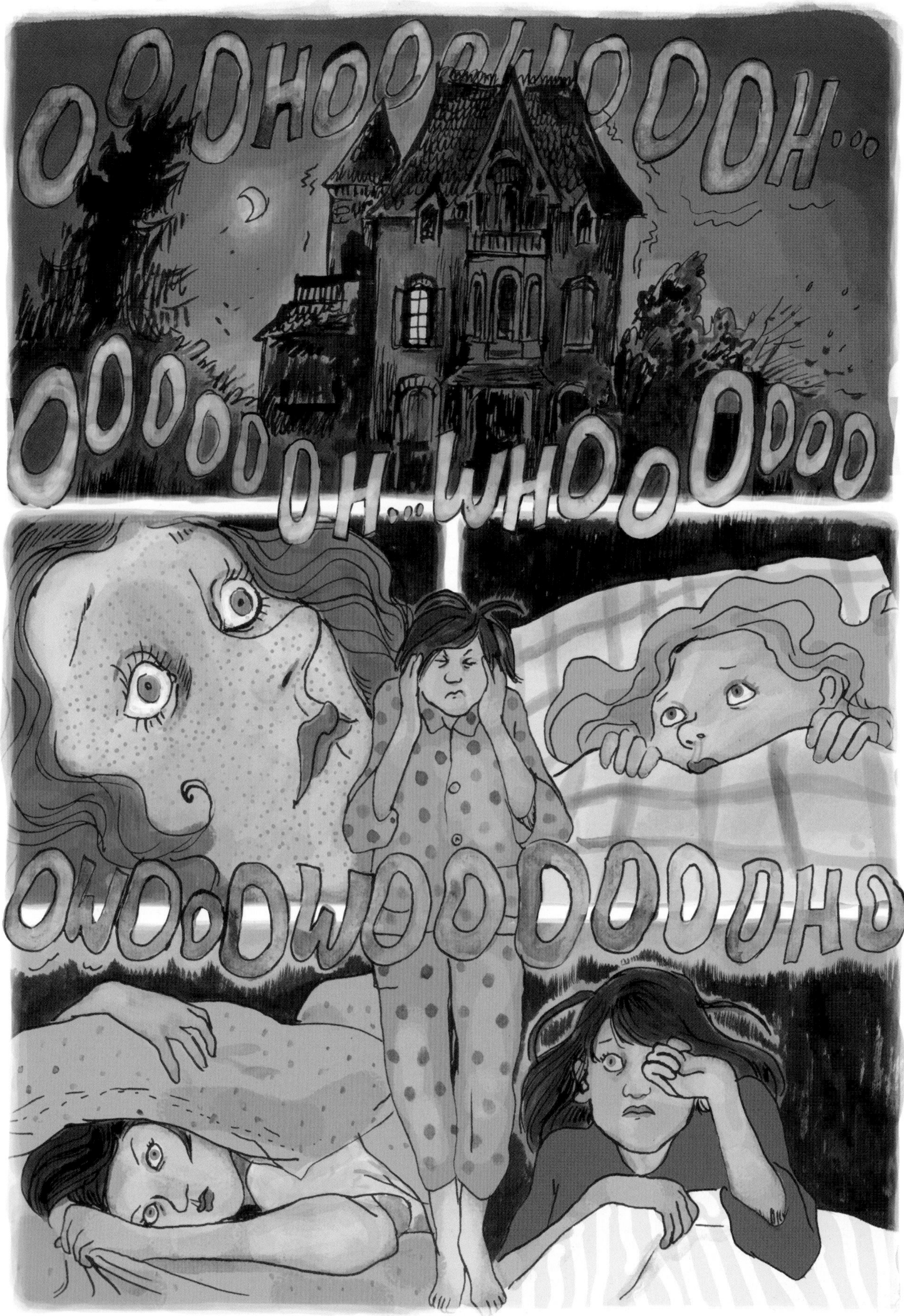

…its wails were carried by the wind and rattled the whole house from top to bottom.

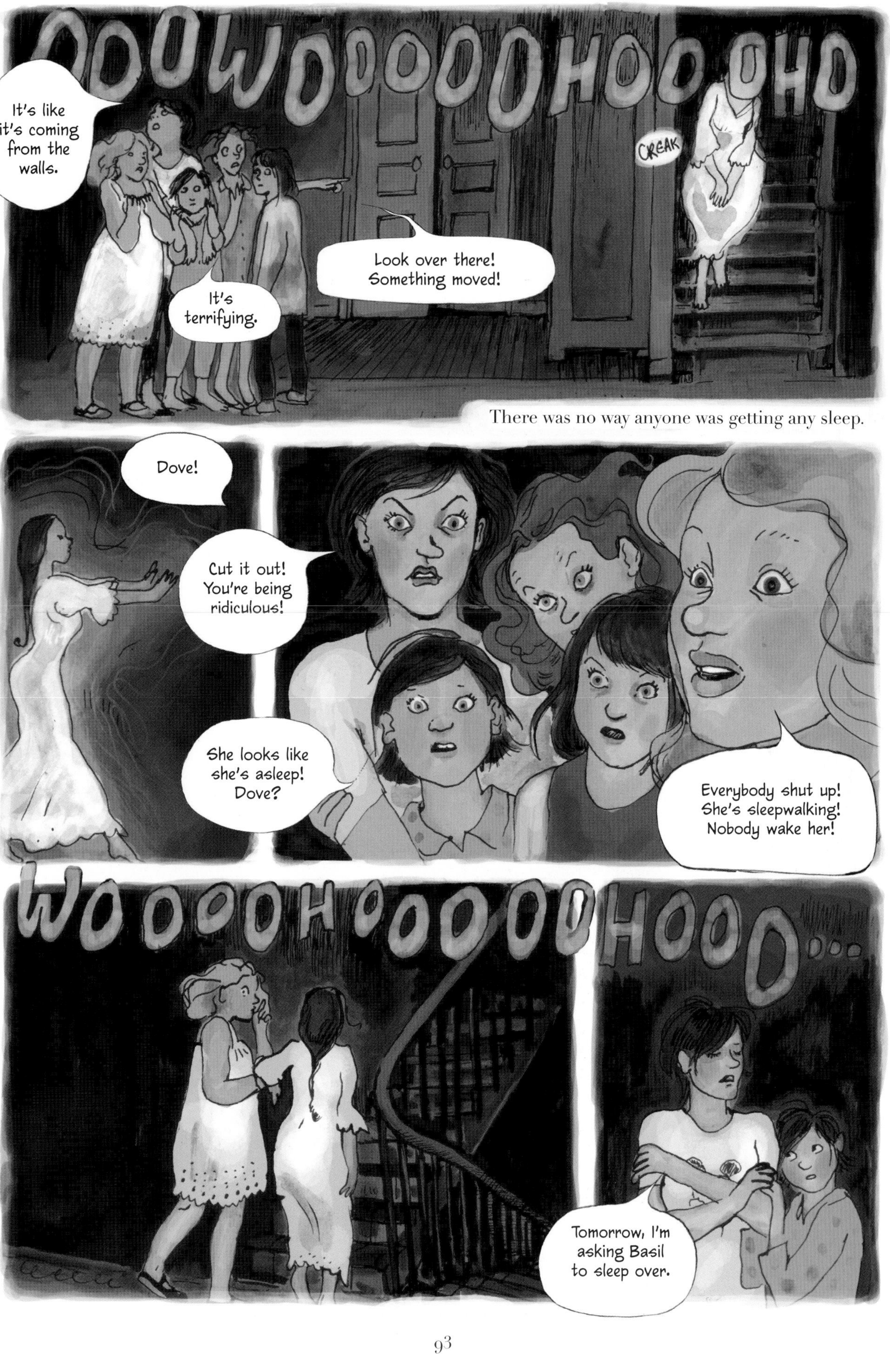
OOOWOOOOOOHOOOHO
It's like it's coming from the walls.
It's terrifying.
Look over there! Something moved!
CREAK
There was no way anyone was getting any sleep.
Dove!
Cut it out! You're being ridiculous!
She looks like she's asleep! Dove?
Everybody shut up! She's sleepwalking! Nobody wake her!
WOOOOHOOOOOHOOO...
Tomorrow, I'm asking Basil to sleep over.

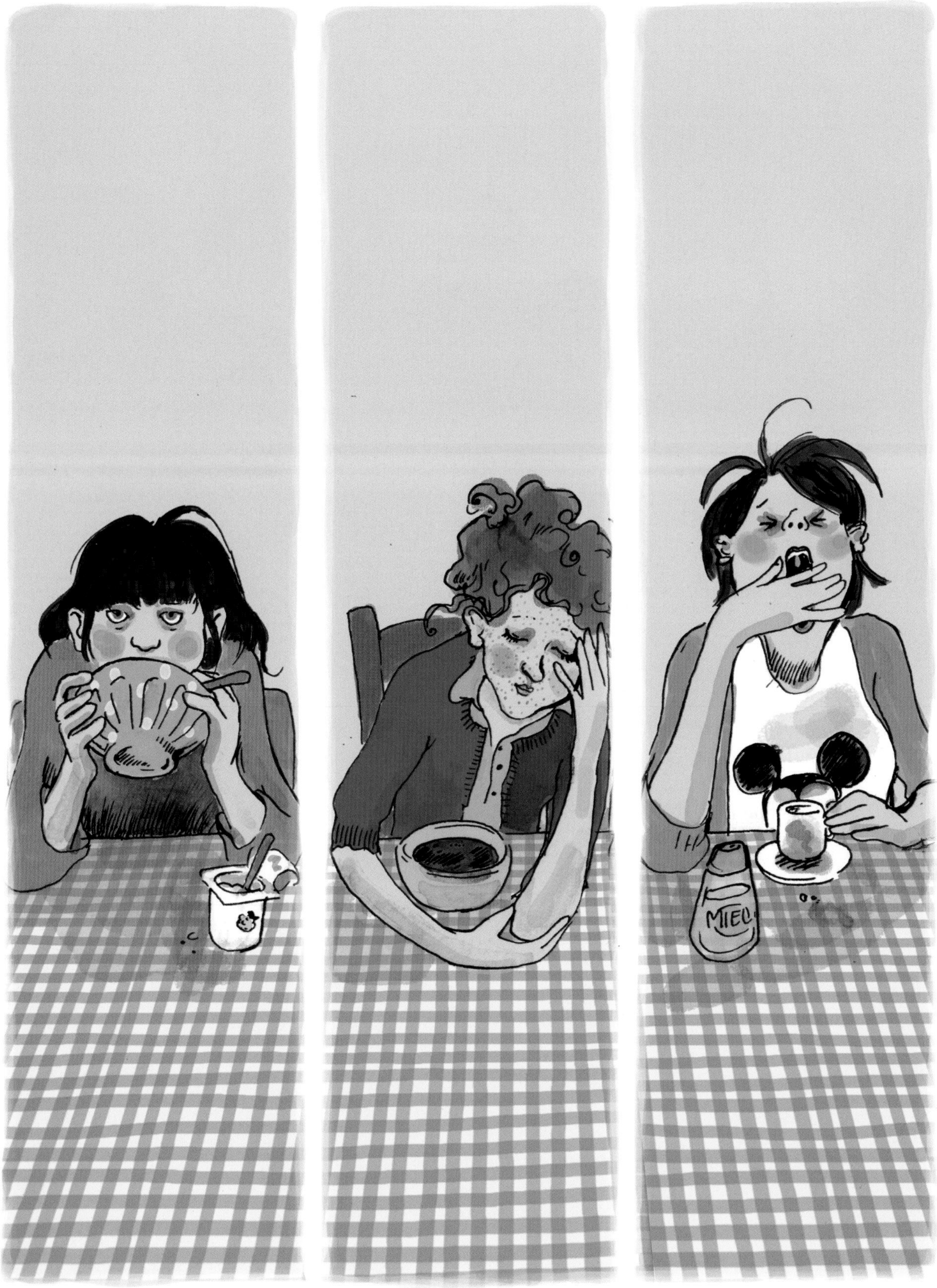
MIEL

Desolation at the breakfast table: no one got a wink of sleep...

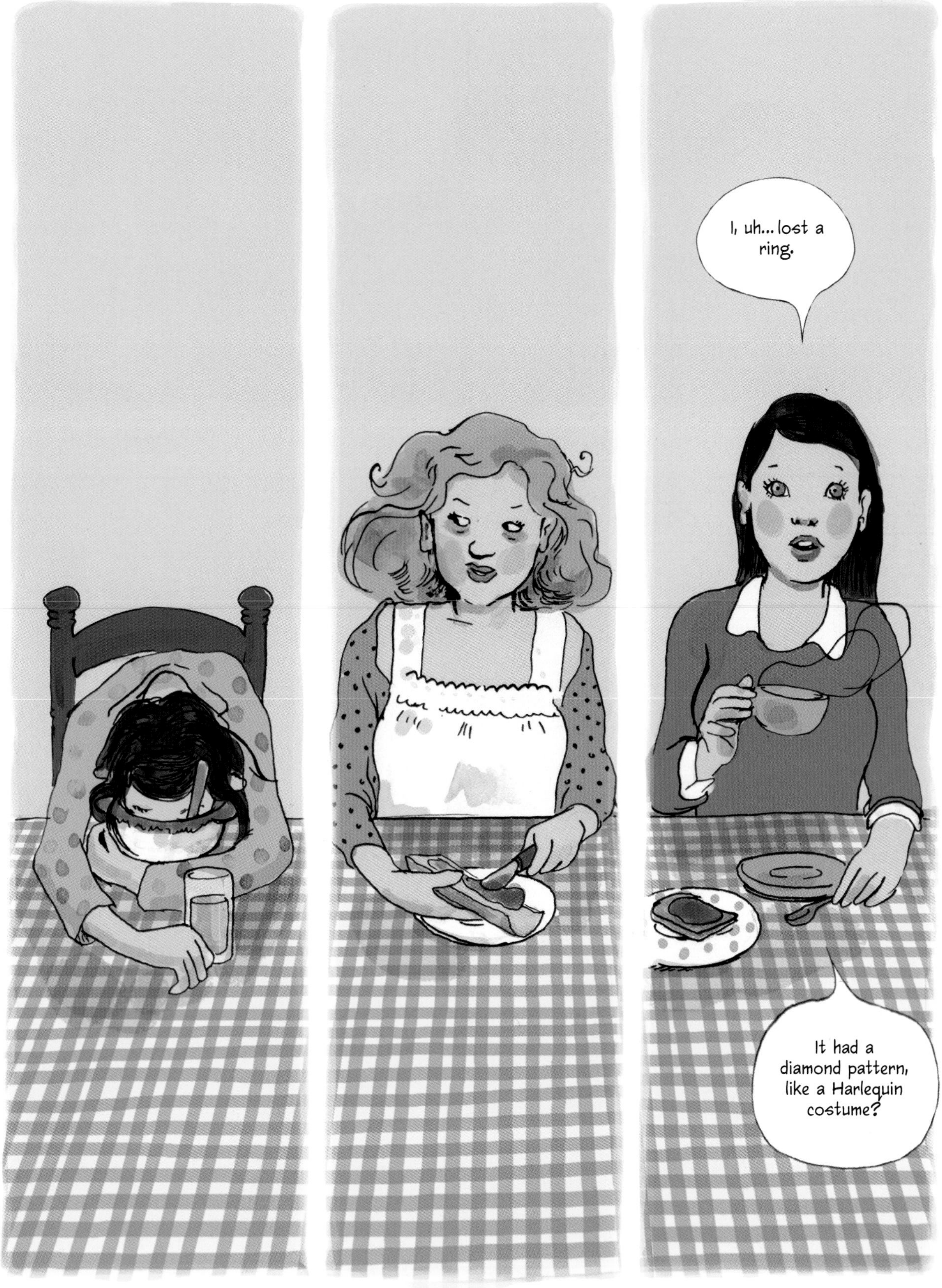
I, uh... lost a ring.
It had a diamond pattern, like a Harlequin costume?

...except Dove.

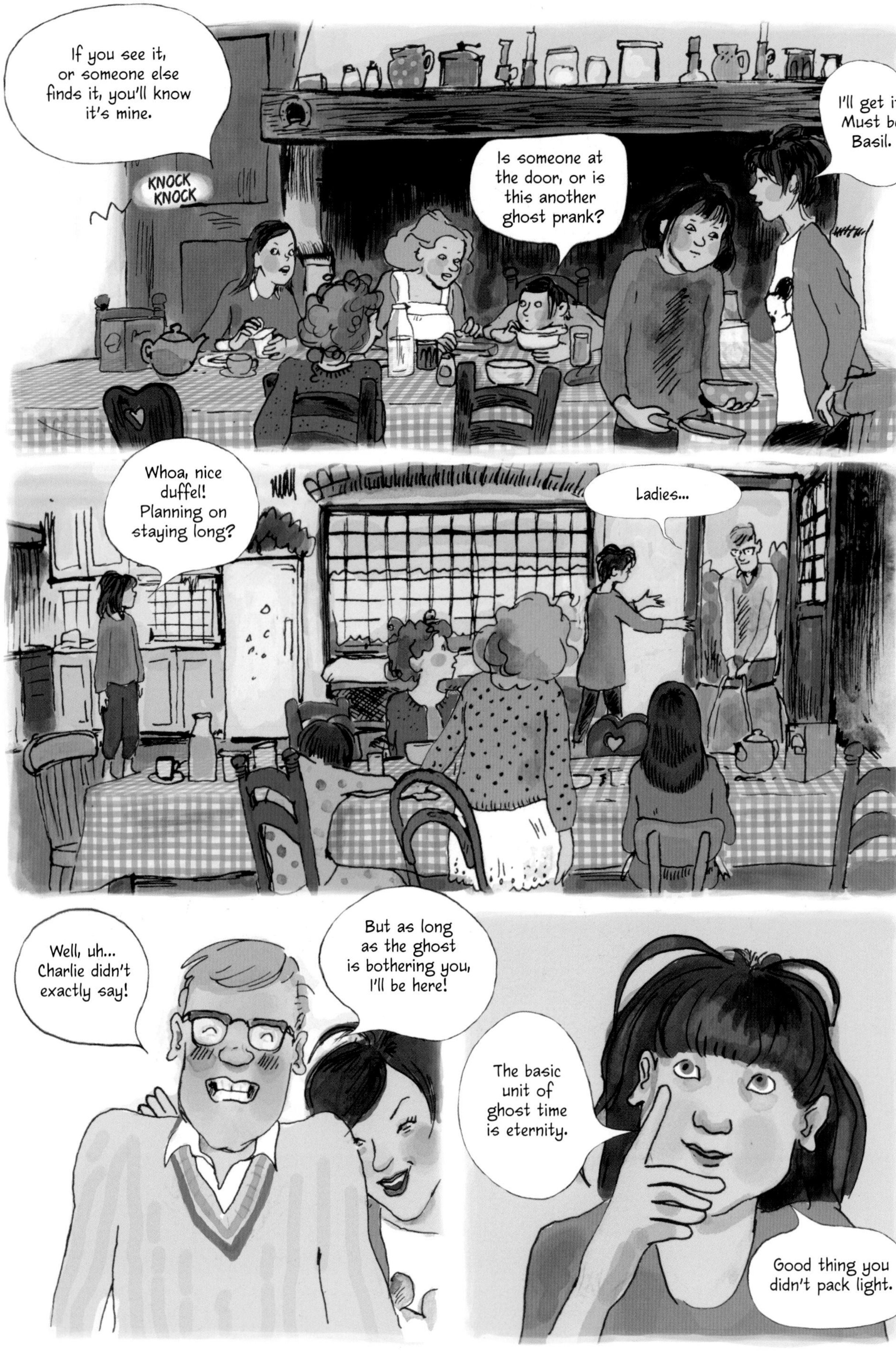
If you see it, or someone else finds it, you'll know it's mine.
KNOCK KNOCK
Is someone at the door, or is this another ghost prank?
I'll get it. Must be Basil.
Whoa, nice duffel! Planning on staying long?
Ladies...
Well, uh... Charlie didn't exactly say!
But as long as the ghost is bothering you, I'll be here!
The basic unit of ghost time is eternity.
Good thing you didn't pack light.

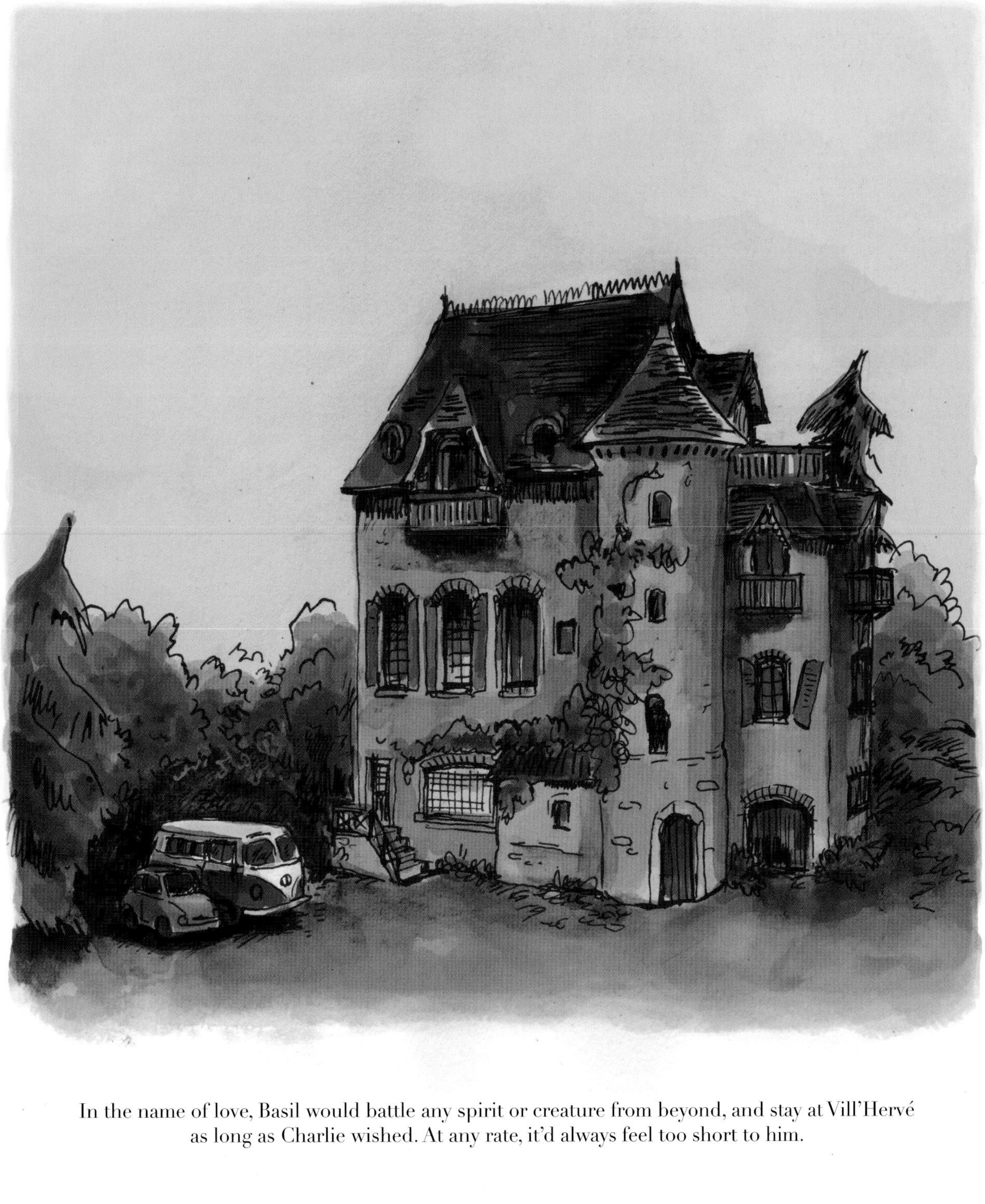

In the name of love, Basil would battle any spirit or creature from beyond, and stay at Vill'Hervé as long as Charlie wished. At any rate, it'd always feel too short to him.

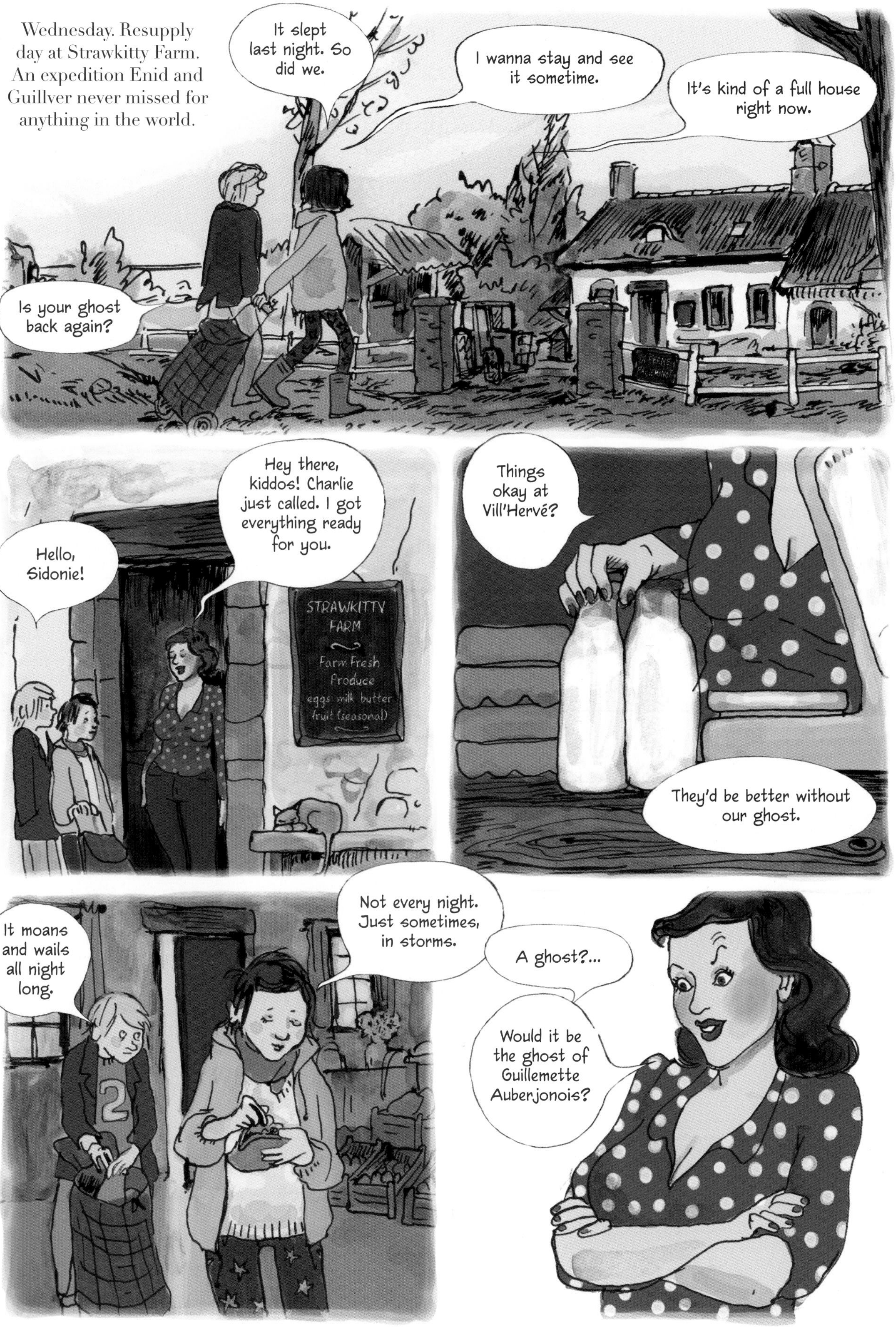
Wednesday. Resupply day at Strawkitty Farm. An expedition Enid and Guillver never missed for anything in the world.
It slept last night. So did we.
I wanna stay and see it sometime.
It's kind of a full house right now.
Is your ghost back again?
Hello, Sidonie!
Hey there, kiddos! Charlie just called. I got everything ready for you.
STRAWKITTY FARM
Farm Fresh Produce
eggs milk butter
fruit (seasonal)
Things okay at Vill'Hervé?
They'd be better without our ghost.
It moans and wails all night long.
Not every night. Just sometimes, in storms.
A ghost?...
Would it be the ghost of Guillemette Auberjonois?

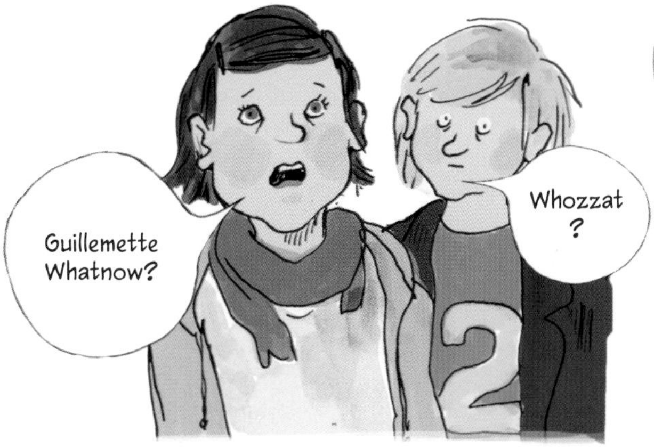
Guillemette Whatnow?
Whozzat ?

For Enid, the name rang a bell. She felt like she'd heard the name before, a century or so ago, before her parents passed away.

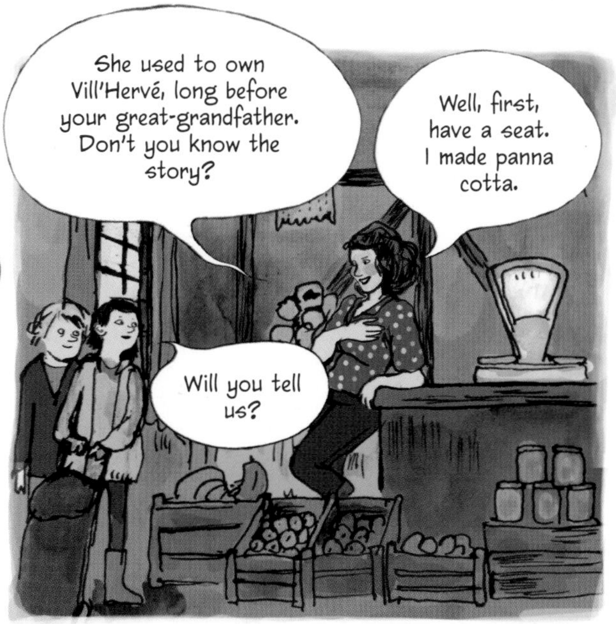
She used to own Vill'Hervé, long before your great-grandfather. Don't you know the story?
Well, first, have a seat. I made panna cotta.
Will you tell us?

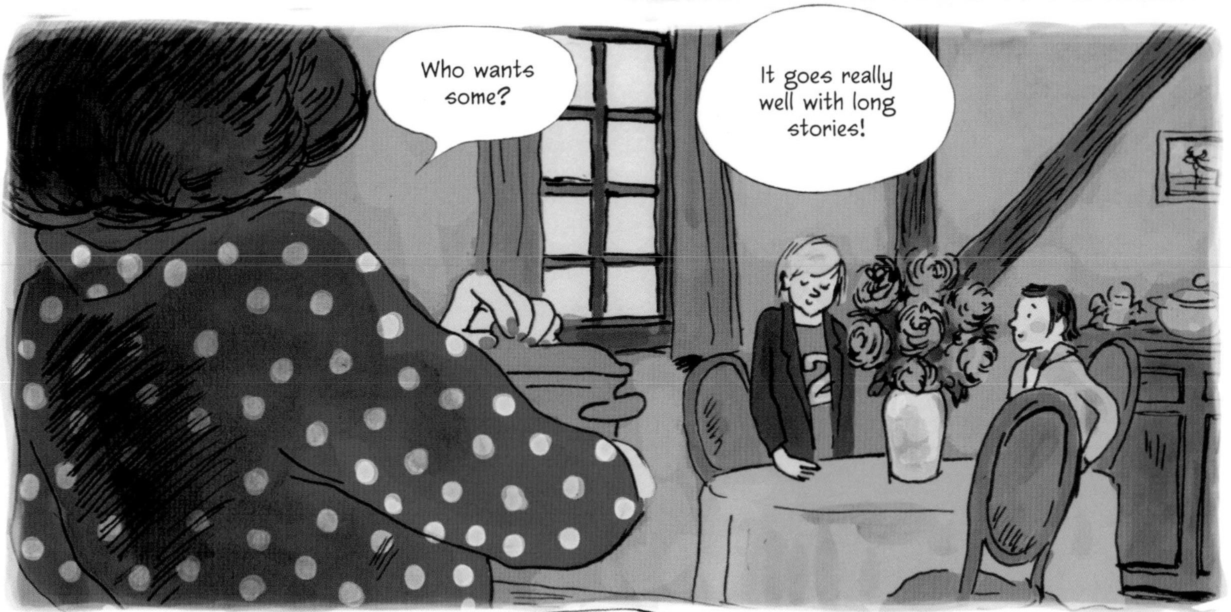
Who wants some?
It goes really well with long stories!

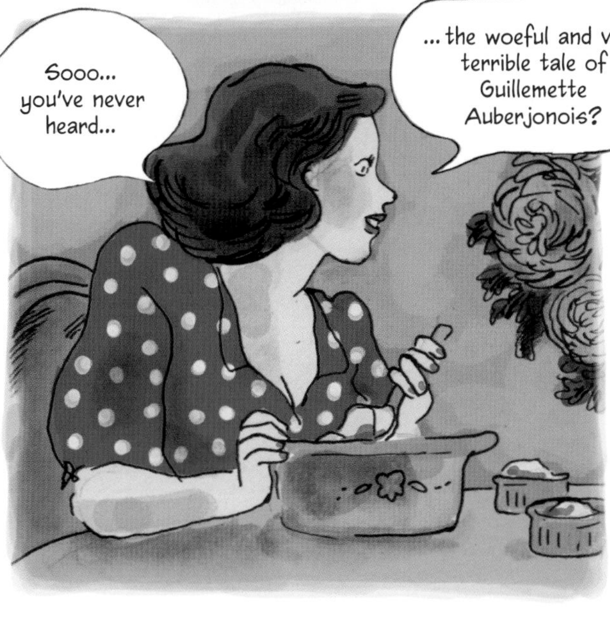
Sooo... you've never heard...
...the woeful and very terrible tale of Guillemette Auberjonois?

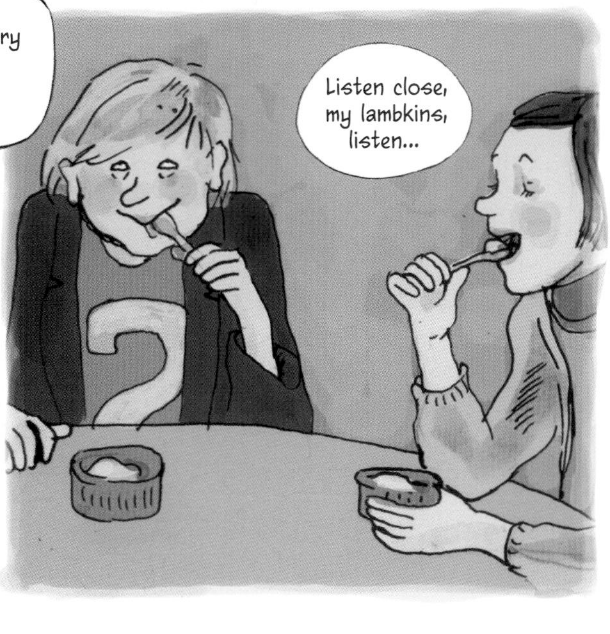
Listen close, my lambkins, listen...

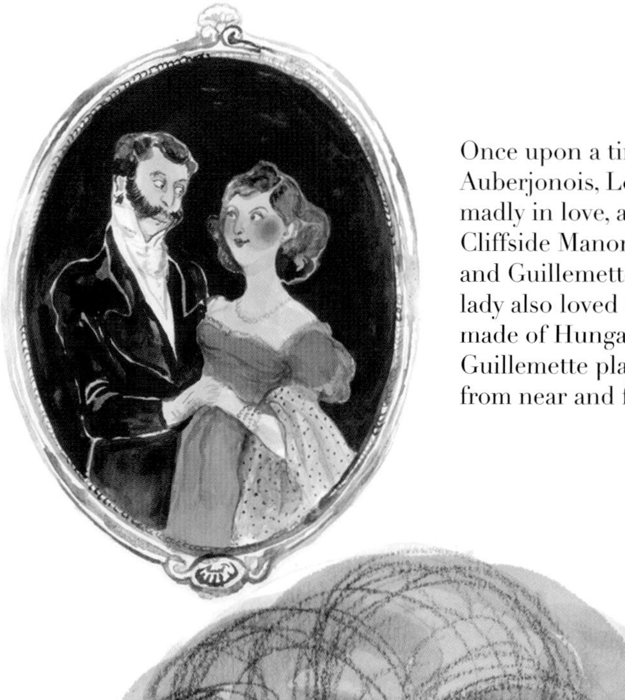

Once upon a time there lived Gildaz and Guillemette Auberjonois, Lord and Lady of Esquille. They were madly in love, and lived in a pretty house called Cliffside Manor. Gildaz lived only for his Guillemette, and Guillemette only for her Gildaz. The beautiful lady also loved to play the harp. Gildaz gave her one made of Hungarian wood with Venetian strings. Guillemette played like an angel, and people came from near and far to hear her.

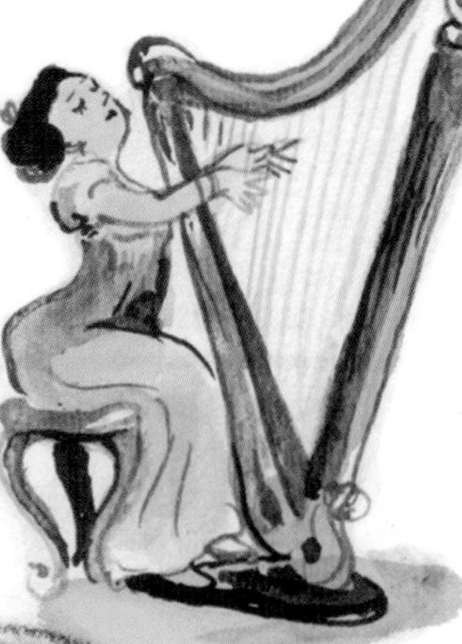

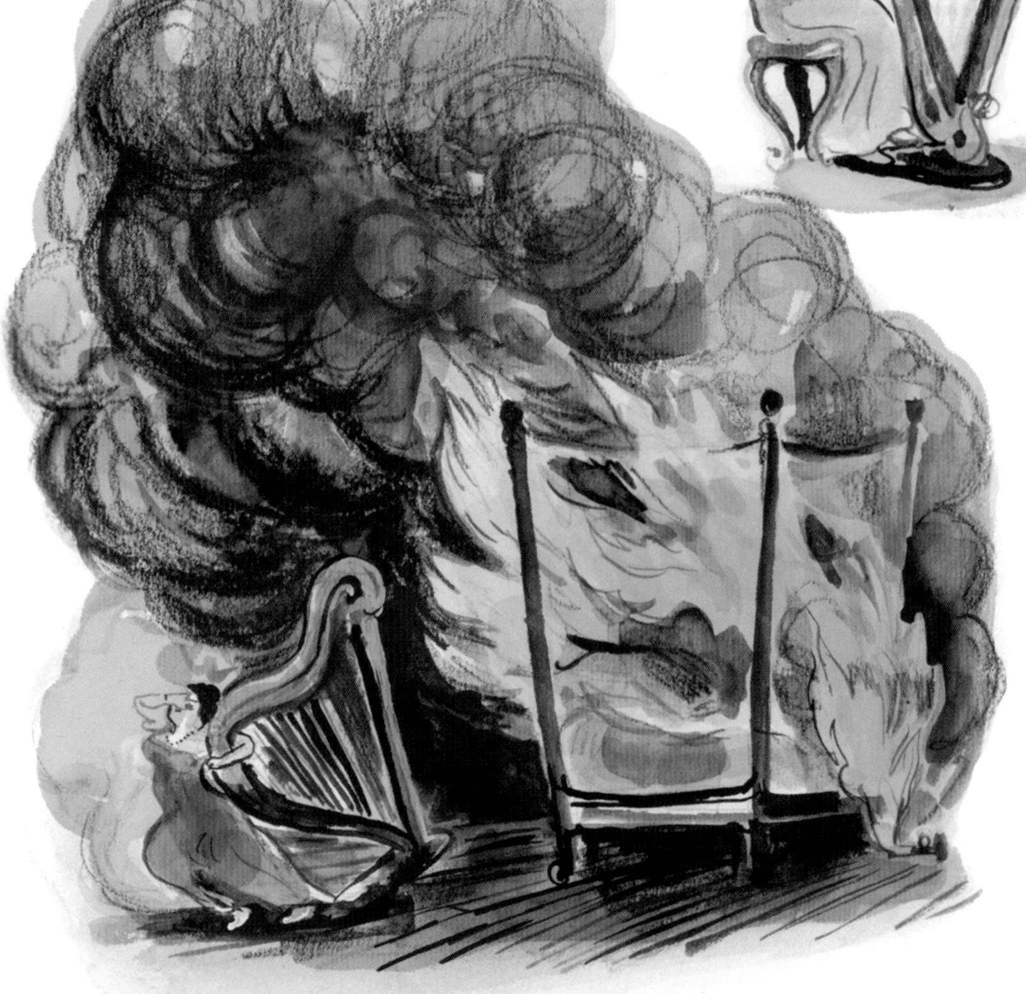

One stormy night in October, tragedy struck. While her husband was away, the canopy above Guillemette's bed caught fire. Soon, the bedroom was in flames. The harp was burning; Guillemette tried to rescue it and drag it to safety. But the instrument proved heavy. Guillemette was spent. The wind fanned the inferno. Surrounded by flames, she burned to death.

Upon his return, Gildaz, overcome with grief, plunged a dagger into his own heart. And Cliffside Manor became a cursed place. Empty. Haunted. No one dared live there any more.

Fifty years later, it lay in ruins. The year was 1918. The year your great grandfather, Hervé Verdelaine, a fisherman, returned from the war. And after all, what was a haunted house after witnessing the horrors of the Great War? Hervé wasn't afraid. He bought the house from the township for a song, and, with his siblings, decided to fix it up. You know the rest. Twelve years of labor, hewing granite block by block, sawing wood for the roof beams, cutting slate for the roof tiles, planting trees in the yard — all so Cliffside Manor could become Vill'Hervé.

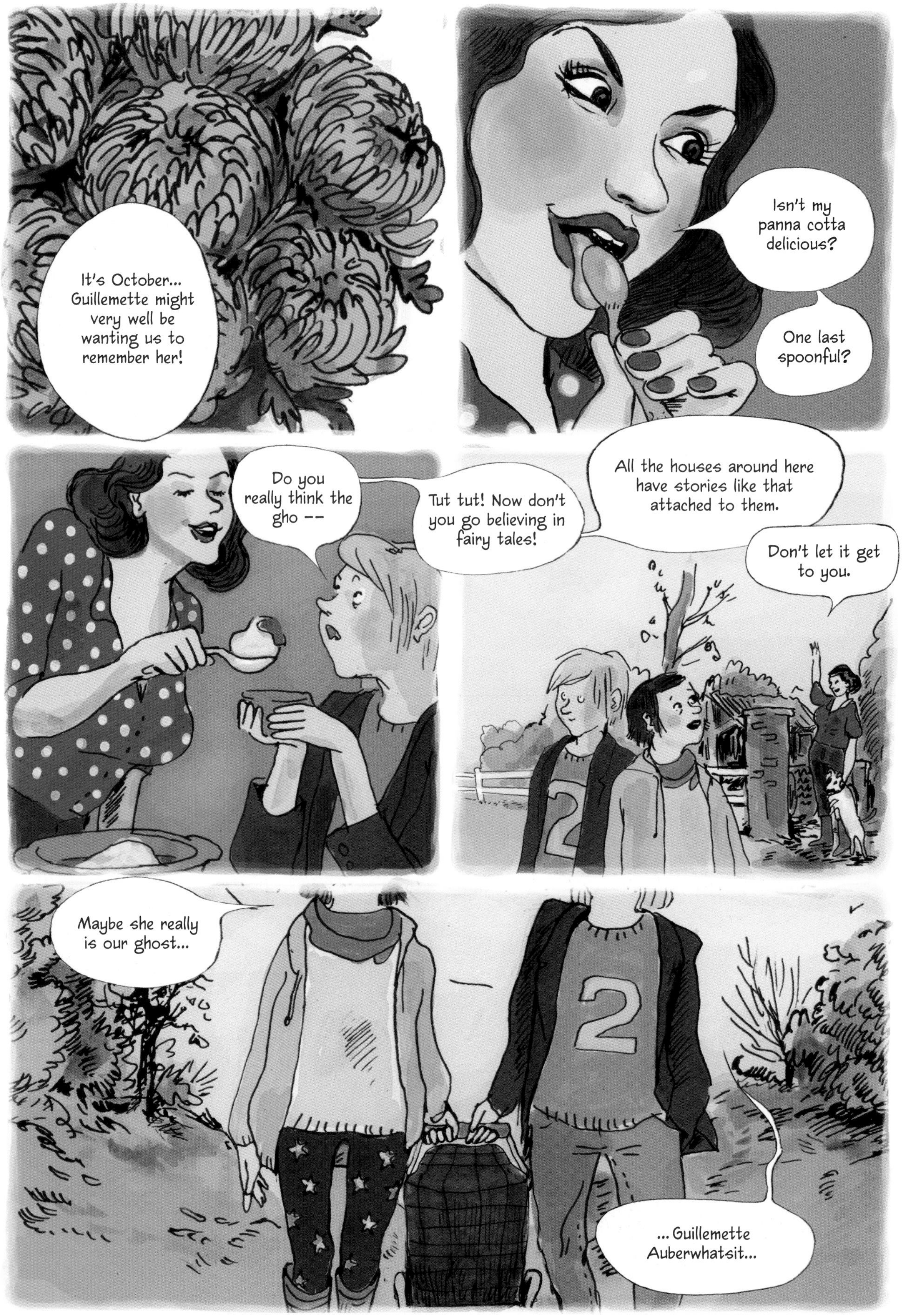
It's October... Guillemette might very well be wanting us to remember her!
Isn't my panna cotta delicious?
One last spoonful?
Do you really think the gho --
Tut tut! Now don't you go believing in fairy tales!
All the houses around here have stories like that attached to them.
Don't let it get to you.
Maybe she really is our ghost...
...Guillemette Auberwhatsit...

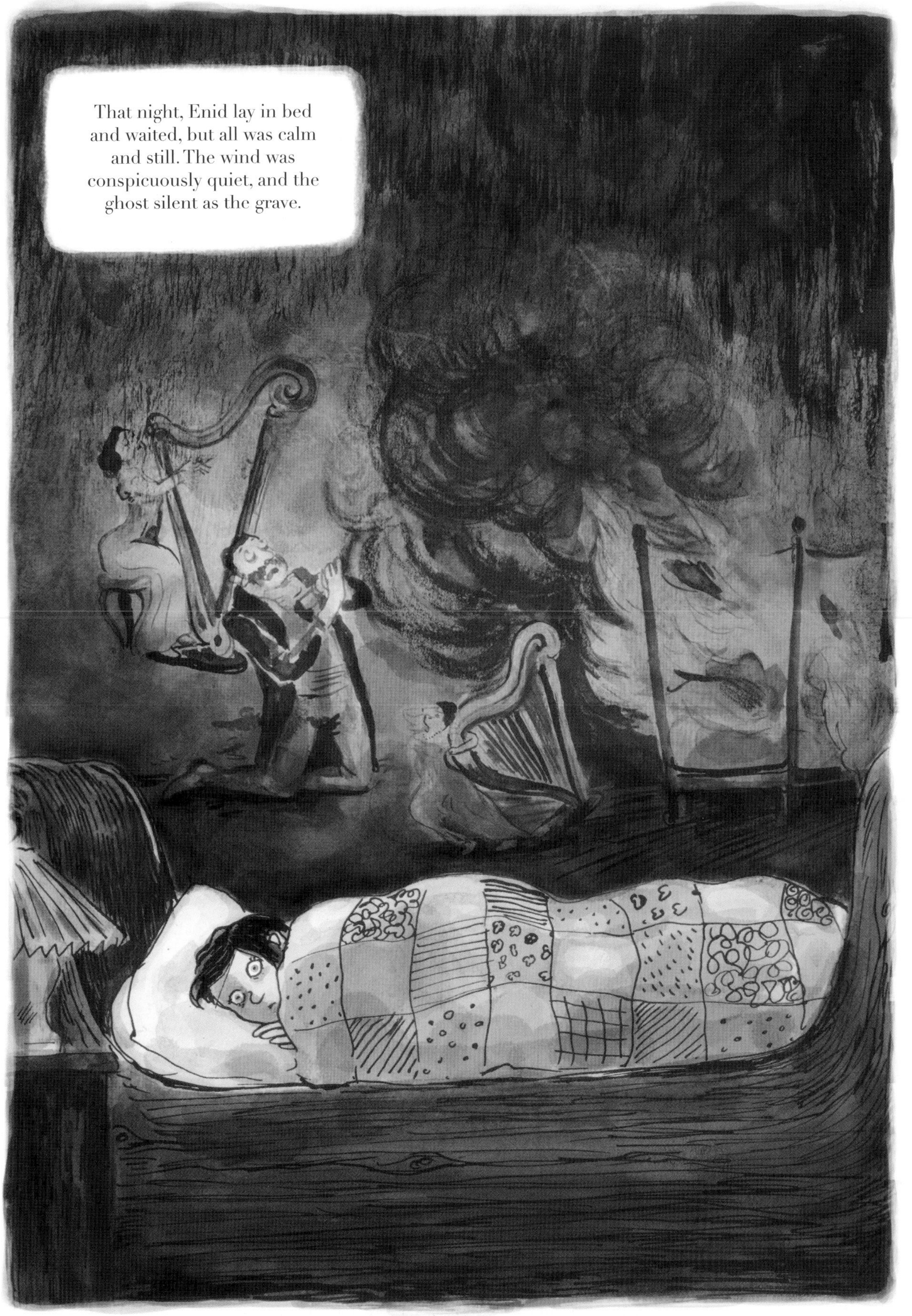
That night, Enid lay in bed and waited, but all was calm and still. The wind was conspicuously quiet, and the ghost silent as the grave.

On Friday nights, Genevieve "babysat for the Deshoulieres twins." It wore her out, but she loved it. Of course, she had no reason to keep her Muay Thai classes with Mr. Qol Moï a secret. But that was precisely why she didn't tell a soul about them.

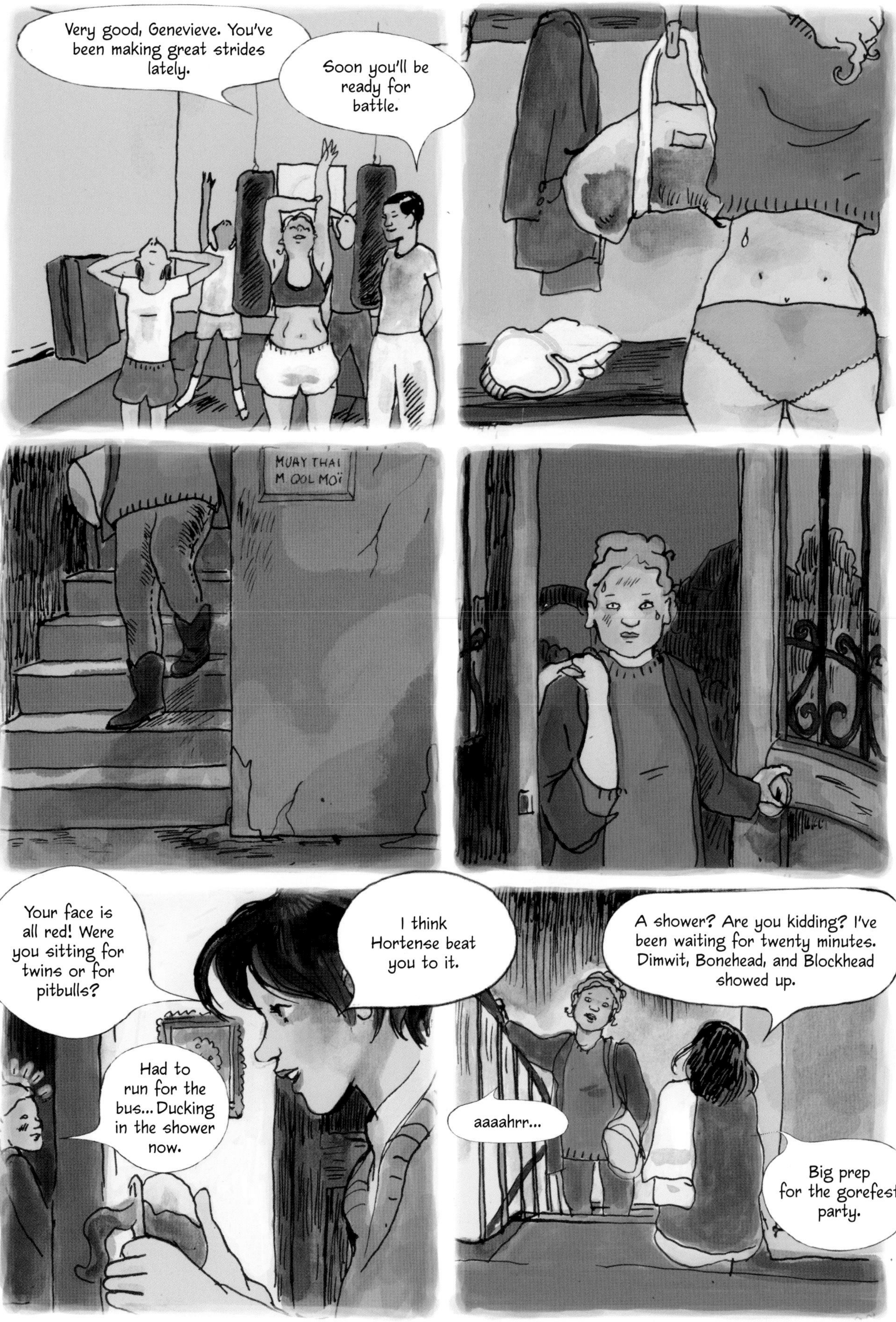
Very good, Genevieve. You've been making great strides lately.
Soon you'll be ready for battle.
MUAY THAI M. QOL MOÏ
Your face is all red! Were you sitting for twins or for pitbulls?
I think Hortense beat you to it.
Had to run for the bus... Ducking in the shower now.
A shower? Are you kidding? I've been waiting for twenty minutes. Dimwit, Bonehead, and Blockhead showed up.
aaaahrr...
Big prep for the gorefest party.

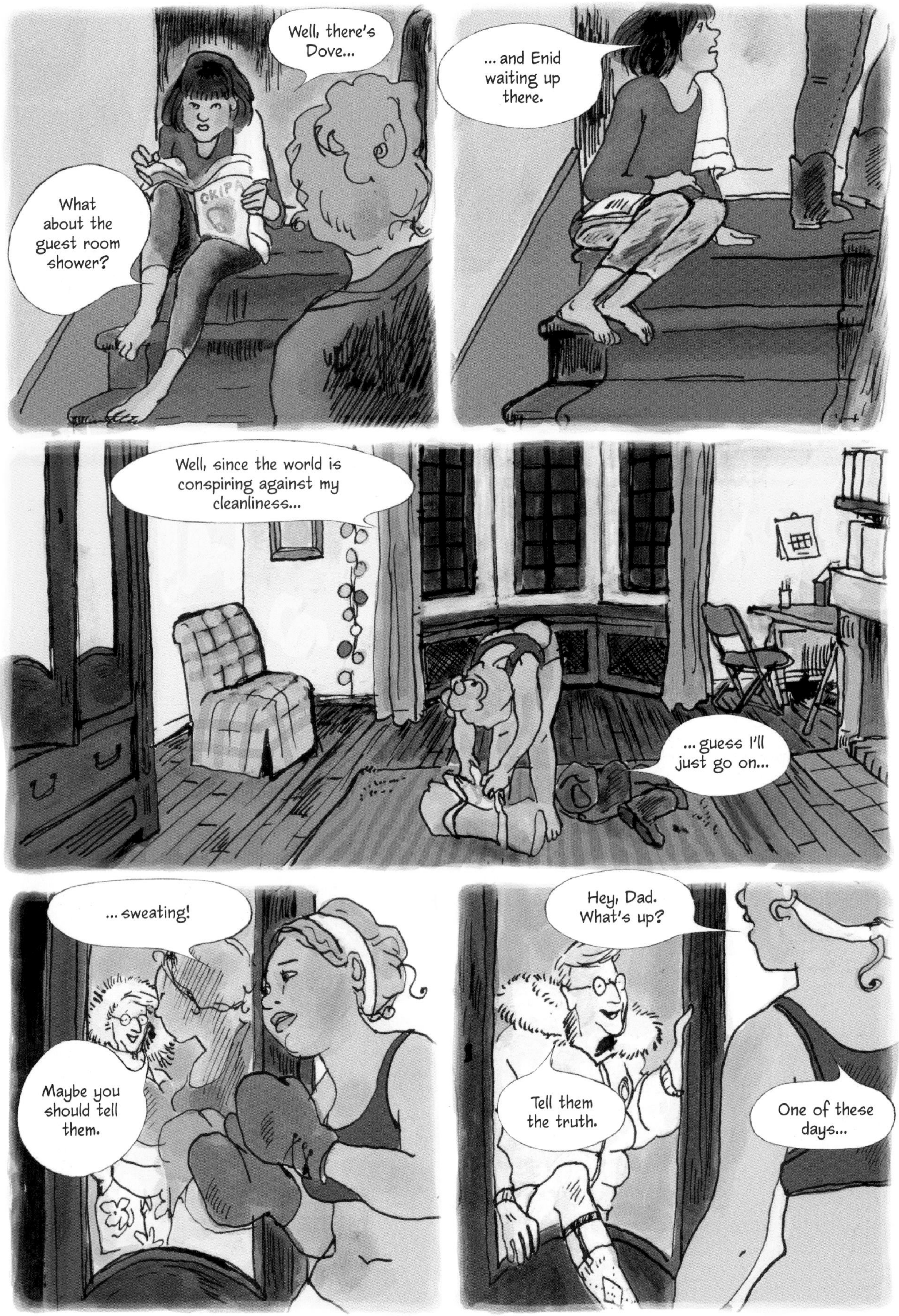
Well, there's Dove...
What about the guest room shower?
OKIPA
... and Enid waiting up there.
Well, since the world is conspiring against my cleanliness...
... guess I'll just go on...
... sweating!
Maybe you should tell them.
Hey, Dad. What's up?
Tell them the truth.
One of these days...

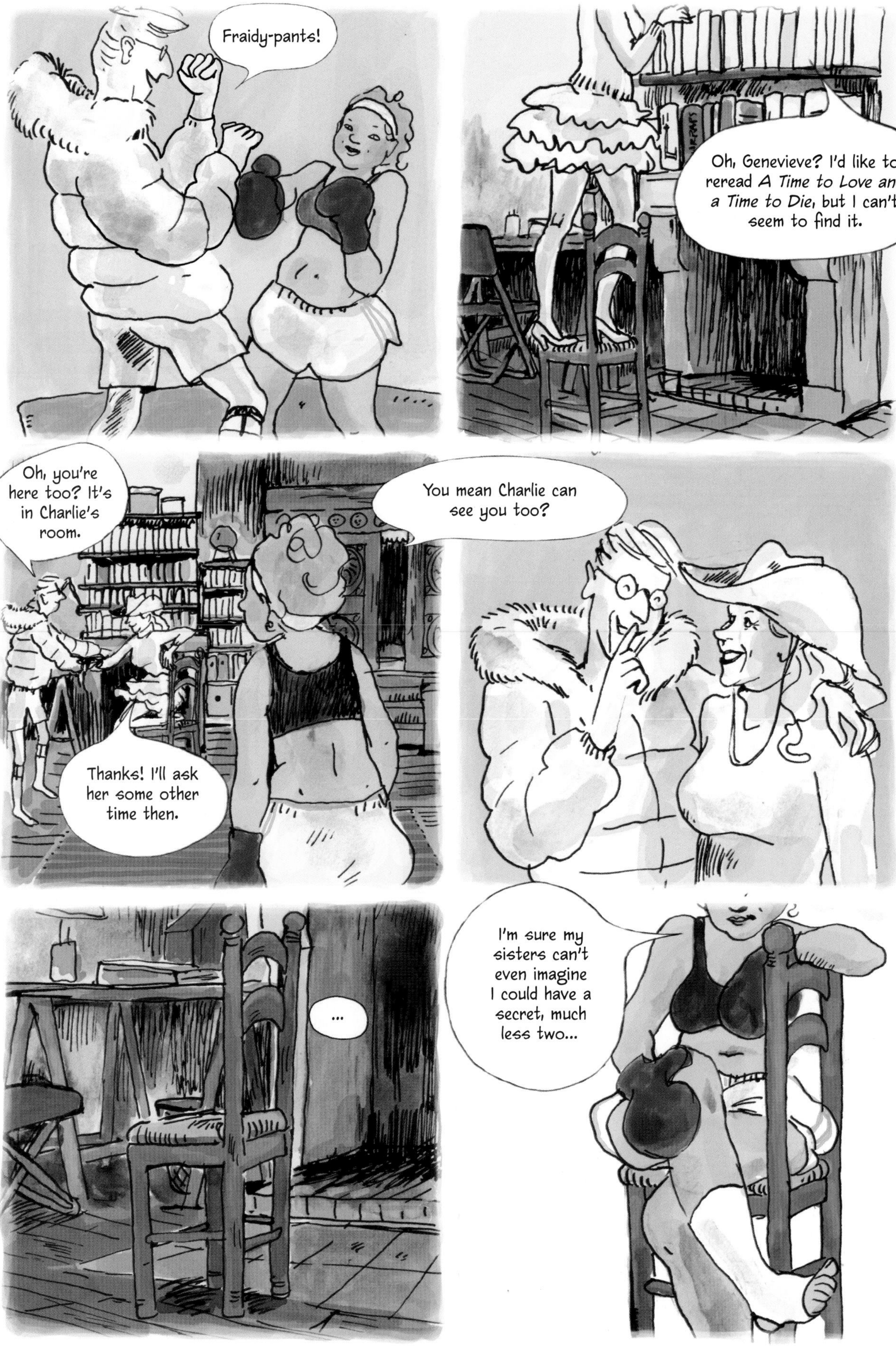
Fraidy-pants!
Oh, Genevieve? I'd like to reread *A Time to Love and a Time to Die*, but I can't seem to find it.
Oh, you're here too? It's in Charlie's room.
You mean Charlie can see you too?
Thanks! I'll ask her some other time then.
...
I'm sure my sisters can't even imagine I could have a secret, much less two...

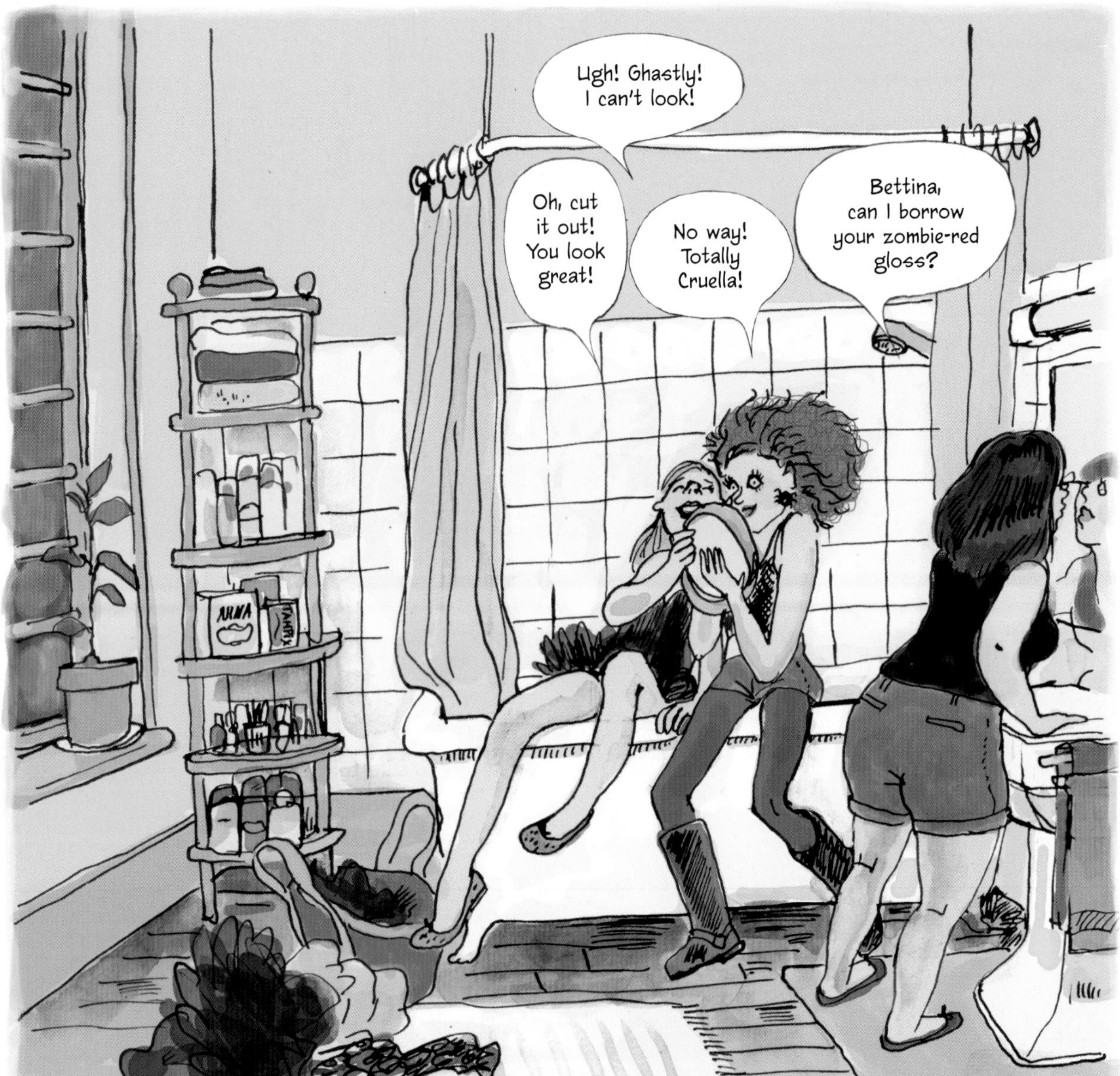
Ugh! Ghastly! I can't look!
Oh, cut it out! You look great!
No way! Totally Cruella!
Bettina, can I borrow your zombie-red gloss?
AMMA
TAMPAX

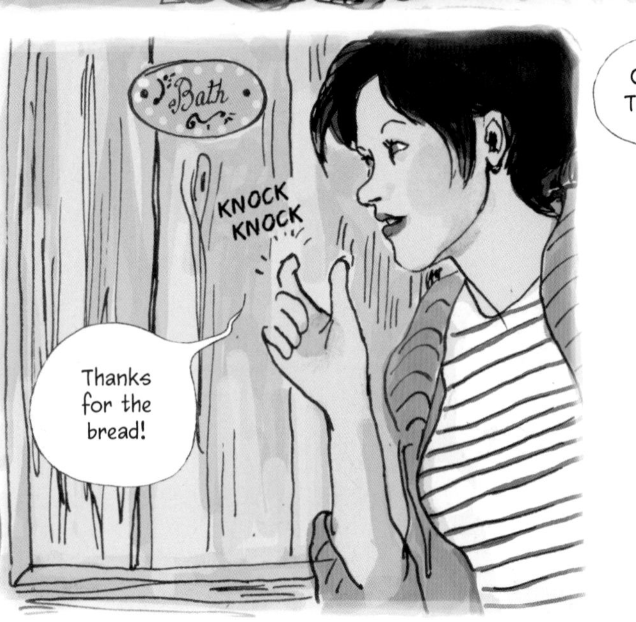
Bath
KNOCK KNOCK
Thanks for the bread!

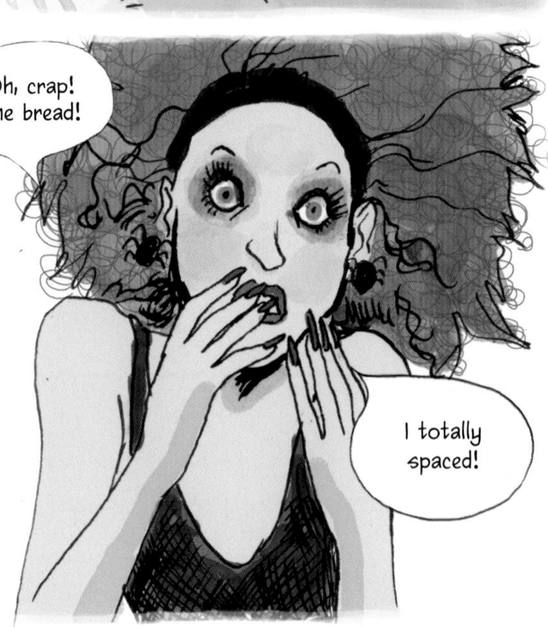
Oh, crap! The bread!
I totally spaced!

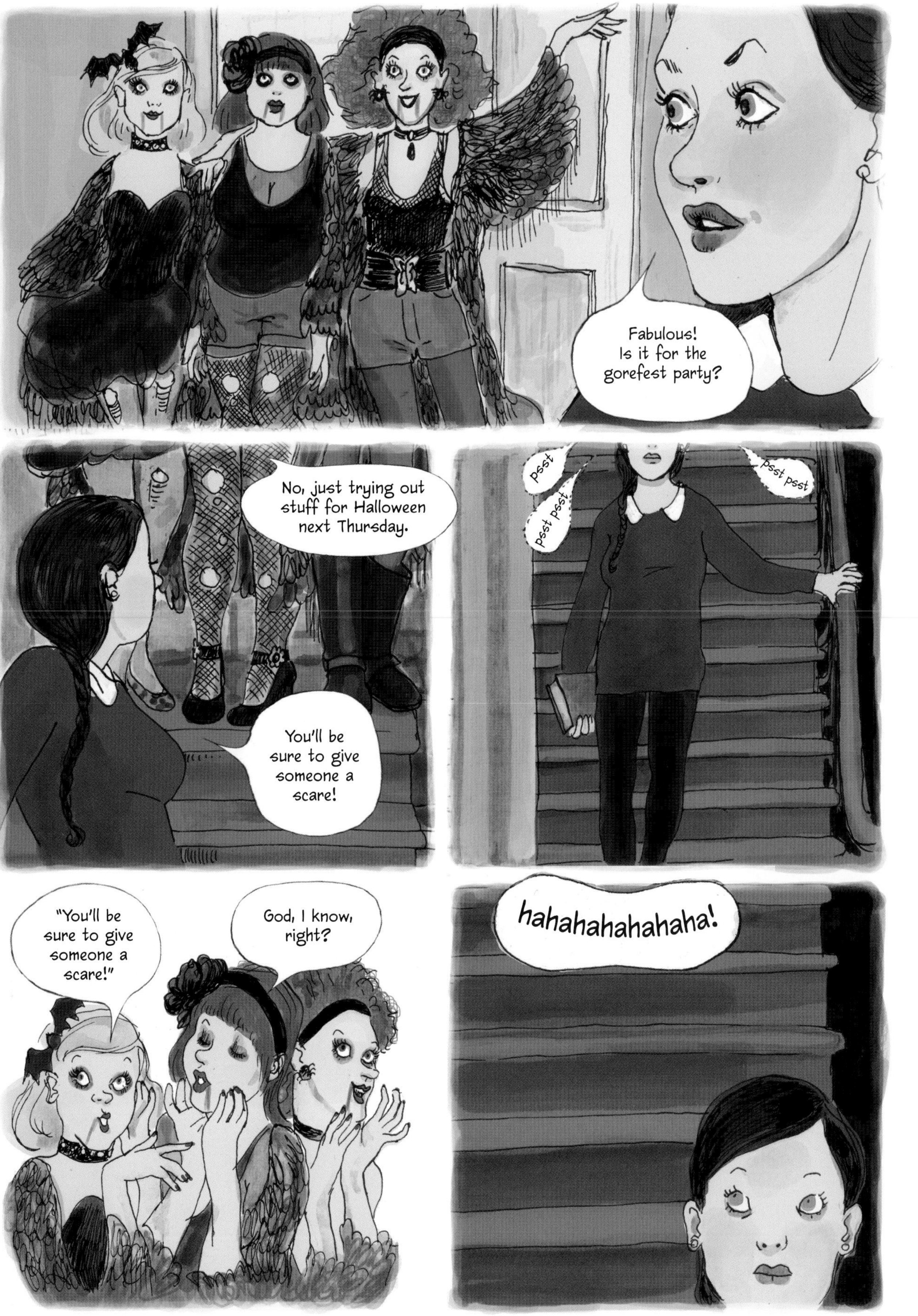
Fabulous! Is it for the gorefest party?
No, just trying out stuff for Halloween next Thursday.
You'll be sure to give someone a scare!
psst
pssst pssst
psst psst
"You'll be sure to give someone a scare!"
God, I know, right?
hahahahahahaha!

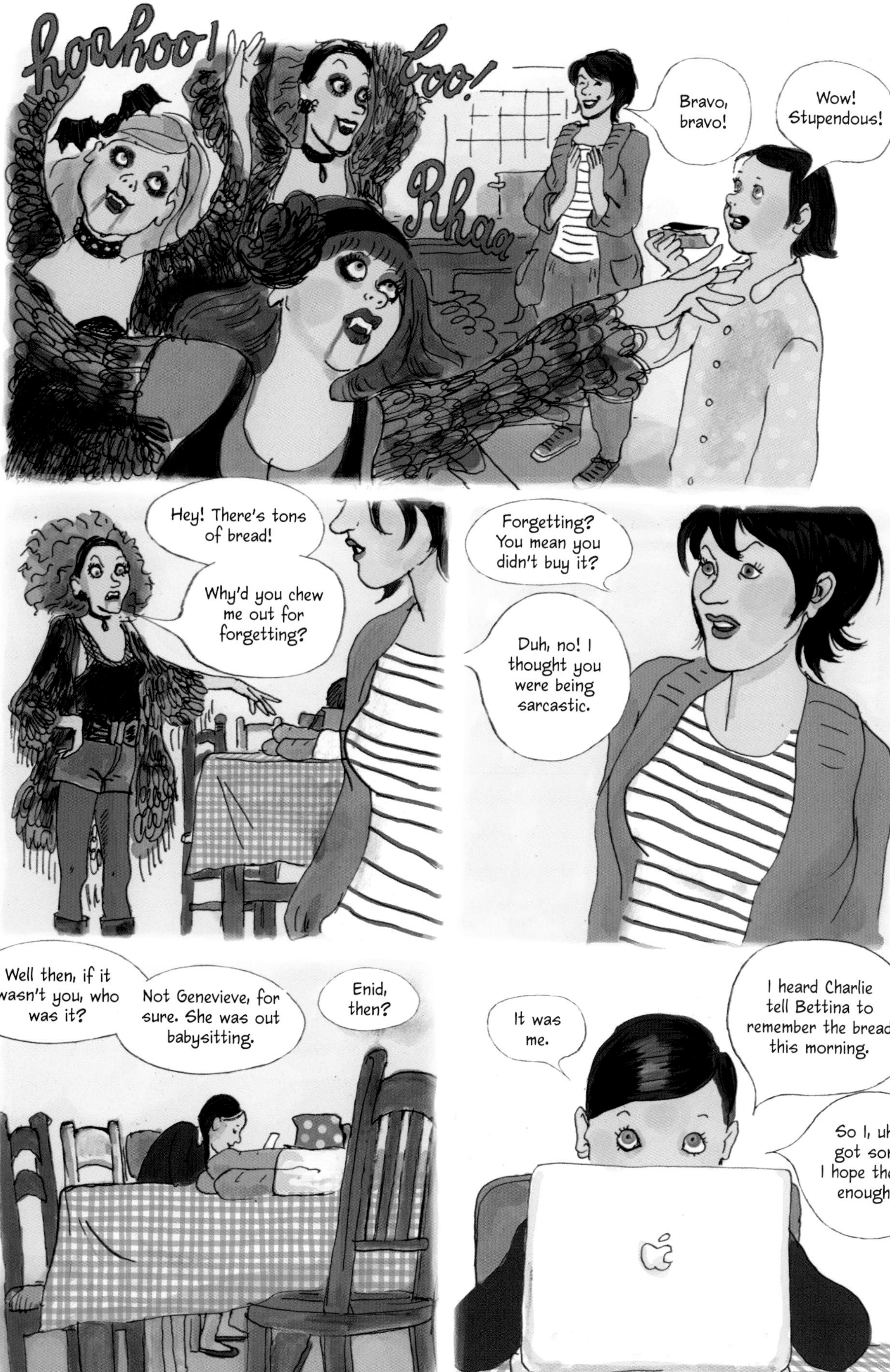
hoahoo!
boo!
Rhaa
Bravo, bravo!
Wow! Stupendous!
Hey! There's tons of bread!
Why'd you chew me out for forgetting?
Forgetting? You mean you didn't buy it?
Duh, no! I thought you were being sarcastic.
Well then, if it wasn't you, who was it?
Not Genevieve, for sure. She was out babysitting.
Enid, then?
It was me.
I heard Charlie tell Bettina to remember the bread this morning.
So I, uh... got some. I hope there's enough...

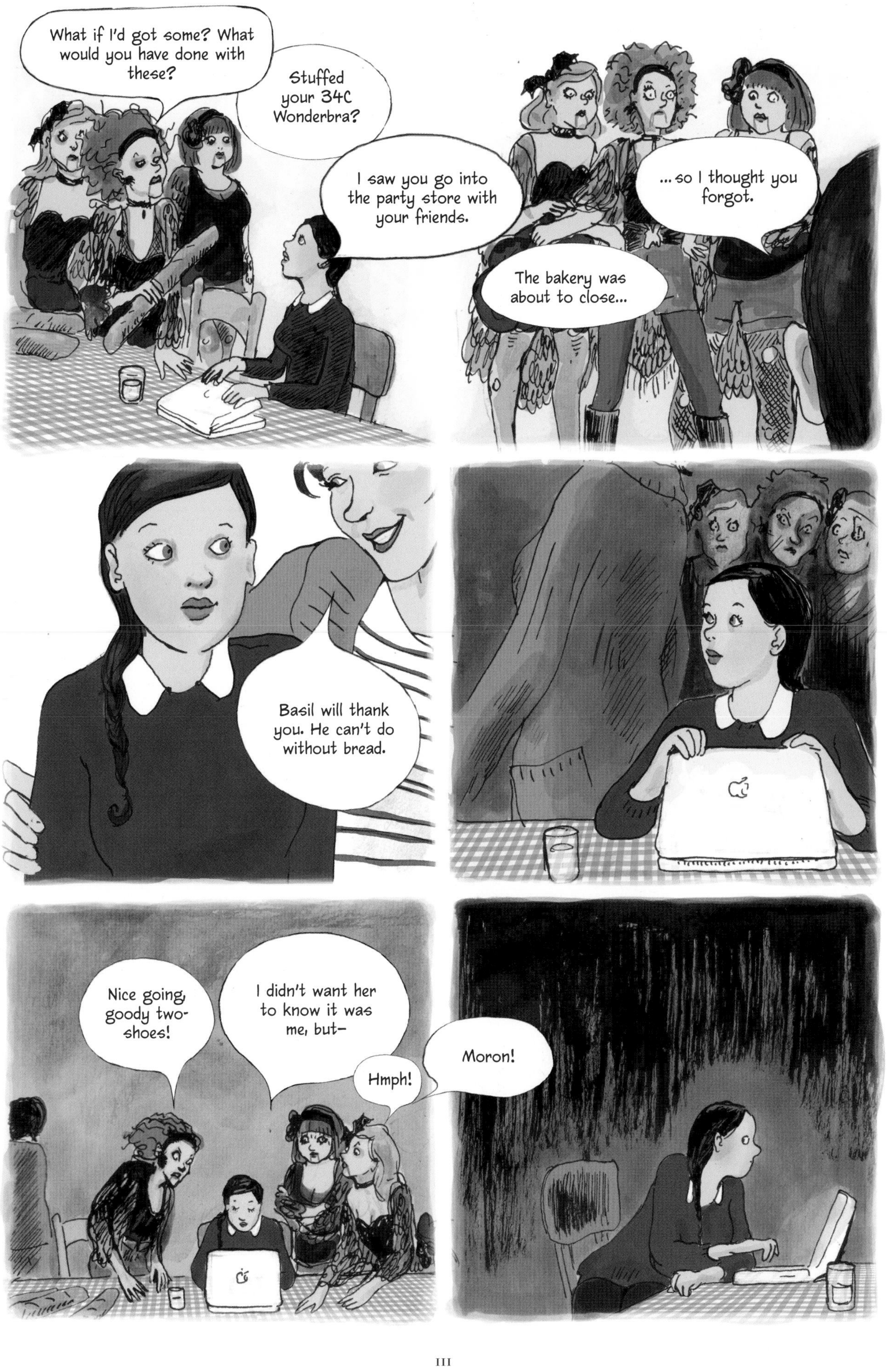
What if I'd got some? What would you have done with these?
Stuffed your 34C Wonderbra?
I saw you go into the party store with your friends.
The bakery was about to close...
...so I thought you forgot.
Basil will thank you. He can't do without bread.
Nice going, goody two-shoes!
I didn't want her to know it was me, but–
Hmph!
Moron!

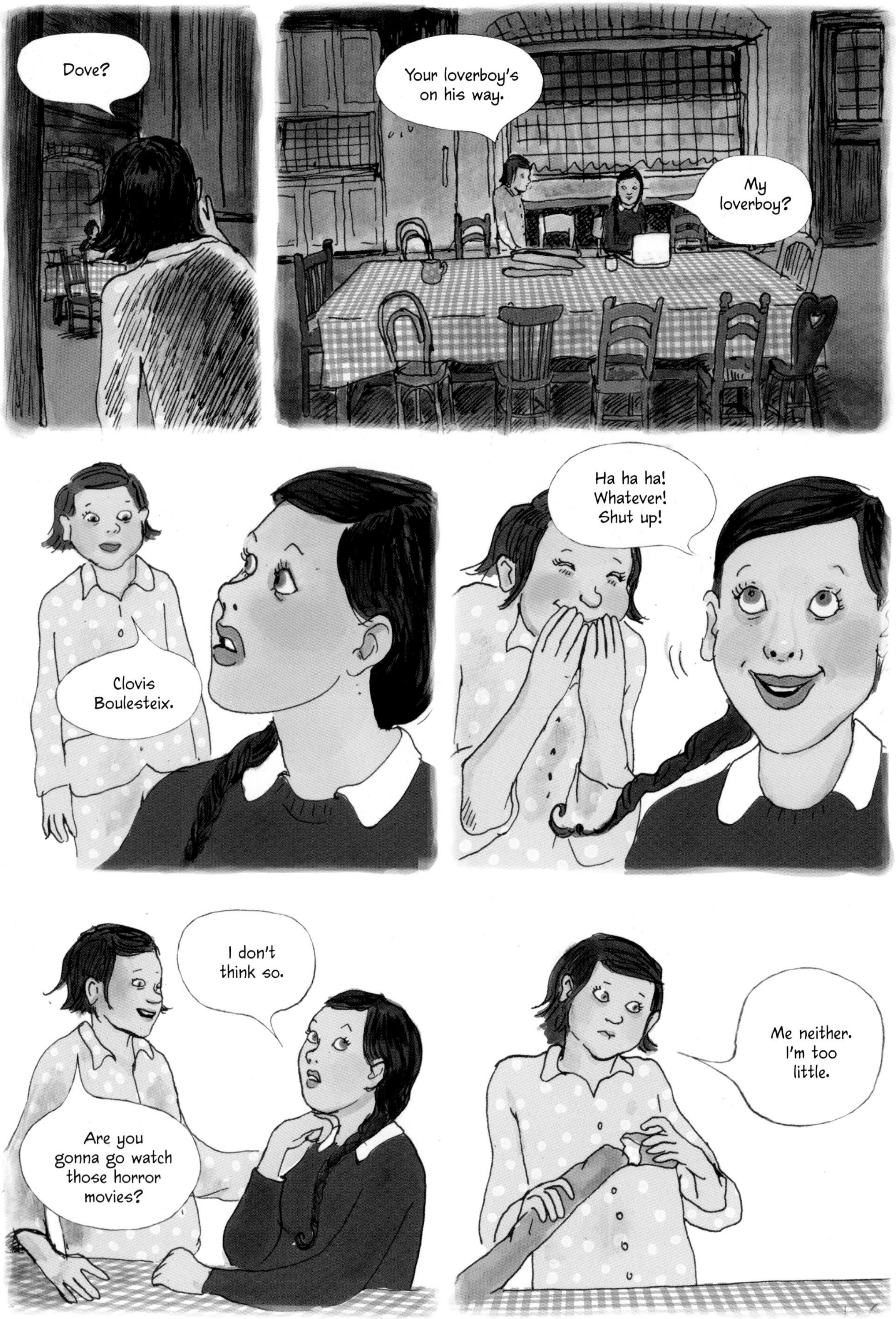
Dove?
Your loverboy's on his way.
My loverboy?
Clovis Boulesteix.
Ha ha ha! Whatever! Shut up!
Are you gonna go watch those horror movies?
I don't think so.
Me neither. I'm too little.

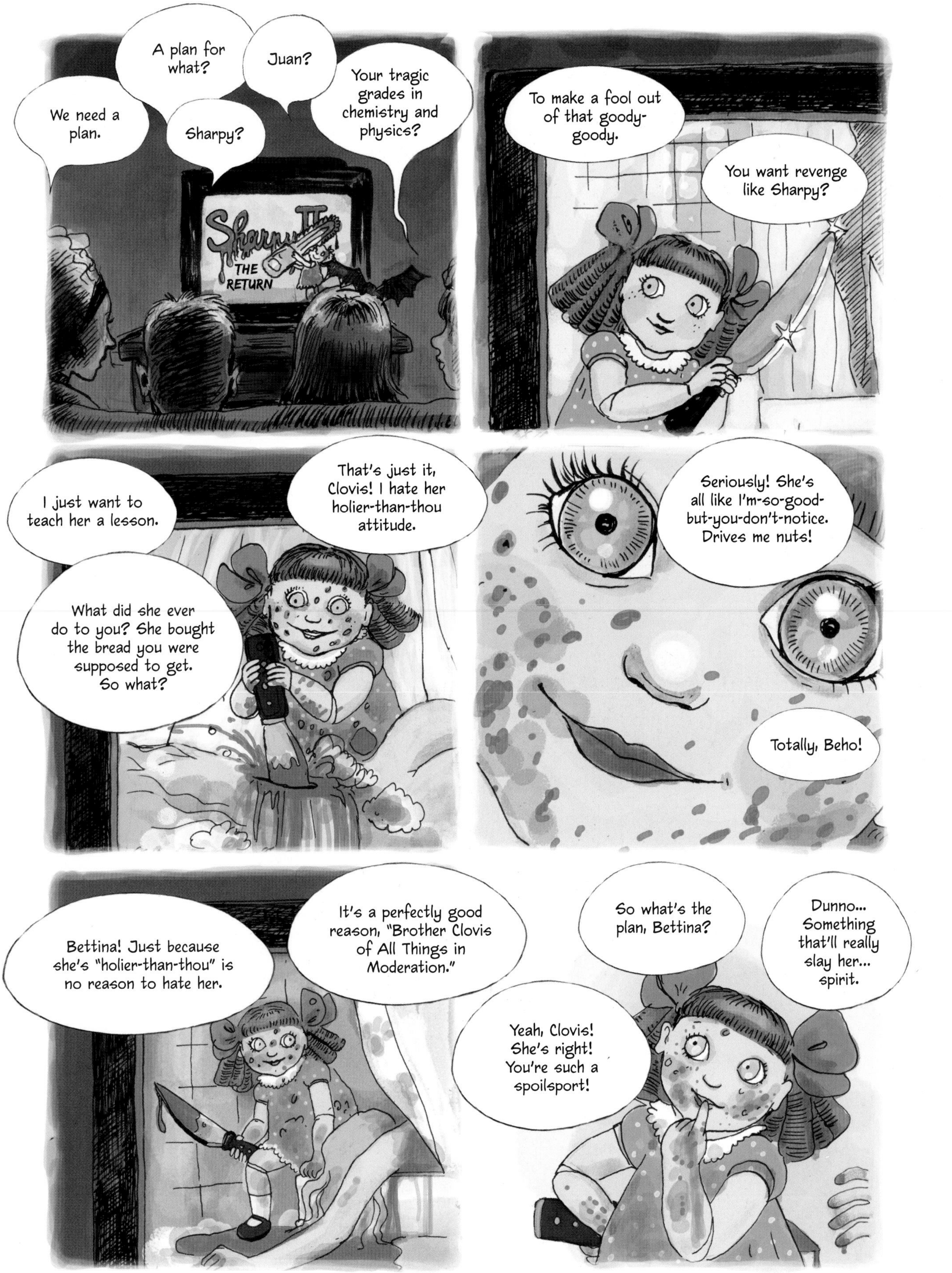
We need a plan.
A plan for what?
Sharpy?
Juan?
Your tragic grades in chemistry and physics?
Sharpy II THE RETURN
To make a fool out of that goody-goody.
You want revenge like Sharpy?
I just want to teach her a lesson.
That's just it, Clovis! I hate her holier-than-thou attitude.
What did she ever do to you? She bought the bread you were supposed to get. So what?
Seriously! She's all like I'm-so-good-but-you-don't-notice. Drives me nuts!
Totally, Beho!
Bettina! Just because she's "holier-than-thou" is no reason to hate her.
It's a perfectly good reason, "Brother Clovis of All Things in Moderation."
So what's the plan, Bettina?
Dunno... Something that'll really slay her... spirit.
Yeah, Clovis! She's right! You're such a spoilsport!

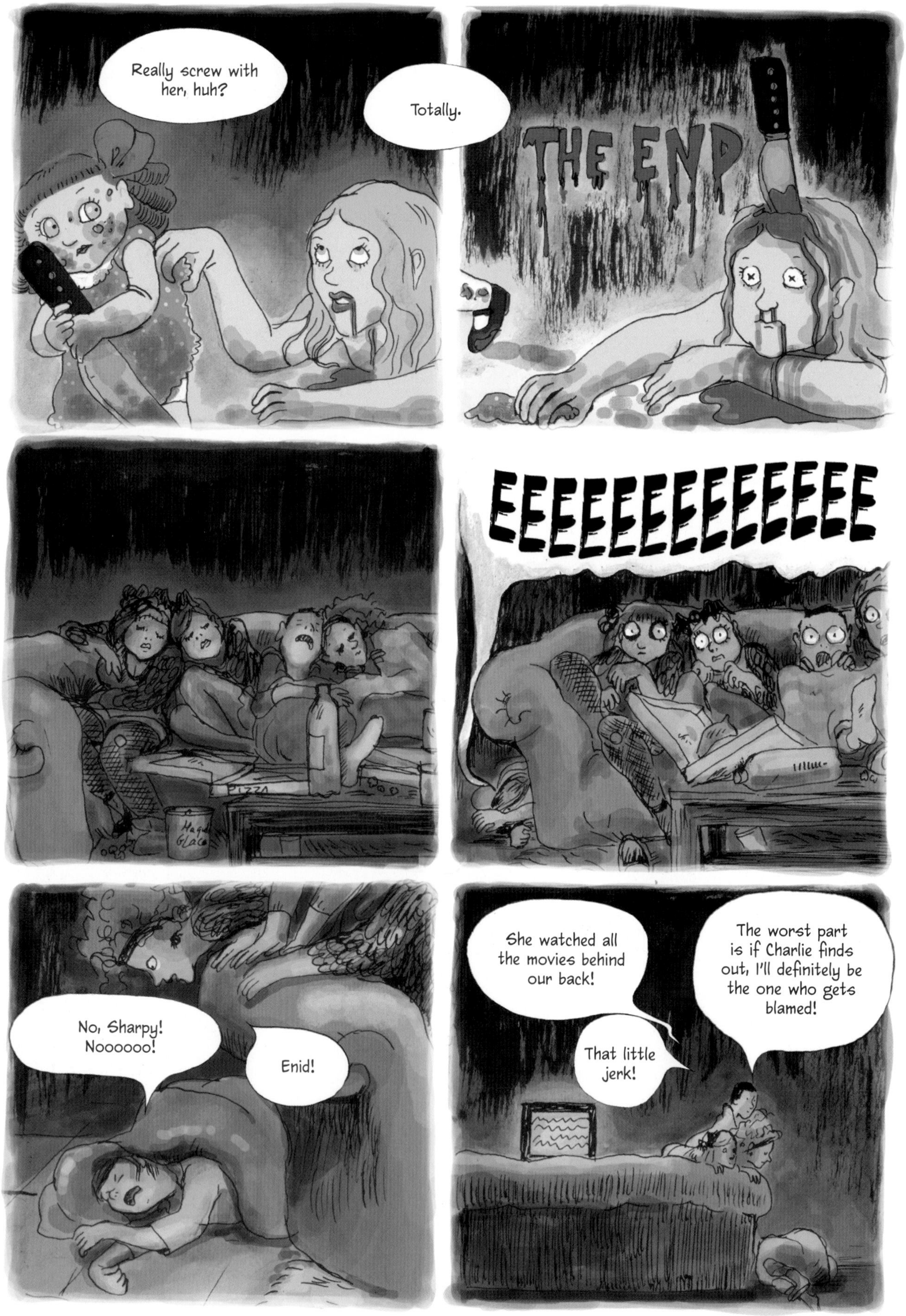
Really screw with her, huh?
Totally.
THE END
EEEEEEEEEEEEEE
PIZZA
No, Sharpy! Noooooo!
Enid!
She watched all the movies behind our back!
That little jerk!
The worst part is if Charlie finds out, I'll definitely be the one who gets blamed!

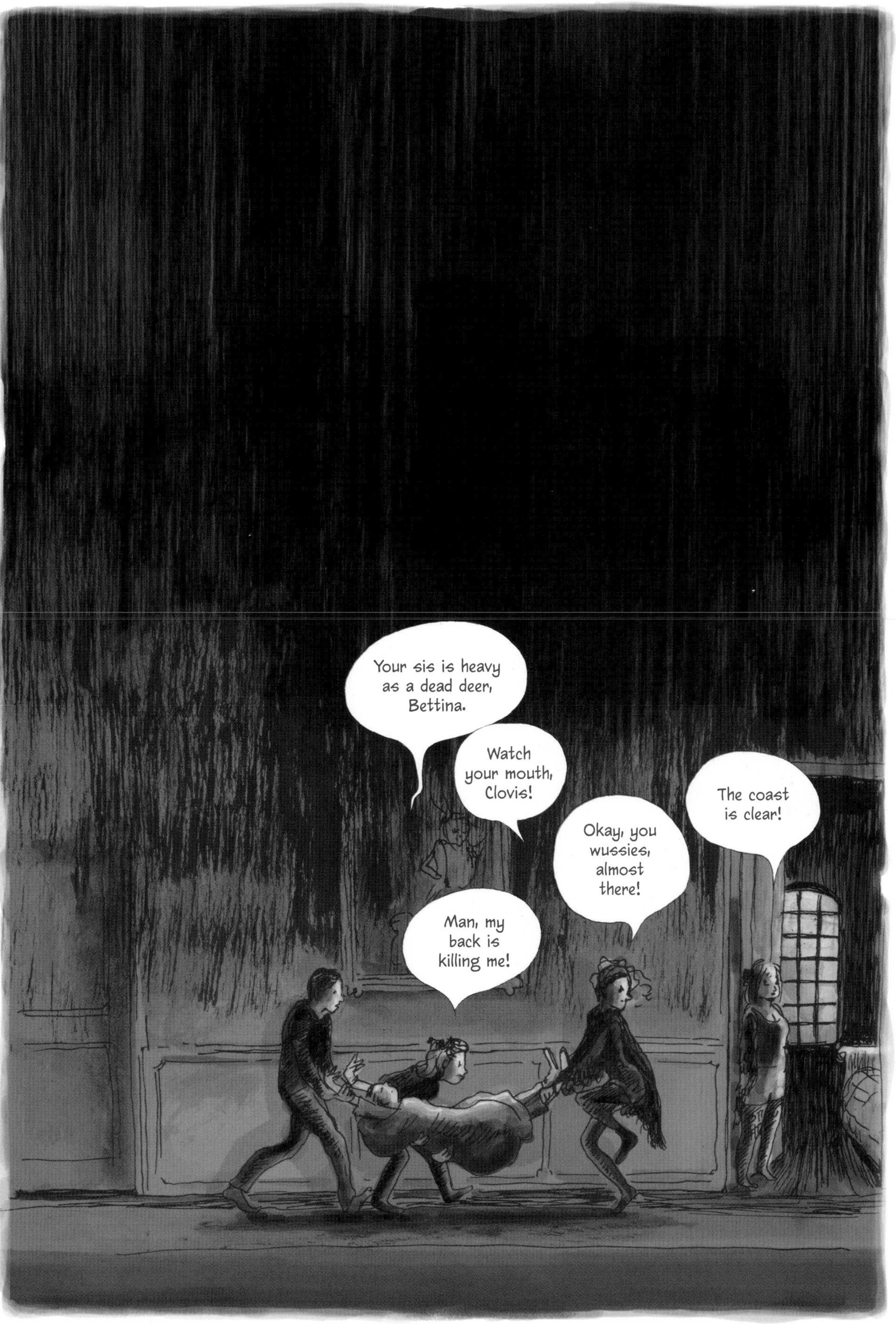
Your sis is heavy as a dead deer, Bettina.
Watch your mouth, Clovis!
Man, my back is killing me!
Okay, you wussies, almost there!
The coast is clear!

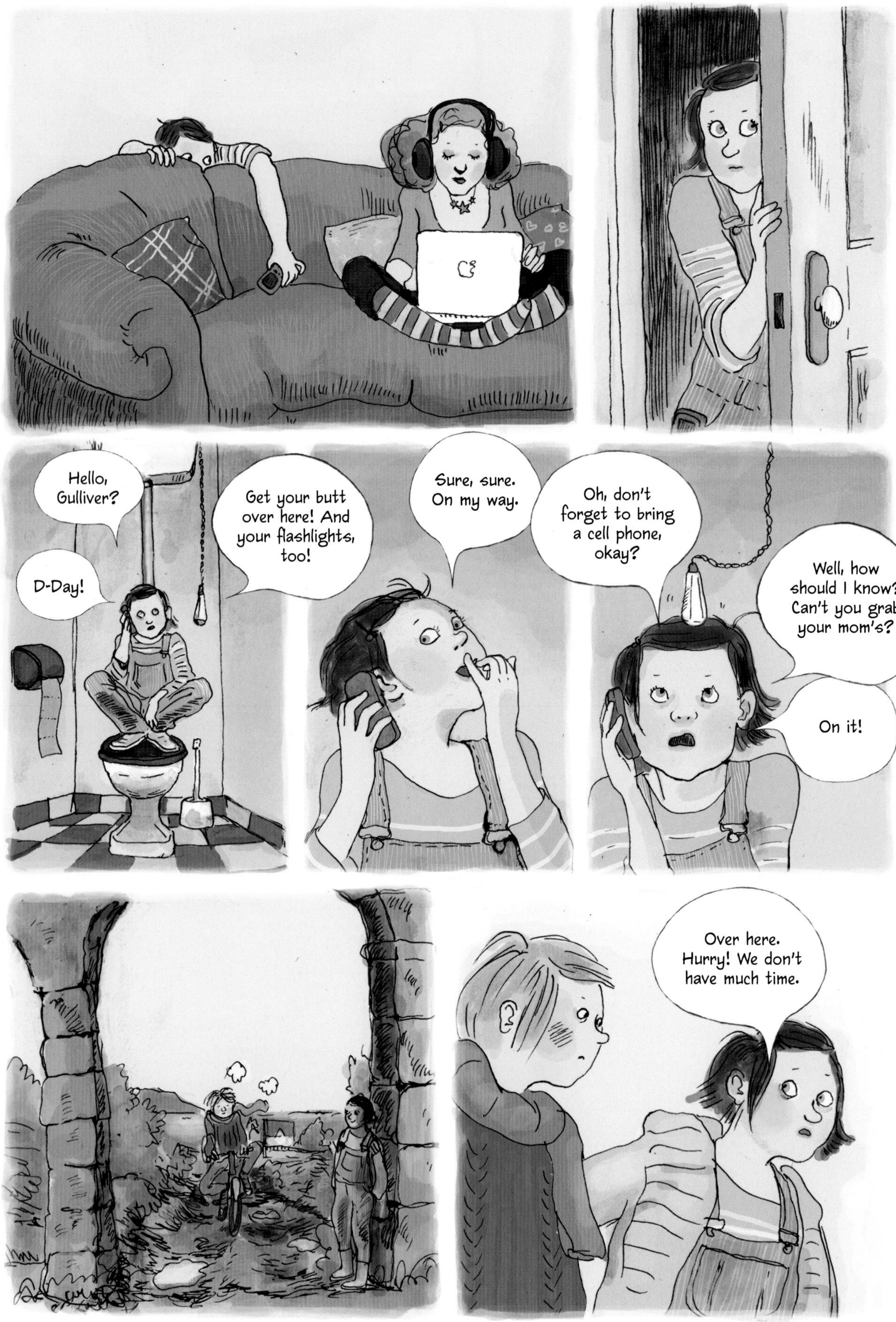
Hello, Gulliver?
D-Day!
Get your butt over here! And your flashlights, too!
Sure, sure. On my way.
Oh, don't forget to bring a cell phone, okay?
Well, how should I know? Can't you grab your mom's?
On it!
Over here. Hurry! We don't have much time.

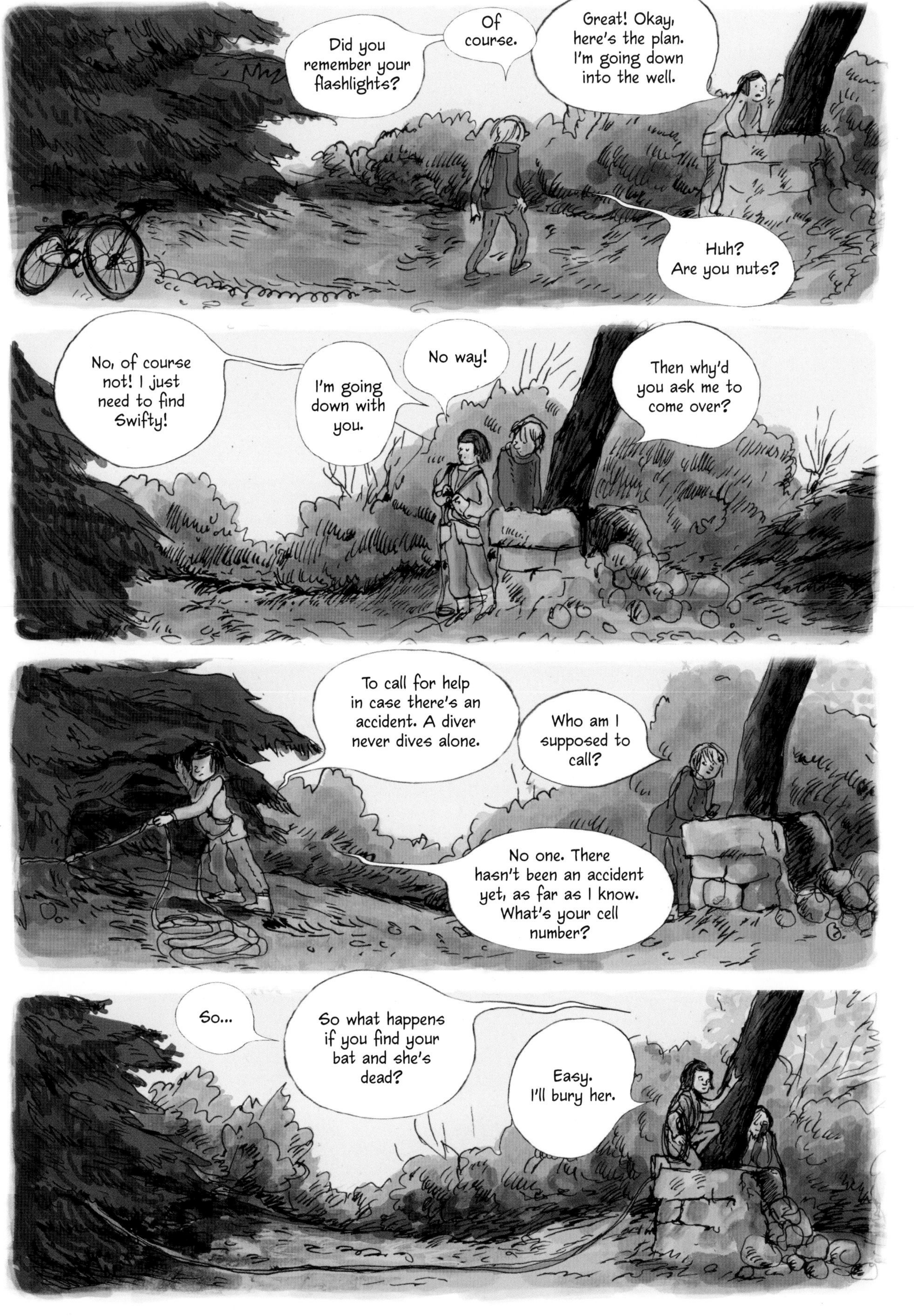
Did you remember your flashlights?
Of course.
Great! Okay, here's the plan. I'm going down into the well.
Huh? Are you nuts?
No, of course not! I just need to find Swifty!
I'm going down with you.
No way!
Then why'd you ask me to come over?
To call for help in case there's an accident. A diver never dives alone.
Who am I supposed to call?
No one. There hasn't been an accident yet, as far as I know. What's your cell number?
So...
So what happens if you find your bat and she's dead?
Easy. I'll bury her.

Enid's parents were never buried. Their car caught fire in the accident, and they were charred to a crisp. There are no bodies beneath the headstone that bears their name.

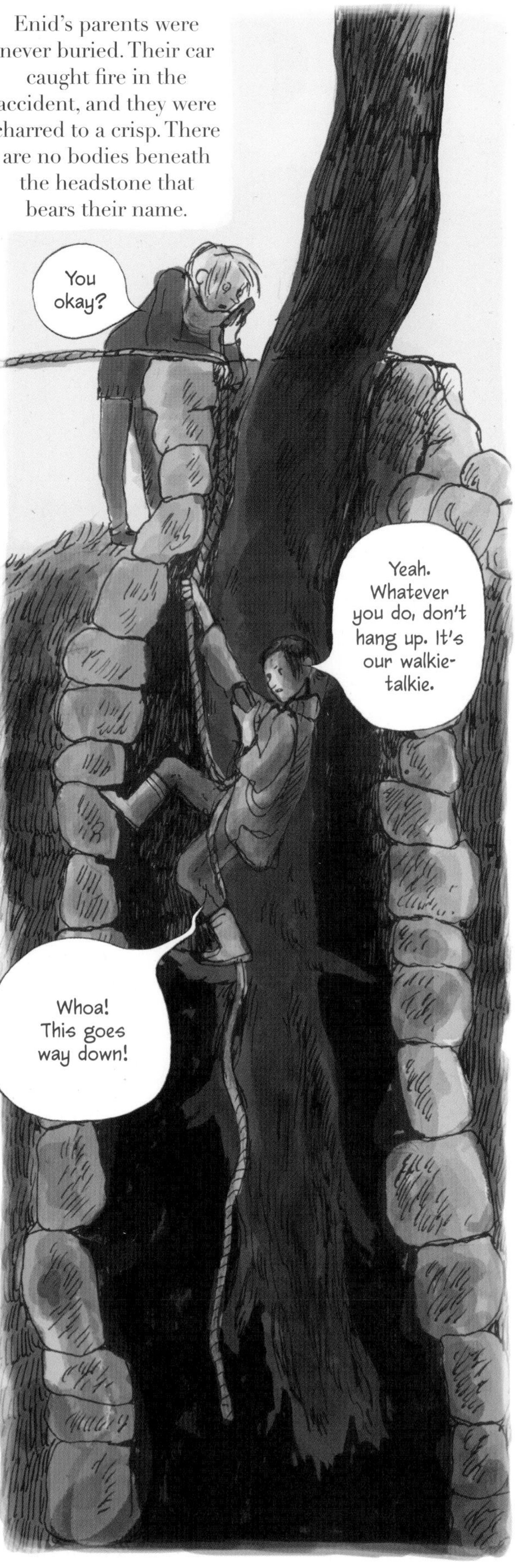
You okay?
Yeah. Whatever you do, don't hang up. It's our walkie-talkie.
Whoa! This goes way down!

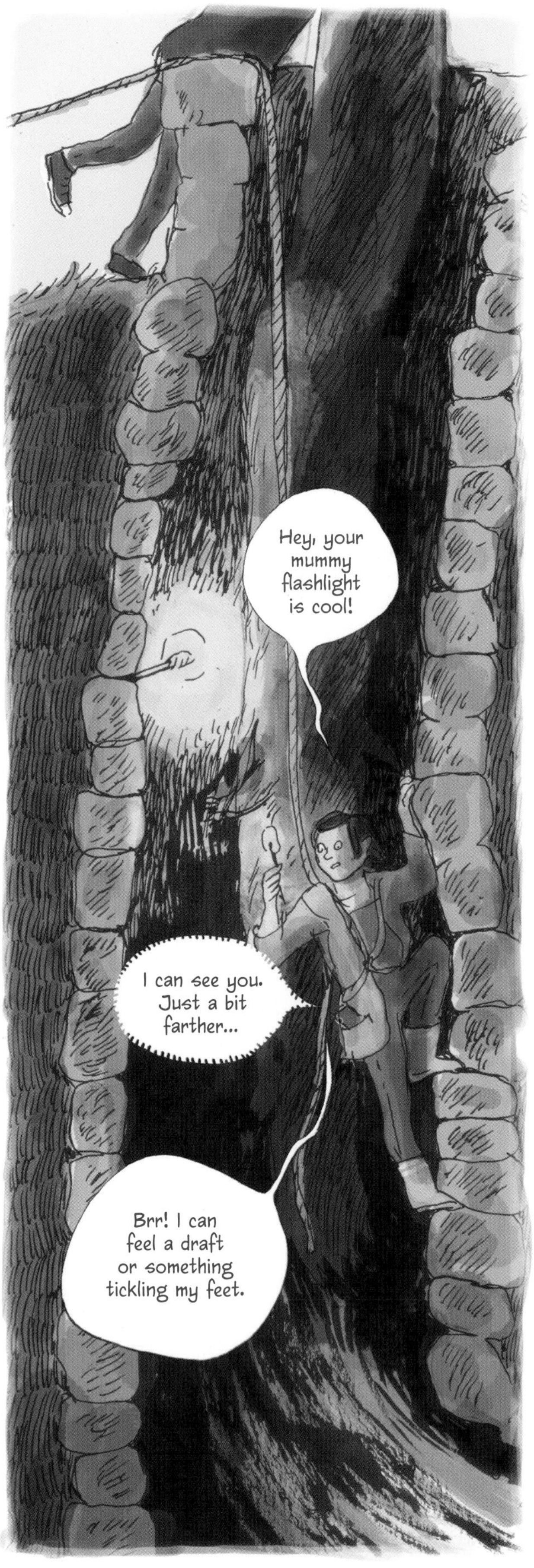
Hey, your mummy flashlight is cool!
I can see you. Just a bit farther...
Brr! I can feel a draft or something tickling my feet.

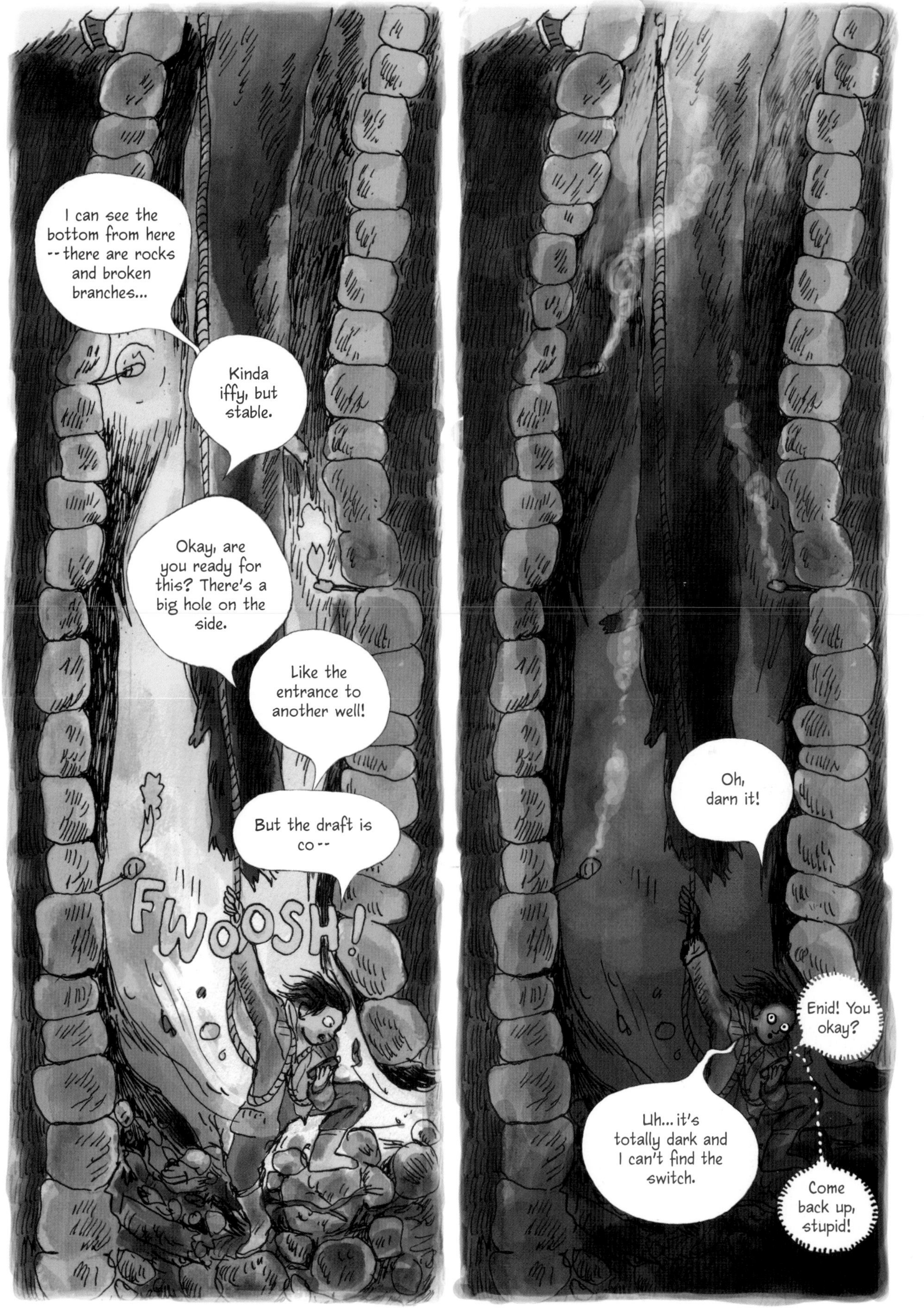
I can see the bottom from here --there are rocks and broken branches...
Kinda iffy, but stable.
Okay, are you ready for this? There's a big hole on the side.
Like the entrance to another well!
But the draft is co--
FWOOSH!
Oh, darn it!
Enid! You okay?
Uh... it's totally dark and I can't find the switch.
Come back up, stupid!

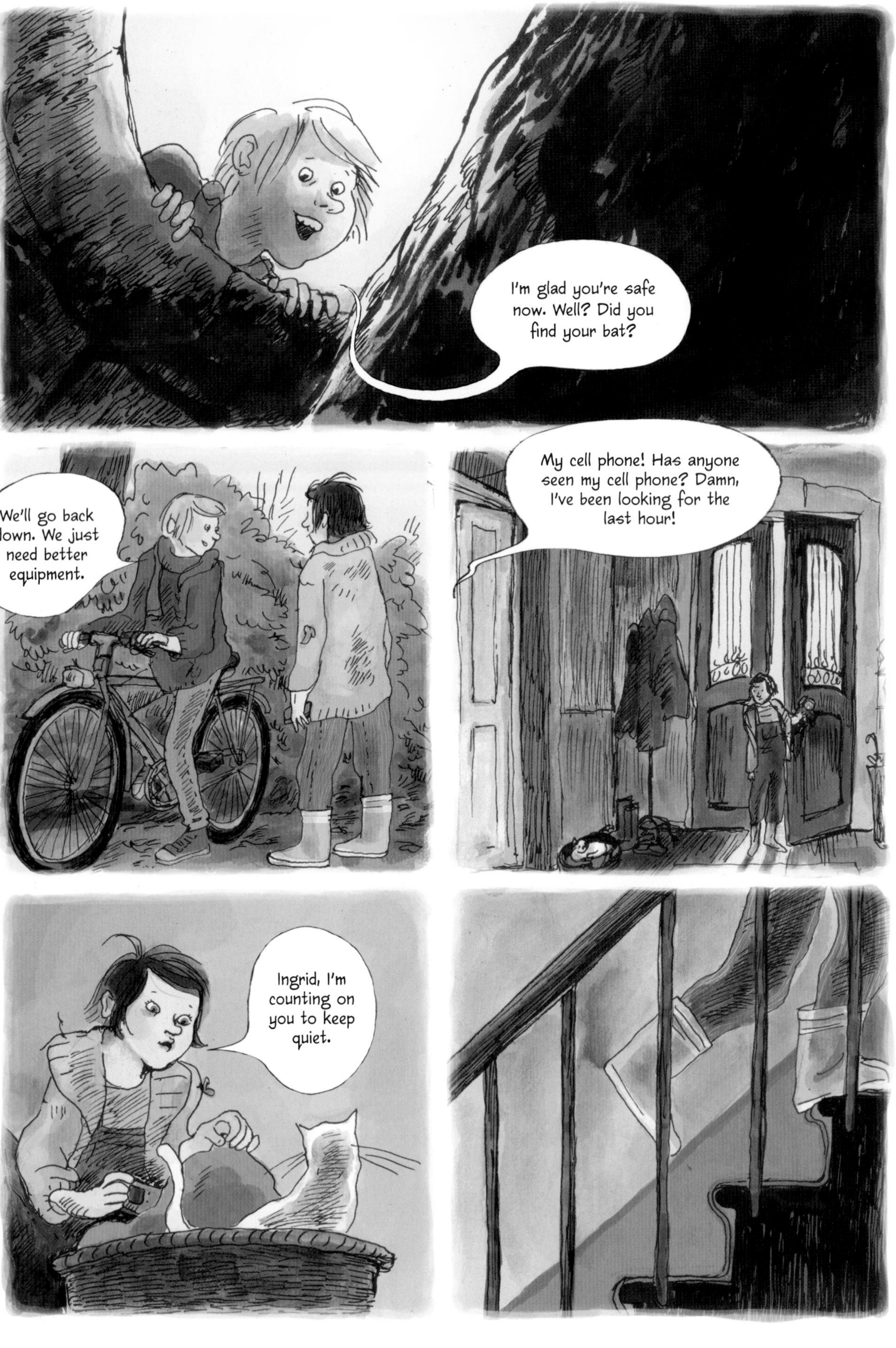
I'm glad you're safe now. Well? Did you find your bat?
We'll go back down. We just need better equipment.
My cell phone! Has anyone seen my cell phone? Damn, I've been looking for the last hour!
Ingrid, I'm counting on you to keep quiet.

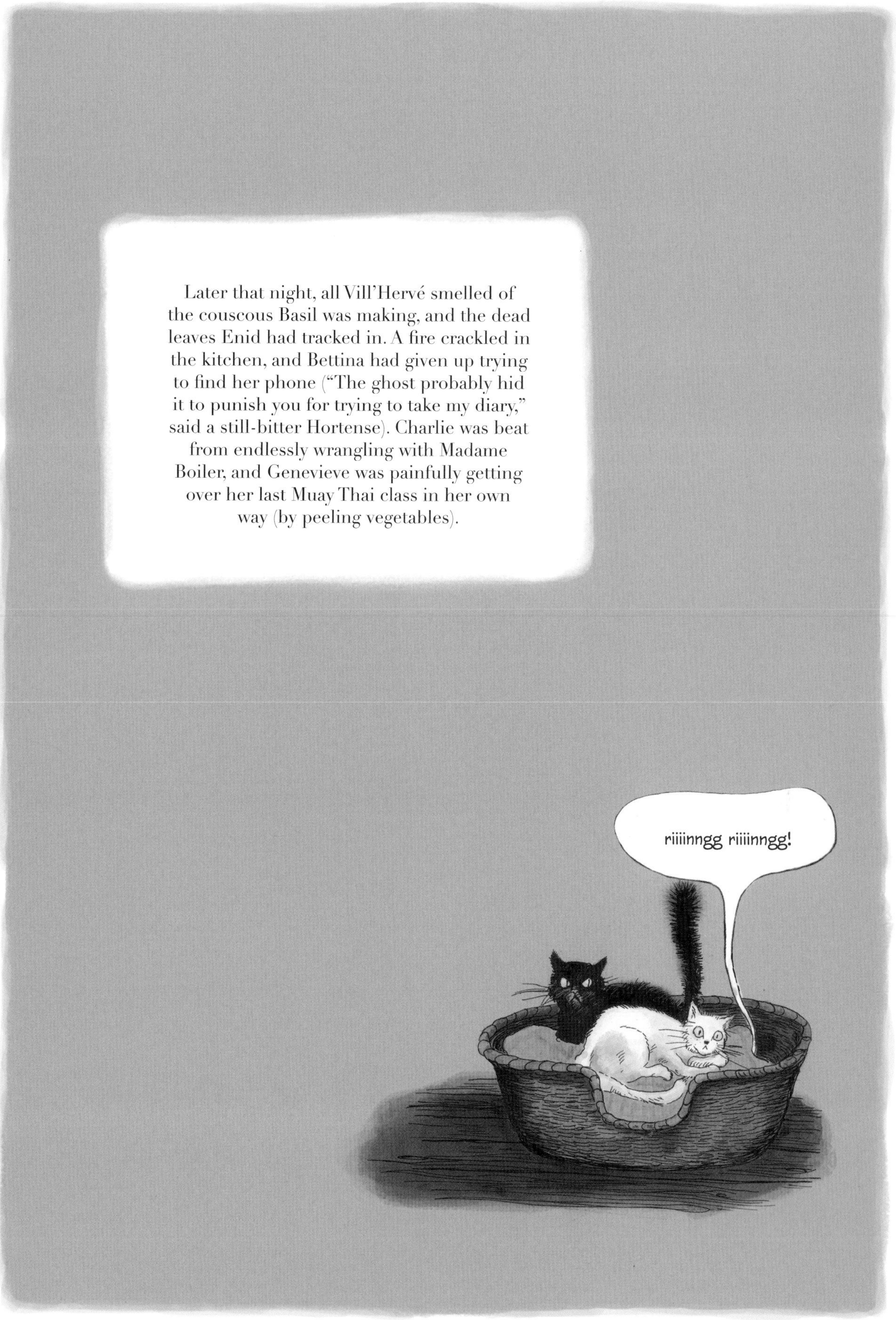
Later that night, all Vill'Hervé smelled of the couscous Basil was making, and the dead leaves Enid had tracked in. A fire crackled in the kitchen, and Bettina had given up trying to find her phone ("The ghost probably hid it to punish you for trying to take my diary," said a still-bitter Hortense). Charlie was beat from endlessly wrangling with Madame Boiler, and Genevieve was painfully getting over her last Muay Thai class in her own way (by peeling vegetables).
riiiinngg riiiinngg!

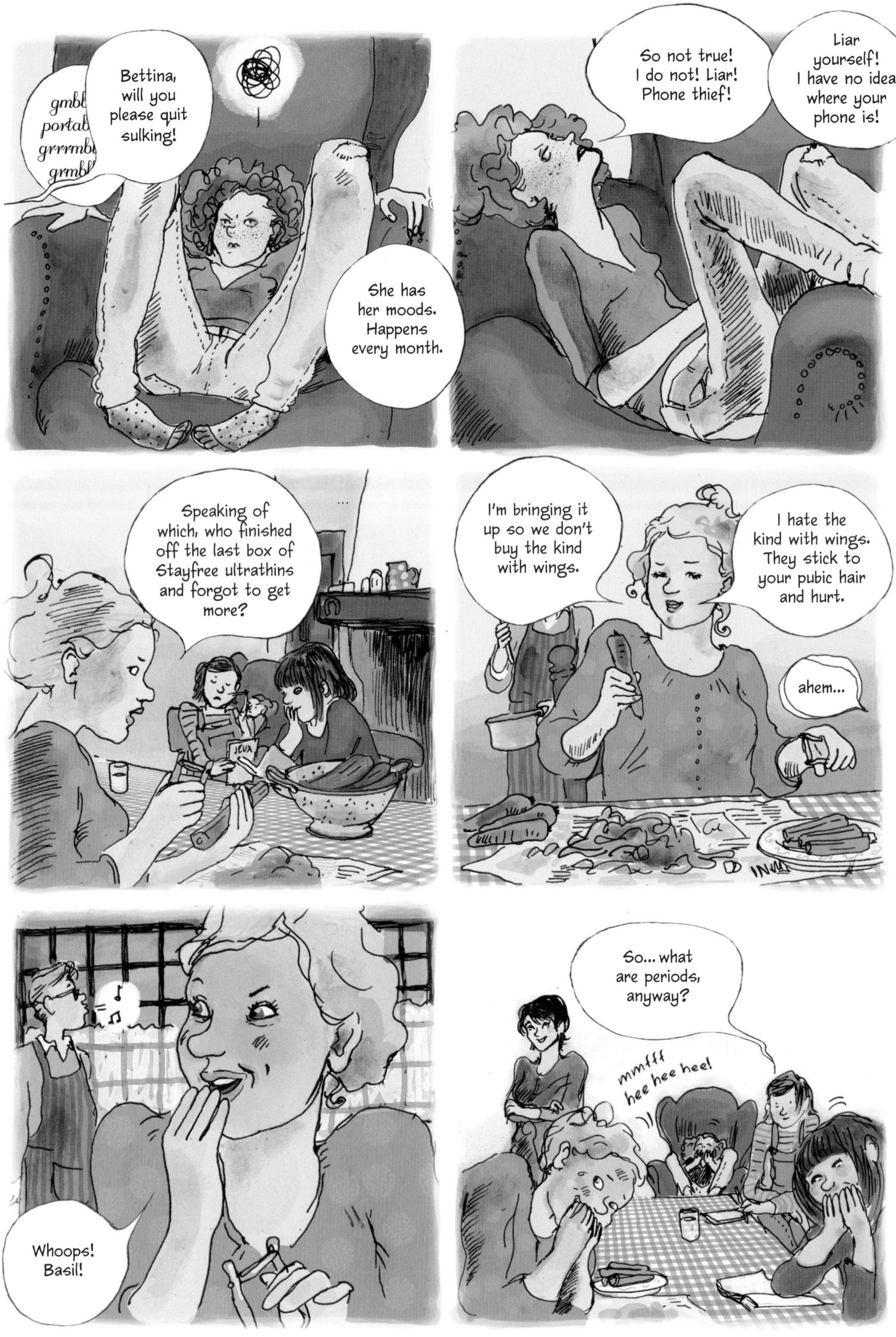
gmbl portab grrrmbl grmbl
Bettina, will you please quit sulking!
She has her moods. Happens every month.
So not true! I do not! Liar! Phone thief!
Liar yourself! I have no idea where your phone is!
Speaking of which, who finished off the last box of Stayfree ultrathins and forgot to get more?
JEUX
I'm bringing it up so we don't buy the kind with wings.
I hate the kind with wings. They stick to your pubic hair and hurt.
ahem...
Whoops! Basil!
So... what are periods, anyway?
mmfff hee hee hee!

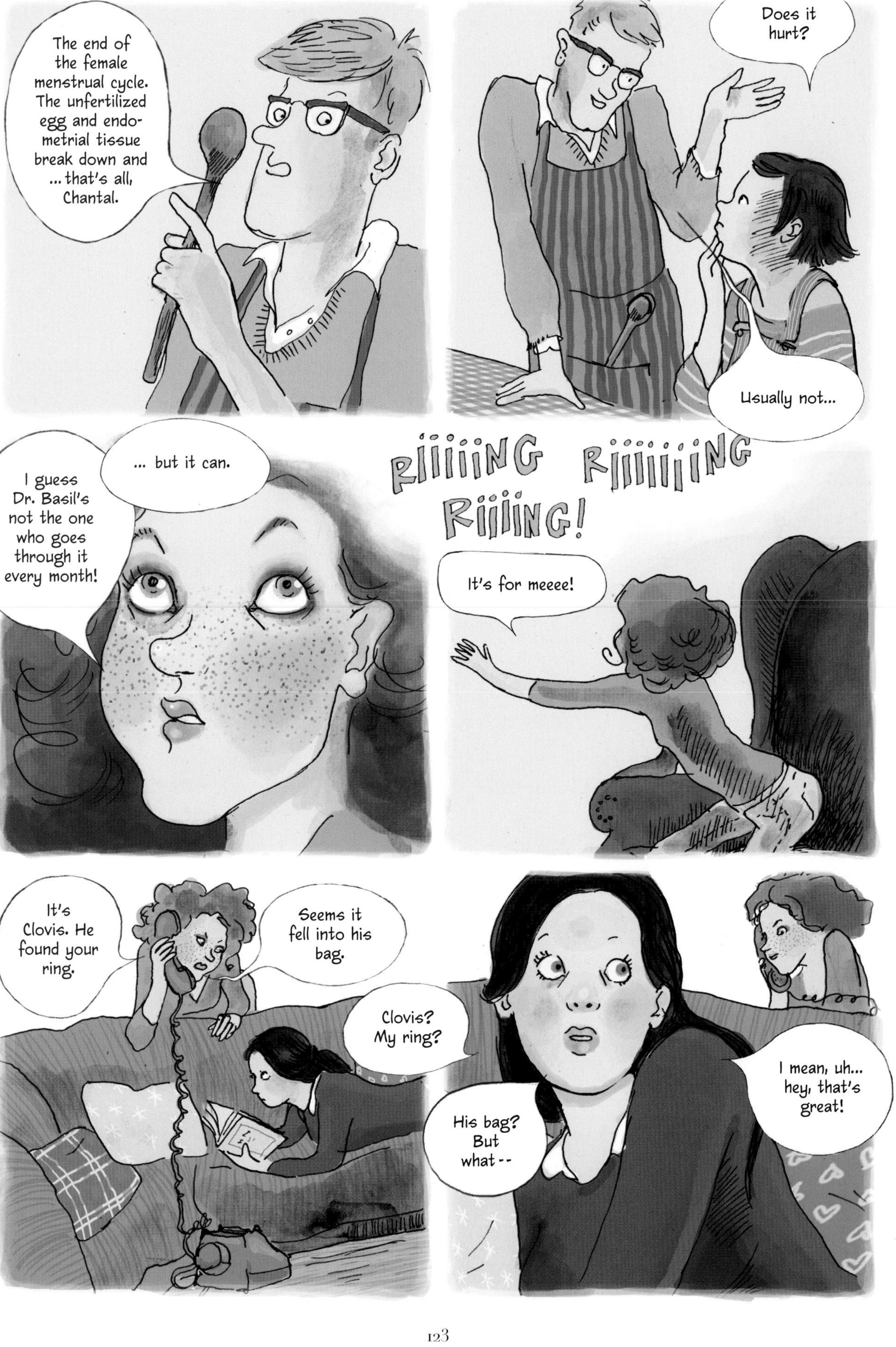
The end of the female menstrual cycle. The unfertilized egg and endo-metrial tissue break down and ...that's all, Chantal.
Does it hurt?
Usually not...
... but it can.
I guess Dr. Basil's not the one who goes through it every month!
RIIIIING RIIIIIIING RIIING!
It's for meeee!
It's Clovis. He found your ring.
Seems it fell into his bag.
Clovis? My ring?
His bag? But what--
I mean, uh... hey, that's great!

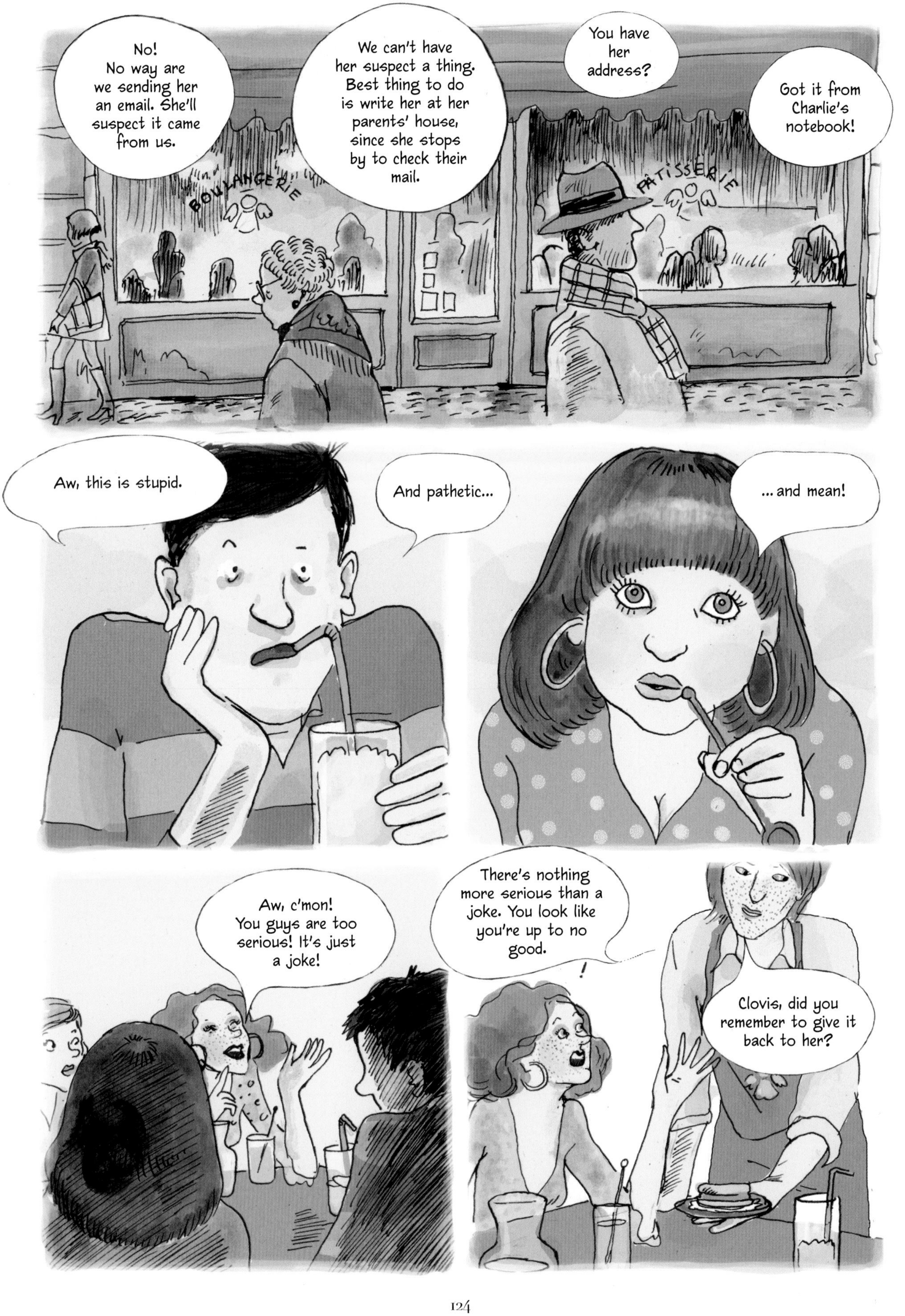
No! No way are we sending her an email. She'll suspect it came from us.
We can't have her suspect a thing. Best thing to do is write her at her parents' house, since she stops by to check their mail.
BOULANGERIE
You have her address?
PÂTISSERIE
Got it from Charlie's notebook!
Aw, this is stupid.
And pathetic...
...and mean!
Aw, c'mon! You guys are too serious! It's just a joke!
There's nothing more serious than a joke. You look like you're up to no good.
!
Clovis, did you remember to give it back to her?

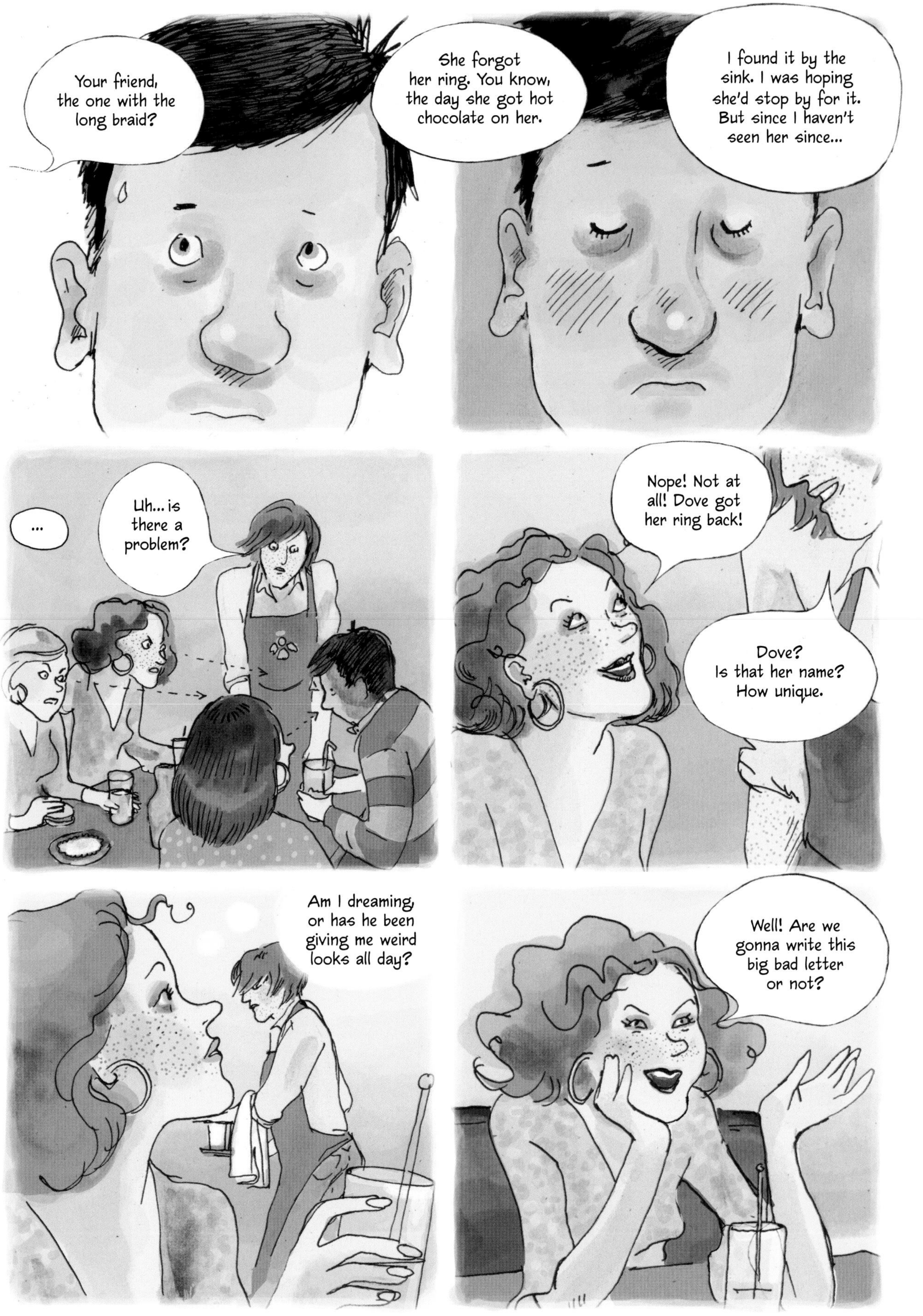
Your friend, the one with the long braid?
She forgot her ring. You know, the day she got hot chocolate on her.
I found it by the sink. I was hoping she'd stop by for it. But since I haven't seen her since...
...
Uh... is there a problem?
Nope! Not at all! Dove got her ring back!
Dove? Is that her name? How unique.
Am I dreaming, or has he been giving me weird looks all day?
Well! Are we gonna write this big bad letter or not?

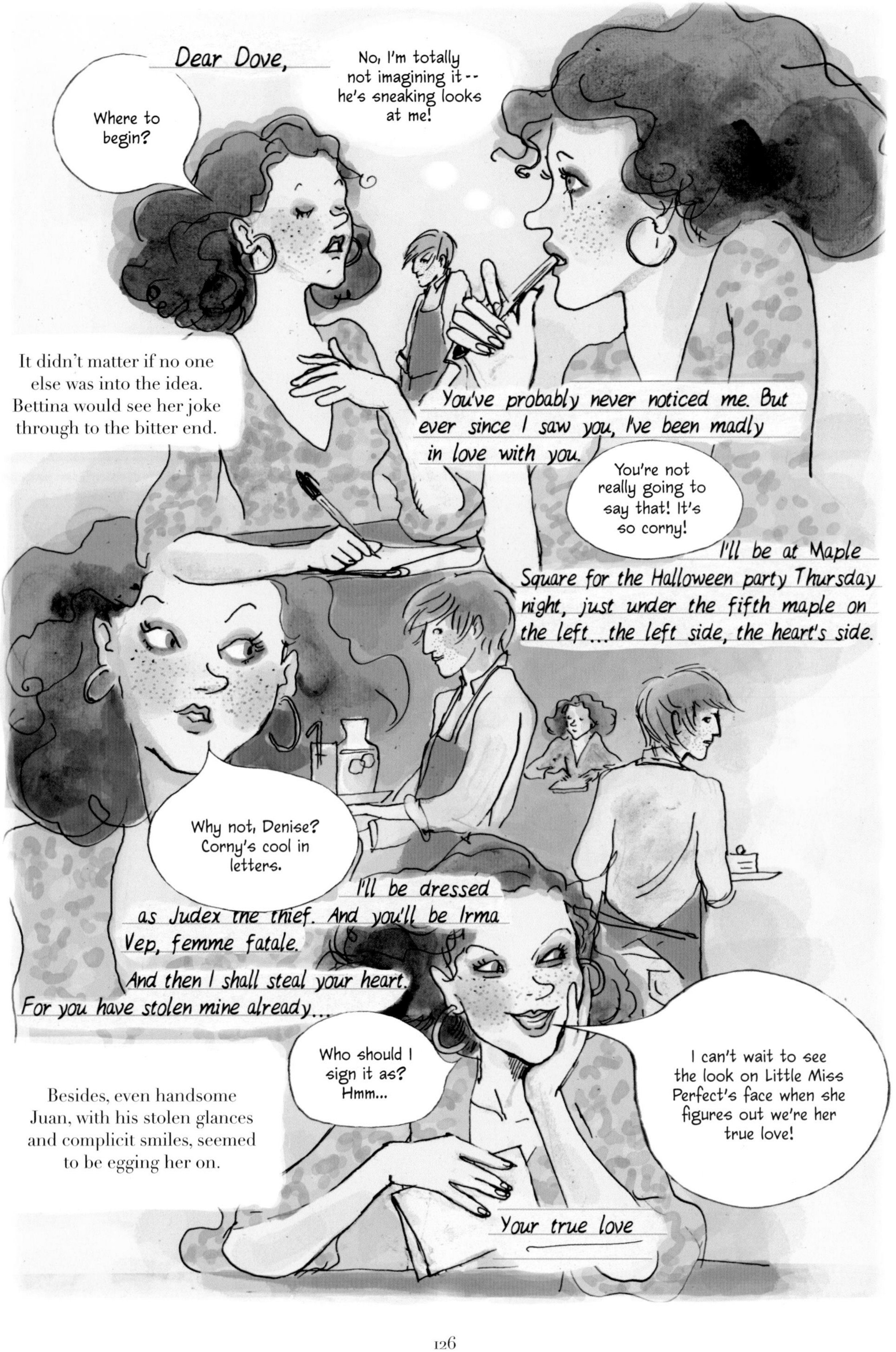

Dear Dove,
Where to begin?
No, I'm totally not imagining it -- he's sneaking looks at me!
It didn't matter if no one else was into the idea. Bettina would see her joke through to the bitter end.
You've probably never noticed me. But ever since I saw you, I've been madly in love with you.
You're not really going to say that! It's so corny!
I'll be at Maple Square for the Halloween party Thursday night, just under the fifth maple on the left...the left side, the heart's side.
Why not, Denise? Corny's cool in letters.
I'll be dressed as Judex the thief. And you'll be Irma Vep, femme fatale.
And then I shall steal your heart.
For you have stolen mine already...
Besides, even handsome Juan, with his stolen glances and complicit smiles, seemed to be egging her on.
Who should I sign it as? Hmm...
I can't wait to see the look on Little Miss Perfect's face when she figures out we're her true love!
Your true love

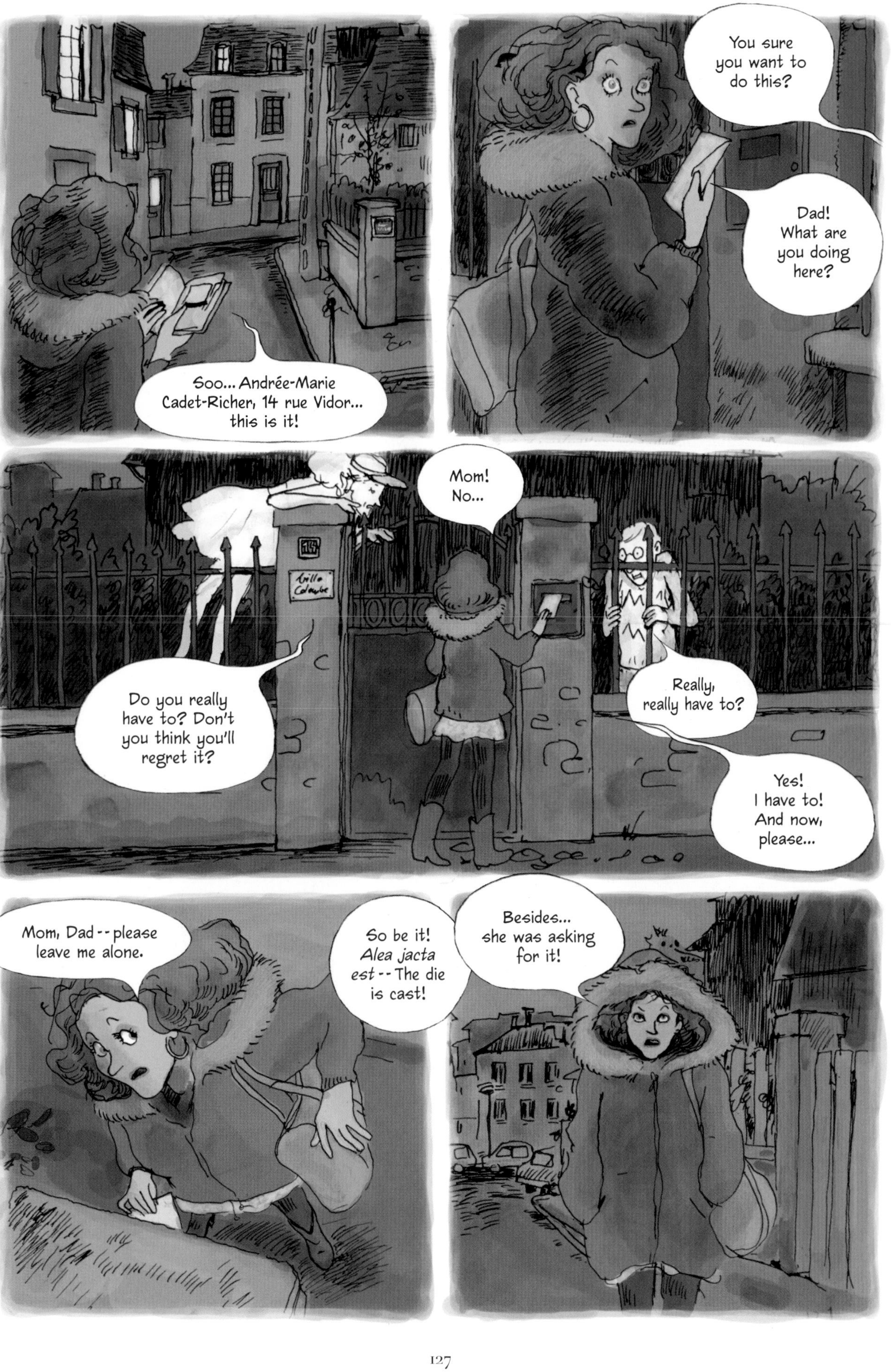
Soo... Andrée-Marie Cadet-Richer, 14 rue Vidor... this is it!
You sure you want to do this?
Dad! What are you doing here?
Mom! No...
Do you really have to? Don't you think you'll regret it?
Really, really have to?
Yes! I have to! And now, please...
Mom, Dad -- please leave me alone.
So be it! *Alea jacta est* -- The die is cast!
Besides... she was asking for it!

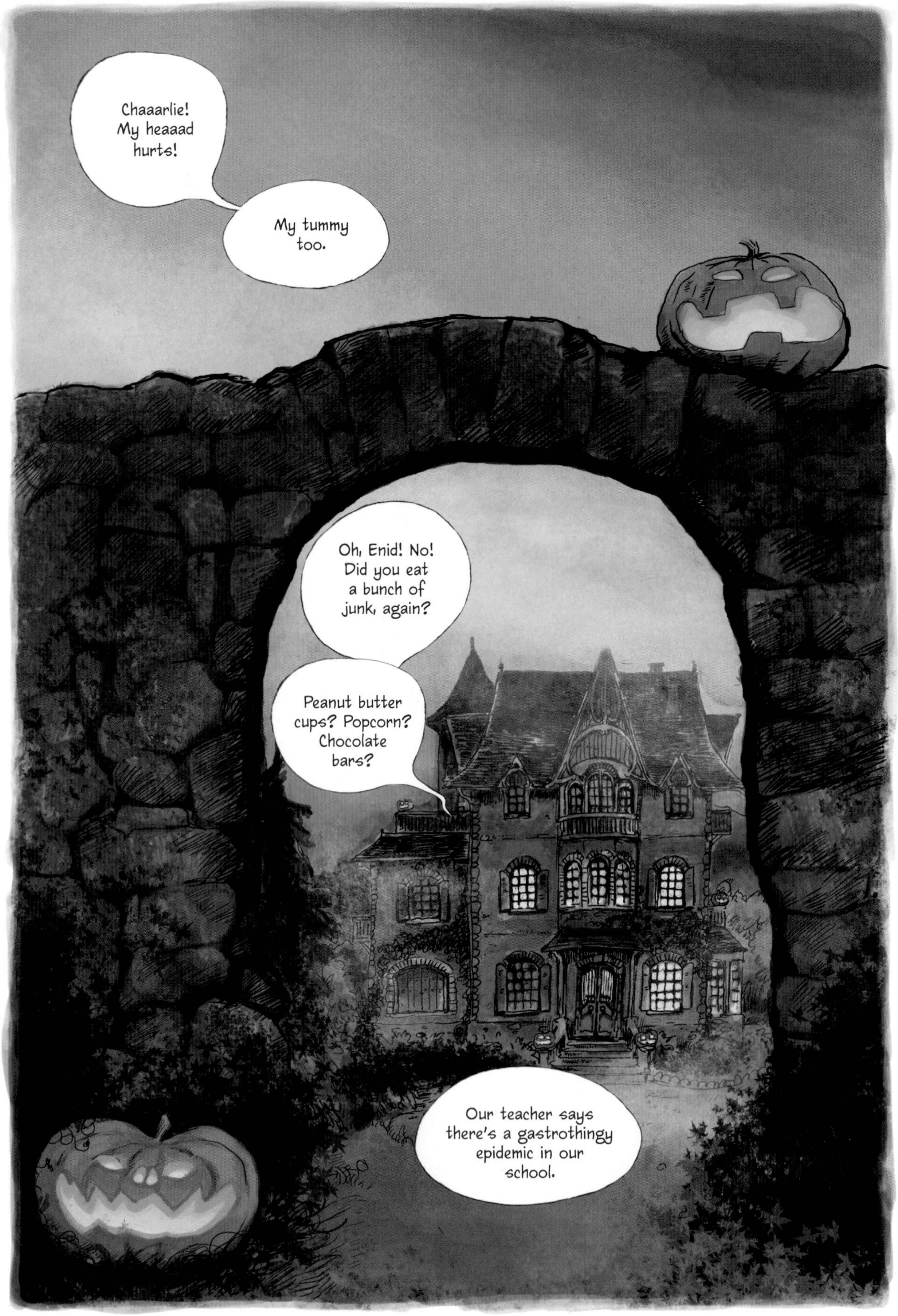
Chaaarlie! My heaaad hurts!
My tummy too.
Oh, Enid! No! Did you eat a bunch of junk, again?
Peanut butter cups? Popcorn? Chocolate bars?
Our teacher says there's a gastrothingy epidemic in our school.

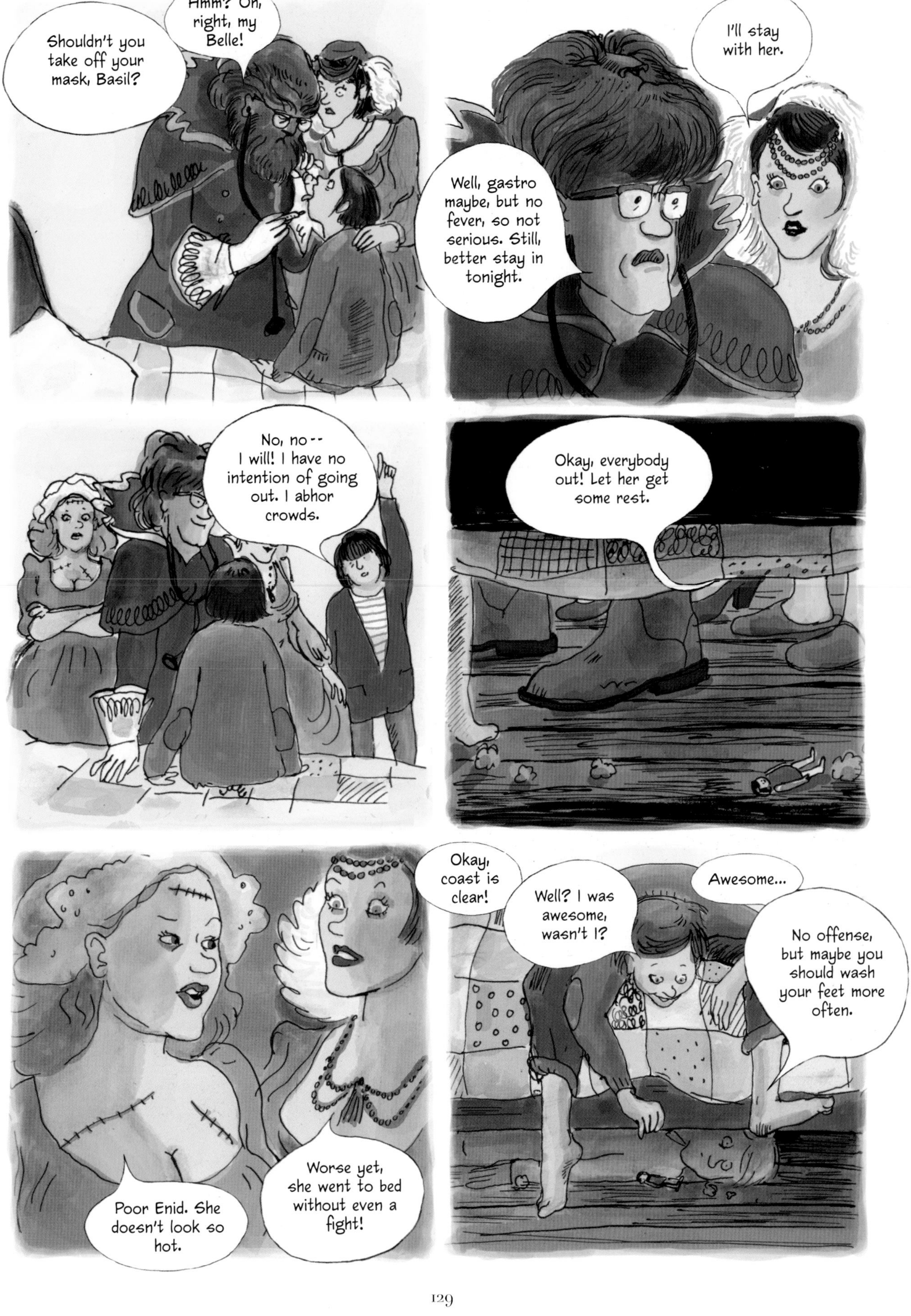

Shouldn't you take off your mask, Basil?
Hmm? Oh, right, my Belle!
I'll stay with her.
Well, gastro maybe, but no fever, so not serious. Still, better stay in tonight.
No, no -- I will! I have no intention of going out. I abhor crowds.
Okay, everybody out! Let her get some rest.
Poor Enid. She doesn't look so hot.
Worse yet, she went to bed without even a fight!
Okay, coast is clear!
Well? I was awesome, wasn't I?
Awesome...
No offense, but maybe you should wash your feet more often.

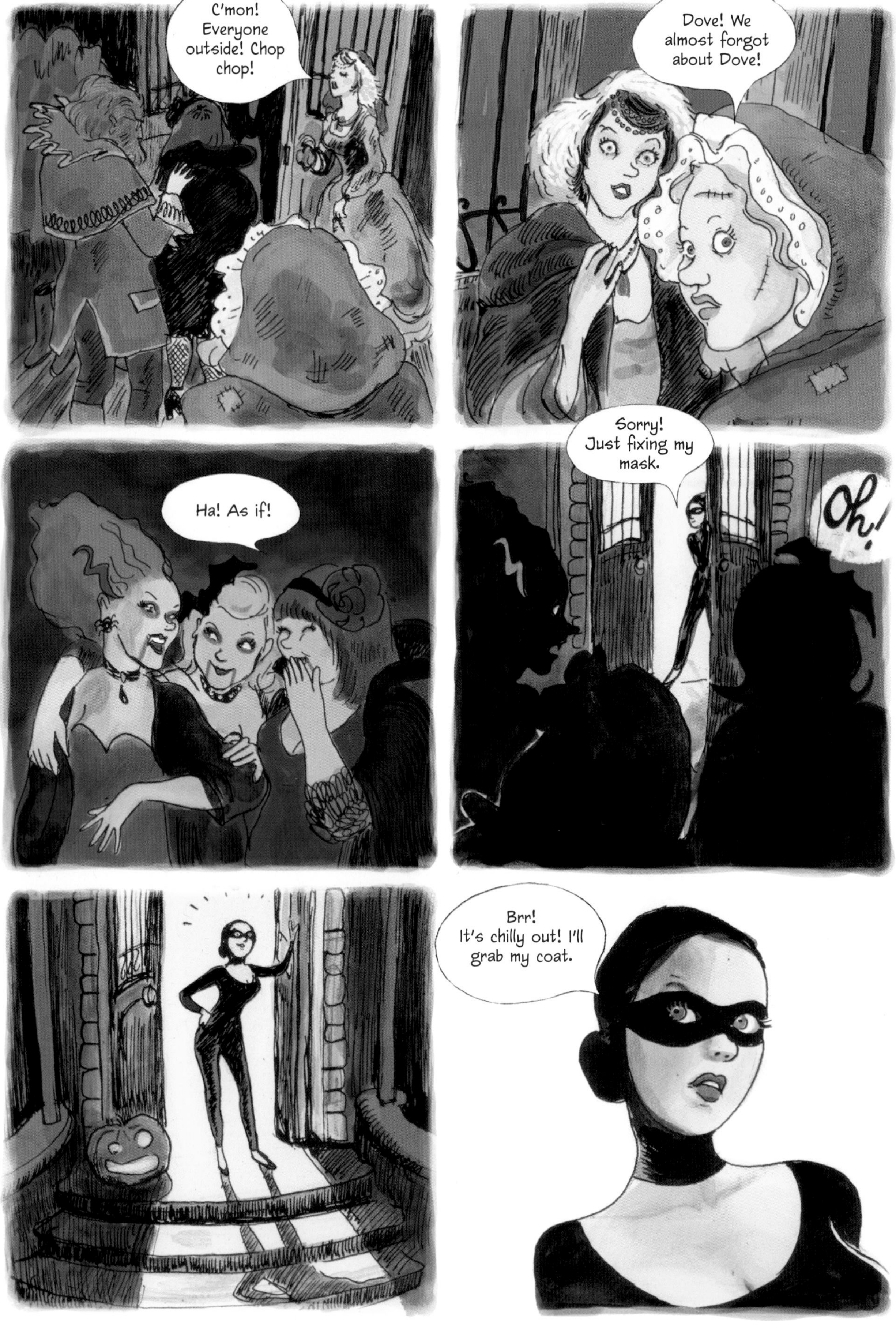
C'mon! Everyone outside! Chop chop!
Dove! We almost forgot about Dove!
Ha! As if!
Sorry! Just fixing my mask.
Oh!
Brr! It's chilly out! I'll grab my coat.

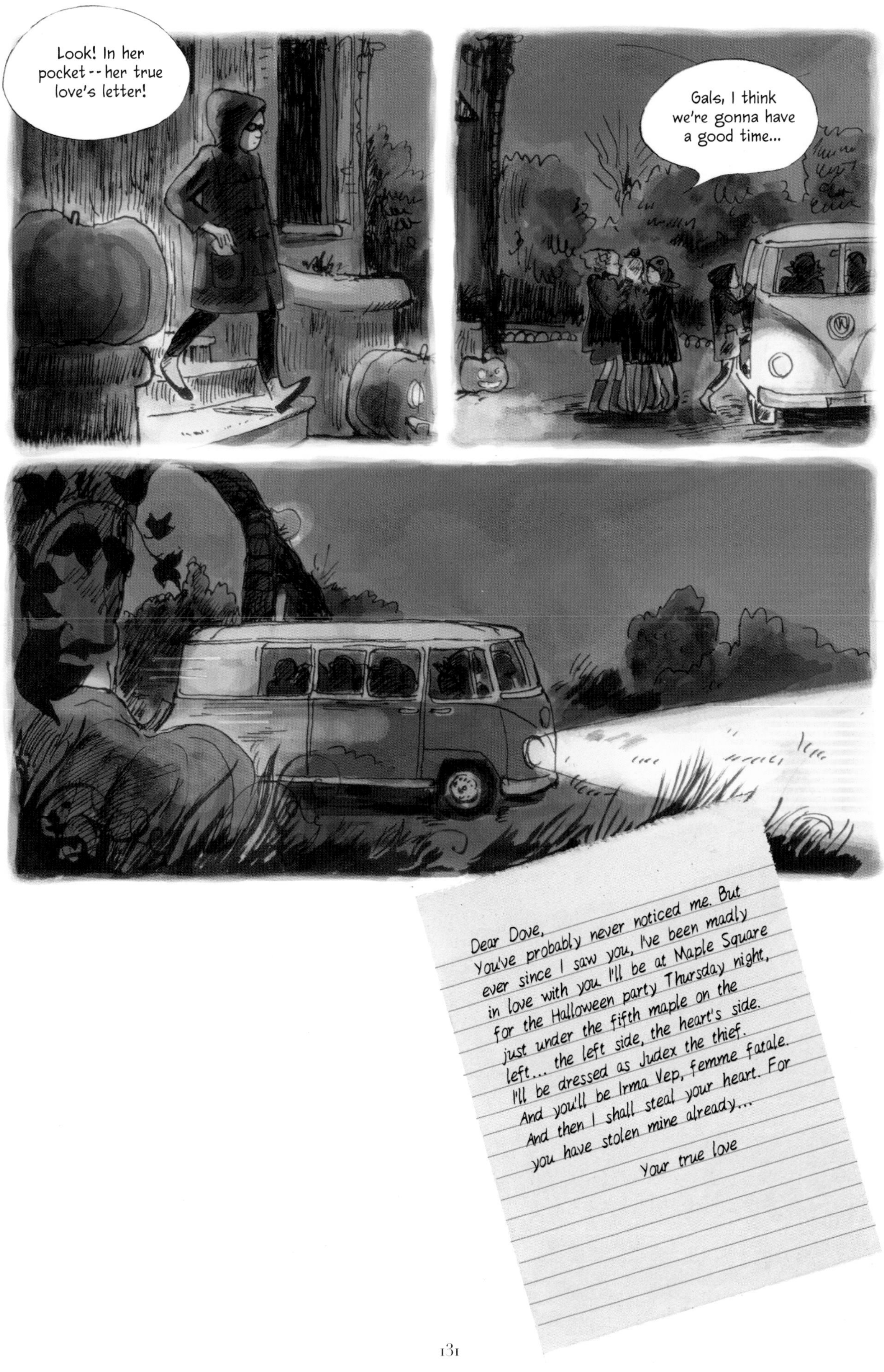
Look! In her pocket--her true love's letter!
Gals, I think we're gonna have a good time...
Dear Dove,
You've probably never noticed me. But ever since I saw you, I've been madly in love with you. I'll be at Maple Square for the Halloween party Thursday night, just under the fifth maple on the left... the left side, the heart's side. I'll be dressed as Judex the thief. And you'll be Irma Vep, femme fatale. And then I shall steal your heart. For you have stolen mine already...
Your true love

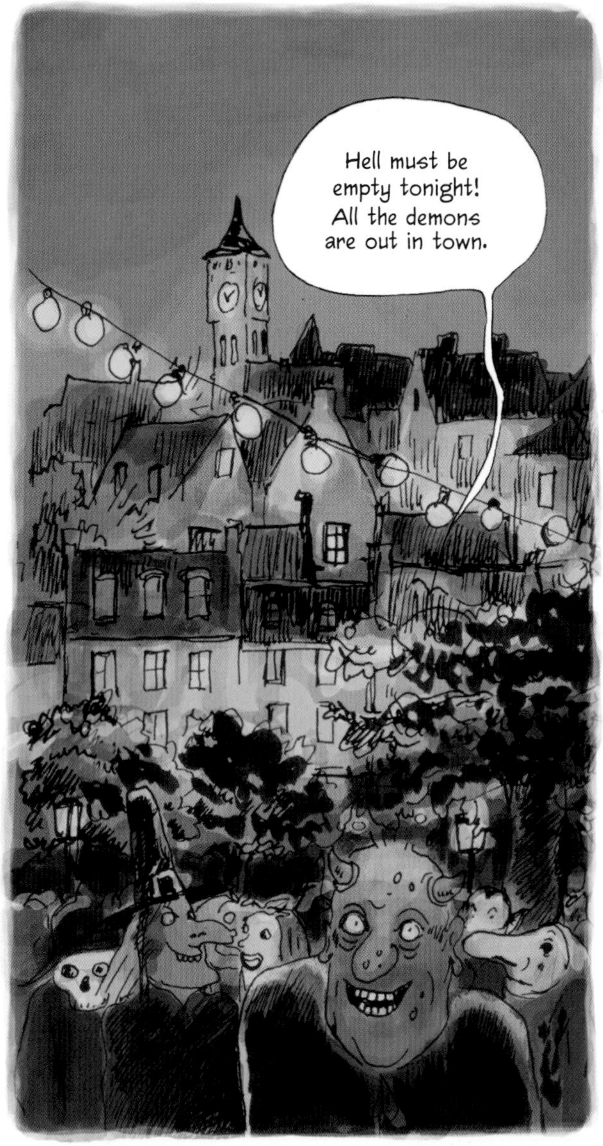
Hell must be empty tonight! All the demons are out in town.

All of them? Almost.... Deep in a half-collapsed well topped with a giant scallion, two little imps were hard at work.

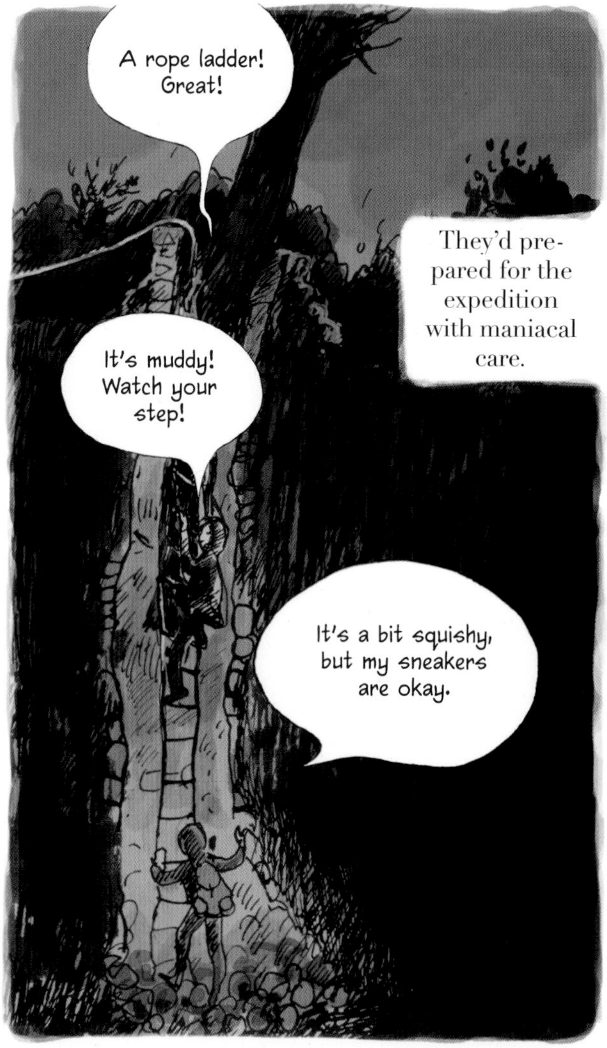
A rope ladder! Great!
They'd prepared for the expedition with maniacal care.
It's muddy! Watch your step!
It's a bit squishy, but my sneakers are okay.

In Gulliver's backpack were a battery-powered flashlight, ginger snaps, pound cake, a small bottle of water, leftover firecrackers from Bastille Day in case of emergency, a compass, and a box of band-aids.

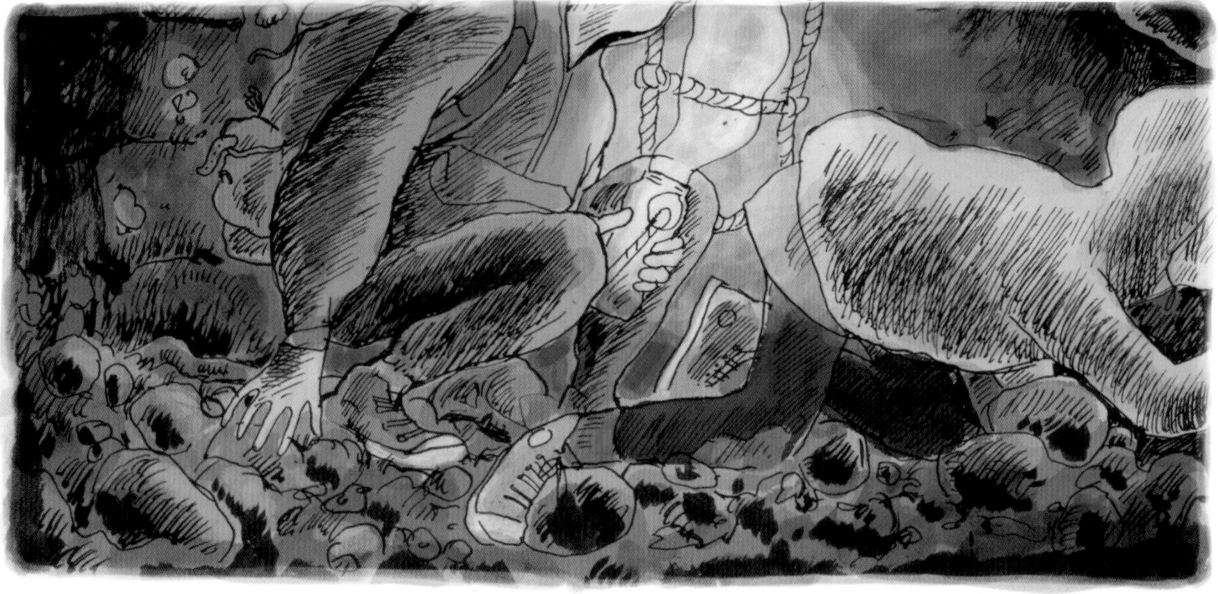

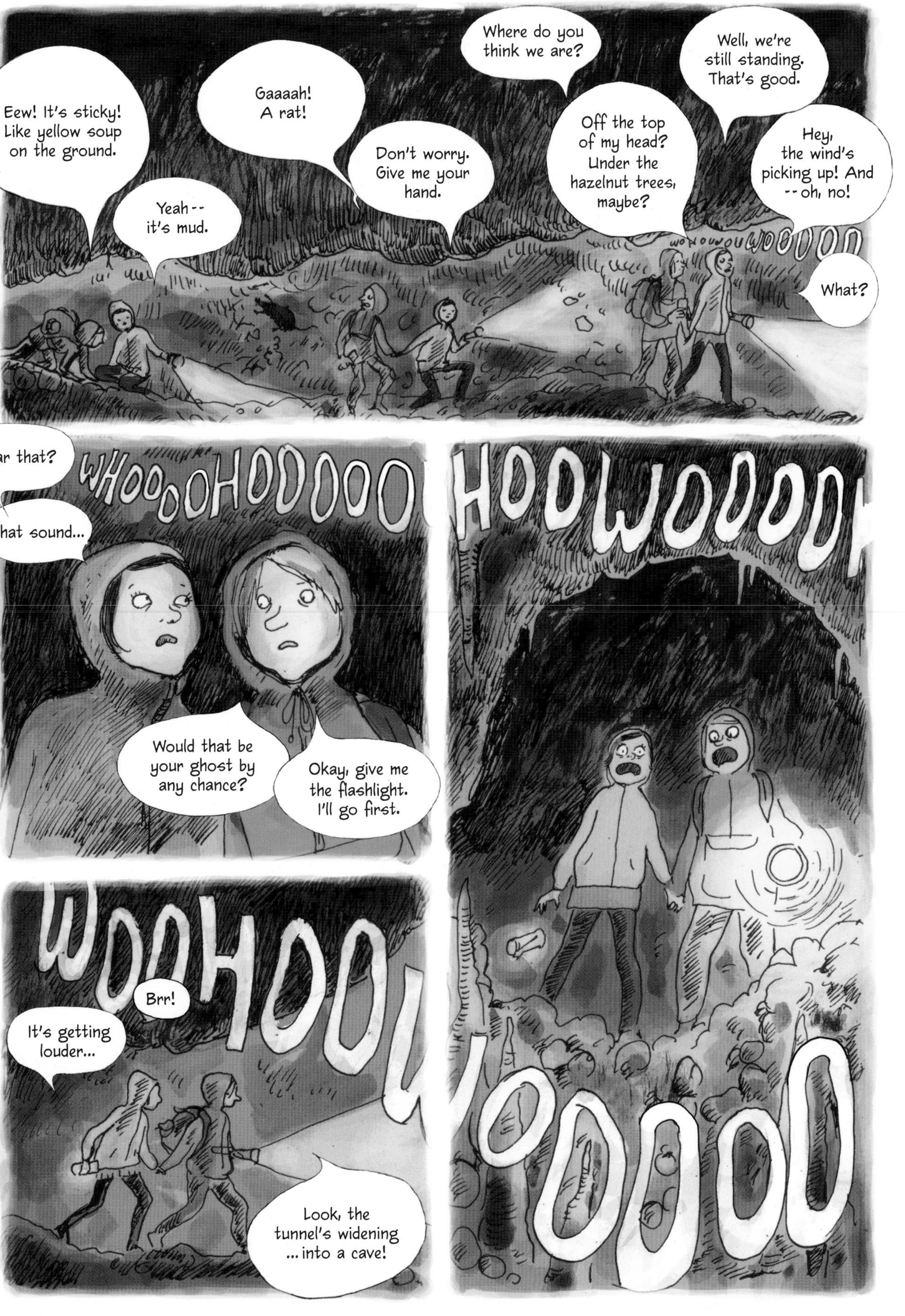
Eew! It's sticky! Like yellow soup on the ground.
Yeah -- it's mud.
Gaaaah! A rat!
Don't worry. Give me your hand.
Where do you think we are?
Off the top of my head? Under the hazelnut trees, maybe?
Well, we're still standing. That's good.
Hey, the wind's picking up! And -- oh, no!
What?
Hear that?
WHOOOOHOOOOO
That sound...
Would that be your ghost by any chance?
Okay, give me the flashlight. I'll go first.
HOOWOOOO
WOOHOOWOOOOOO
Brr!
It's getting louder...
Look, the tunnel's widening ...into a cave!

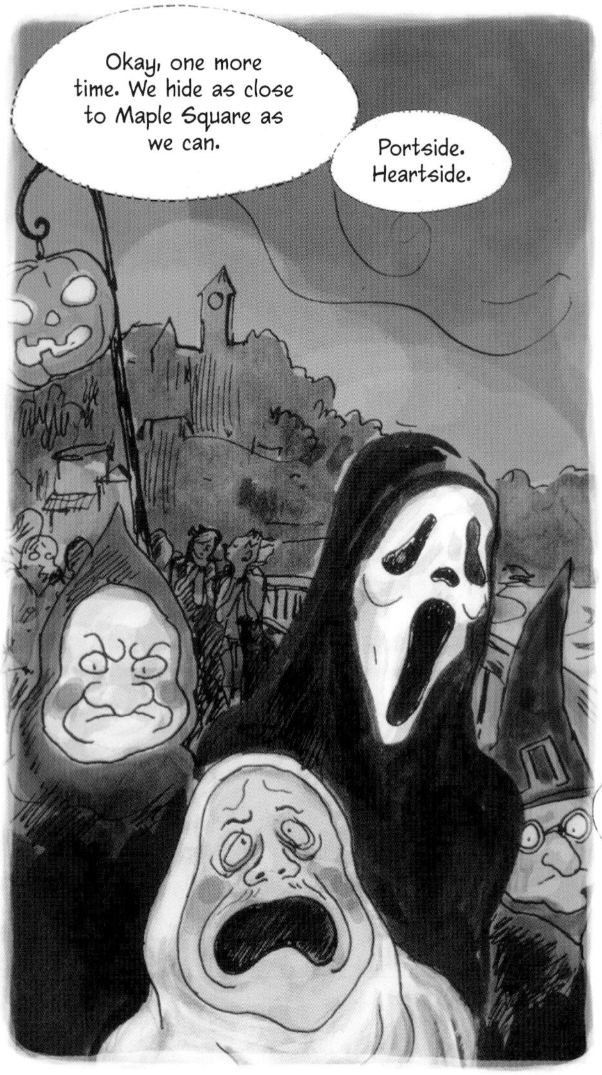
Okay, one more time. We hide as close to Maple Square as we can.
Portside. Heartside.

While Beauty and the Beast headed to the ball, unaware of all the other mischief underway, DB&B set out to ditch Dove and find Clovis, one Harry Potter out of about twenty-eight others at the party.

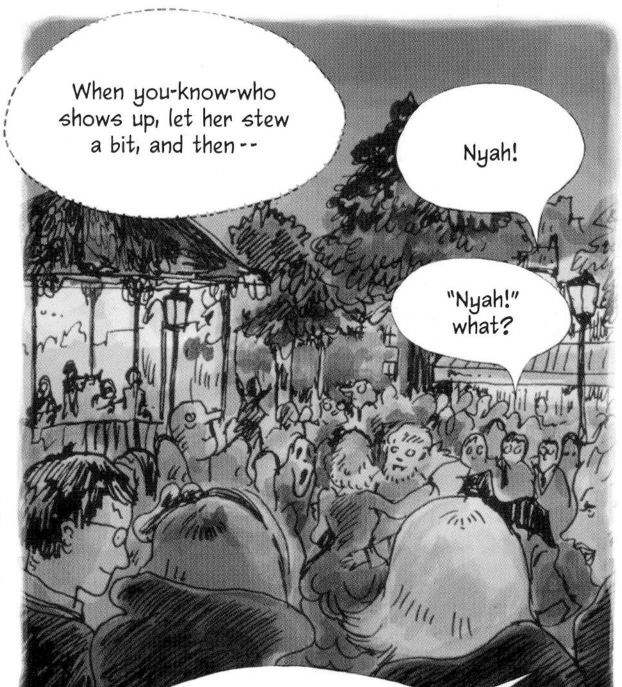
When you-know-who shows up, let her stew a bit, and then--
Nyah!
"Nyah!" what?

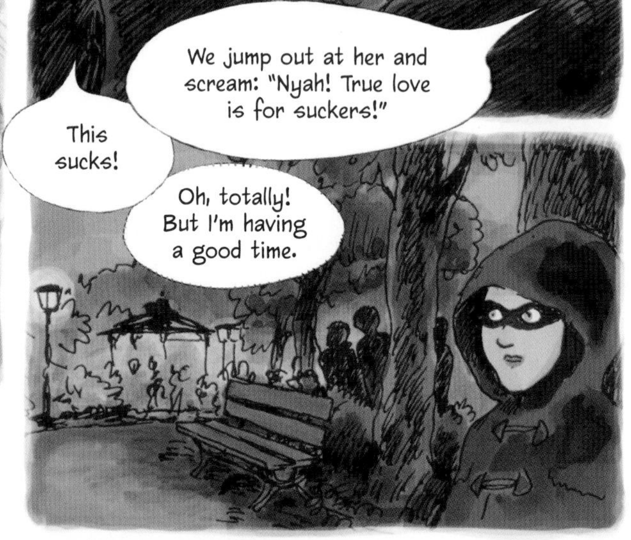
We jump out at her and scream: "Nyah! True love is for suckers!"
This sucks!
Oh, totally! But I'm having a good time.

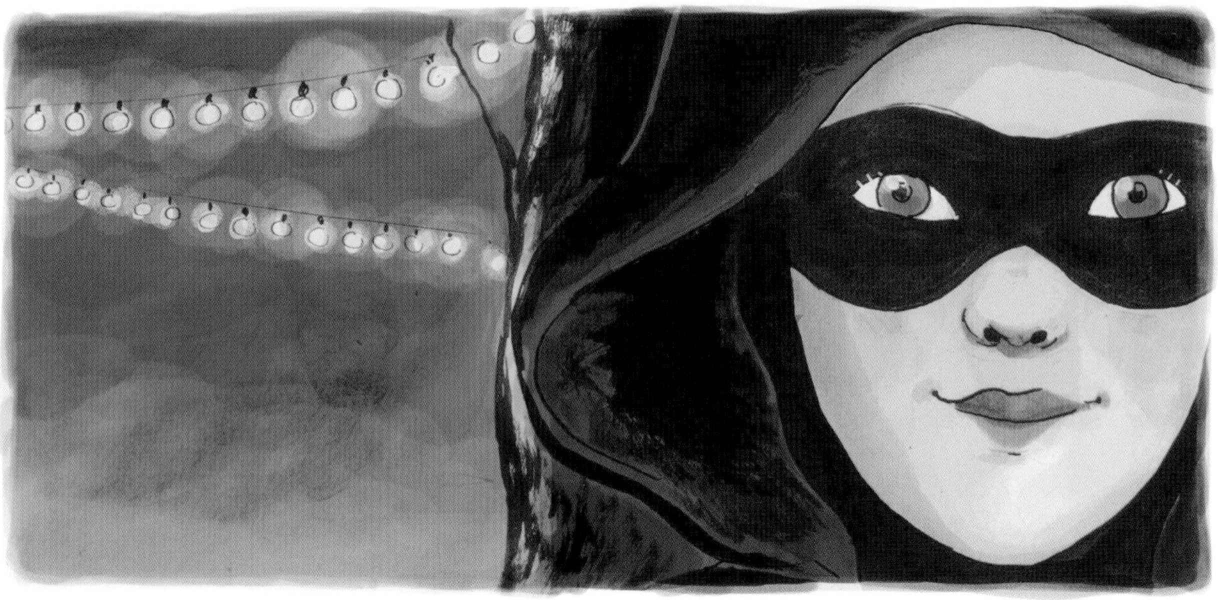

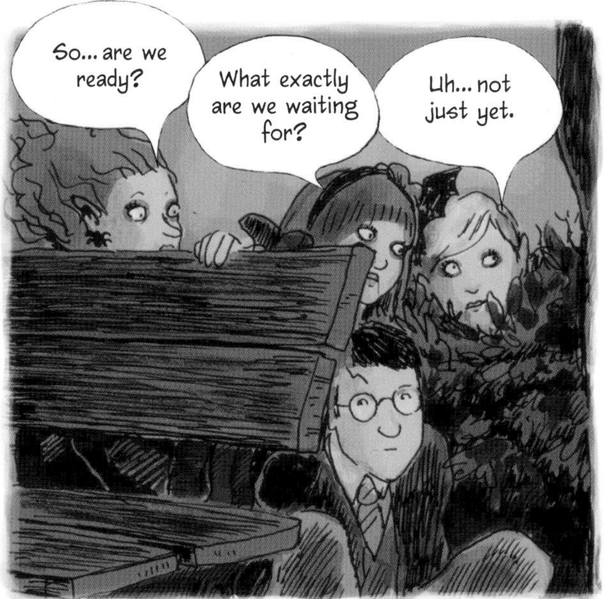
So... are we ready?
What exactly are we waiting for?
Uh... not just yet.

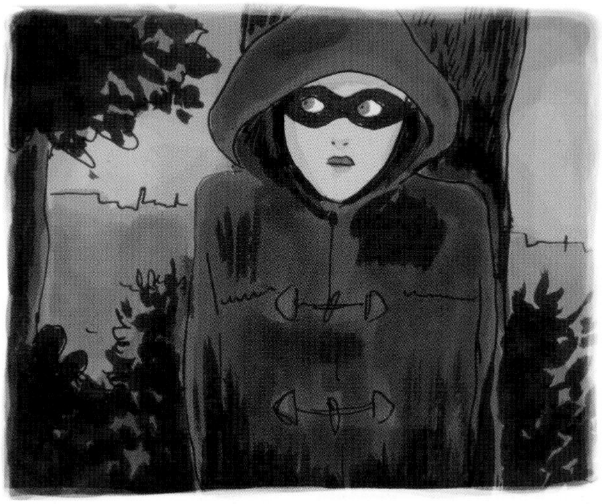

When? No one knew. They felt foolish all of a sudden, wondering if they shouldn't just hightail it out of there. But no one dared say so, of course.

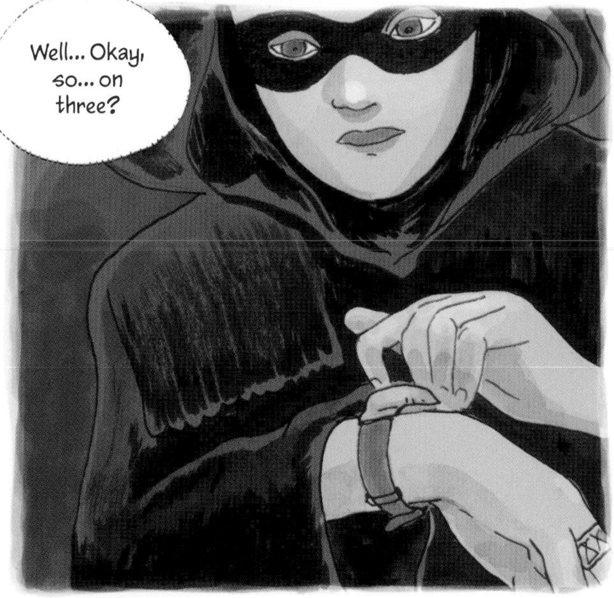
Well... Okay, so... on three?

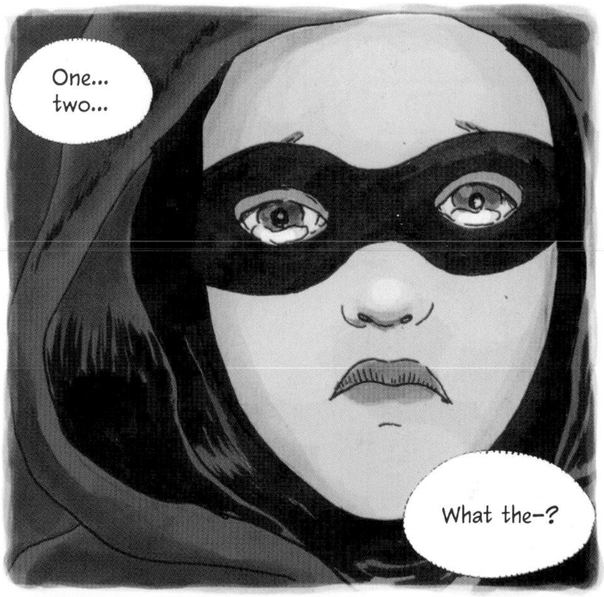
One... two...
What the-?

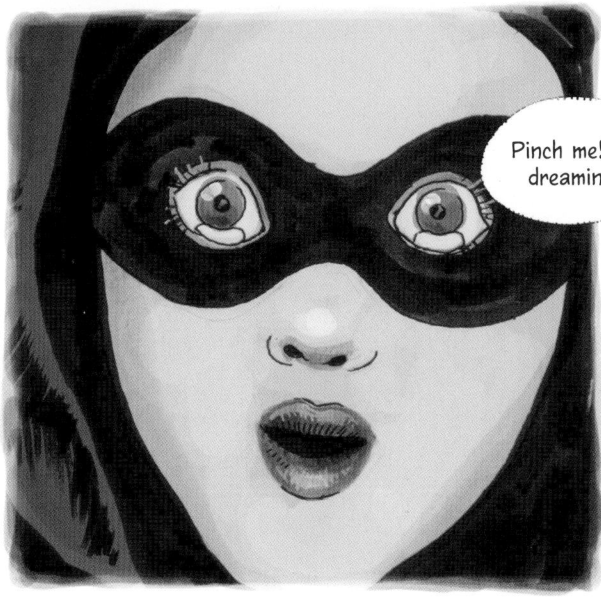
Pinch me! I'm dreaming!

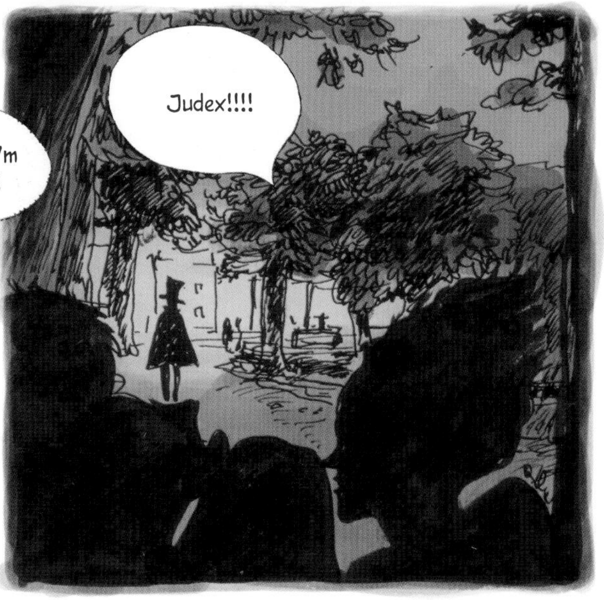
Judex!!!!

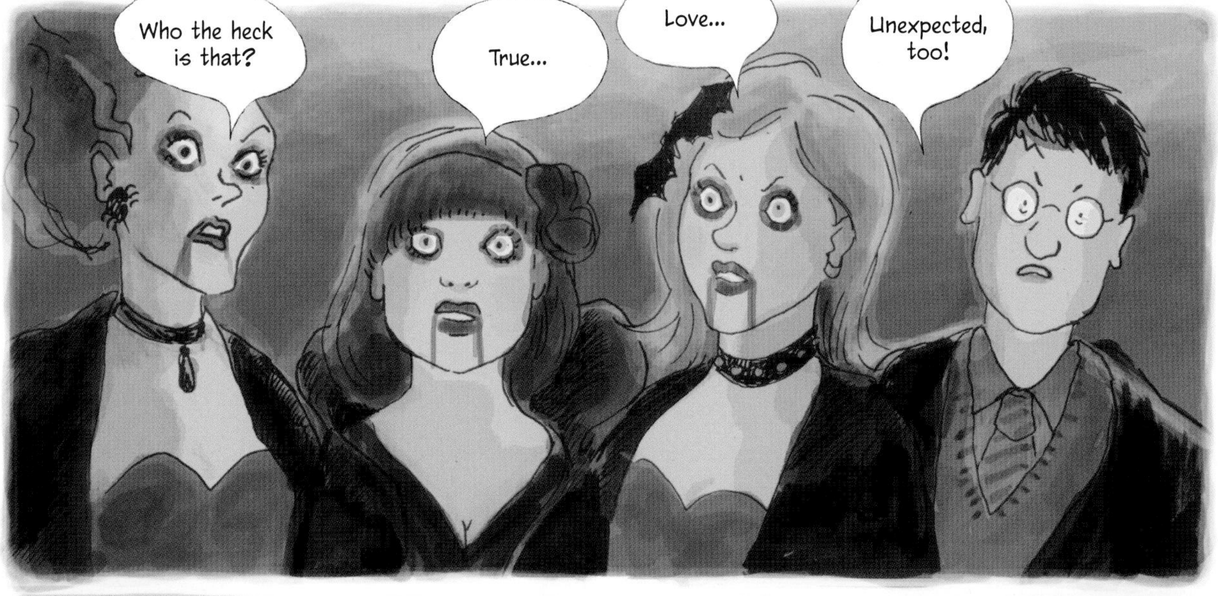
Who the heck is that?
True...
Love...
Unexpected, too!

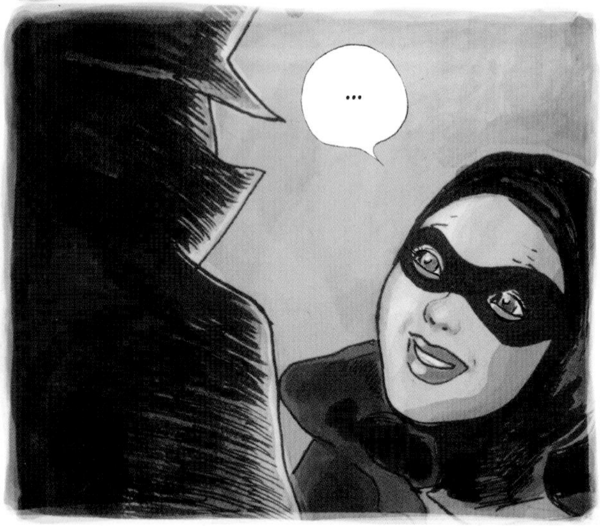
...

None of them found words for the happiness that shone unabashed from Dove's face just then.

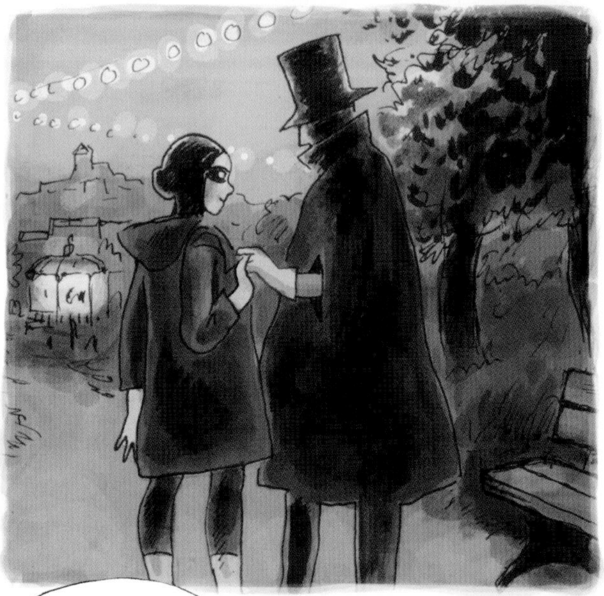

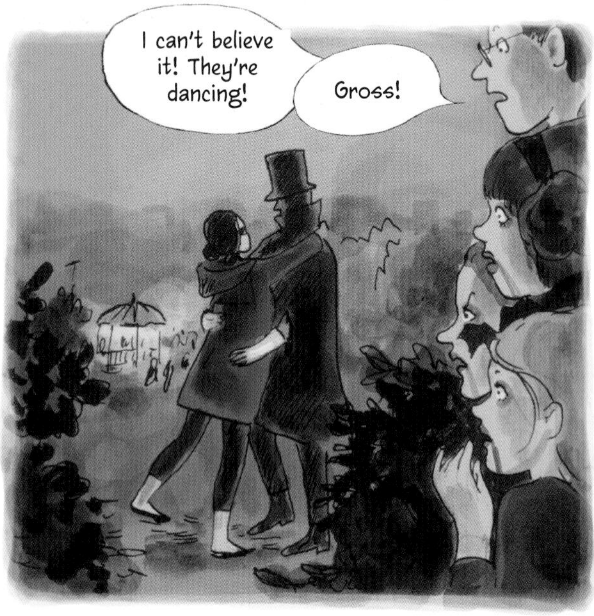
I can't believe it! They're dancing!
Gross!

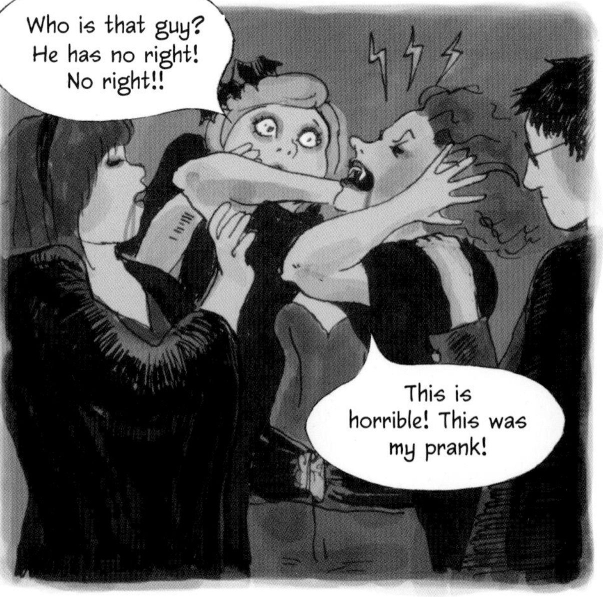
Who is that guy? He has no right! No right!!
This is horrible! This was my prank!

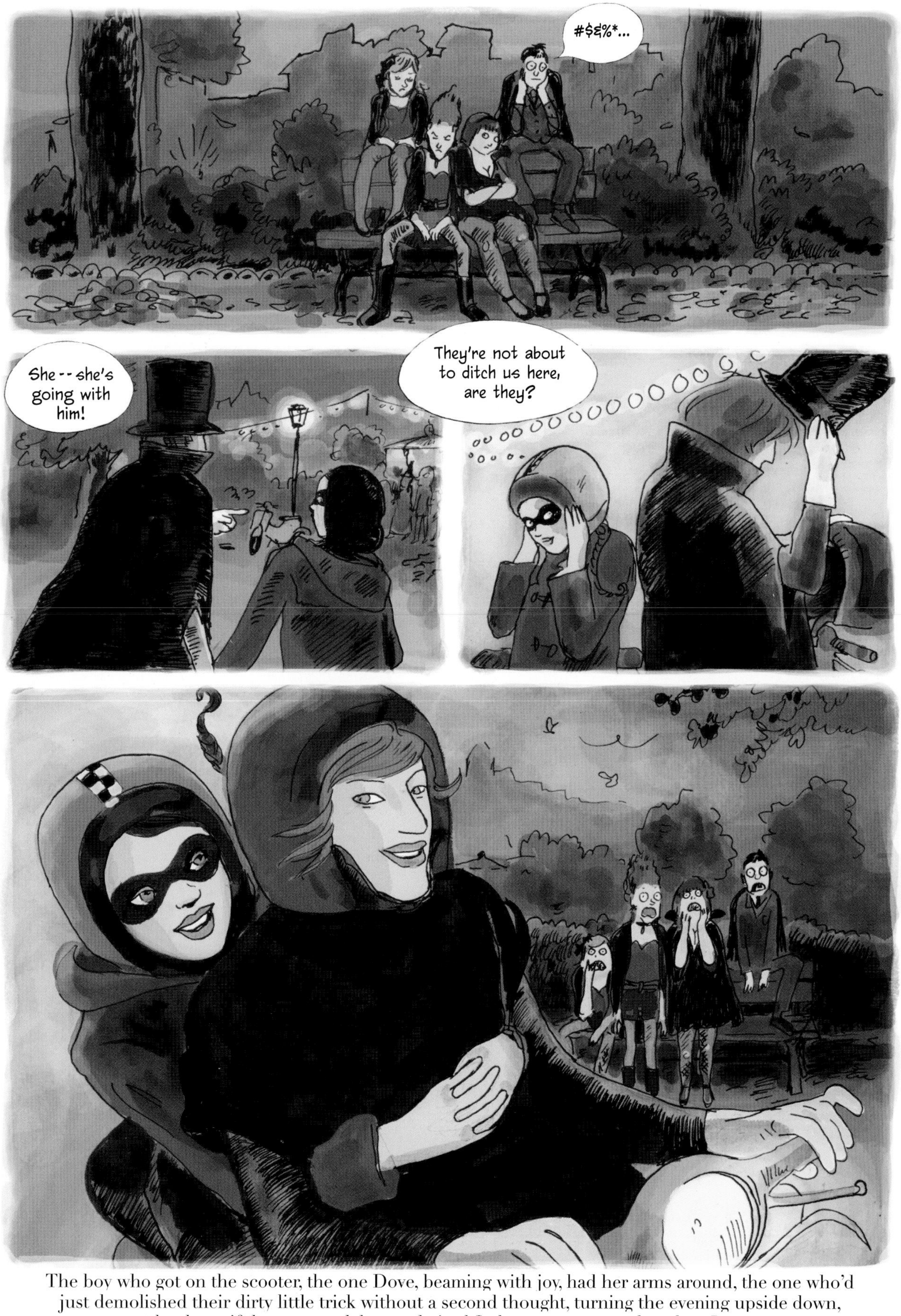
#$&%*...
She -- she's going with him!
They're not about to ditch us here, are they?

The boy who got on the scooter, the one Dove, beaming with joy, had her arms around, the one who'd just demolished their dirty little trick without a second thought, turning the evening upside down, that beautiful green-eyed, brown-haired Judex… was none other than Juan.

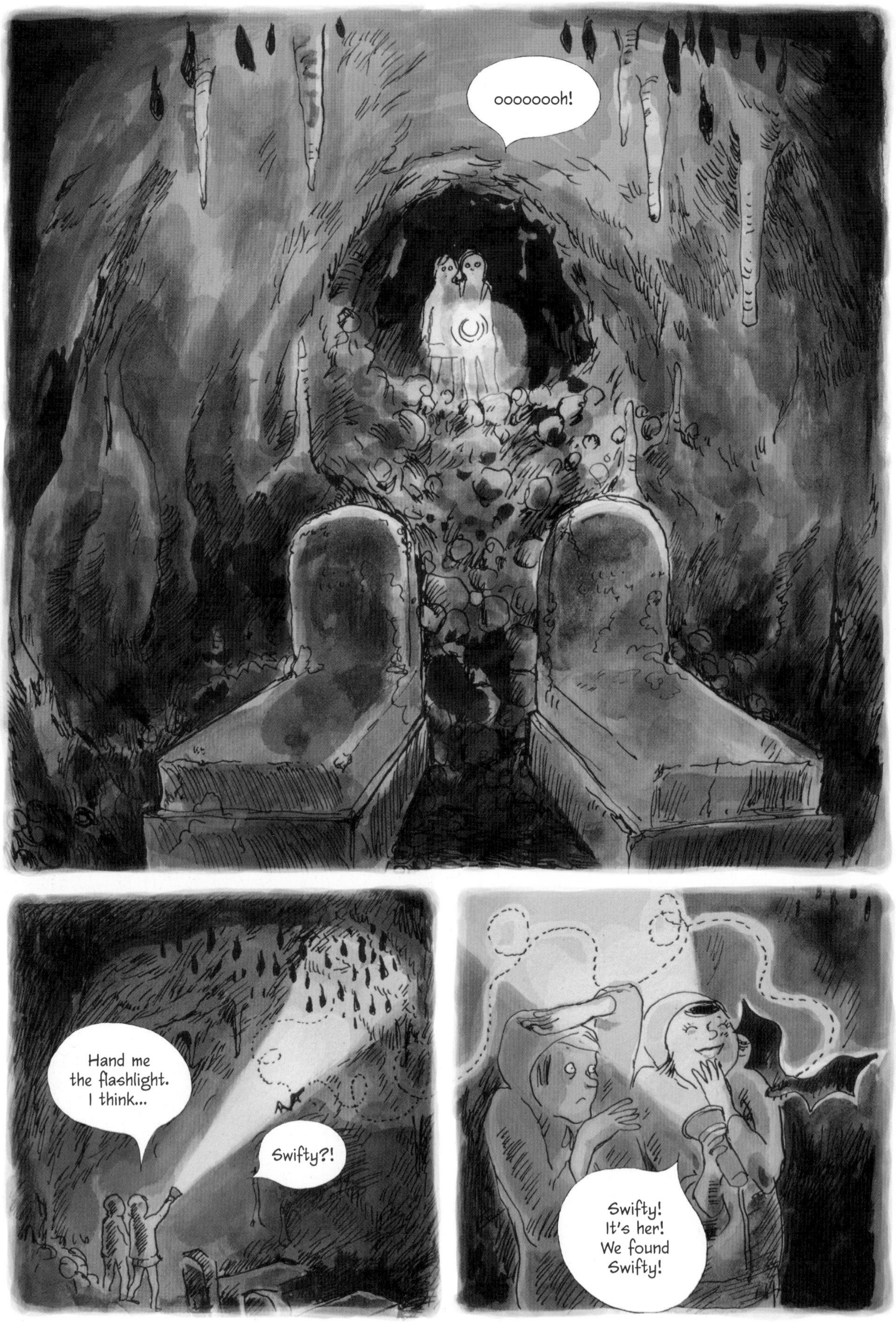

oooooooh!
Hand me the flashlight. I think...
Swifty?!
Swifty! It's her! We found Swifty!

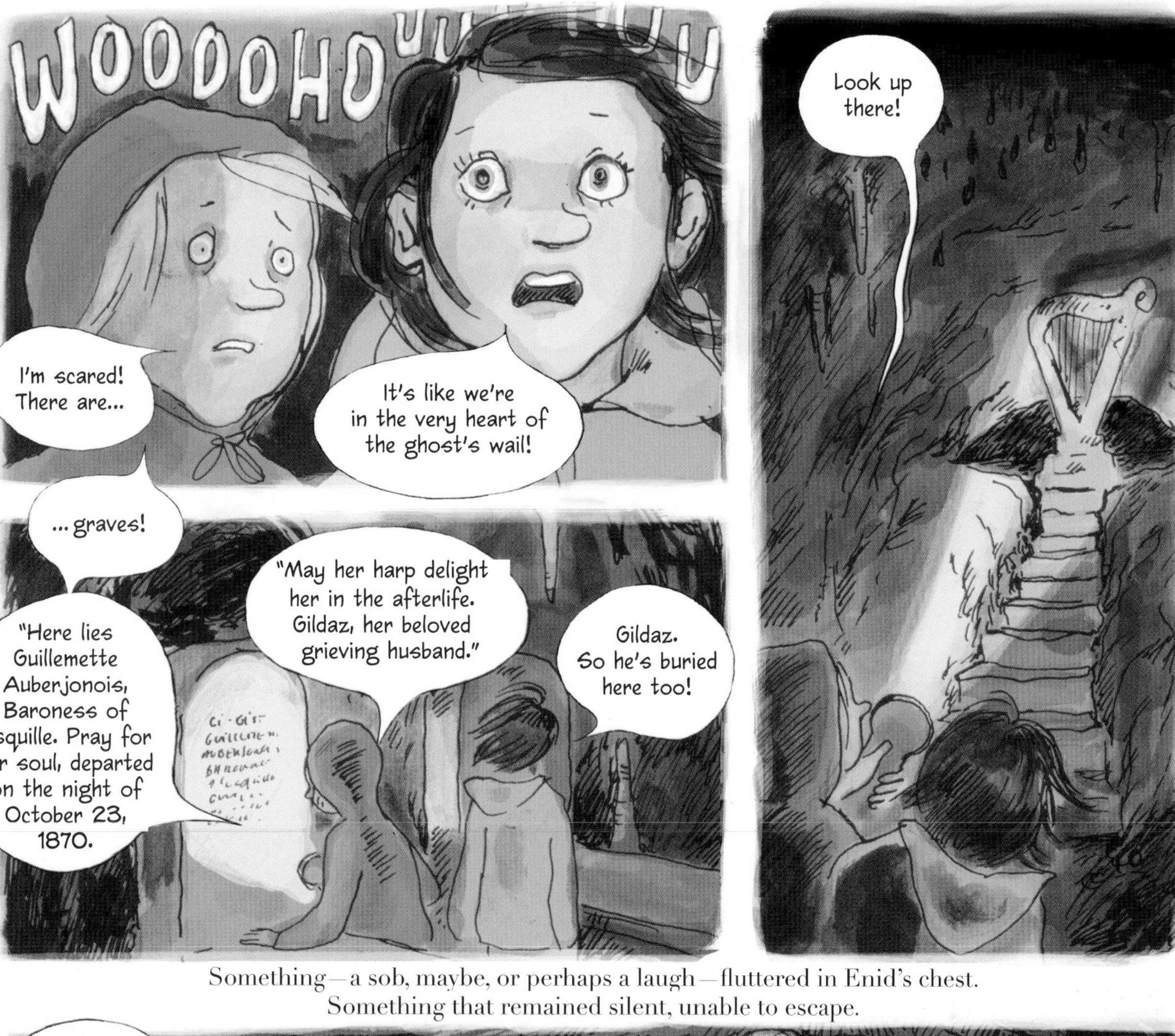
WOOOOHOU
I'm scared! There are...
It's like we're in the very heart of the ghost's wail!
... graves!
"Here lies Guillemette Auberjonois, Baroness of Esquille. Pray for her soul, departed on the night of October 23, 1870.
"May her harp delight her in the afterlife. Gildaz, her beloved grieving husband."
Gildaz. So he's buried here too!
Look up there!

Something—a sob, maybe, or perhaps a laugh—fluttered in Enid's chest. Something that remained silent, unable to escape.

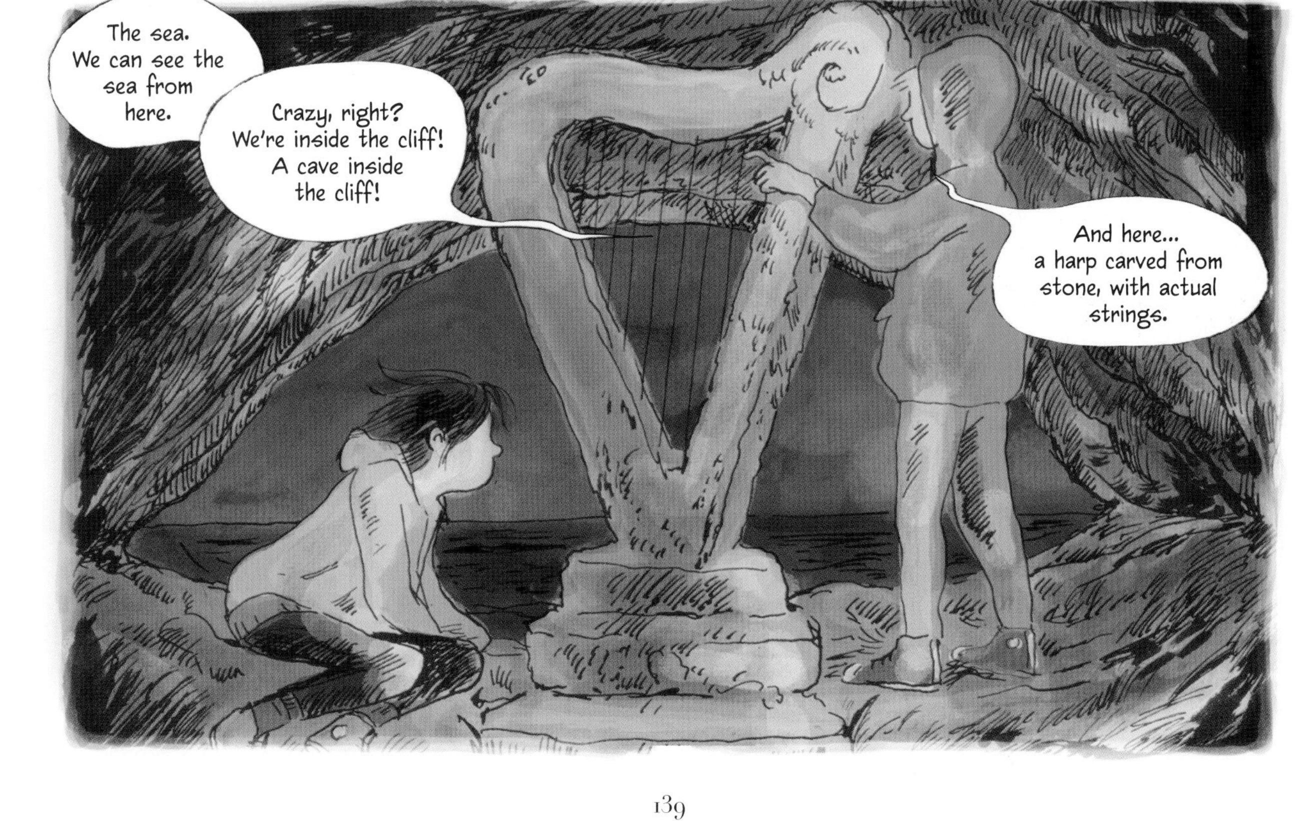
The sea. We can see the sea from here.
Crazy, right? We're inside the cliff! A cave inside the cliff!
And here... a harp carved from stone, with actual strings.

Suddenly, everything became clear. Enid knew who the ghost was. The sea wind with its thousand fingers came bursting in like a genie into a bottle, swept the crypt, hammered the harpstrings, rattled them, tormented them, and brought them to life, at long last liberating that vibrato heartrending as an open wound: the sad lament of Guillemette, her way of speaking to the living.

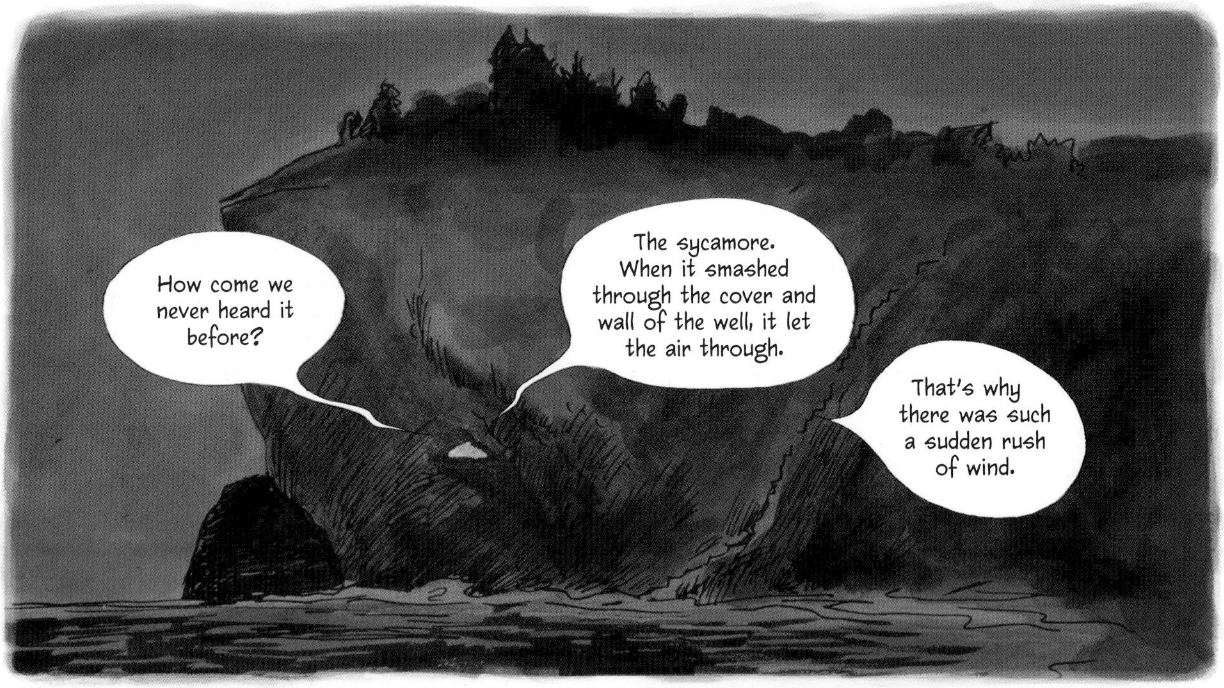
How come we never heard it before?
The sycamore. When it smashed through the cover and wall of the well, it let the air through.
That's why there was such a sudden rush of wind.

Then, and only then, did Enid let her own thoughts turn to her deceased parents, who had also been burned alive in their crashed car.

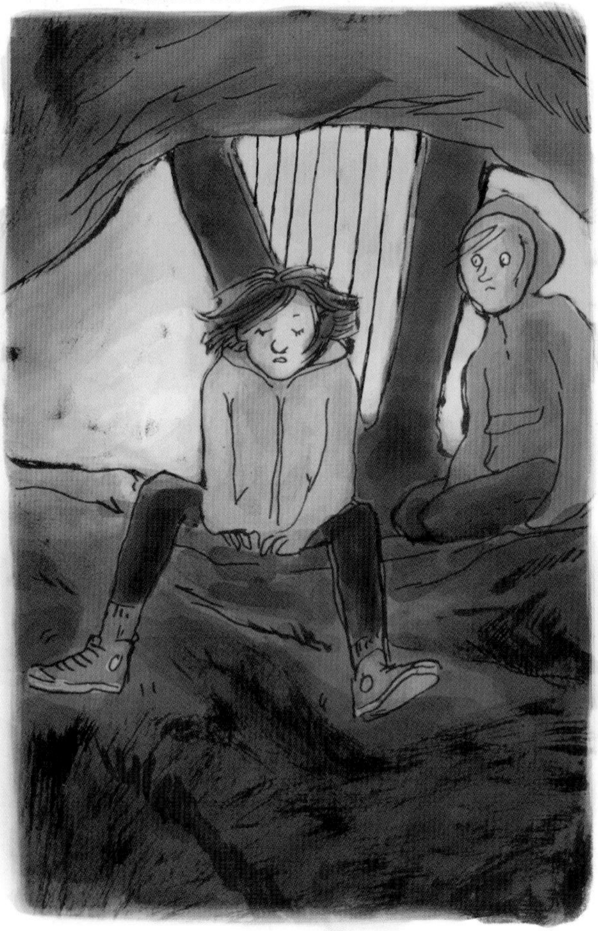

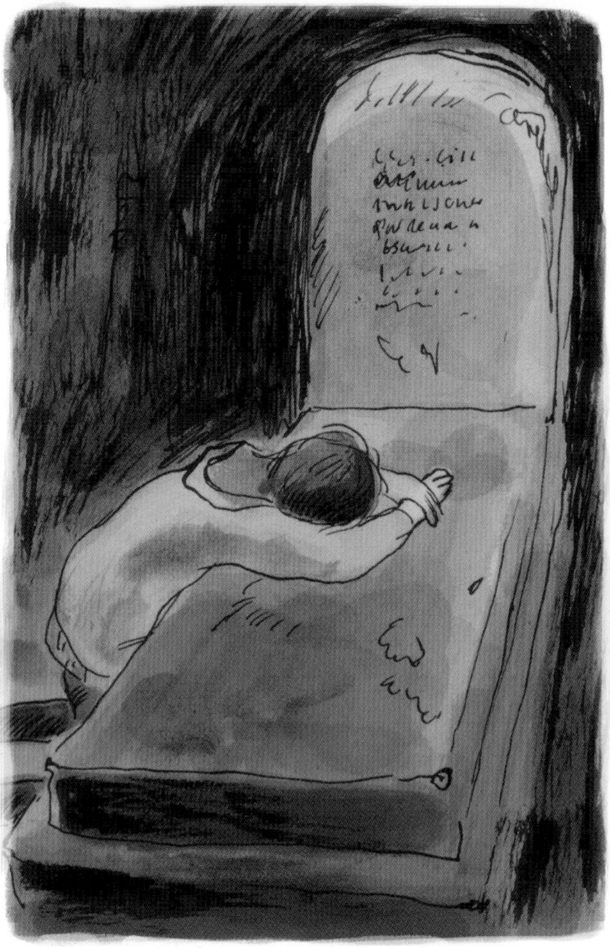

And suddenly, her sobs exploded in a tempest of tears as hot as they were soothing.

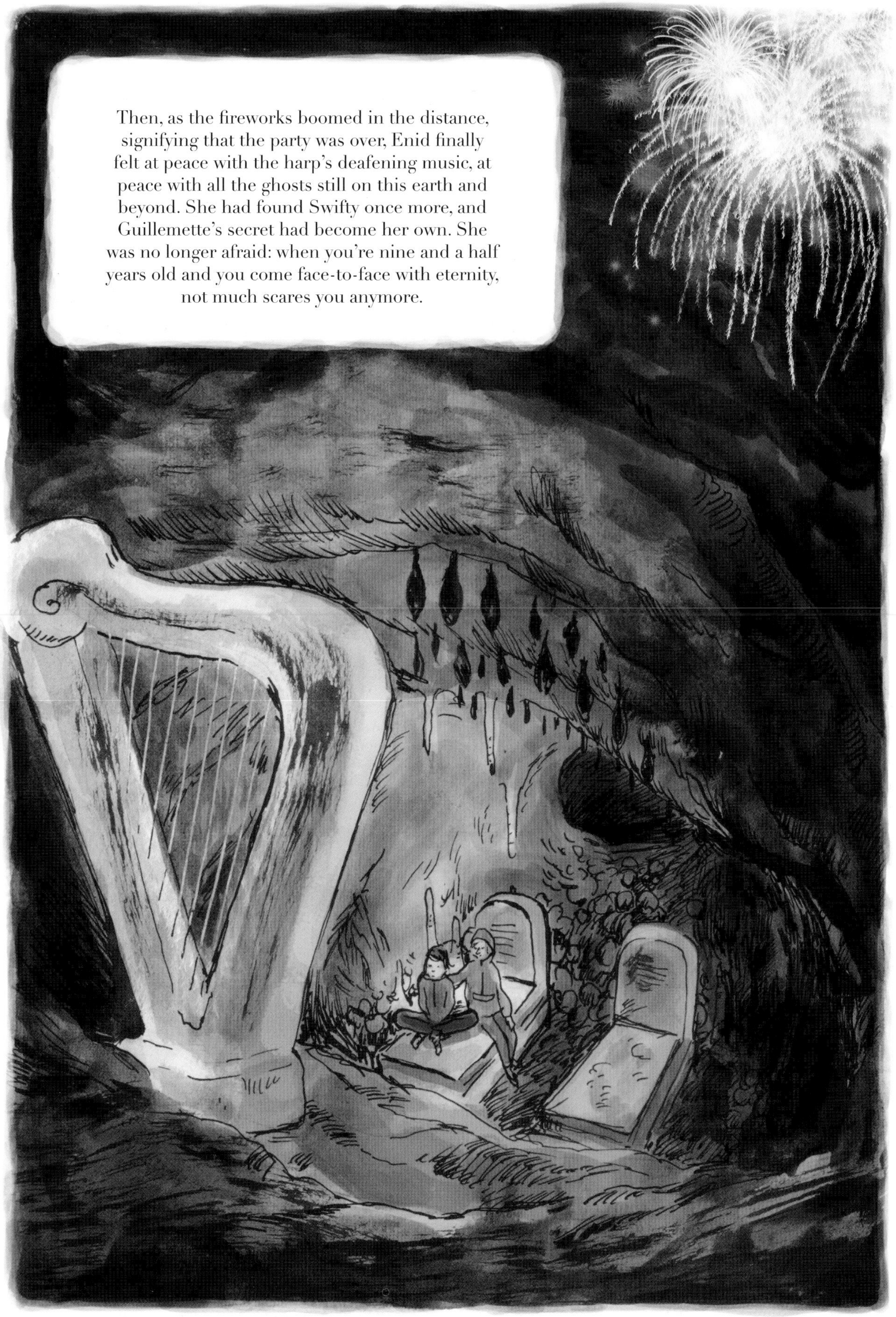
Then, as the fireworks boomed in the distance, signifying that the party was over, Enid finally felt at peace with the harp's deafening music, at peace with all the ghosts still on this earth and beyond. She had found Swifty once more, and Guillemette's secret had become her own. She was no longer afraid: when you're nine and a half years old and you come face-to-face with eternity, not much scares you anymore.

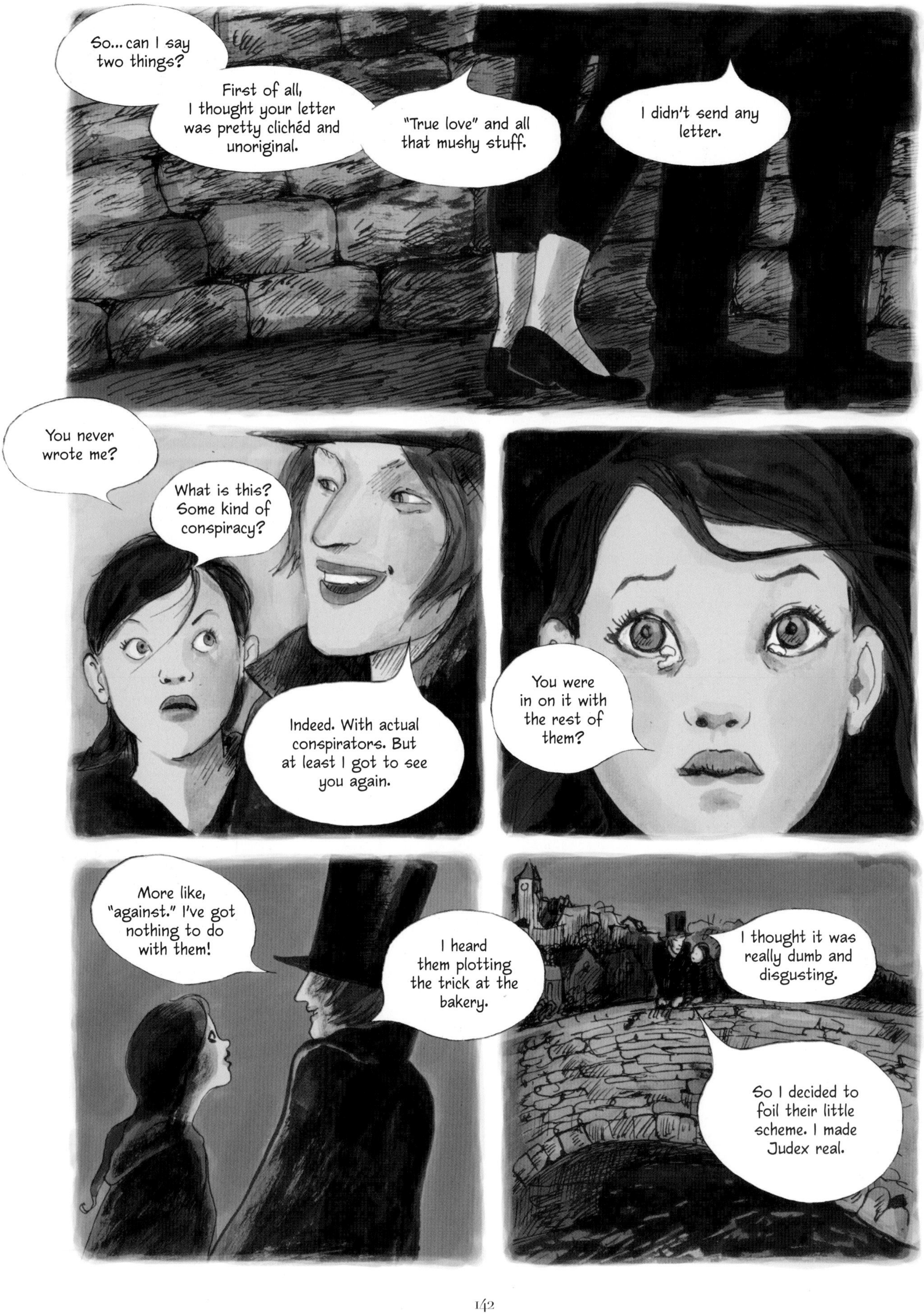
So... can I say two things?
First of all, I thought your letter was pretty clichéd and unoriginal.
"True love" and all that mushy stuff.
I didn't send any letter.
You never wrote me?
What is this? Some kind of conspiracy?
Indeed. With actual conspirators. But at least I got to see you again.
You were in on it with the rest of them?
More like, "against." I've got nothing to do with them!
I heard them plotting the trick at the bakery.
I thought it was really dumb and disgusting.
So I decided to foil their little scheme. I made Judex real.

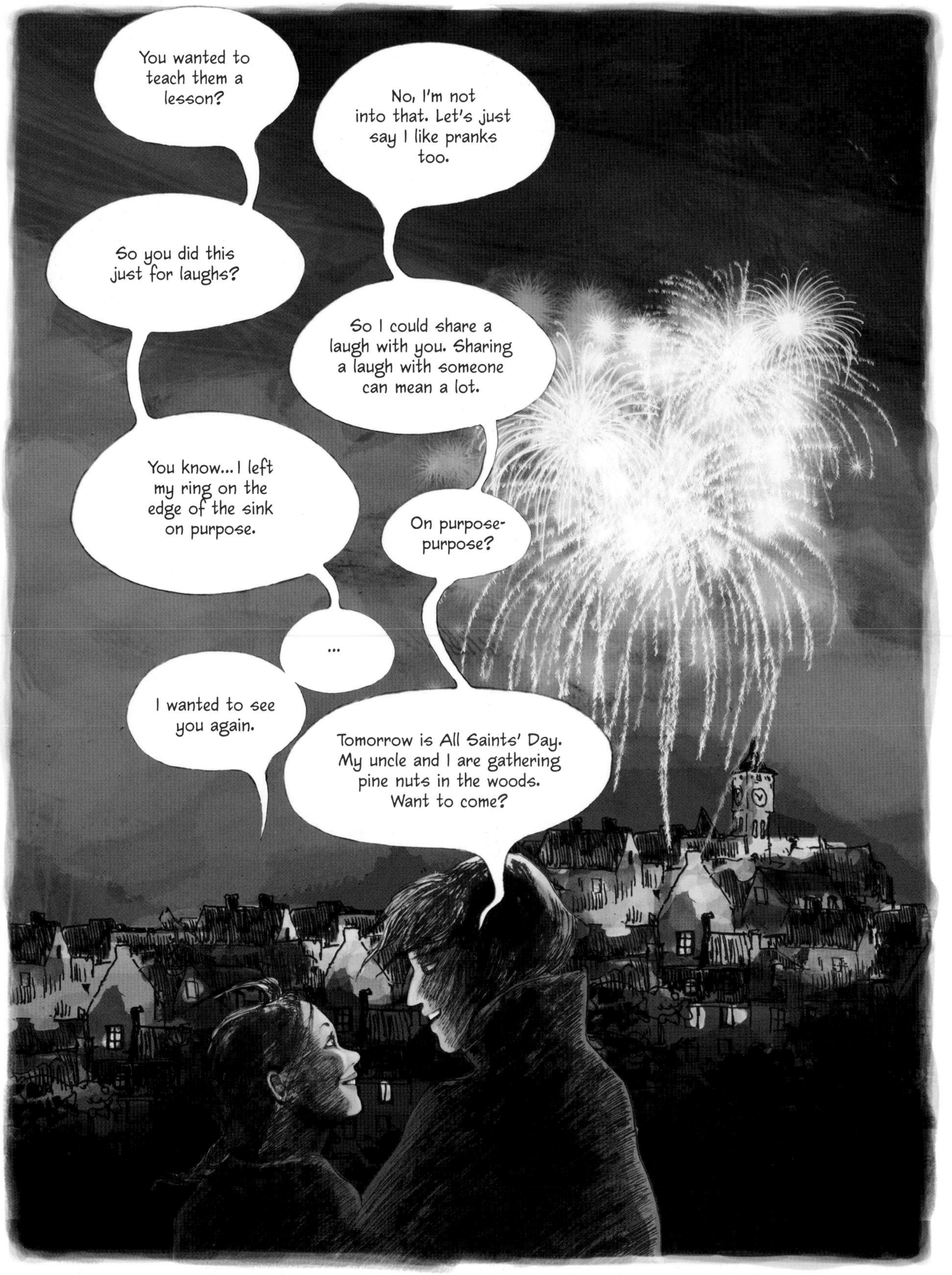
You wanted to teach them a lesson?
No, I'm not into that. Let's just say I like pranks too.
So you did this just for laughs?
So I could share a laugh with you. Sharing a laugh with someone can mean a lot.
You know... I left my ring on the edge of the sink on purpose.
On purpose-purpose?
...
I wanted to see you again.
Tomorrow is All Saints' Day. My uncle and I are gathering pine nuts in the woods. Want to come?

Only three more days, Dove thought. Try not to think about how short that is. But tomorrow will be the first. And it will be wonderful. Just absolutely wonderful.

For several hours now, the whole of Vill'Hervé had been winding down, tuckered out after a night of laughter, discoveries, and emotions. Bettina lay choking like a drowning woman in the darkness of her bed. What filled her with rage, with wrath and shame, was ever having thought Juan was interested in her. She wanted to scream with all her heart, but all she could do was gnaw on her pillow and gulp down her tears. Juan's betrayal had been a slap in the face. There was no other word for it: be-tray-al. How could he have been on the side of that stuck-up twit? How could he be into her? How? Bettina couldn't wrap her head around it, and kept replaying the night's events in her mind.

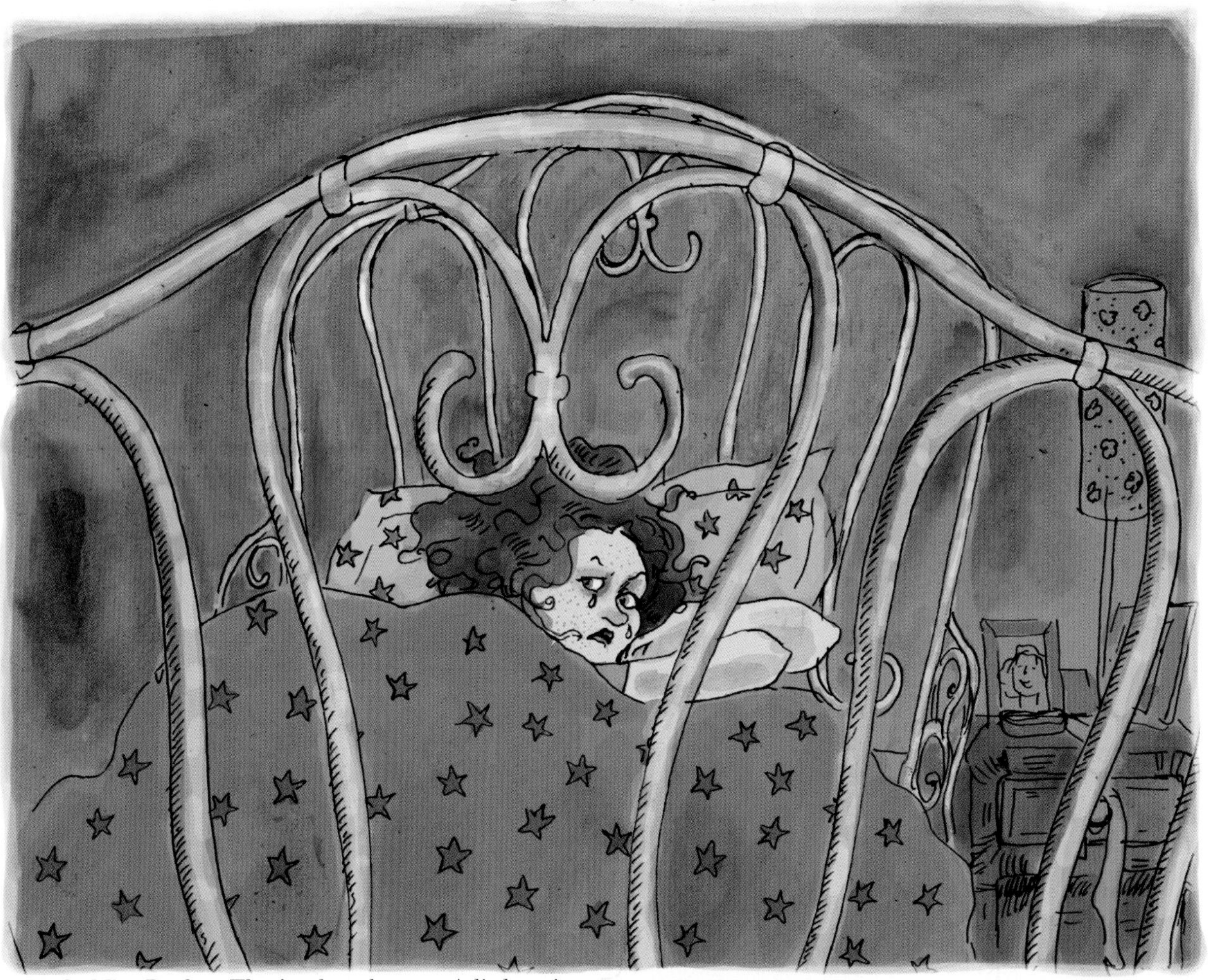

Little Miss Perfect. That's what she was. A little prig who hid her ploys well. Just trash. Out-and-out trash.

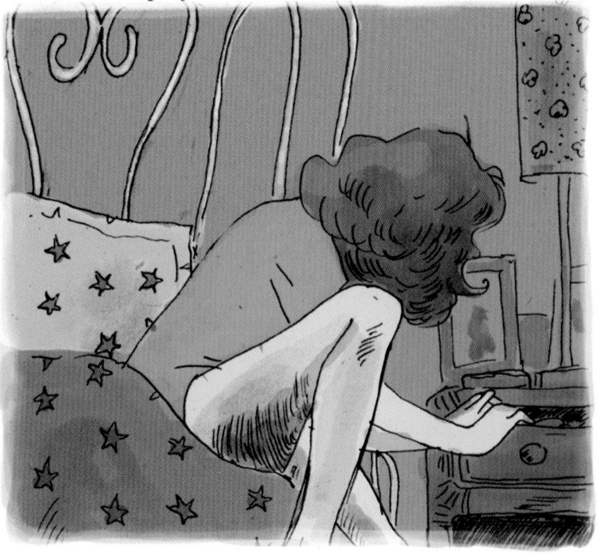

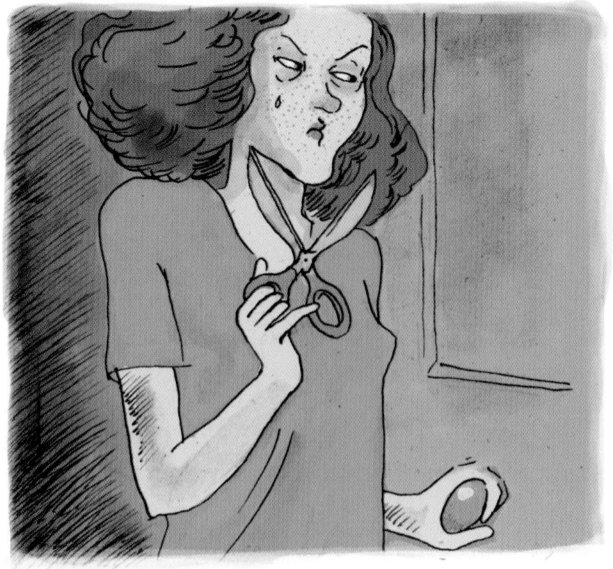

Bettina had to do something.

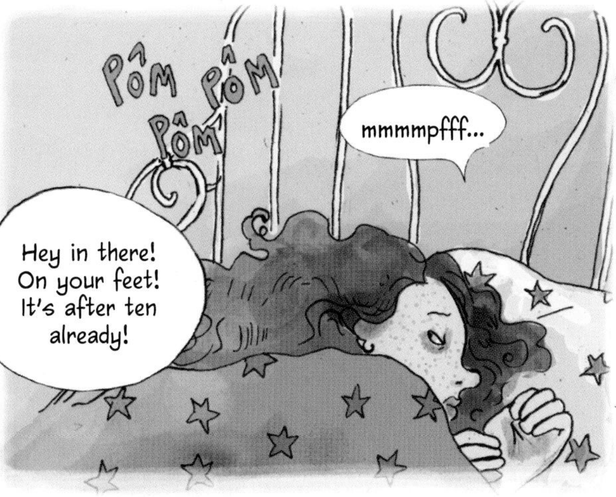
PÔM PÔM
PÔM
mmmmpfff...
Hey in there! On your feet! It's after ten already!

For an instant upon waking, Bettina felt exactly like she did every other morning: a fairly good-looking girl without a care in the world and nothing on her conscience but a D in science…

In short, as happy as you can be at age fourteen and a half. Then, she remembered.

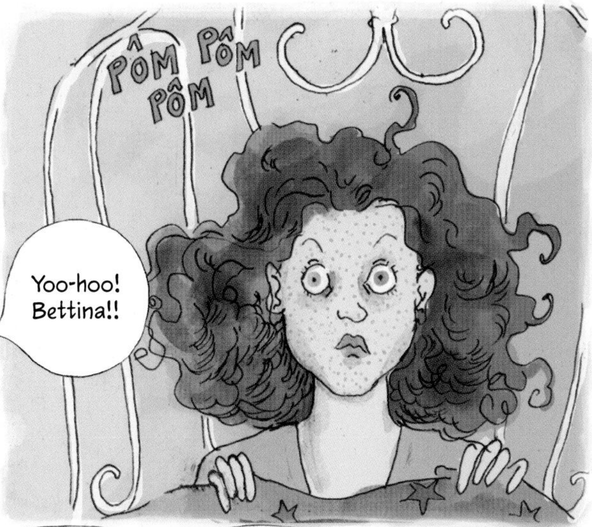
PÔM PÔM
PÔM
Yoo-hoo! Bettina!!

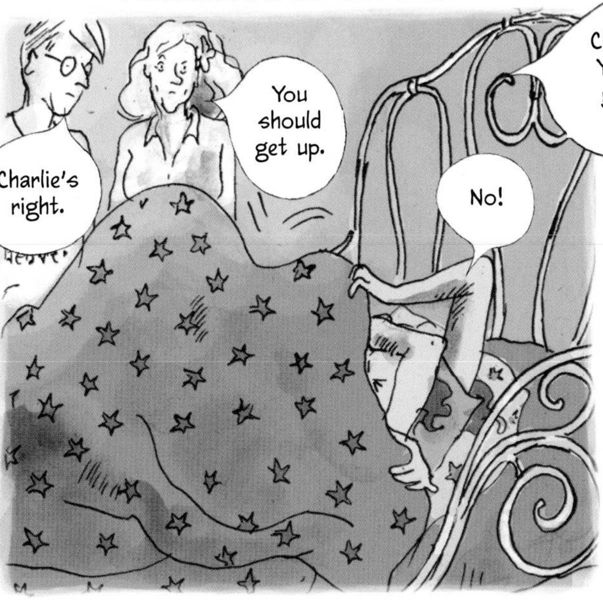
Charlie's right.
You should get up.
No!

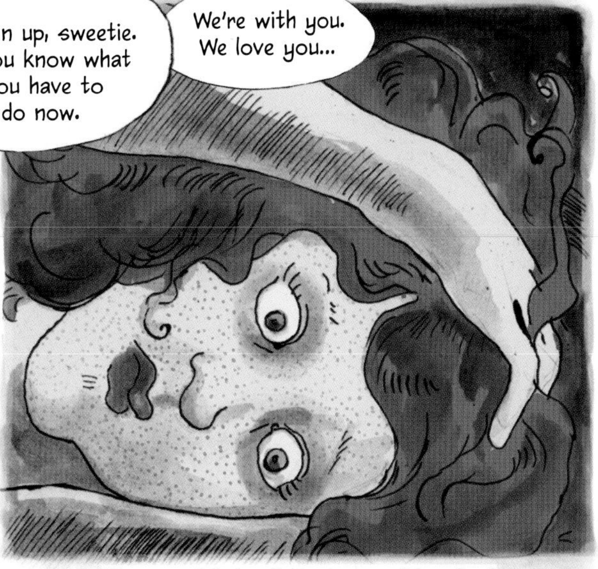
Chin up, sweetie. You know what you have to do now.
We're with you. We love you...

How could she face the world today?

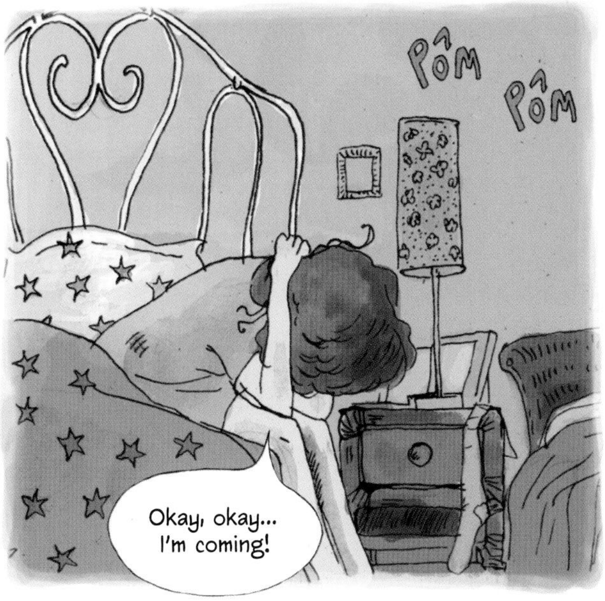
PÔM
PÔM
Okay, okay... I'm coming!

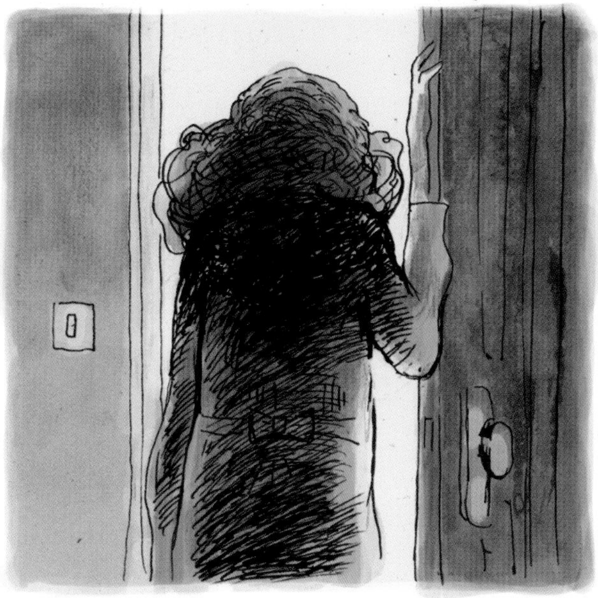

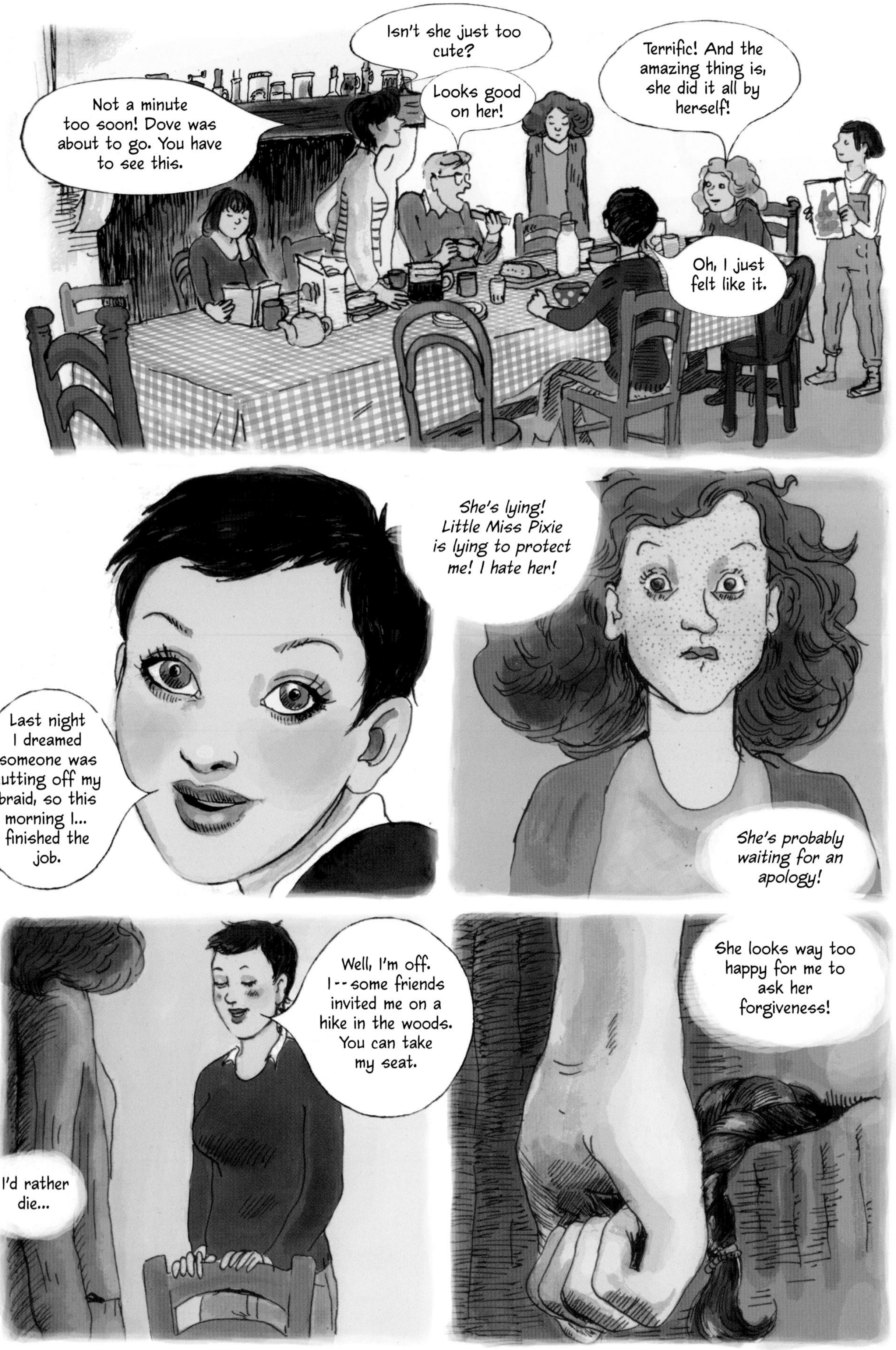
Not a minute too soon! Dove was about to go. You have to see this.
Isn't she just too cute?
Looks good on her!
Terrific! And the amazing thing is, she did it all by herself!
Oh, I just felt like it.
Last night I dreamed someone was cutting off my braid, so this morning I... finished the job.
She's lying! Little Miss Pixie is lying to protect me! I hate her!
She's probably waiting for an apology!
Well, I'm off. I -- some friends invited me on a hike in the woods. You can take my seat.
I'd rather die...
She looks way too happy for me to ask her forgiveness!

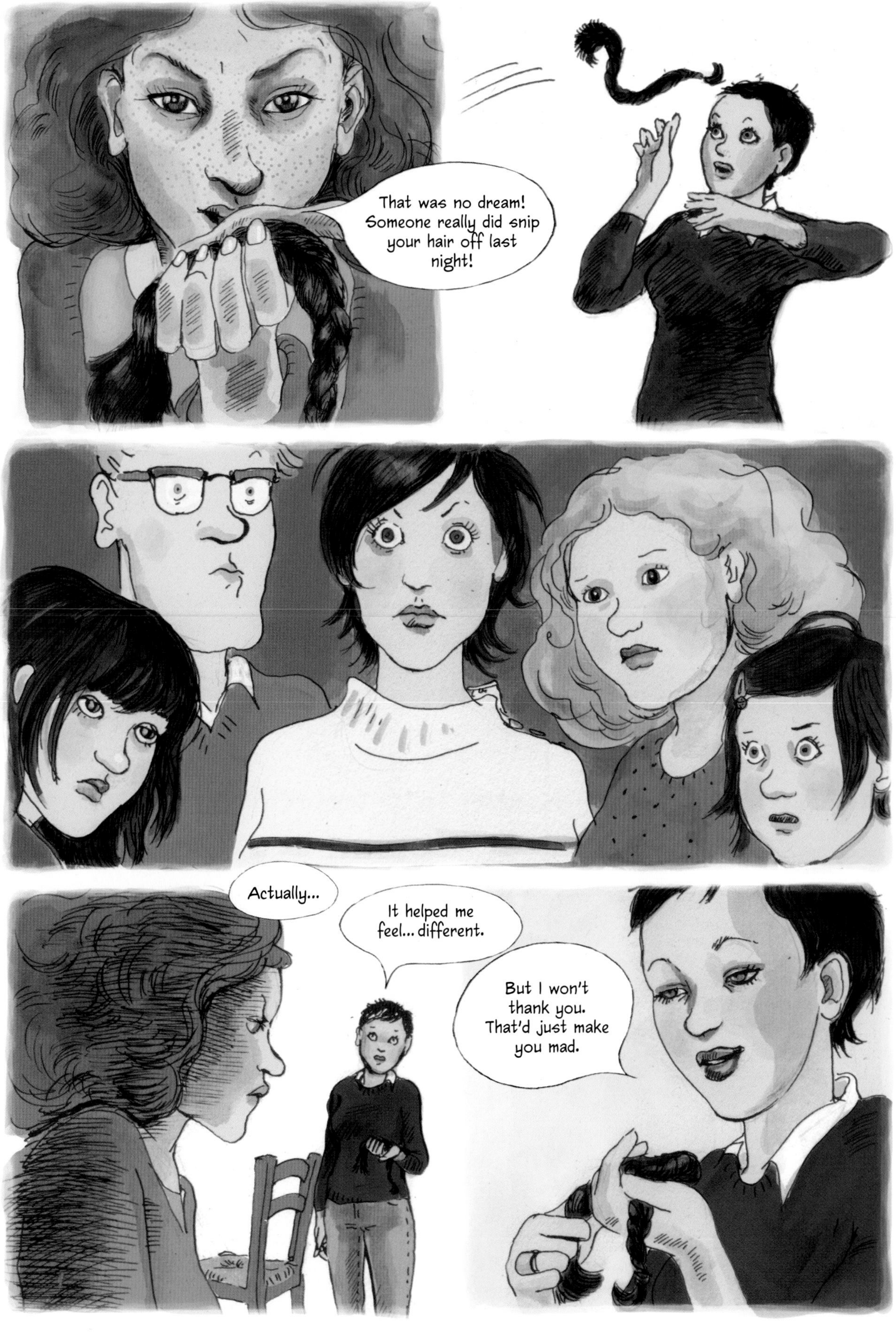
That was no dream! Someone really did snip your hair off last night!
Actually...
It helped me feel... different.
But I won't thank you. That'd just make you mad.

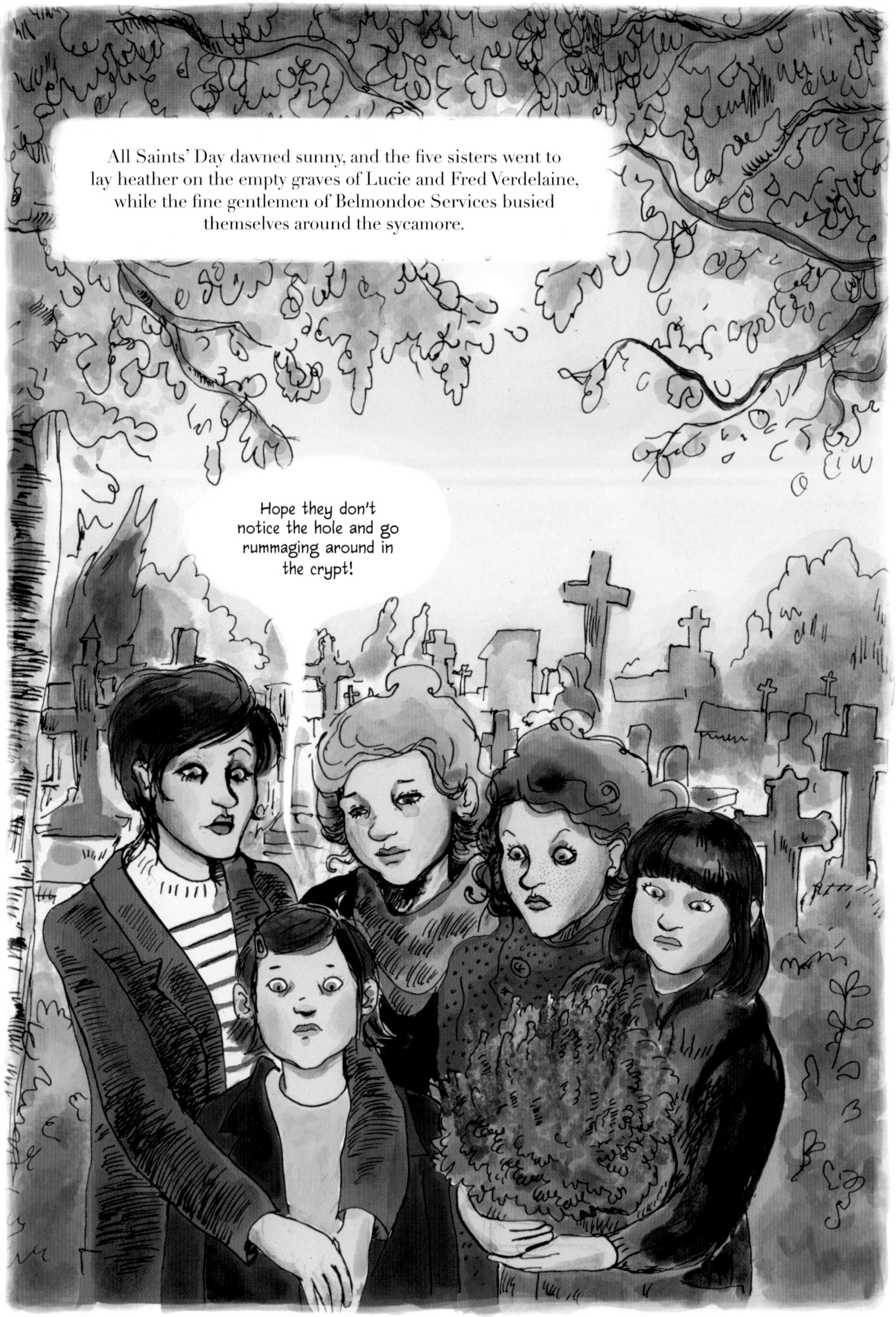
All Saints' Day dawned sunny, and the five sisters went to lay heather on the empty graves of Lucie and Fred Verdelaine, while the fine gentlemen of Belmondoe Services busied themselves around the sycamore.
Hope they don't notice the hole and go rummaging around in the crypt!

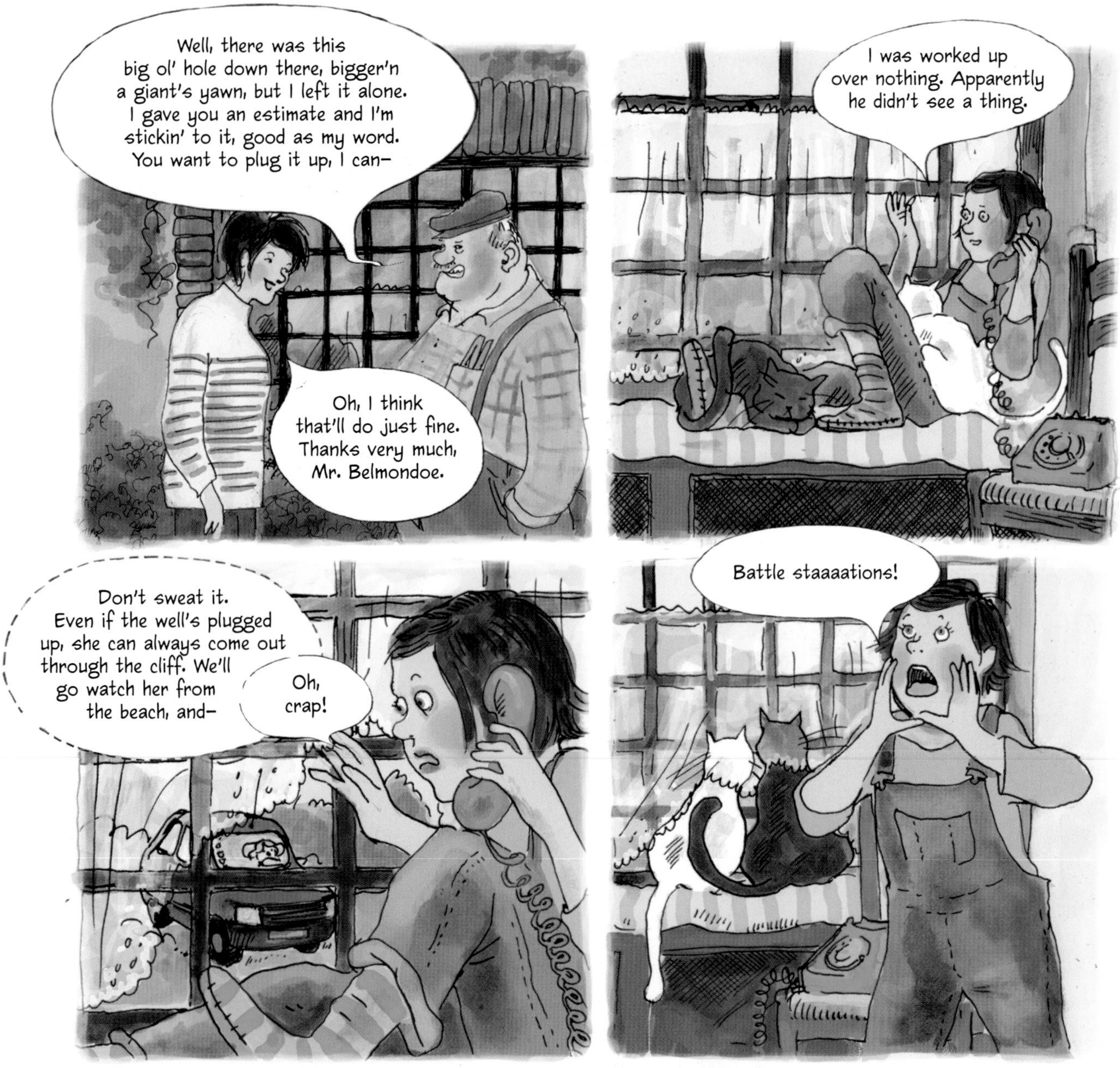
Well, there was this big ol' hole down there, bigger'n a giant's yawn, but I left it alone. I gave you an estimate and I'm stickin' to it, good as my word. You want to plug it up, I can–
Oh, I think that'll do just fine. Thanks very much, Mr. Belmondoe.
I was worked up over nothing. Apparently he didn't see a thing.
Don't sweat it. Even if the well's plugged up, she can always come out through the cliff. We'll go watch her from the beach, and–
Oh, crap!
Battle staaaations!

No mistaking those words: at Vill'Hervé, "battle stations" was the ultimate battle cry. The goal being, in exactly sixty seconds, to hide the overflowing mess and make as much dust and as many animals as possible disappear before the arrival of…

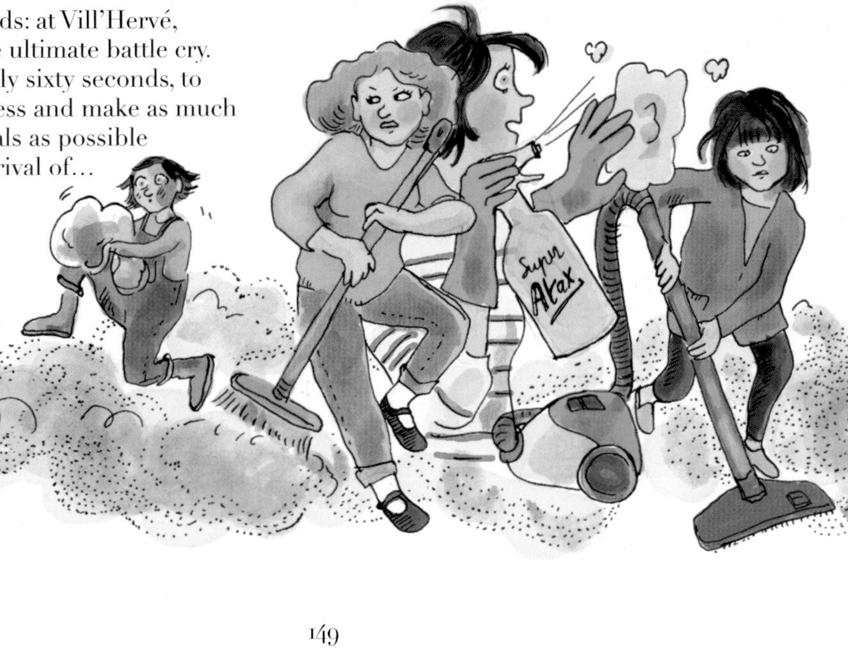

… Aunt Lucretia.

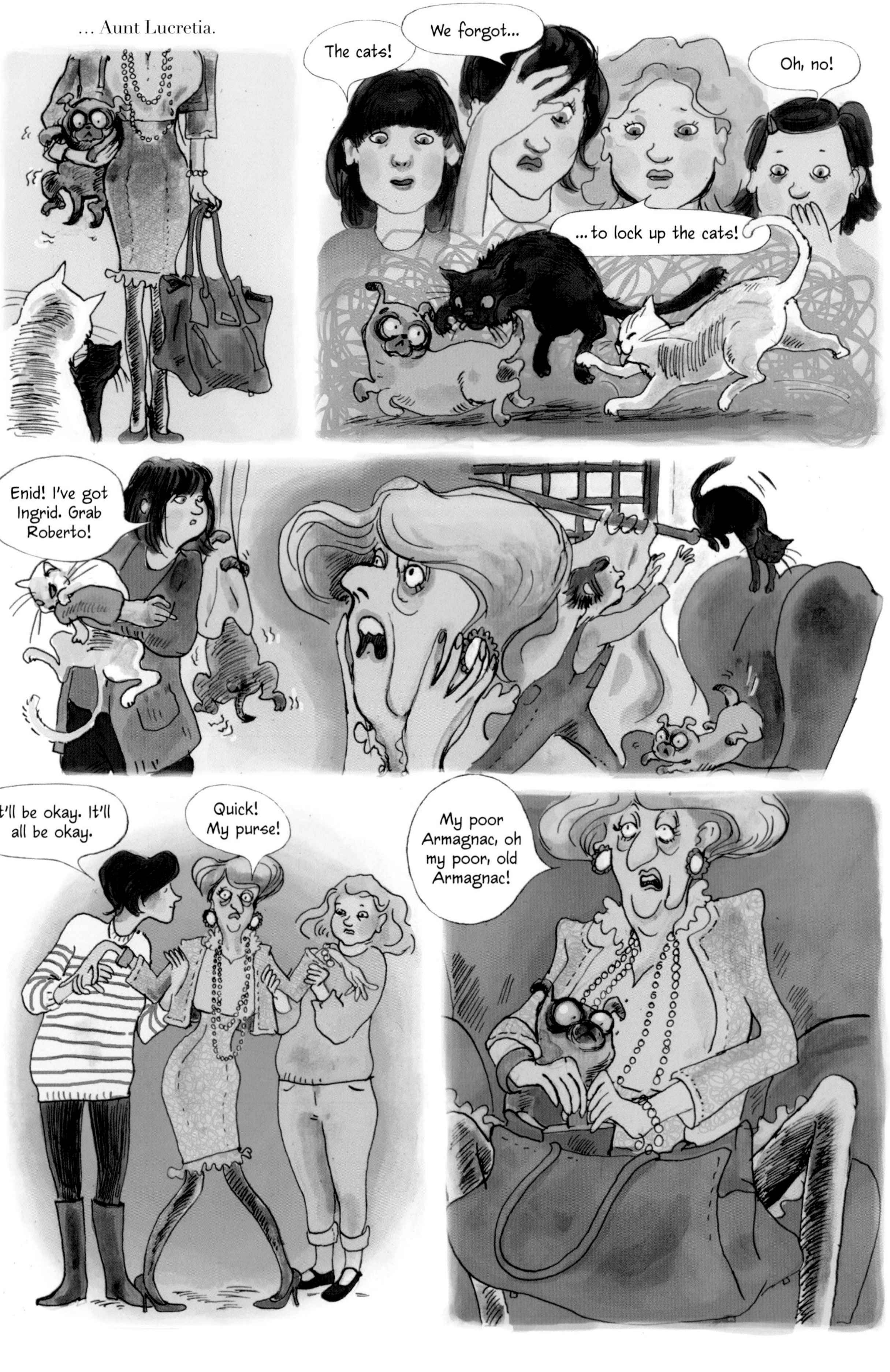
The cats!
We forgot…
Oh, no!
…to lock up the cats!
Enid! I've got Ingrid. Grab Roberto!
It'll be okay. It'll all be okay.
Quick! My purse!
My poor Armagnac, oh my poor, old Armagnac!

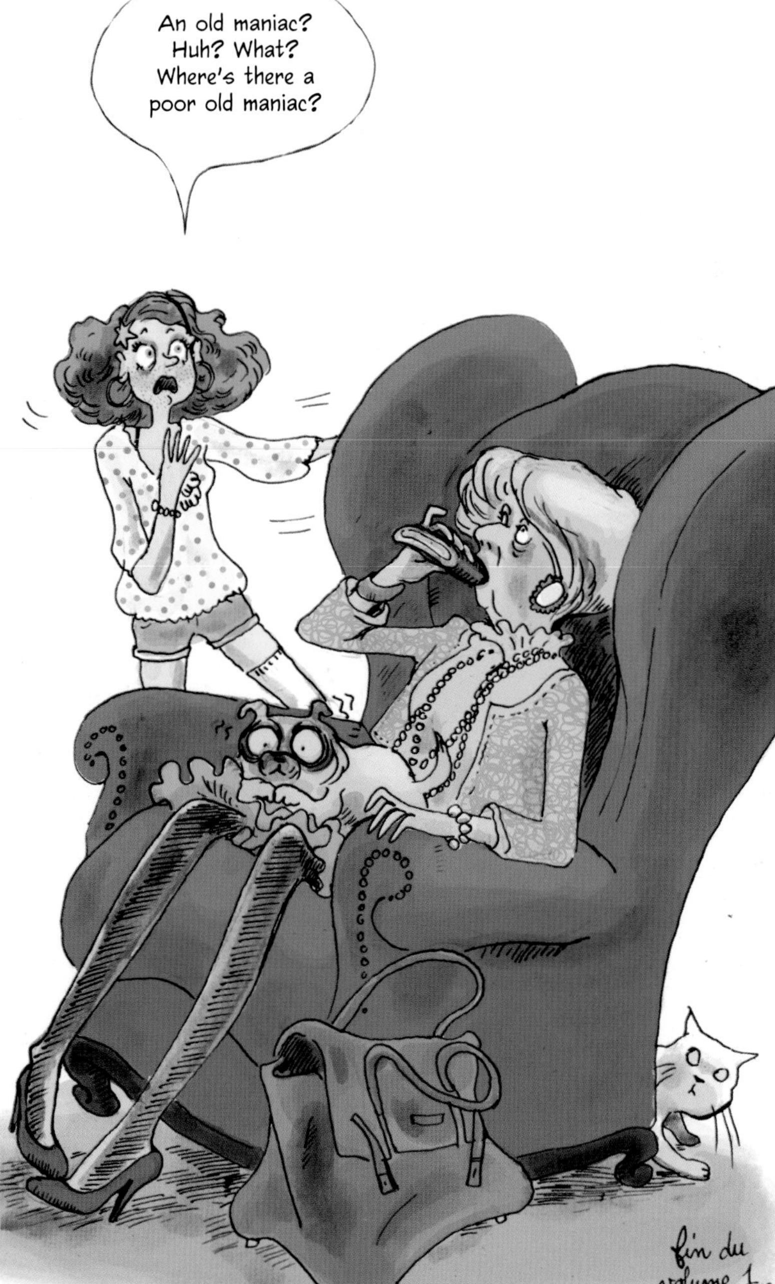
An old maniac? Huh? What? Where's there a poor old maniac?
fin du volume 1.

Four (or Five) Reasons
to Say Yes to Cati

by Malika Ferdjoukh

Cati Baur's first email came in on tiptoe, peeked through the crack in the door, wiped its heels on the doormat of the Internet.

Shyly, it whispered: You probably don't like comics. "But what if I said I wanted to draw those sisters you once wrote about?"

People who ask you for things, all pigeon-toed and timid about it, make you want to say yes. So I did. That was my first reason for doing so.

My second was, it was December and cold. My pen, my ink, my fingers, and my writer's brain were freezing—and this unexpected query revived me right away!

We decided to meet in person, she and I…and soon realized we lived two blocks apart, that we bought our clementines, our chocolate, and our bottled water at the same Franprix supermarket…. And that was an excellent third reason.

(Besides, me not liking comics? So not true. I adore Alex Raymond, Harold Foster, Milton Caniff, George McManus, Winsor McCay!)

But the most amazing, most flabbergasting reason of all, the magic reason that bowled me over and still dumbfounds me to this day:

Cati stopped by my place one day so I could show her some movie scenes, a few reels of actors and actresses that might provide some atmosphere for her, images I'd had in my head when I was writing my quartet of books.

•••

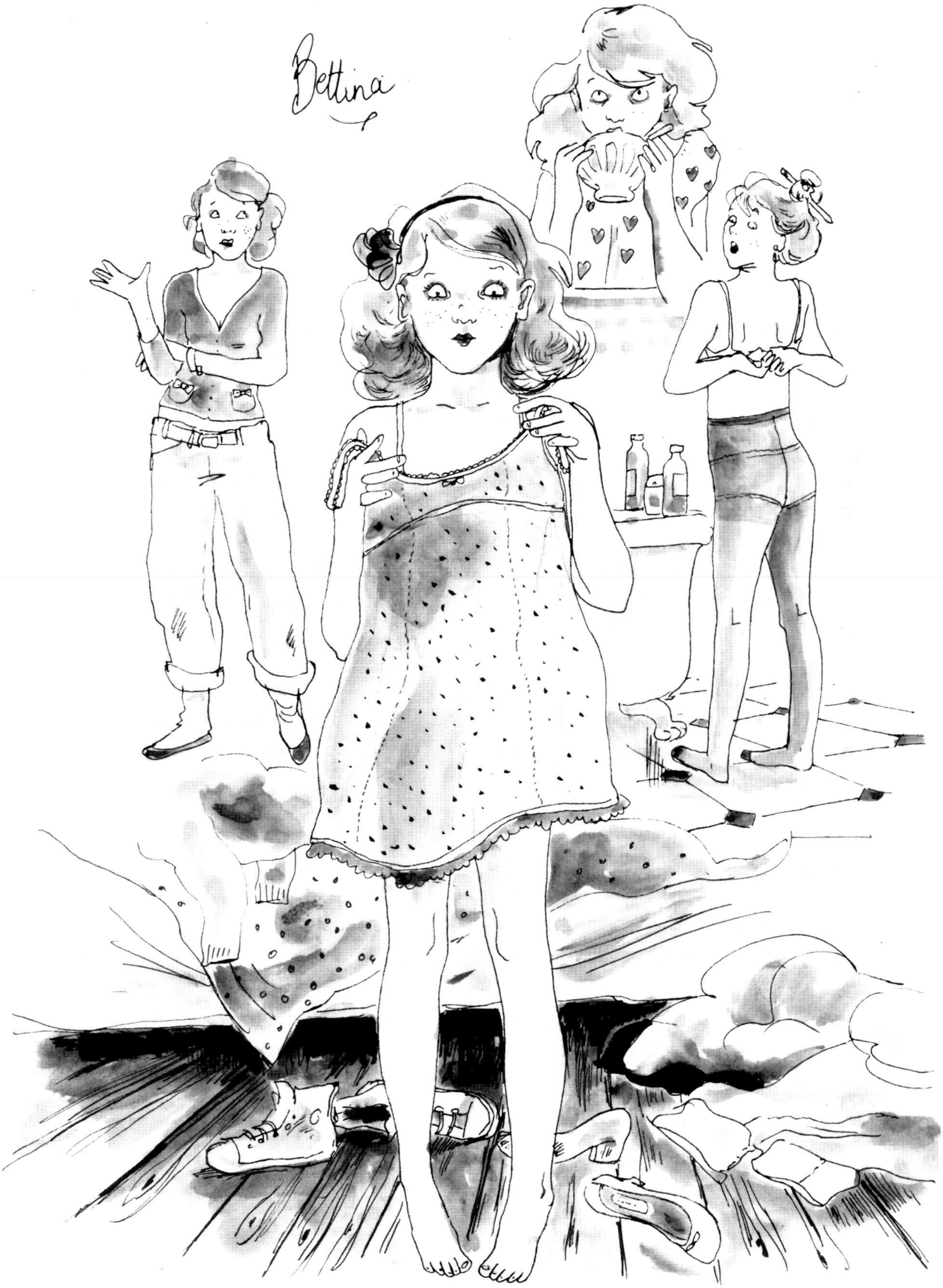
Bettina

I told her about Dick Van Dyke, the chimney-sweep from *Mary Poppins*, for Basil, about Shirley MacLaine and the 1950s model I'd borrowed Bettina's name and red hair from; I showed her Priscilla Lane, Cary Grant's fiancée in *Arsenic and Old Lace*, for my idea of Genevieve. Priscilla who, by the way, was one of Hollywood's four famous Lane Sisters—of which there were, in fact, five! (Ring a bell?)

In short, I was bombarding poor Cati with my personal movie library and we got around to Aunt Lucretia. How did I picture her? That was when I introduced Cati to Kay Thompson. You may remember her as the fifty-something fashion editor in Stanley Donen's *Funny Face*, the one who sings "Bonjourrr Parrris!" with Fred Astaire and Audrey Hepburn. Brusque, insane, stylish, despotic, and dressed in pink from head to toe.

Cati watched, nodded, took notes, warning me all the while that she might not wind up using any of this. Which seemed a wise and healthy attitude to me!

Then came the moment when Cati began talking about her drawing style… The name Eloise, came up—the little heroine of a series of children's books. Eloise was six years old and lived in the palatial Plaza Hotel in New York, where she drove everyone crazy: the manager, the bellboys, the front desk lady, the guests, the hotel detective, et al.

I'd never heard of Eloise. But as a girl Cati had devoured these books a hundred times over; had pored over, scrutinized, inspected, and dissected every last illustration in them the way only someone who will someday become an artist can.

As a matter of fact, these illustrations (a delight!) were by Hilary Knight. And the words were written by…Cati pulled the book she'd brought to show me out of her bag. The author's name fairly leapt from the cover: Kay Thompson!

The very same.

●●●

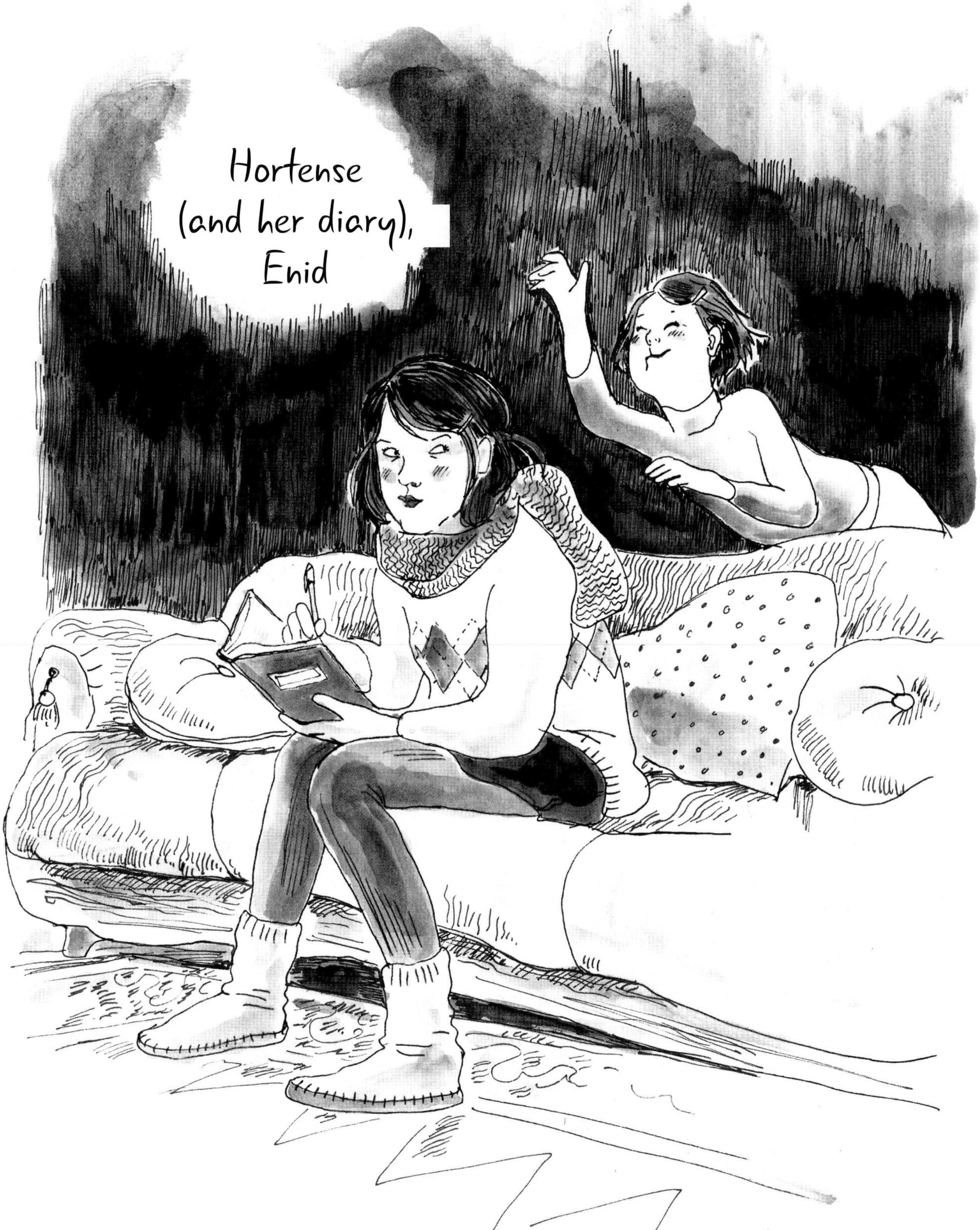
Hortense
(and her diary),
Enid

Abracadabra! And so at that moment we knew that we had each, without knowing it, been under the spell of two facets, two different sides of a single artist! After that, I learned that Thompson's character Eloise had been inspired by her goddaughter, Liza Minnelli, who as a child lived at the Plaza, the forlorn little girl of two geniuses of musical comedy and melodrama (my favorite genres), Judy Garland and Vincente Minnelli.

After such a magical coincidence, there was no doubt the Verdelaine daughters were about to embark on a graphic adventure under the finest, most beautiful auspices, and in wonderful company! All the more so because, while Cati was busy giving them new life, fate would slip me a little sign now and then.

Like the Engelbert Humperdinck (he really does exist, Virginia!) giving one and only one concert at the Grand Rex—which is to say, two hundred yards from where Cati and I lived…

Signs: all you have to do to see them is keep your eyes open.

And now, faced with the beauty, the absolute elegance of Cati Baur's pages, I think to myself what incredible luck it was that they appeared so unmistakably in my life.

M. F.
October 2010

•••

Volume 2:
Hortense

CATI BAUR and MALIKA FERDJOUKH

FOUR SISTERS

2.Hortense